CLOWNS

FIRST CONTACT

Peter Cawdron

thinkingscifi.wordpress.com

Imprint: Independently published

ISBN: 9798827331117 — Paperback

            9798827362357 — Hardback

*To the teachers that shaped my curiosity and imagination at
Penrose High School in Auckland, New Zealand*

"Life's but a walking shadow, a poor player
That struts and frets his hour upon the stage
And then is heard no more: it is a tale
Told by an idiot, full of sound and fury,
Signifying nothing."

Shakespeare: Macbeth

PREFACE

First Contact occurred a decade ago with a traveling circus in the high-altitude desert plateau of Uzbekistan. The US Government has been covertly monitoring extraterrestrial activity around Earth since then but has struggled to make contact. They've kept tabs on the circus and its founder, Buster Al-Hashimi.

Four years ago, Buster returned to the US to start a counter-culture group called The Clowns, challenging the sociopolitical status quo in America.

MELEE

Breezy walks into a drug store at the back of a hospital in Washington, D.C. Hair dye, nail clippers and tweezers line the aisle. The store is a blend of the mundane and exotic—licorice and laxatives. Hard drugs are kept in a safe in the storeroom. Breezy isn't here to get a prescription filled. She got bored waiting for her partner to sneak out of the emergency department for a few minutes, so she snuck inside to get a drink. Back in the parking lot, parched lips demanded a bottle of chilled water. Now, it's a question of Coke or Pepsi.

She opens the fridge door and grabs a soda. Fuck the gym. Spin class can wait. The label on the back of the can says, no sugar, no caffeine, no calories. Hell, it's only a few steps away from being tap water.

Breezy pulls out her smartphone and checks her socials while waiting in line to pay at the counter. Facebook is meme central. Twitter is for whiners. Telegram is encrypted comms for bitching about work. Tiktok is for extroverts on steroids and their wannabes. She ends up on Instagram, knowing it's full of pretty little lies. Ah, the serene lives of everyone but her. Photogenic smiles, slender arms, full busts, slim hips and chiseled abs—it all looks so goddamn easy. She looks down at the can of soda in her hand, wondering if hitting the gym is a better idea. Of course, it is. If the claims of no sugar and no caffeine are correct, it shouldn't matter—and yet somehow it does. 'Both' is an option but she knows only one will win. Breezy needs a dopamine hit, and now! *Fuck the 'gram.* She closes the app, ignoring all those perfect smiles, stunning backdrops and carefully manicured lies about being happy. Breezy's mind doesn't work like that.

Perhaps the wiring is crossed somewhere deep within her central cortex. As much as she says she hates it, deep down, she loves the rollercoaster ride that is her life. The slow clank of the chain drawing her car up high on the narrow track is always followed by the screaming terror of rushing down the other side. Somehow she always survives, at least so far. Besides, if the *'gram* were honest, her buddy Helena would admit lying on the beach in Cancun is more novelty than nirvana. Breezy would be bored within minutes. Fucking sand gets everywhere.

She looks at her nails. They could do with a fresh coat of acrylic. Her cuticles are visible as her nails grow out. Why bother? Fashion is an endless cycle of keeping up appearances, but who cares? No one she knows will notice either way.

Four men enter from the street. They're dressed in jeans and long sleeve plaid shirts. It's hot outside. Checkered tartan is horribly out of fashion, even for hillbillies. Baseball caps sit low against their ears, hiding their eyes from security cameras. Bandanas hang loosely around their necks. Within seconds, each piece of cloth is raised, being positioned over the nose. What is this? A covid outbreak or the wild west?

Don't do it, she thinks. Don't fuck up my Saturday. Please.

Breezy's already dialing 911. She lowers the volume on the side of her phone. This is a one-way call. She knows what's about to unfold. Shit is going down. It's the way the team moves. Two out wide with the lead asshole jogging up to the counter. That leaves one guy by the main door. After spotting them in the mirror, Breezy keeps her head forward, pretending to be caught unaware. No eye contact. She slips her phone behind a sign advertising incontinence pads, putting it face down in the shadows. On the other end, there's a whisper as someone says, "911. What's your emergency?" Listen up, babe. You're going to have to figure that shit out for yourself.

"Hands in the air," a shotgun says just inches from her head. "Phones! I want your goddamn phones!"

The old lady ahead of Breezy surrenders her phone. A puddle forms on the carpet around her feet.

Breezy's got her hands up. She gets a barrel shoved into her shoulder.

"Your fucking phone!"

"It's up in the room," Breezy says, slipping in a stutter for realism. "I—I'm visiting my aunt. I'm just down here to get a Coke. Please—don't shoot."

There. That should be enough for 911 to get a handle on what's going down.

Visiting your aunt, seriously? That's the best you got, Breezy? What's her name? Aunt May? Who do you think you are? Gwen Stacy? Mary Jane Watson?

"Get down on the floor!"

Breezy ain't no hero, not in the traditional John McClane sense of the term. She knows the drill. Compliance is the best strategy for surviving an armed robbery. Hugging the carpet ain't a bad option, but she starts by sliding down the side of the counter and sitting with her back against the thin chipboard panel. Breezy puts her arm around the old lady, comforting her, wondering how much this punk will let her get away with. She has no desire to be taken hostage, but if possible, she'd like to feed a little more information to the 911 operator.

These fuckers only see two things—speed bumps and the open road. Get in their way, and they'll run a steamroller down the street. Stay calm. Blend in with the curtains. That's the strategy. Breezy needs to look scared. She keeps her head low. They're after a haul of class-one drugs. No tricks. Only treats. But this ain't Halloween.

Breezy knows the odds. These damn fools will be sitting in a jail cell by this time tomorrow. And she'll be lounging on the couch with a tube of Pringles, watching TV and laughing about this with her daughter. Just give it time, Breezy. No one needs to get hurt.

Perp number one jumps the counter. He yells at the attendant, rattling off the drugs he wants. The poor girl is shaking like a leaf. From the acne on her face, she's in her late teens. She's probably working here as a side-hustle while at college. She doesn't seem to know what he's after. A senior clerk comes over with hands raised and points at the back room. The perp unzips a backpack and starts the harvest.

Breezy pushes her head against the counter behind her, trying to get as close to her phone as possible. In a whisper, she says, "Mount Hermon Hospital. Drug heist. We're in the drug store on the main road. Four perps. One out the back raiding the place. One watching the street. The others are on the hospital entrance and the fire exit. I make six civilians and two staff. Best option: Let the team leave. They're not interested in hostages, so don't give them a reason to change their minds. Corner them on the street for an easy takedown."

The older woman looks up at her with alarm. Breezy holds a finger to her lips. She's regretting leaving her government-issued Glock locked in the glovebox. Fuck. What the hell is she doing here? Breezy was supposed to be doing Susan a favor, dropping off an early dinner, so she didn't have to wait until her shift finished. Why the hell are there so many assholes in this world?

The guy she's designated as perp number three is the internal lookout. He's over by the entrance to the hospital, and he's as nervous as hell. A long corridor links the drug store with the hospital reception area. Rather than being part of either building, the corridor is a covered walkway connecting the two. Perp number three is hating this. He's got regret written all over his furrowed brow. Yes, fuckwit. This is a bad idea! Going along with these guys is the worst idea of your stupid, miserable life.

It's all Breezy can do not to shout at him.

Dumbass!

He fidgets, waving his gun around as he dances on the spot. Does he need to pee? His poor gun discipline is going to get someone killed. Breezy's tempted to get up and help perp number one with the loot. The sooner these idiots get out of here, the better. Every additional moment perp number one spends messing around in the storeroom erodes their chances of survival a little further. Perp number three's got his finger on the trigger of his gun. If he gets panicked by a car door slamming, he'll fire off a round.

A security guard comes huffing down the corridor from the hospital reception. Someone's alerted him to the robbery, but he's making as though he's rushing for a slice of birthday cake. He's got his hand on his holstered revolver, but he doesn't draw. He doesn't seem too concerned about the prospect of being shot. White shirt. Polished shoes. Shiny badge. Get the fuck out of here, Chief Wiggum! Leave this to the professionals.

"Put down the gun," he says to the perp with the full bladder.

It's four against one. What the hell is this guy thinking? Wait for the cavalry, Wiggum.

Breezy's heard plenty of gunfire. Usually, it's at the range. Noise-canceling earmuffs transform it into little more than a pop! Even in the street, gunfire is loud but not impossibly so. Within the confines of the store, though, it's as though the god of thunder has descended on Earth.

BOOOOOOM!

The crack of gunfire is so loud and sharp it hurts her ears.

This heist is going south fast.

Chief Wiggum still hasn't drawn his clunky old revolver from the thick leather holster wrapped around his oversized waist. He clutches a red patch soaking through his white shirt and falls into a shelf, knocking it into the aisle. Pepto-Bismol scatters across the floor. The sheet metal shelving collapses along with him, leaving panels and cross-braces scattered on the carpet.

"What the *fuck*?" perp number one yells from the other side of the counter, shouting at number three. He's angry. He looks as though he could shoot his own man.

Breezy has no choice. Well, she does, but she can't let someone bleed out in a goddamn hospital. Slowly, she gets to her feet, holding her hands high.

7

"What do you think you're doing?" perp number one says to her with utter disbelief in his voice. He's not very bright, but she keeps that thought to herself.

"He's dying," she says, crouching slightly as she walks. Breezy makes herself as small as possible while still keeping her hands raised. Small target. No threat. Come on, asshole. Grow a conscience. Perp number one is caught in indecision, which is a decision in itself. He lets her continue.

"I'm a nurse," she says. It's yet another lie, but who's counting. Sure, Breezy. Nothing says nurse like a death metal t-shirt, torn jeans and dark regrowth coming through from the straggly bleached blonde hair roots on top of her head. Ah, so you're a nurse that works here, but you also happen to be visiting your aunt upstairs and left your phone there—no inconsistencies detected!

Perp number one trains his shotgun on her.

Breezy is bold. Shock is her only ally. As big and as bad and as tough as perp number one thinks he is, he's an amateur. He's on the verge of panicking. It's the old no-one-was-supposed-to-get-hurt mantra. He needs convincing. She looks at him and adds, "I can help."

Perp number one tightens his lips. He's on the verge of making a very bad decision. Goddamn, you stupid control freak. Let it go. His hand tightens on the grip of his shotgun. His white knuckles don't inspire her with confidence.

"Listen," she says, coming to a halt by an aisle with feminine products on display. "You've got what you want. No one has to die. This is a hospital. I can save him. This doesn't have to become a murder scene."

Oh, yeah. The M-word gets him. A felony murder conducted in the course of a crime carries a minimum 30-year sentence in the District of Columbia. He does not want that hanging over him or his crew. He waves her on with his shotgun and rushes back to collect more drugs. Time is the enemy, not her.

Breezy grabs a packet of tampons and a couple of sanitary pads. She's deliberately sloppy, dumping entire boxes on the carpet in front of the fallen guard. Chaos needs to be met with chaos to succeed. Anything less is a position of weakness.

"Don't you fucking do anything dumb," perp number three says, still waving his handgun around. He's stepped back from the guard, but he's towering over her. Breezy is tempted to quote the criminal statute for murder at him and ask what he wants for Christmas in twenty-fifty-five, but a nurse wouldn't know that. Come on, nurse Gwen Mary Jane Stacy Watson. Get it together.

"I'm not going to let him die," she says, tearing open some packaging.

"What the *fuck* do you think you're doing?"

Breezy ignores the perp, opening the guard's shirt. She shoves a tampon into the gunshot wound. She uses a cardboard insertion tube to work the tampon deep within the bloody mess, leaving the thin, trailing string visible against his skin. She's bluffing. A tampon isn't going to stop internal bleeding—only direct pressure will do that, but pressure is imprecise. Press where? Directly over the hole? Off to one side? Where the hell are his arteries located? Besides, pressure will only delay the inevitable. He needs surgery. She's got to get him the hell out of here.

Breezy's trying to look confident in front of the perp. She needs him to forget about her. She needs him to see her as a medic, not a threat. It's only then she can make her move.

She takes the dying man's hand and makes eye contact with him, saying, "Hang in there, okay?"

Breezy tears open a sanitary pad and pushes it into the guard's palm. She drags his hand up to his chest, saying, "Press here."

"Why aren't you pressing?" perp three asks. It's a good question. Perhaps he's not that dumb after all.

Breezy empties the cardboard carton containing the tampons, spilling them on the floor beside the guard. She's using that confusion as cover to make for the guard's gun, but he's got a secure holster. It's the kind that only allows someone to draw straight up, reducing the chance anyone could grab it from the side. It's likely to snag if she grabs the pistol grip. Damn it!

Breezy thinks about her options. The guard's carrying a Smith and Wesson snub-nosed .38 Special. He might as well be carrying a Nerf gun. The standard operating procedure for US security guards is to only load five of the six chambers to avoid an accidental discharge. From her perspective, that means there's a minimum of four to five seconds from snatch to shot. It's too goddamn long. By the time she pops the leather catch on his holster and draws—assuming she can pull the gun along the length of his body without the holster impeding her—the gun will be useless. Perp three will have plenty of time to react. Besides, she needs to turn the cylinder to a chamber with a live round and cock the hammer. By that time, she'll have already taken two slugs to the chest from perp number three. Great. That's just *fucking* great.

The perp over by the front door sticks his head around the corner to see what all the yelling is about. The perp on the far side of the store, over by the fire door, looks along the front of the aisles at the three of them. Okay, so these guys are easily distracted. Fucking clowns!

"Get away from him," perp three says, seeing her hands drifting close to the holster as she gathers the tampons.

"Easy," Breezy says, pulling a second sanitary pad from its wrapping. She's stalling, looking for other options. She shoves it under the guard's fingers—not that it's helping. Blood pools on the carpet. He's bleeding out. There's an emergency department not more than fifty yards away down the corridor, just past the hospital reception. After the gunshot, it'll be in lockdown, but the doctors there could save the guard's life. Besides, her partner Susan won't leave anyone behind. If she can, she'll roll her patients into one of the other wards, but she won't abandon anyone in need.

"Listen," Breezy says to perp number three, trying to appeal to reason. "I need to get this guy into the emergency room. I'm going to drag him down that corridor, okay?"

"You're not going anywhere."

Breezy closes her eyes, pressing them shut for a moment, wanting to manage her frustration. Although it might look like she's trying to flee, she's not. Breezy's no coward. She's trying to save a life—and she'd like to provide the cops outside with some intel, but that motive is secondary. Perp number three is backing her into a corner. Breezy will not sit idly to one side while the guard slips away.

"He's going to die. Do you really want that on your conscience?"

"You're not leaving."

Conscience? Breezy should have said rap sheet. She should have needled the guy about going to prison. As it is, her ire is raised.

"Oh, don't worry. I'll be back," she says, but coming from a short Hispanic woman in her mid-thirties, this isn't the threat she'd like to think it is. Breezy's no muscle-bound robotic terminator sneering as he drops his lines with a thick Austrian accent. If anything, her comment is perplexing. From the furrow on the perp's brow, it seems he can't figure out what she means.

Even if there are only five rounds in the .38 Special, Breezy's happy to give these chumps a run. She'll take her chance in the shooting gallery at the county fair. Four-to-one odds are still in her favor.

"It's the hair, isn't it?" she says, confusing perp three even further. With blood sticking to her fingers, she reaches up, touching her center part. Dark regrowth is pushing out the peroxide blonde strands. Breezy should have colored her hair about two weeks ago.

Nobody takes Breezy seriously, which is just the way she likes it. In her experience, there's no such thing as a fair fight. Violence is inherently unfair by design. Breezy will take any advantage she can—and if that's some dumb mark underestimating her because she's a woman or because her dad is from El Salvador, so be it. This asshole is about to learn pretty damn quick that she's no chump.

"Cops!" the perp at the front of the store yells.

Blue and red lights flicker over the windows. Goddamn it, 911. You were supposed to keep them back. You were supposed to draw these assholes out into the open. Pushing them into a corner is not smart.

Pushing them into a corner with her on the inside is exceptionally dumb. It must have been the gunshot. The 911 operator would have heard both the shot and the discussion following it. They're expecting this to be a bloodbath. They're trying to contain the violence and stop it from spilling into the hospital itself.

Breezy is out of time but not options. She can't risk going for the guard's gun, but there are plenty of other possibilities.

"Are you a fan of medieval conflict?" she asks perp number three, raising an eyebrow as she adds, "LARPing?"

"What?" he replies, screwing up his face with disdain.

Breezy gathers twenty to thirty loose tampons in front of her. "A word of advice: never use a ranged weapon in a melee."

The tampons are individually wrapped in paper along with a cardboard applicator, making each of them slightly longer than a fountain pen, but they're far lighter. There are so many she can't grab them all with her hands. Instead, she bundles a bunch between her palms. Breezy throws them up at the perp, tossing them toward his face along with a few sanitary pads. The delicate feminine products tumble through the air, spinning and colliding with each other like oversized confetti. They're harmless, and yet they elicit a predictable response. The perp steps back, shielding his face with his hand raised. And with that, he's taken his gun off her. And that split second is all she needs.

Breezy launches herself from the ground, springing out toward him, leading with her arms. She's going for the Glock.

When it comes to raw strength, fingers suck. As someone that's fallen while rock climbing more times than she cares to remember, Breezy knows this better than most. Fingers rely on tendons for what little strength they have. Thank God for nylon climbing ropes. A bit of slack, a little momentum when her foot slips and her tiny fingers can't hold onto much of anything.

Breezy grabs the Glock with both hands. She directs the gun at the ceiling as she turns into him, flying past and knocking him backward. The gun fires as she knew it would. The recoil, combined with her motion, allows her to rake the Glock from his fingers. Breezy rolls on the carpet, landing on her right shoulder and rocks around onto her feet. In an instant, she's taken up a kneeling stance facing back the way she came. She levels the Glock at the front counter.

Perp number one appears with a bag full of drugs over his shoulder. He sees her and raises his shotgun. It's the last mistake he'll ever make.

Perp number three's Glock has a magazine that extends only a fraction of an inch from the butt of the grip. It's a standard mag rather than an extended one. The gun's heavy. It feels as though it's carrying a full magazine, which is good. With two rounds already expended, Breezy suspects she can rely on anywhere from ten to fifteen rounds remaining. It's rare anyone loads all seventeen possible rounds into a Glock as the pressure on the spring within the magazine resists those last few casings, but this gun has enough weight to suggest the mag is over half full. It sure beats the five rounds in the 38 Special.

Breezy sets the tritium dot at the end of the barrel over the sternum of perp number one. She's unsure whether perp three has loaded the standard 9mm rounds or the show-stopping 147-gram rounds. Given they have different recoil profiles, she settles on the sternum rather than a headshot. After the crack from the shot that hit the guard, she suspects it's firing the lighter 115-gram rounds, but she can't risk missing. From her time on the range, she knows the 115s have less recoil but are slightly faster than the 147s. They're supersonic rounds which gives them a flatter trajectory over distance. The crack she heard from the first two shots had to be the equivalent of an indoor sonic boom. This gives her a good idea about what to expect as she squeezes the trigger.

Of all the days to rob the hospital drug store, these chumps had to choose the one when a United States Secret Service special agent was buying a can of Coke.

Breezy's USSS assignment is to blend into the outer perimeter when the President decides to walk around outdoors. What may look informal and casual is carefully rehearsed. Breezy doesn't wear the classic formal dress or dark sunglasses of the Secret Service. She doesn't even have a radio earpiece or body armor in her kit. Hell, most of the time, she's in a t-shirt and shorts to throw any would-be attacker off the scent. Usually, she keeps her service Glock in a streamlined, modified, quick-draw holster held flat against her stomach. Breezy wears a C-cup bra, but when she's on duty, a little padded foam allows her to slip into a D-cup, and the Glock is all but invisible beneath her loose t-shirt. If shit goes down, the close contact team is responsible for protecting the principle while she and the outer perimeter take down the assailant. Breezy can hit a fly crawling over a paper target at fifty yards—well, she thinks she can. To be fair, there's nothing left to confirm the kill on the range, but there aren't too many flies buzzing around either.

One shot is all she needs.

The bullet lashes out of the barrel of the Glock at over a thousand feet per second. Within five milliseconds, the copper slug is plunging deep into the man's chest, shattering bones and tumbling as it tears through soft tissue. It's the exit splatter that confirms the nature of the bullet for Breezy. She wasn't sure if these were hollow-point rounds, but from the fine arc of blood on the door behind perp number one, she's firing cheap-ass solid spun copper. Okay, good to know. They don't have quite the stopping power of a hollow point, but they still make one helluva mess.

As for perp one, he's in disbelief. Guns are so much more fun when you're the one squeezing the trigger. When you're on the other end of the barrel, the fun comes to a thundering halt. He drops his shotgun and clutches at his chest. To him, it'll feel like he's been hit across the ribcage with a baseball bat. He's not dead. Not yet. But it won't take long. It's the shot placement that induces the shock he's experiencing. Hit someone in the shoulder or the gut, and they'll keep coming. Even the ribs are survivable. Strike the sternum, though, and it's like cracking an eggshell. It's central, so the shockwave reverberates outward, fracturing ribs. Behind it lies the windpipe, arteries and spinal column. Clip just one of those, and the body's critical support systems unwind in seconds.

Perp three is still trying to figure out what just happened. It's the two shots in rapid succession that leave him stunned—one into the roof, the other into his buddy. It'll take his mind a moment to reboot. That gives Breezy an opening to focus on the others.

Damn, she wishes she had ear protection. The ringing inside her skull makes it impossible to hear the screams of the woman beside the counter. The lady's mouth is open. The veins on her neck are taut. Her fists are clenched, and her face is flushed with color, but she's silent as far as Breezy can tell.

The curious perp by the front door shows his face again, positioning it in precisely the same location as before. He's in line with the fourth shelf and has not more than half of his profile peering around the edge of the aisle. And he gets a tiny red dot in the center of his forehead for his trouble. For Breezy, it's an easy shot. She's got the feel of the Glock and the kick of the ammo down. She lined him up before he appeared. He walked into the round. She doubts he even saw her; it was so damn quick. His body tumbles backward. A gun falls from his hands. Blood splashes across the window behind him. Cracks run through the glass, telling her the round exited out the back of his skull. Beyond him lies the parking lot and a concrete retaining wall. What's left of that slug is either embedded in the door frame of a car or has dug into the brickwork. The forensics team will find it when they reconstruct the scene.

The other lookout is at the end of the five aisles within the store. From what Breezy can tell, the team was probably planning to exit through the fire door, and his assignment was to keep it clear. Perhaps there's someone in a car waiting for them in the alley. If the driver's smart, he will have left as soon as police lights lit up the parking lot.

From where she is near the walkway leading to the hospital, Breezy can see across in front of the aisles. A dark silhouette crouches behind bottles of shampoo. He has his hands up near his face. Through the bottles and shelves, Breezy can see the outline of a gun pointing up at the ceiling. He's readying himself to swing around the corner. If he had leveled his gun at the old lady, Breezy would be in trouble. As it is, hair dye and conditioner are no match for a 9mm slug moving faster than the speed of sound. She fires. The bullet strikes him before he can react, before he even hears the report of her Glock. Based on his side profile, she estimates it struck him just behind the temple. A gun tumbles out into the walkway. Fingers twitch before lying still. The remains of the bullet are embedded in the steel fire door.

Perp three has lost all the color in his face. He's got his hands up. His bandana has slid down around his neck, exposing his neatly trimmed mustache. His mouth hangs open. Breezy is back on her feet with the hot barrel of the Glock inches from his head. This is not where she wants to be. Ranged weapons and melee and all that shit. She'd rather there was a good fifteen to twenty feet between them, but he's shaking like a puppet on loose strings.

"Grab him," she says, stepping back and gesturing to the security guard. "Pull his arm over your shoulder."

Perp three does as he's told.

"Now, move, move, move," she yells, grabbing the young man by the back of his collar and pushing the hot barrel of her gun against the back of his neck. She runs, keeping the perp out in front of her. Perp three drags the security guard along with him. Breezy has no desire to shoot this perp. She's already removed her finger from the trigger, laying it along the side of the Glock. So long as he's not a threat, he'll live. Perp three, though, doesn't know that and runs as though his life depends on making it to the emergency department.

They crash through the doors into an empty triage unit.

"Get him on a gurney," she yells, letting go of the perp's collar. Breezy steps into the nursing station and grabs the intercom. "This is Secret Service agent Breanne De la Cruz. The active-shooter incident is over. I have a wounded security guard in Emergency, requiring immediate assistance."

No sooner has she finished speaking than Susan appears, peering around the corner of the swinging doors leading to the operating theater. She's wearing blue scrubs with a stethoscope around her neck and has a name badge on a lanyard. Susan rushes over to tend to the guard.

Perp three is standing beside the wounded guard, towering over him with what Breezy can only describe as a look of satisfaction on his face. He really thinks he helped save a life. Breezy slips the Glock into the small of her back and grabs his arm, twisting it up behind him. With one hand on his collar and the other driving his arm hard up against his spine, she marches him out into the reception area.

Several police officers come running in with guns drawn. Breezy identifies herself, but they're not going to believe anyone until every firearm is secure and the place has been thoroughly searched—and she agrees with that approach. If this were her patch, she'd take no chances either.

"United States Secret Service," she says, letting perp three go and pushing him forward toward one of the officers. Perp three staggers like a deer on the freeway. He can't even blink before he's taken down. Two officers crash tackle him, throwing him around like a rag doll.

Breezy drops to her knees with her hands interlocked behind her head, saying, "I'm law enforcement. I'm armed. I'm carrying a Glock in the small of my back."

"On the ground," is the reply. "Now!"

Breezy knows what's coming next. It's going to hurt, but there's no other option.

The only way for her to lie prone on the ground is to remove her hands from her head and lower herself, but that isn't happening. She's wearing a bloodstained t-shirt and torn jeans. Her hair's a goddamn mess. She's got blood on her hands. In the eyes of the officers staring at her down the barrel of each standard-issue police sidearm, she's a threat. If she moves her arms, she's inviting a response. She remains stationary regardless of their illogical, non-sensical demands for her to drop. It's better they take control of her by force. Making any movement when staring down the barrel of a gun isn't smart. She could move slow, but not slowly enough. They're nervous. They've walked into the unknown. Fingers are already itching against the trigger of various guns. Cops take no chances. And that's understandable. Breezy lowers her head, showing she's submissive, but she's not making any movement that could be misinterpreted. Her head motion, though, isn't enough. She knows that, but it's all she can do.

From the side, a cop crashes on top of her. The Glock is tossed across the floor. Breezy goes limp, offering no resistance even though the takedown *fucking* hurts. The cop grabs her arms and jerks them back. The bloodstained gun clatters across the linoleum. Cuffs are ratcheted around her wrists and tightened to the point she's in agony, but she doesn't say anything. She grits her teeth, working through the pain. Breezy tells herself it's only temporary, only for a few minutes. Hang in there, girl.

Two of the cops retreat, keeping their guns on her as she lies on the floor in front of the hospital reception. The other cop plants a boot in the middle of her back, pinning her to the linoleum. With both her and perp three effectively neutralized, they can talk among themselves, reducing the tension.

There's shouting from the drug store as more cops move in, but the show's over in there.

"ID? Where's your ID?" one of the cops says to her, holstering his weapon.

Blood drips from her mouth. She's split her lip on the floor.

Where the *fuck* is her ID?

"Ah," she says, trying to think through the pain in her shoulders and her crushed ribs. As it is, she can barely breathe. It would help if the asshole behind her took his boot off her back. Or is it his knee? She can't tell. "In the store. Back in the drug store. On the counter."

One of the cops walks away along the corridor toward the drug store. There's a lot of chatter over various radios. Red and blue lights compete with each other in the parking lot. At least there's no need to call for an ambulance.

"Could you?" she says with her face still flat on the floor.

The officer behind her drags her to her feet. Steel fingers grip her upper arm. Breezy is all of five foot four. She gets blown away in a storm. And not figuratively. If there's a decent gale pushing in from the Atlantic, she gets tossed around trying to run from her car to her apartment. There's not much meat on her bones. Oh, there's plenty of padding around the middle, and her thighs are like those of a weightlifter, but she's never had a lot of upper body strength. It only takes a steady arm and a gentle squeeze to fire a gun.

Perp three is blabbering. He's talking about everything. The cops will have to read him his Miranda rights just to get him to shut up. Nothing's his fault, of course. The damn fool has no idea police body cameras are recording everything and from multiple angles. At least it'll make for a brief court appearance. Besides, the drug store has its own security cameras, and they will have captured everything.

19

Breezy is marched back into the drug store.

What a fucking mess!

Blood soaks into the carpet. Shelves lie scattered on the floor. Bottles of just about everything clog the aisles along with colorful cardboard boxes. Breezy could have sworn it wasn't this chaotic when she left.

"No phone," the lead cop says, turning back to them from beside the counter.

"Behind the sign," she says, unable to point with her hands. She nods, directing the officer where to look. "You'll find my driver's license and Secret Service ID in the pouch on the back of the phone."

The lead cop picks up the phone, turning it over. Immediately, the screen comes back to life. There's an active call in progress. The number displayed is 911. He raises it to his ear and identifies himself to the dispatch operator. She must fill him in on what she heard as he turns to the other officers, saying, "Uncuff her."

"Thanks," Breezy says as blood rushes back to her fingertips. She shakes her hands.

"You did this?" the cop asks, gesturing to the bodies on the floor. "All of this?"

Breezy's sure he doesn't mean to sound patronizing. She understands how unassuming she appears. That's how she got her job with the Secret Service.

"Yes."

Now that they're over by the cashier's register, Breezy gets her first good look at the perp by the fire door. She hit him behind the ear rather than near his temple and struck much lower than she thought. The round removed the back of his skull but didn't pierce his brain. It wouldn't have

20

made any difference, though. The shockwave would have turned his grey matter into mush, and the bleeding was profuse.

"I had no choice," she says. "Once they shot the guard, the meter was running. He wasn't going to last long."

"I—ah," the officer says, handing her the phone along with her ID. "I'm going to need you to accompany me to the station."

"Sure. No problem. I understand."

Susan stands back by the reception area with her arms folded across her chest. Breezy offers her a slight wave, just a subtle flick of her fingers in acknowledgment as she's led away out of the drug store. The cop beside her carries the Glock in a zip-locked plastic evidence bag.

It's the only handgun they bag.

SHOOT

Sweat beads on Olivia's skin. Droplets glisten in the twilight, threatening to roll down her neck and ruin the shot. She shifts, laughing with coy ambiguity, hiding the way she's perspiring. As night falls, a cool breeze blows in from the Potomac. The air is soothing on her naked body. Lace curtains sway. There's talking in the distance, probably down by the river, but the shotgun mic won't pick that up. Her groans, though, oh, hell yeah. The mic won't miss those.

Olivia rides back and forth on a man twice her age, working her pelvis with a steady motion. She moans softly, arching her back and playing to the camera.

Olivia rolls her head, letting her hair rest on her back as she straddles the stranger, grinding her hips over his loins. For his part, there's no acting. From the look on his face, he's somewhere between Mars and Jupiter. His eyes are bulging from his head. He has a grin a mile wide. Some jobs are more fun than others.

Olivia's not even sure what this chump's name is—she was introduced to him using a pseudonym before they got to work. Such

23

pleasantries are meaningless. Olivia was more interested in the room than his fake name. She was curious about the setup. She knows the drill. The producers never give anything away, but there are always tells. For all she knows, it'll be her and not him that's ultimately used as a deep fake, but they'll both be scrubbed to hide their identities. Olivia's learned more about the industry than they realize. Most people think porn stars are dumb, and that's exactly what the stars want them to think, so they don't see them coming—or cumming, depending on perspective. Sex doesn't so much sell as blind.

Olivia reaches forward, clutching at the sheets on either side of her mark, letting her hair fall off her shoulders toward him. Without taking her eyes off his, she giggles, acutely aware of the camera placement. A slight flex of her arms allows her to arch her back, ensuring her breasts are visible through her long, flowing hair. She writhes, rocking upon him, ensuring her nipples protrude past her extensions.

This guy can't help himself. The rule for this shoot was 'no hands.' It's not that Olivia doesn't enjoy being touched, but that the camera angles are set to accentuate her form and highlight her bust, not his stubby, hairy fingers. The director lets it slide, probably because he wants the footage to remain uninterrupted. He's using multiple cameras, but she overheard him talking about going with one continuous shot. It seems he's not sure which one he'll use until he reviews the imagery. Yep, this is definitely a deep fake and not a porno, regardless of what Snow White said to her. One angle is usually a giveaway for a fake security camera or for mimicking covert surveillance footage.

Olivia goes along with *Mr. Handsy*. His fingers might be a little calloused, but he's gentle. He knows how to touch a woman. There's respect. Rather than treating her breasts like water balloons at a children's party, he caresses them, running his fingers around the curves leading down to her nipples. She smiles, enjoying herself. Actual pleasure makes the job a little easier.

Someone's pacing in the background. No one gets nervous on a porno shoot. They get as hard as a goddamn rock. This has got to be a blackmail play. They'll use AI to change appearances and set up some poor sap. It's the ambient light that's revealing. It's seven-thirty in the evening. Shooting in the middle of a sweltering summer, with the sun catching the smog as night descends over the capital, might not be romantic, but it gives the room a natural, soft focus.

Fading sunlight reflects off the wardrobe mirror. Hints of yellow and orange catch her dark hair. There are some things computers can't fake. Ambient lighting is one. Oh, in theory, they can. In practice, they miss the subtleties of how light scatters in a million directions.

The crew must have some other footage they're working with as the cameraman was surprisingly precise with the timing of the shoot and the location of the cameras. He knew exactly what he wanted. Before they got started, he had a light meter out, pointing at the sky. He checked the reflected light from the walls and the floor, reading whites, blues, reds and greens. He turned on half the lights within the room, which seemed unduly strange to her. They didn't need any additional lighting for the shoot. Then he held up production until he was satisfied the exact moment had arrived.

Olivia's been reading up on the additive model of color theory. Although she doesn't know the exact combination he was after, she knows why he went to these lengths. He must have a clip of the mark in similar lighting, probably taken from a similar angle using a concealed camera. He's recreating the scene.

That's the thing about deep fakes—she thinks, making sure she's got good contact with this guy's pelvis and riding him like a bronco— everyone assumes the best fakes are CGI, but that's not true. Get a computer to fake a video. That'll work, right? The only problem is, if a computer can fake it, another computer can detect it. Artificial intelligence is an arm's race. As fast as one adaptive program figures out how to fool people, another machine learning algorithm works on exposing fakes. Ah, but *blended* fakes, deep fakes that use the bare minimum of retouches, can still slip through the net. Most of Snow White's fakes are composites made using old-school techniques, making them harder to detect. For now, they can still fool the best filtering software. After all, the censors can't block everything. Something's got to be real.

Both Olivia and Prince Charming, as the director calls the guy groaning beneath her, have roughly a hundred tiny dots painted on their faces in a carefully choreographed lattice. In the past, motion-capture would use maybe fifty such dots in bright greens or blues, but the two of them have been painted with invisible dots that will only show up in ultraviolet. They don't appear on the primary camera, only on the secondary UV tracking camera. Not all of the dots will be used, but they're concentrated around the nose, eyes and mouth, allowing for subtle changes to be made to transform their appearance in post-production. The process took almost two hours to apply, with Olivia sitting patiently in front of a blue light as her skin was touched up with meticulous care. She was fascinated by the process, watching it in the mirror. Rather than being evenly spread, the dots follow tendons, muscles and the ridge of various facial bones. This allows the SFX team to better map structures and overlay their deep fake image. Damn, the budget for this fake must be insane.

Olivia bites at her lip. She closes her eyes for a few seconds and works herself into a frenzy. With her legs spread wide and her pelvic bone rubbing against his, she rocks back and forth. Olivia squeezes her thighs over his hips, bringing her legs in. She shivers a little, flexing her stomach

26

muscles. Faking an orgasm for the camera is an easy payday. He's finished, so why go on? Time to wrap things up.

And the Oscar goes to...

Olivia opens her eyes and slowly unfolds her facial expression into a huge sense of relief. Who says Hollywood is dead? Olivia knows the routine. It's important to make sure her smile reaches high into her cheeks. Being fake is one thing; looking fake is another. Olivia's a pro. With a slight tilt of her head, she leans forward and kisses him softly on the cheek, lingering for a second before working down his neck, following the script. Olivia pauses, biting at his skin, knowing this will elicit a genuine response from him. He flinches, reacting, but he too has script prompts to follow. Her little buddy breathes deeply, sinking back into the pillow. He stares at the ceiling as she climbs off him. She moves to her left even though she'd normally go to the right. She turns in the manner prescribed in the dress rehearsal.

No one speaks. The cameras are still rolling. Olivia picks up her silk gown and drapes it over her shoulders. She offers one last look, peering at him as she saunters off to the bathroom.

"...and cut," is called by the producer. "Nice work."

Yep, work—that's what it is. Nothing more than a lousy buck.

Olivia loves a bit of bling, but she's not allowed to wear any during shoots as it's too easy to identify, so she idles her time away as the crew mill around, putting her rings and necklaces back on. She doesn't get dressed as she dreads the possibility of a callback. Someone somewhere will be reviewing the footage. Sometimes it's a close-up out of frame or a bird squawking at the wrong time that will demand a reshoot. Given they want something spontaneous, she hopes they let those slide. As the seconds pass in silence, Olivia becomes more confident. She might actually get out of here a little early. She slips on some underwear. Already she's feeling more comfortable.

"Are we good?" she calls out from the bathroom.

"We're good," is the reply.

Olivia lets her silk gown fall to the tiles. She pulls a bra from her purse. It's been folded up. The cups are creased. She straightens them. Olivia hasn't worn a bra today, but she brought one with her for after the shoot. Clients are often picky with subtle details most people would overlook. In this instance, they didn't want to see the distinct imprint where the elastic in her bra would have sat up against her skin. Olivia gets it. Deep fakes succeed because of their attention to detail. Although most ordinary people wouldn't realize it, seeing a slight imprint tells an astute observer precisely how long she's been undressed. Not everyone stares at nipples. No, the thin imprint around her ribs would have told them she'd only just whipped off her bra. The lack of bra straps suggests she's been relaxing in the apartment for most of the day. Illusions are all about maintaining plausibility. Every detail tells a story.

As for leaving the silk gown collapsed on the floor, it's all part of the plan. Silk is easy to examine for hair. The cleaning crew will remove any strands, swapping them out with samples collected from some other poor bitch. They'll ensure the crumpled clothing looks precisely as it does now—right down to the direction it was discarded, how it folds on itself and even the placement of the sleeves. Deep fakes are nothing without corroborating evidence.

Olivia works her legs into a pair of tight jeans. Ziggy Stardust rocks her t-shirt. She slips on some shoes but doesn't bother with socks, leaving them in her purse.

Dopey, as she likes to think of him, tosses his used condom in the toilet. He flushes, watching as it circles the bowl briefly before disappearing. Then he slips on a pair of boxer shorts. His rotund belly sags over his waistband.

"Damn, that was good," he says, looking her up and down now that she's dressed. It seems he can't help himself. He has to know. "So... did you?"

"No," she replies coldly. Olivia keeps her back to him. It's all an act, buddy. You knew that when you took the job. Although she does appreciate that even he wasn't able to tell. Seriously, why do men ask?

Olivia pulls some more jewelry out of her purse. She looks down at her rings. Diamonds glisten in the bathroom downlights. Dopey wanders off while Olivia smiles at the irony. Her diamonds are as beautiful and as fake as her performance. They're synthetic. They're too good to be real, which is crazy. Actual, natural diamonds have flaws and imperfections. Jewelers even have a term for it—*inclusions*. The defects and imperfections in a natural diamond are like fingerprints, revealing not only how that particular rock formed but where it was mined. Like her deep fakes, slight flaws make them more real. That's why there's little or no CGI in her line of work. If it looks too good to be true, it is. A little grit keeps things real, at least as real as a deep fake can be.

"Not bad," the producer says, walking up beside her. Snow White is in her sixties, but apart from a few hairline wrinkles, she looks as though she's in her late thirties. She's got a damn good surgeon. With her pale skin and bleached hair, she's only missing a pretty skirt and a blood-red apple to complete the look.

From the doorway behind her, one of the women on the production crew says, "Minnie, you were smoking in there."

Olivia ignores her. She fiddles with her rings. She's not being rude. She's forgotten that's her stage name for this particular gig. The woman is indignant at being snubbed. "Well, fuck you too, bitch," she says, wheeling in front of Olivia and storming out.

"W—What?" Olivia says, looking up. She thought it was a background comment to someone else, perhaps the camerawoman packing up her equipment.

"Don't worry about her," Snow White says.

"Why can't we use our first names?" Olivia says, still reeling from being insulted. "I'm fucking Olivia." She points at Dopey, saying, "Well, technically, he's fucking Olivia, but I'm Olivia. That's me. That's my name."

Dopey says, "I'm Dave."

As well-meaning as he is, those two words don't help. Olivia wants an apology from the wicked witch of the west storming down the corridor. She can see her down the hall, coiling a cable. She goes to walk down there when Snow takes her by the arm.

"Just leave it. Shit happens. Move on."

Snow is right.

Olivia grabs her purse. She's done with fucking around in this mansion. She's ready to leave.

"Where's the drop?" she asks.

"Arlington Cemetery. There's a construction site well back from the main road, just off York Drive. Be there at nine."

"Nine?" Olivia says, realizing it's already 7:30 pm. "Tonight?"

"Yes."

"And you want to meet in a cemetery?"

"Yes."

"That's a little macabre, don't ya think?"

"It's dead quiet," Snow replies without a hint of irony. "Is that going to be a problem?"

"No."

"Good."

"I'll be there," Olivia says. She'd rather be paid on-site, but she understands Snow White's concerns. It wouldn't do for Olivia to be pulled over by a cop because she failed to signal while changing lanes or didn't come to a complete halt at a stop sign, only to have her car searched and twenty thousand dollars found in a duffle bag hidden in the trunk.

"Client's a bit edgy," Snow White says. "Can't afford any publicity. No links. Clean scrub. They want this kept on the down-low. You know the drill. Quiet as a church mouse."

Olivia replies, "Blackmail is always best served in silence," not that Snow White bites. It's probably not that she wants to be discreet. At a guess, even she doesn't know who the client is and what they're after. High-value ops like this tend to go through brokers, so there's a dead-end if anyone picks up on the trail. At first, Olivia assumed this was a bitter ex wanting something incriminating to stack up in divorce proceedings. That would explain the UV motion capture dots.

It's the timing that bothers her. The team isn't recreating something that happened months ago. They're staging something that happened yesterday or earlier this week. To her mind, that means the actual mark has got to be someone at the federal level, perhaps even in the senate. This isn't a corrupt mayor they're shaking down.

"Where's the exit?" Olivia asks.

"There's a ladder at the back of the garden. Once you're on the wall, drop down and follow the path along the river back to the parking lot."

Olivia nods.

The film crew isn't taking any chances being picked up on some nosey neighbor's surveillance camera pointing out on the street. Operational security has been tight. As it was, the team had Olivia hire a rental car using cash under an alias and park it nearby. Then she took a ferry across the Potomac and had lunch in a cafe where she would be captured on at least one security camera. They gave her five designer shopping bags to make it appear as though she were on a spending spree, but these were stuffed with empty boxes. Then she slipped back into a waiting speedboat that ferried her across the river, avoiding any known cameras. From there, she slipped into the back of a cleaning van by the docks and waited. When the driver came back from a fake bathroom break, he drove on to park undercover on the adjoining property. If anyone does connect her with the shoot, the best they'll be able to do is identify her as being on the other side of the river at the time.

After the shoot, the team will do something overt. They need to get caught on surveillance to establish a credible alibi. The house next door will get the best clean it's ever had. Then they'll do something dumb to throw any private eyes off the scent. If anyone backtracks them, they need to lead them to a dead end. They'll do something like drive the van straight from here to the local McDonald's for a bite to eat. Then they'll open the back in full view of the parking lot security cameras. This will 'clean' them if anyone gets too nosey. Anyone digging that deep will move on at that point as there's nothing to see. That's the thing about deep fakes. There's always a trail left behind. Always. Even the best of dead ends will inevitably lead somewhere, so the best strategy is to give up a plausible lead to investigators. Leaving a cold trail is a good way to shake a tail. Leaving no trail at all raises too many goddamn questions. Snow White could fake the security camera footage on the ferry or at McDonald's, but every touch leaves the potential for compromise. By appearing innocent and misunderstood, they're more likely to fade into the shadows. If the heat comes down, they want to be struck off the list of suspects asap.

As Olivia walks downstairs toward the back door, Snow says, "Don't be late."

Oh, when it comes to money, Olivia's never late.

The bitch that insulted her sees her coming and turns away into a side room. Yeah, you'd better hide, Olivia thinks, still feeling angry. Ah, let it go.

She slips her hand under her t-shirt and grabs the door handle through the cotton, opening the door without leaving any fingerprints. The handle will be cleaned, but she's not taking any chances either. Twenty grand for a quick shoot screams of the need for caution. Someone's about to get buried, and it isn't going to be Olivia.

Once outside, she keeps to the shadows as she walks through the manicured garden. The bushes are shaped like lollipops. How fucked up is that? An elongated water feature stretches into a tiled forecourt and a carefully mowed lawn, which looks as though it doubles as a putting green. Goofy is standing by a rendered wall at the back of the garden, holding a ladder.

"Damn, you were hot tonight," he says.

"Thanks," she says, appreciating the compliment. This is their fourth job together. It's the closest they'll get to being friends. She knows she'll never learn his real name.

Olivia climbs the ladder. She's careful not to grab the rungs with her hands. Instead, her fingernails glide over the aluminum, guiding her on as she steps up.

Behind her, the sun is setting. The ladder has been placed in the shadow of a poplar tree, allowing her to slip over the wall without being seen. On the other side, the brickwork is rough. Whoever built this mansion skimped on the render. As the wall backs onto a narrow strip of land running along the river, it's only ever visible from a distance. Olivia crouches on top of the wall and jumps, bending her legs to soften the landing. She hits with a thud resounding through her feet.

At low tide, the Potomac smells like a fish market. Tiny crabs pop in and out of holes in the mud as she creeps along beneath the trees, walking away from the home. The bank has eroded, giving her not more than a few feet to work with. A recent storm has felled a pine tree, causing it to fall into the river, blocking what little of the path she has to walk along. Olivia tries to climb over it, but the branches are too densely packed. Pine needles irritate her skin.

"Fuck," she mutters, looking at how the tree has crushed a brick wall before hitting the water. Her options are: push through the needles and suck up the scratches, or wade around the tree and sink up to her knees in the mud, or climb over what's left of the wall into the backyard of some stranger's home and risk being picked up on someone's security surveillance system. From what she can tell from staring out of the shadows, no one's home. This is probably a vacation spot as whoever owns the house has ignored the damage caused by the tree, which is all the more reason for there to be cameras.

"Damn it!"

The only option she hasn't considered is backtracking past the shoot, heading upriver to the Mount Vernon Estate and then cutting inland from there. That turns what should be a ten-minute walk into an hour-long detour. She's going to have to hotfoot it to shave off some time. She'll have to go back as far as the ferry terminal and then trace a U-shape back to the boat ramp where her car is parked.

"There has got to be an easier way of making a buck."

It's just after eight in the evening when she turns around. There's barely an hour till the money drop. There's no way Olivia's wading through the mudflats. She power walks, lengthening her stride as she heads back toward Mount Vernon.

Several properties have private docks stretching out into the river, reaching beyond the low watermark. The tide is coming in. Waves begin to lap at the mud, submerging the flats. There's a couple out walking two small dogs on a joint lead. Seagulls scatter on seeing the dogs even though their combined lead prevents them from rushing across the narrow strip of sand. Olivia warns the couple about the fallen tree further along the path. They continue on regardless. She should have kept her mouth shut. She's just made herself memorable. Chances are they'll never be identified as bystanders. If they are, she'll be a hazy blur.

Right now, Olivia simply needs to blend in. Be pleasant but not friendly. The technical term is *grey*—neither black nor white, just some indeterminate shade in between. Forgettable. No one special. Just another faceless stranger enjoying the cool breeze coming in from the river.

Olivia's hungry. As tempting as it is, she resists the urge to grab a burger from the van in the parking lot opposite the ferry terminal. Day trippers linger, chowing on fries. She needs to be a ghost, blending into the background. If she were to stop and order something, she'd be memorable. Pretty girl on her own. Paid cash. Yeah, she can wait and get something to eat later.

An Uber would be nice, but that would leave an electronic fingerprint. No, she's got to walk around the block. Olivia heads up a couple of streets and doubles back toward the boat ramp and her waiting car. She keeps her head down as she walks, staring at her phone. It's bogus, of course. There's no SIM and the battery has been pulled out. She won't connect until she's at least a suburb away, but those driving past won't know that. Besides, staring at the blank screen keeps her face from appearing on dash cams.

Once Olivia makes it to the boat ramp, she drives to the mall, where she can switch cars and slip a charged battery into her phone. It's 8:30 pm. She's got to hustle if she wants to be paid.

CLOWNING AROUND

"What the hell were you thinking?" Director Johnson asks. He's grumpy because he's been called in on a Saturday evening. From his attire, he was heading out for dinner. It's the pressed business shirt that's the giveaway. The lack of creases tells Breezy he changed into it. Whoever he was meeting, it was important rather than social. He's probably left them at the restaurant while he rushed in to deal with her.

She drops her head, looking down at her hands resting in her lap.

"I couldn't let him die."

"I know," the director says. "I get it. You did the right thing. I only wish you hadn't left a trail of dead bodies."

"I was out of options," she says, twisting her lips sideways. It's perverse to distill lives down to a few choices, and yet it's honest. To her, it wasn't about life and death. It was about *whose* life and *whose* death. When it came down to her life or the lives of the staff and customers being weighed against the robbers, there was no choice. Once that guard was shot and they refused him medical assistance, there was only ever going to be one outcome in her mind. With cop cars turning up outside and their lights flashing, the prospect of being held hostage was looking all too real. Breezy wasn't going to wait for things to get any worse.

The director is stone-faced. "I know, but you've created one helluva mess. It's going to take time to clean this up."

The Secret Service has a good working relationship with the DC Metro Police. Allowances are made to accommodate their operations, so it isn't unusual to be sitting in a police precinct talking to the USSS director. Already, the police captain is running interference with the press.

The director reaches up and undoes his bow tie. He loosens the top button, relaxing a little, but to Breezy, it seems staged. He could have done that at any point in time. Why now? He's getting ready to deliver the bad news.

There's an awkward silence between them—which tells Breezy everything she needs to know. She's going to be stood down. It's the Secret Service. The clue is right there in the title: *secret*. As they speak, her face is being plastered all over the evening news. She's being hailed as a hero. She would have preferred the opportunity to drag the injured guard down to the emergency department without any additional shots being fired.

"How did you do it?" the director asks. Breezy is quiet, so he continues. "Three shots—on target—under pressure—all in under ten seconds."

"I cheated," Breezy says, knowing the director will understand. "All three had shown their faces earlier. When the shooting started, they all appeared at the same spots around the store, at the same height, in the same way. It was like being on the range shooting targets. All I had to do was swivel and keep my aim level."

The director nods.

Their discussion would seem unusually cold and detached to anyone listening in, but there's method to the approach. Killing someone is a horrific act. There's no avoiding that brutal reality. Dwelling on it is a recipe for PTSD. Breezy needs to get it out of her system. The shock will hit her at some point. They both know that. Disengaging is a coping mechanism. She's trained for this—not merely the act of pulling the trigger but living with the consequences. Being on the outer perimeter of the Presidential detail, Breezy has been trained not to hesitate. Her prep for a moment like this has been brutal.

Back at Langley, a pop-up target of an assassin would appear with the image of a pregnant woman thirty feet beyond it, just off the line of sight. What if she misses and hits the woman? Hell, the bullet could pass right through and still hit her. It doesn't matter. The trigger must be pulled. Movies like to romanticize the idea of special agents sacrificing themselves for the President. What they don't realize is that sacrifice happens long before anyone squeezes a trigger. The challenge isn't to take a bullet for the President—it's to live with the consequences of a lethal decision made in a fraction of a second. If that consequence is waking in a cold sweat night after night because a stray round hit a five-year-old kid in the crowd, so be it. There's no second-guessing. In the moment, it's always the right decision to act.

"Well, from the photos I've seen, you were on point."

"Thank you, sir," Breezy says, avoiding eye contact even though he's looking to connect with her. Killing someone is nothing to be proud of. Breezy needs to focus on the lives saved, not the shots taken, but she struggles to express herself in terms beyond that of following through on her training.

The director says, "You took one helluva risk in there."

"I did, sir."

"I respect that."

"Yes, sir."

"Breezy," he says, pausing for a moment. "You know what comes next, right?"

"Yes, sir."

The bullshit and bravado are over.

"I'm going to put you on administrative leave with full pay. There's no doubt about your actions. No question about your integrity. You understand that, right?"

"Yes, sir."

"I need to give you a cooling-off period. My problem is that you're no longer invisible. Hell, the mayor called me. He wants to award you a medal. You understand the position that puts me in, right?"

"Yes, sir."

"I can't have you on the outer perimeter. You're too high profile. You'll draw attention to the broader operation."

"Yes, sir."

"I'll talk to Mathers about having you moved to close protection detail. We'll get you in a nice dress and put you on the front row."

"Yes, sir," Breezy says, hating the loss of freedom that comes from being on show in front of *The Boss*.

The Secret Service is as much for show as it is for protection. It's designed to project strength and deter aggressors. Most of the close protection detail are gym junkies. Their thick chest muscles struggle to remain hidden behind their dark suits. With black sunglasses, visible earpieces and padded jackets, they're as much a *don't-fuck-with-me* message as the quills of a porcupine or the tail of a rattlesnake. Breezy enjoys being on the outer perimeter precisely because she doesn't fit that stereotype. She hangs her head.

"But not right away. I need the heat to die down."

"How long, sir?" she asks reluctantly, not wanting to hear the answer.

"Eighteen months."

"Eighteen months!" Breezy buries her head in her hands for a moment. She composes herself, sitting back in the chair, wanting to remain focused.

"Maybe longer."

Breezy closes her eyes, pinching them shut for a moment.

"There's going to be an investigation. It's the fourth guy. He's going to go to trial. That will drag you through the news cycle for at least the next six to nine months. I can't have that kind of distraction hanging over the department. You understand?"

"Yes, sir."

"We'll put you behind a desk. You'll push paper for a while, but we'll get you back out in the field. I need this to fade into the background."

"I understand."

"On Monday, I want you to undergo a full debrief with the team psych. We'll get through this, okay? We'll find something for you to focus on until this runs its course."

"Yes, sir."

Breezy appreciates the director's use of the word, *We*. He doesn't want to do this to her. He's trying to show her she's not alone, but he's out of options. Eighteen months to two years is a long time to sit on the bench.

In ten seconds, three lives were lost, and her career was effectively destroyed, but, hey, the guard lived. It's a bitter consolation for killing three people. As much as the two of them may talk about taking slick shots and being *on point*, the reality is that three families have lost someone they cared about. Oh, for her, they were three creeps—three crackheads. They knew what they were doing when they busted through those doors. They all contributed to the guard being shot. But theory never matches practice. On paper, she did the right thing. That makes it easy to justify. The unavoidable truth is that she killed three young men. Breezy knows she'll see each face down the barrel of that goddamn Glock several hundred times before she dies. They'll haunt her dreams regardless of any macho bluster she engages with during the day.

There's a knock on the glass door. The police captain is outside. The director signals it's okay for him to come into his own office.

"Hey," the captain says. He pauses, unsure if he should continue in front of Breezy.

"It's okay," the director says. "What is it?"

"We've got Buster."

The director jumps down from the edge of the desk. He points at the floor. "Here?"

"Right here."

"How?"

The captain says, "He just walked in the front door. Said he wanted to talk."

"Just like that?"

"Just like that. I've got him in a holding cell."

"Who's going to talk to him?"

"I've got a couple of detectives working the case. They're in with him now."

"Can we observe?" the director asks, pointing at himself and Breezy.

"Sure," the captain says, beckoning them to follow.

"Come on," the director says, gesturing for Breezy to join them.

"What's going on?" she asks as they walk down the corridor toward the internal stairwell.

"You've heard about the clowns, right?"

She shrugs. "A little, I guess. They're like a crazy fringe cult or something. Always complaining about human rights. Mental as fuck."

"They're a crazy cult with an eye for radical political change," the director says. "They want to disband our sociopolitical and judicial systems. And that puts them on my radar."

As they walk down the internal concrete stairs to the basement, the captain says, "We're working a murder case involving them. We found a body floating face-down in the river last week. All identifying marks were removed. No fingerprints. No teeth. No face."

"Damn," Breezy says. It's one thing to kill someone. It's another to desecrate a corpse. It just seems wrong on every level. The thought sends a chill through her.

The director explains. "DNA matched the body to the FBI. He was a deep-cover agent tasked with infiltrating the clowns."

"Oh."

"I need to know if these guys are a danger to national security," the director says.

"And I need to catch a cop killer," the captain says.

"And now, Buster Al-Hashimi has voluntarily walked in off the street!"

"And waived his Miranda rights," the captain says.

The director is brutal in his assessment: "Idiot."

The captain leads them into a dimly lit anteroom and from there into a darkened room behind the interrogation cell. Although it looks as though they're peering through a window, it's a one-way mirror. They could sit, but the three of them stand, peering in at the tiny man on the other side of the glass. They lean against the desk, sitting half on it. Buster looks up. His eyes dart around the mirror. He seems to make eye contact with Breezy, which is impossible.

"He can't see us, right?" Breezy asks, pointing at the bright downlights within the interrogation room.

"Not a chance," the captain says.

Buster is squat in stature. He's not a dwarf, but he's short. His feet swing from the chair, not touching the floor. At a guess, Breezy would put him at five foot two inches. His hands rest on the table. A pair of chrome handcuffs locked around his wrists catch the downlights, shining like bracelets. A steel chain leads from the cuffs to a ring on the metal tabletop, forcing him to keep his arms out in front of him. To Breezy, at least, Buster looks harmless. He's balding on top with thin wisps of hair combed over his scalp. He's looking at her. She's sure he can see her. His expression, though, is blank. It's as though he's confused by her presence.

"Fascinating," the director says, leaning back on the table. He sits up on the edge. "What's the plan?"

The captain says, "I've got—"

"Now that we're all here," Buster says, "we can get started."

44

Buster peers at the captain with eyes that seem to pierce the soul. For someone that can only see his own reflection in a darkened mirror, he's picking his focal point with startling precision. Perhaps it's an educated guess. He may have heard the anteroom door open. Given the width of the mirror and its placement, it easily fits several people. He could have heard their muffled voices outside and guessed three officers were watching rather than one or two. It's not difficult to imagine the spacing and height.

Breezy mutters, "Damn, this guy is good."

In a heartbeat, Buster's expression goes from flat to a broad smile revealing his teeth. It's as though he heard her, but that's impossible. His cheeks lift. He twists his head sideways, looking precisely where she's leaning against the table behind her. He makes as though he's being warm and friendly—inviting. He's a clown on stage, ready to perform. His hands rise with chains dangling from them, limiting his range of motion.

"The spotlights are on," he says. "The curtain's drawn. The audience awaits. Send in the clowns! It's showtime! Let the spectacle begin!"

The captain talks into a radio. "Send in Connor and Zara."

The door to the interrogation room opens. Two detectives enter wearing plain clothes. Breezy smiles. They've gone with good cop/bad cop.

Connor is six foot four and imposing. He's got to be able to bench press two-twenty with ease. Breezy struggles with anything over fifty. Her personal best is a hundred, but that would be a warm-up weight for him. He looks down at Buster with unveiled disdain. He could crush him like a bug.

Zara smiles warmly. She's a pretty blonde with long hair falling off her shoulders. She's got the dreamy 36-26-36 measurements Breezy would die for. She's showing a little cleavage beneath her buttoned shirt. Are her breasts natural? That ass ain't. Well, maybe if she's still in her twenties. She's got to be a gym bunny. There's no way she could maintain that hourglass figure without a helluva lot of time on a cross-trainer. Her thighs are muscular. Perhaps a Peloton is more her style.

"Before we get started," Connor says. "I need to remind you that this interview is being recorded. I also need to remind you that you can reassert your right to have a lawyer present at any point in time. You do not need to talk to us without your lawyer. Do you understand?"

"Yes," Buster says, holding out his wrists, appealing to be uncuffed.

"And you're happy to proceed?" Zara asks, leaning against the wall and folding her arms. She looks relaxed. It's a lie.

Buster appears naive. "Yes."

Breezy thinks he's mad, waiving his rights. These two seasoned detectives are going to eat him alive. It's the power imbalance. They do this all day, every day. For him, this is an unnatural setting. They've got nothing to lose while a few loose words from him could see him spending the next thirty years behind bars.

Connor reaches in with a key and unlocks the cuffs, leaving them on the table.

"Was that really necessary?" Buster asks, rubbing his wrists. "I came here openly, freely, willingly. I'm talking to you of my own accord."

Zara says, "You're a suspect in a murder case."

"Me?" Buster asks, feigning surprise. He points at the center of his chest, but the expression on his face is almost comical. Connor looks pissed. He's not here to play games.

"You," Zara replies, pointing at him. "You're in deep shit, buddy. There's an FBI Special Agent in the morgue because of you."

"You need to ask me questions," Buster says, which is a curious point for him to make. They're the ones conducting the interview.

Breezy squints, looking carefully at the tiny, middle-aged man. He appears harmless enough. On the surface, he seems hopelessly out of his depth. Breezy's not so sure. She's been underestimated her entire life. She knows a pro when she sees one. This is the kind of guy that looks befuddled at the blackjack table in Vegas, but it's all an act. The others may not realize it yet, but Breezy knows they're being played.

Connor snaps. "Did you kill him? You want questions. That's a question."

"That's the wrong question."

"Okay. What question should I be asking?"

"Why?"

"Why seems obvious," Zara says in a relaxed tone, setting herself in contrast to Connor. "You found a mole. You eliminated the problem."

"You're still not asking the right questions," Buster says, remaining calm. "You shouldn't be asking why I or anyone else would kill your John Doe. You should be asking why I or anyone else would let the body float away?"

Zara and Connor exchange a quick glance.

"It's obvious once you think about it," Buster says. "Why go to such extreme lengths to hide the identity of the victim? Why remove the fingerprints, the teeth and even the guy's face, only to leave his body drifting on the tide?"

"You wanted us to find him," Zara says.

"Not me," Buster says, shaking his head. "I would have buried him alongside Jimmy Hoffa."

"You're saying someone's trying to set you up?"

Buster smiles. "And they say cops are dumb."

Within the observation room, the captain picks up a phone and dials the interrogation room.

"He's playing with you," the captain says, talking to Connor. "No one outside of this precinct knows the state of the corpse. We never released how it had been mutilated. He couldn't possibly know that from the news."

Connor hangs up. He turns to Buster, asking, "How did you know about the fingerprints and the teeth?"

Buster points at the mirror.

"What?" Zara says, not making the connection. She knows they're back there, but she also knows Buster has no way of knowing who's watching him.

"I heard them talking about the poor guy as they walked here."

Buster reaches up beside his face, using his thumb and forefinger to pull a tiny device from his ear. He places it on the desk, saying, "You'll find this is a military-grade A14 Motorola covert earpiece with a range of two hundred yards and three hours battery life."

"What?" Breezy says, jumping forward and touching the glass from the other side of the room. "He was listening to us? That whole time? While we were walking? The three of us together? How?"

The captain says, "No one was near us for more than a few seconds. How the hell did he hear us?"

The director asks, "Has the precinct been bugged?"

Breezy says, "Or one of us?"

Buster points at his own reflection in the mirror, addressing Breezy as he says, "She's asking the right questions."

48

"Jesus," the director says. "What the hell are we dealing with here?"

"Power," Buster says, although that one word seems out of context to the two officers inside the room with him. They have no way of knowing what's been said in the observation room. Breezy wants to speak up. She wants to point out to the others watching the interrogation that Buster no longer has his earpiece. She wants to ask how he can still hear them, but she dares not speak.

Within the room, Connor's confused. "Power?"

"You're powerless," Buster replies, facing the muscular detective. "You hold no power over me other than that which is given to you—and that which is given can be taken away."

Zara takes offense at his comment. She swings around in front of him, leaning forward on the table and towering over him. "Oh, I think you'll find we have plenty of power, buddy."

"With what?" Buster asks, laughing. "A pair of handcuffs? A jail cell? All your police in their pretty little uniforms, sitting behind their messy desks?"

"That's power," Connor says.

"It's an illusion," Buster replies. "It's a cheap magic trick that's easily dispelled. That's not real power."

"So show me real power," Zara asks, being flippant. She steps back, inviting him to respond. "What? Are you going to shoot lasers out of your eyeballs? Bend steel with your bare hands?"

Buster turns sideways on his chair. The metal legs scrape on the tiles as he drops to the floor. He says, "Take off your clothes."

"What?" she says, recoiling from him. "No!"

"See," Buster says. "You're powerless. You think you're dressed, and yet to me, you're naked. I see through the facade."

"Sit down," Connor says.

"Or what? Are you going to shoot me? Unarmed? Here in an interrogation cell? In the middle of a police station? Are you going to beat me to death?"

Buster unbuttons his shirt. As it's baggy, he appears overweight. Once it falls open, though, his well-defined stomach muscles are apparent. His shoulder muscles are taut and lean.

"Are you trying to impress me?" Zara asks.

Buster throws his arms back, saying, "Power is the ability to project strength."

The flimsy material falls to the floor. He might look ordinary. His face may appear bland. He might be short and stocky, but his chest is enormous. Large pectoral muscles stretch across his ribs. His chest is hairy, but that doesn't hide the scars. Dozens of marks crisscross his skin. They're old, having healed long ago, but the thick scar tissue makes them apparent. More scars wrap around his arms and shoulders, forming stripes of mutilated flesh reaching down to his wrists.

Buster holds onto the chair back, lifting each of his legs and taking off his shoes. He tosses them on the floor. He's not wearing socks.

"Leave your clothes on," Connor says.

Buster ignores the detective, undoing his trousers and letting them fall to the floor. The skin on his hips, loins and thighs has been subject to third-degree burns, leaving it looking as though melted wax has been poured over a storefront mannequin. His penis is deformed, while his pubic hair is patchy.

"What the *hell* are you doing?" Zara asks, even though it's apparent.

Buster steps toward her. "What's the matter? Are you scared?"

Zara shakes her head. "I'm not scared of you."

"Your heart rate just tipped over a hundred. Your breathing is shallow. Perspiration is breaking out on your forehead. Go ahead," he says, snarling. "Deny it."

"I—I'm," she stutters, stepping away from him.

Connor steps between them, blocking Buster's path. "What about me? Am I scared of you?"

"You?" Buster says, coming to a halt in front of him and looking him up and down. He sniffs the air. "You smell of fresh semen. It drips from the end of your cock."

"Fuck you," Connor yells, thumping Buster with both hands. He slams his palms against Buster's chest, forcing him to step back.

"Where were you?" Buster asks, smiling. "Before you walked in here? What were you doing? Imagining her naked as you crouched inside a bathroom stall?"

"You *fucking* asshole," Connor yells, throwing a punch.

Buster weaves in place, dodging his fist with ease and leaving Connor swinging at the air. A second punch lands, catching Buster on the side of his jaw. His head rocks back, but he doesn't fall.

"No, don't," Zara says, grabbing Connor and pulling him back. "The cameras!"

Buster laughs. Blood drips from his lips. He grins. A single word slips from his mouth. "Power."

"Get them the hell out of there," Breezy says from within the observation room. "It's a trap!"

"A what?" the captain says, confused.

Buster parades himself naked before the one-way mirror. He stands in front of it with his arms raised and his muscular, scarred body in full view. He flexes his thighs, tightens his stomach muscles and pumps his biceps.

"You want to see power? Real power? Here it is, baby."

There's a knock on the door to the interrogation room. It's not polite. Someone pounds on the metal.

Connor leans down, picking up Buster's clothing and throwing it at him. "Get dressed."

Buster ignores the clothing, letting it fall to the floor. He's staring through the mirror at Breezy, making eye contact with her—which is impossible.

"I hope you enjoyed the show," he says, holding his arms out wide and bowing to the mirror. "Thus ends the first act of this illustrious play."

Zara opens the door. A uniformed police officer stands there with a woman in a business suit. She's holding up a typed sheet of paper as though it were a poster.

"This is a writ from Judge Albert Canton ordering the release of my client. Unless you have due cause to charge him, you are instructed to release him into my care immediately."

She points at the red LED glowing beneath the camera in the corner of the room, adding, "And I want that footage. Now!"

The captain rushes out into the hallway. He grabs the writ and reads it, but the lawyer doesn't give him a moment's breathing space. She peppers him with questions, not giving him the ability to comprehend the legal prose unfolding before him, let alone its implications. He tries to get her to stop, raising his hand and wanting a moment, but she fires concepts at him like a machine gunner in World War II. She has her phone out, facing up, recording video and audio, making it apparent she's gathering additional evidence. The pressure on the captain is obvious from his trembling hands. He stands there in the open doorway, flustered by the lawyer.

Zara turns to Buster, looking at him with exasperation.

He laughs, saying, "This is what true power looks like."

Buster strikes a series of body-building poses in the mirror. He performs a front lat spread, with the muscles on his shoulders flexed and the triangular *latissimus dorsi* on his back fanning out like wings beyond his biceps. Then he turns into a classic side-chest pose with one leg slightly raised and his arms pumped. His body is hideously scarred and yet there's something regal about him. Far from being vulgar or pornographic, his body is dignified.

"We're all actors," he says, assuming another pose. "We're caught in *The Spectacle*. Each one of us has a role to play."

Buster is grandiose, accentuating his actions. It's as though he were performing on a stage. He turns side-on, crouching slightly with his arms raised together at an angle. He's holding something up high and yet he isn't. There's nothing there. His motion is reminiscent of an actor performing Shakespeare. He talks to the invisible prop. He speaks with a distinct British accent as though he were performing at the Royal Albert Hall in London.

"Alas, my poor fellow. Such misery is the life we lead. We take to the stage, speaking lines written for us by strangers. We're clothed and yet naked, wise and yet fools, alive and yet dead inside. And for what?

All for the applause of a crowd we neither know nor understand. Adoration, my dear friend, is poison to the soul."

"He's mad," the director says.

"He is," Breezy says, shaking her head. Buster, though, doesn't seem to care. He drops into another body-building pose. She has to admit his rear double bicep pose is impressive, especially as his glutes are as taut as a kettle drum. Buster flexes his bum cheeks, apparently realizing they're the focus of her attention.

The director says, "This is a disaster."

"That was always the plan," Breezy says, watching as Buster moves into a side tricep pose. He's rambling about *The Spectacle,* but she's stopped listening. His muscles ripple beneath the thick scar tissue. She says, "He knew exactly how this would play out. Oh, not all the details, not Connor jerking off in the bathroom, but he knew he could provoke a response and catch it on camera."

"Police brutality," the director says. "It makes for a good defense."

"Play that video in court, and he could get off on both police brutality and an insanity plea. Hell, that lawyer has probably already prepared a defense that says he was incapable of waiving his rights and that the detectives should have known this from his rambling comments."

Out in the hallway, the lawyer wins her argument with the captain. Buster gathers up his clothes and leaves with her, but not before taking one last look at the one-way mirror. He doesn't bother getting dressed, carrying his clothing in front of him.

"Come with me," the captain says, leading Buster out into the hallway. Breezy and the director open the door to the observation room and peer down the corridor. Buster and the lawyer disappear into an elevator further along the floor. Breezy catches one last glimpse of his pumped, sweet ass as the doors close. Michelangelo couldn't have done better.

The director leads Breezy to a side door and out into a secure parking area behind the precinct.

"We've got a problem."

"We?" Breezy asks, raising an eyebrow.

He laughs. Cop cars sit idle in multiple rows, waiting to go out on patrol. Given it's Saturday night, shouldn't they all be out there somewhere?

"Who the hell was that guy?" Breezy asks. "I mean, where did he come from?"

"We don't know much about Buster, but he's an American national. His mother was born in Kansas, while his father is an Iraqi. Buster was a guest of the Iranian secret police for about eight years before escaping across the border to Turkmenistan. He turned up here about four or five years ago."

Breezy says, "Right when the clowns first appeared."

"I need you," the director says, surprising her.

"Me?"

"I need you on the inside."

"Of the circus?" Breezy replies in disbelief. "With the clowns?"

"We'll discredit you," the director says, walking down a row of squad cars, making sure they're well out of earshot. "We'll frame it as though you used excessive force in the drug store. We'll make out that there's an ongoing investigation to give you a cover story. They'll see you as bitter—an outcast."

Breezy says, "In case you forgot, they cut the face off the last guy that infiltrated the Three Rings. And then they fed him to the fishes."

"You were unarmed," the director says. "You took down three robbers in under ten seconds. I can't think of anyone more capable."

"Well, now you're blowing smoke up my ass," Breezy says.

"I need this," the director says. "We're leaking like a sieve. You saw it yourself. The clowns were able to bug a cop precinct. I need to know if there's a mole inside the service. I need to know if they have allies in Congress or the Senate. Given that only four people knew the identity of the FBI agent, I'm worried there's a leak in the White House."

"That bad, huh?"

"That bad," the director says, coming to a halt by a chainlink fence. "FBI Agent Zambarrow was killed within four hours of the President being briefed."

"And me? How are you going to keep me safe?"

"I'll be the only one that knows. You'll report to me and no one else."

"Understood," Breezy says, looking down at her feet. "Ah, how am I supposed to find these guys?"

"You don't," the director says. "They'll find you."

GETTING PAID

Before she gets out of the rental car at the local mall, Olivia dons a broad, floppy summer hat. She drapes a shawl over her shoulders, obscuring her identity on the parking lot's security footage. It's not that she's paranoid, but rather that she understands how easy it is to get caught by a simple mistake. Criminals don't get busted because they're dumb. They get caught because they're lazy.

Olivia knows the blind spots within the mall. She works her way toward the women's public toilets by the food court. She doesn't need to pee. She needs to hang her beautiful hat and designer shawl on the back of a stall door, leaving them for someone to snag. They'll think they're lucky. They'll think someone accidentally left these designer items behind. They'll be sure they've scored, but they're providing her with cover.

Time is short. She's got twenty minutes to get to the drop. Usually, Olivia would go straight to the opposite parking lot and head off to collect her pay, but she feels uneasy. She can't shake the feeling she's being watched. It's irrational. Most mall stores have only one entrance/exit, but the bigger department stores span multiple floors. They have storefronts on each level and sometimes several on the same level. This gives her the opportunity to apply a little tradecraft and set her mind at ease.

When being followed, it's essential not to react or panic. Olivia wanders into the cosmetic section of a large store, knowing there are mirrors everywhere. She sniffs at a sampler and sprays a little perfume on her wrist. She might look distracted, but she's not. She's using that motion to hide the way in which she's scanning the mirrors for a tail. Out of all the people in the store, the two that catch her attention are a young woman looking at manicure sets on the far side of the cosmetic counter and a thin guy in a black jacket loitering just outside, pretending to look at polo shirts on a rack.

She asks the attendant where the elevators are, knowing precisely where she'll point ahead of time, and then thanks her. Being five foot six inches in height has its advantages. Olivia walks briskly out of the centrally-located cosmetics department. She strides past the billboards with perfectly bronzed models advertising the latest designer perfume. On any other day, she'd peruse the new styles. She cuts through the store at an angle, heading toward the elevators. As Olivia passes out of sight behind a pillar, she crouches slightly, hiding behind a rack of dresses on sale. Sure enough, they take the bait. The guy walks through the men's department toward the distant elevator while the woman power walks through sportswear, peering around, trying to pick up on her trail. Olivia backtracks through cosmetics and out into the main concourse. She makes a beeline toward one of the mall exits.

Depending on whether these guys are law enforcement or private eyes, they'll either have a backup crew or access to mall security cameras. Either way, Olivia won't get the chance to fool them again. They'll ratchet up the tempo, even if it means going overt. She does not want to be corralled like a steer.

As the automatic doors open, Olivia's aware she's probably just been pegged on a security monitor somewhere via facial recognition. She keeps her head down, reducing the profile of her face to the cold, electronic lens.

"You're living in *The Spectacle*," a voice calls out, appealing to the mall crowd as it surges in both directions, going into and coming from the mall in a frenzy of activity. People arrive empty-handed and leave with shopping carts full of junk. "Roll up! Roll up! This is the greatest show on Earth! Whether you realize it or not, you're part of the circus!"

A middle-aged woman with a rotund belly stands on a low brick wall under the watchful eye of mall security. The crowd around her is three to four people deep, partially blocking the entrance. Were it not for her makeup, her bellowing could be mistaken for a preacher warning about the end times. Green dye has been sprayed over her slicked-back hair, making her look like a female version of *The Joker*. White face paint covers her cheeks, chin and forehead, but not her neck. Thick black eyeliner rings her eyes. Red lipstick has been smeared around her mouth. No attempt has been made to ensure precision or beauty. It looks like her makeup was applied by a chimpanzee during an earthquake.

"Our lives unfold in a three-ring circus," she yells, holding up one finger at a time as she counts out, "Religion, politics and ego. You can't escape. All you can do is play to the crowd. The circus is all around us every day, demanding we perform. Fake smiles on selfies. Post that shit on Instagram. It's all a goddamn lie!"

Under her breath, Olivia mumbles, "Fucking clowns." She pushes through the crowd, looking for an opportunity to hide.

"We were all born into *The Spectacle,* and in *The Spectacle,* we'll die!"

Boots pound the pavement behind Olivia. Someone comes to an abrupt halt beside her. She doesn't look. Instead, she reaches out and pushes forward toward the front of the gathering. She taps a man on the shoulder, saying, "Tell me about *The Spectacle*?"

The guy that turns back to face her is dressed in an old, torn business suit. He has a fake flower for a lapel pin. Makeup is smeared on his collar. Olivia's not sure she can take him seriously, but this is a ruse on her part. Situation blindness is a great way to hide. Her pursuers are looking for someone fleeing the mall. The clowns might as well be storefront mannequins. Anyone interacting with them is an idiot or an anarchist. Security is looking for someone on the run. Hundreds of people are coming and going. Car trunks open. Van doors slam. Vehicles reverse out of parking lots. There's too much to focus on. The confusion allows her to hide in plain sight.

Olivia's clown has been plastered in the typical white paint that makes him appear like a corpse. It's no wonder kids are afraid of clowns. The red plastic nose in the middle of his face looks comical. Dark black brows have been drawn on his forehead. His actual eyebrows have been smothered in white face paint, making his features appear elongated. Thin black lines peel away from his lips like whiskers.

Beyond him, the lead clown—if that's the correct term—continues addressing shoppers.

"From birth, we're taught to lie," she says, trying to make eye contact with someone pushing past through the crowd. "Who are you? What do you feel? You're more than a number, more than a worker, more than a statistic, more than just another consumer. Smile, they say. You need to be happy. You need to be an individual—just like everyone else. And with that, your sense of self is gone."

From the crowd, an overweight guy in an NFL shirt yells, "Go back to the circus!"

"This *is* the circus," she replies. "It's all around you. Nothing is real. Everything is for show. The lights. The trinkets. The clean aesthetic. It's a con. All they want is your money."

The dead-looking clown gestures for Olivia to sit on the low wall beside the battery-powered speaker used by the lead clown. Olivia hangs her head, knowing the shadows cast by the crowd obscure any security camera footage of her. By dropping below head height, she's effectively invisible.

A couple of teens stand at the back of the entrance, over by a streetlight. They're chatting to each other, holding up their phones, taking pictures and posting videos. For them, this is entertaining.

"Social media is a lie," the clown yells, pointing at them. "It's anti-social. It tells us we have to compete for happiness. Smash that *like* button—*like, like, like!* In *The Spectacle,* everything's an act—you're never good enough on your own. Never. And the *likes* turn us into junkies. We're addicted to the fake adoration spewing out of our phones. Pose for a smile, and you're lying to everyone, including yourself. None of it is real. We're so busy doing something we don't stop to realize we're doing nothing at all."

The clown with Olivia looks serious. His eyes narrow.

"Tell me about yourself."

Olivia expected the usual cult sales pitch, not any interest in her. Given half a chance, most religious nuts will blabber on for hours with their psychobabble. Clowns, it seems, are more reserved. They won't spring the trap until they're ready. For her part, Olivia doesn't want to talk—she wants to hide. She's killing time. She peers through the sea of arms and legs as several additional pursuers speak with the woman that was following her. They're looking out across the parking lot. Damn, they're serious about finding her, but why? This is not good. Public places like malls are usually good melting pots. They're places she can blend in and disappear. Not today.

"Ah, well," Olivia says. "I was born in Poland. Moved to the US when I was ten. Lived mainly in the southwest. Earned a degree in fine arts from Trinity here in DC."

"And never went back to Europe," the clown says.

"No."

"Why are you here?" he asks.

"Here as in at the mall? Or here talking to you?"

"Here on Earth."

Olivia laughs. "You guys are nuts."

"Hey," he says. "You tapped my shoulder, remember? What do you want to know?"

"Hmm. Okay. I want to know why you're doing this. You guys are always popping up on the news. It's weird, you know, grownups dressing as clowns. I saw you guys here and figured I had the chance to ask why."

"What do you know about us?" he asks.

"You don't give much away, do you?" Olivia replies. She hasn't answered his question, so he doesn't elaborate. There's an awkward pause. Social pleasantries demand a response and yet he's comfortable remaining silent, forcing her to continue. "You're strange—and deliberately so. Clowns are a counter-culture, right? You're a backlash against social media and mass consumption."

"It seems you have all the answers you need," he says, getting up and handing her a business card. "Call me if you ever really want to talk."

"That's it?" she says, remaining seated on the wall. "You're not going to give me the spiel?"

"You can smell my flower if you like."

He squeezes a tiny plastic ball in the palm of his hand. The fake flower on his lapel squirts a thin stream of water out into the crowd. Several droplets reach her t-shirt.

"You guys really are weird," she says, slipping the card into the back pocket of her jeans.

"And you have somewhere you need to be," he says. "And someone you're trying to avoid."

"How did you...?" she asks, squinting as she peers at him with suspicion.

Olivia glances up at the digital clock—8:45 PM.

"Damn it," she says, peering through the bustle of shoppers, unable to make out any of her pursuers.

"Go left," he says. "Dart behind the bushes. And I'll go right."

With that, he pushes through the crowd. The lead clown is still waffling on about the evils of god-knows-what.

Her clown calls out, "Come to the fair! Stay for the circus! We've got it all. Freaks. Clowns. Elephants, lions and tigers. Grab a Coke. Buy your popcorn."

As he does this, he begins juggling tenpins. Where the hell did he get those? He must have grabbed them from the crate in front of the impromptu stage. He backs up, juggling five bowling pins, sending them sailing high in the air. The crowd parts around him. Occasionally, he bumps into someone facing the wrong way, but he doesn't drop any of the pins. They soar through the air, tumbling end over end, much to the delight of onlookers.

Olivia creeps behind the bushes, staying low. He knew she was hiding from someone but couldn't know who or why. For all he knows, he's breaking the law by aiding a criminal on the run, but he doesn't seem to care.

"It's all a game," he yells, but he never takes his eyes off the sky, watching as the pins cross each other without colliding. "It's *The Spectacle!* Your brand new sweatshirt. Your shiny phone. Your video games and your fast food. They're all a distraction."

Olivia drops down from the raised garden bed, landing on the concrete ramp of a nearby loading dock. She scoots behind a dumpster and out into the parking lot, making for her car. She's parked near one of the side exits.

When she gets to Arlington, she will have to report this to Snow. The old lady always wants to hear about anything out of the ordinary. Someone's getting close.

Fifteen minutes. She slips into her car and drives out onto the boulevard, leaving the clowns behind. Even if she catches a few red lights, she can make it to Arlington in fifteen minutes without speeding.

Olivia's no more than a quarter-mile from the drop when she hears the rhythmic slap of loose rubber hitting the concrete, repeating in time with a wicked shudder through the chassis of her car.

"What the...?"

She pulls to the side of the road and into a breakdown lane.

"You have got to be fucking kidding me," she says, slamming her hand against the steering wheel. Getting out of the car, she kicks the rear tire in disgust. The sidewall has blown. The steel rim of the wheel has dug into the flattened tire wall, perforating the rubber. "Damn it!"

She kicks the tire out of frustration.

An old black car pulls over, slowing but not stopping. Olivia can't see much beyond the glare of the headlights. Duct tape holds a plastic bumper in place. Instead of pulling in behind her, it seems the driver's curious, coming alongside her aging Volvo. The passenger's window lowers, allowing the driver to call out across the empty seat.

"You okay, honey?" a woman asks. From the crow's feet forming on either side of her eyes, she's in her forties. Perhaps in her fifties. Her make-up, though, is on point: deep eyeliner, foundation, cheek blush and glossy lipstick all make her appear younger. She's wearing black, skintight jeans and a strapless corset that pushes her breasts up so they appear high and full. She's working this area, looking for a trick.

The backseat is full of junk. Some of it spills into the gap between the front seats. A couple of pillows and a sleeping bag tell Olivia all she needs to know. This gal is a wanderer—a prostitute living out of her car. Olivia's heart aches. There's a basket with neatly folded clothing, but it's been shoved on top of something else and is leaning against the rear window. Were it not for her Polish heritage and flawless complexion, Olivia could be staring at herself in a decade or so—and that's harrowing. As much as she thinks the clowns at the mall are creeps, they have a point. Society cares only for money. If you don't have it, you're refuse. This woman's eking out an existence on the edge of civilization. She's disposable. She's despised by all.

"Ah, flat tire," Olivia says, gesturing to the rear wheel.

"You be careful out here, hon," the woman says, driving off. "This is a rough area."

"Thanks," Olivia says, throwing her arms up and letting them fall by her side. She continues in a mumble. "Thanks for the help."

Olivia might have felt an affinity for a fellow woman living on the fringe, but that woman's got to turn a trick. She's got to make a buck. She's got to survive. She has no time to play Good Samaritan.

Olivia pops the trunk and rummages around beneath a lone street light, pulling out a spare tire along with a jack. She tosses them on the road behind the car and slams the trunk. One look at the tire iron in her hand has her realize this isn't a five-minute task. Not for her. The cemetery is across the road. The white headstones are shrouded in darkness, but they're visible through the shrubs and trees. She's here, and yet she's not. Arlington is huge. Goddamn it! Olivia's not sure who's running the bag on this op, but they'd better wait. Snow was unusually adamant about the drop time. If Olivia doesn't show, they're likely to get spooked and leave.

"Why me?" Olivia yells into the night, brandishing the tire iron like a club. At this point, if anyone pulled over to help, she's liable to hit them with the iron, steal their car to make the drop and then claim self-defense if/when she gets caught by the cops. She's so angry she could crack a few skulls just for kicks.

"Fuck it!"

Olivia leaves her car where it is. She runs across three lanes, vaults the concrete median barrier, and jogs across another three lanes, much to the disgust of oncoming traffic. Horns sound even though she's in no danger. Within a hundred yards, what seemed like a viable option is looking decidedly stupid. Olivia isn't as fit as she thinks. She stays in shape with stomach crunches and squats, but she's regretting skipping cardio. Running on a treadmill has never made sense to her—it's literally a road to nowhere.

Satellite maps are deceiving. Although the drop point looks close on her phone, it's still quite far away. Green patches that appear to be grass in the satellite view are dense thickets of shrubs, making it impossible for her to go cross-country. The ditches are boggy, having soaked up a summer storm earlier in the day. This portion of the cemetery is underdeveloped. Roads wind through grassy fields with the odd ornamental tree marking various boundaries.

"I don't have time for this shit," Olivia mumbles, checking her location and seeing she's still several hundred yards away. She leans forward on her knees, sucking in the cool evening air.

Olivia hates the dark. She tells herself she's not afraid of the night—and that's no lie. She's scared of what might be in the dark. Here at Arlington Cemetery, that's got to be no one and nothing—not at this time of night. Well, perhaps, zombies. They come out of graves, right? She grips the tire iron a little tighter in her hand.

Car lights sweep across an empty field.

Someone's pulling into the fenced area in the distance. It looks like a construction depot. There are piles of gravel and front loaders in the yard ahead. The chainlink fence appears temporary. The various sections are mounted in plastic footings instead of being driven into the ground.

Olivia jogs on. Pale white tombstones fill the field to her left. They've been meticulously spaced, forming lines of sorrow. To her right is a fresh field of neatly mowed grass awaiting the bodies of the fallen.

Olivia reaches the corner and leans forward on her knees again, breathing deeply, cursing her idle treadmill back at home. Ahead of her, someone gets out of a car parked in the shadows. He walks over to the woman that has pulled up in the black hatchback. Her engine is still running. The brake lights are on. He's got to be the bag man. This is going to be confusing for both of them.

A woman turns on an interior light and leans toward the passenger's seat. It's the prostitute from the main road. She's looking for a quick squeeze. She probably saw him drive in here and followed along, wanting to earn a buck. Once, she would have stood on a street corner, but being mobile opens more venues. In the early days, Olivia gave public sex work a try, but she never took to humping in the backseat of a car. There were too many nosey cops willing to shine a patrol light in the back of a rocking Caddie. Olivia's always preferred hotel rooms to darkened alleys. Besides, having a madam or a pimp offers a little protection. This gal probably cases this place from time to time. But what kind of sicko comes to a cemetery to jerk off? The kind that pays well, apparently.

Is this her money man or someone else? Fuck it, Snow. Why couldn't you just dump a suitcase full of money in the trunk of the rental car?

Olivia walks forward, still trying to catch her breath. She cuts across the grass, waving with her hands, wanting to get the man's attention. He needs to dump that bitch. A name drifts on the wind.

"Olivia?"

A gun is drawn. The silhouette is unmistakable against the dark sky. There's denial along with pleas for mercy from within the car, but the poor woman's cries are ignored. Gunshots ring out, causing Olivia to drop to her knees on the edge of the cemetery. One, two, three, four shots shatter the silence, each being directed into the woman's chest. She slumps on the steering wheel. Her car rolls forward, turning aimlessly with its lights flickering over the grassy slope.

The car swings in an arc, drifting forward even though the accelerator isn't being pushed. Her foot has come off the brake. For a moment, Olivia's caught in the headlights. As quickly as they came, they wander on, illuminating headstones. The car noses into a ditch, kicking up dust as it comes to an abrupt halt.

Olivia squats behind a white headstone.

James Joseph

D'Angelo

PVT

US Marine Corps

Her knee sinks into the grass over his chest. Her fingers clasp the cold stone that holds his memory. Her heart is on the verge of beating out of her chest.

The assassin gets back into his car and drives off.

Olivia trembles.

For once, being late has saved her life.

SUSAN

Saturday night is when the ghouls come out to play. Long hot, lazy days lead to nights of utter mayhem as the cool of the evening descends. The precinct is alive with police officers and fresh arrests.

Breezy chats with the lead officer on the hospital drug store case. He's trying to wrap things up and get them in a state where he can rest the case until next week. The sole surviving robber is hemorrhaging information. Even with a lawyer sitting next to him in an interrogation cell, he's divulged that the team was high on crack. They thought they would score big and pay down some drug debts. The lawyer tries to keep him quiet but coming down off a rush has turned him into a blubbering mess. Breezy watches the video feed from the next room. Technically, she should stay at arm's length from the investigation. There's a danger that her casual conversation with one of the lead officers could compromise the prosecution's case, but she needs to decompress.

"One more bullet," the officer says, leading her out into the hall at the end of the session. "And you could have saved us a helluva lot of paperwork."

"Hah," Breezy says, enjoying a bit of banter with the officer. "Oh, I thought about it!"

As tough as she sounds, Breezy could never do that. She couldn't shoot an unarmed man. Pulling the trigger of a gun is a sacred act. All the bullshit bravado down at the shooting range while poking holes in stupid paper targets at a distance of fifty yards is as dumb as dog shit. Lashing out with lethal force is not a game—it's not fun, it's not enjoyable, it's not trivial, it's not a power trip. There's nothing glorious about it. Breezy did what she had to do, not what she wanted to do. It was a cold, hard calculation: *who is going to die?* When the situation was reduced to, *someone is going to die in the next few minutes, you get to decide who,* Breezy had no choice. She did her job. She did what she was trained to do. And she did it well. It doesn't mean she enjoyed it. Fuck, she's not getting any sleep tonight. All these thoughts will keep ricocheting around her head until the sun comes up. They'll bounce off her brain cells like a pinball. Even the slightest touch on the bumper will cause that shiny chrome ball to shoot off in another direction. It's going to be one helluva long night.

Her phone beeps.

"Hang on."

She checks her messages.

r u ok? I'm outside.

Breezy uses her thumb to gesture to the main door on the other side of the floor. "Hey, I need to..."

"No problem," the officer says. "Don't you worry about a thing. I've got your back. Talk to you next week, okay?"

"Okay," Breezy replies, wondering if she should be worried. She wasn't worried. Now, she's unsettled. She didn't do anything wrong. She saved lives. Why did the officer need to say he has her back?

The officer escorts her over to the processing desk. Bulletproof glass separates the uniformed police officers within the precinct from the reception area, allowing them to respond to various queries from the public. The glass is so thick the room on the other side has a greenish tinge, making it seem as though it's submerged underwater.

The officer swipes his keycard over a secure lock next to the broad desk. There's a clunk in the door. Breezy pulls on the handle. The quarter-inch plate steel ensures the door is far heavier than it looks. This thing isn't so much bulletproof as blast-proof. Being slight of build, Breezy has to plant her shoes to swing the door open. She pulls it back toward her and steps into a narrow anteroom that acts as a man-trap between the precinct and the reception area. There's a small camera on the roof along with a black and white video screen on the intercom beside the next door. The officer smiles on the tiny screen. He presses the outer release button. A buzz, a click and a loud clunk within the lock and she's free.

Breezy steps out into a wall of noise and chaos in the precinct's reception area. An elderly couple waits nervously on seats to one side. They're wearing face masks. Given the smell of sweat in the air, that's not a bad idea. Officer safety might have been a crucial factor in the design of the reception, but ventilation clearly wasn't a consideration.

A tall dude with a thick British accent is arguing with the night sergeant on the other side of the bulletproof glass. Next to him, a woman holds a baby. She clutches the crying child against her shoulder. Blood trickles from a gash on her forehead.

Someone limps toward the counter with a chainsaw. Breezy does a double-take on this guy. The chainsaw's not running, but it's alarming to see a chainsaw in the middle of the city. It makes a switchblade look positively civilized. This guy is as nervous as Lucifer himself. His eyes dart around, wanting to assess any threats. Easy, chainsaw-dude, they're all here for the same reason as you. They're all willingly coming forward to talk to a cop, and on a hot summer Saturday night, that's a miracle. Behind him, a female uniformed officer marches in from outside, pushing a male suspect in cuffs up the stairs. This guy has a torn shirt. He's yelling something about knowing his rights.

As he stumbles by, Breezy mumbles, "Yeah, I'm sure you were top of your civics class."

He glares at her. The officer pushes him past the guy with the chainsaw without batting an eyelid. Breezy isn't quite as relaxed about the lumberjack. He's holding the chainsaw by the guardrail, making it a quick drop away from screaming into life. All he needs to do is grab that starter cord and *vroom*—chaos and heartbreak. That he has blood splatter on his checkered shirt is disconcerting. It's not his. Breezy doesn't understand why the senior sergeant's ignoring him. Sure, the sergeant's safe behind the thick glass. Everyone else in that confined space, though, is in danger. A grenade would cause less damage than that damn thing. At a certain point, Breezy has to turn her back on the lumberjack, but as she heads down the stairs outside her ears are pricked for the start of a two-stroke engine roaring over the trucks rumbling by on the street.

Susan's sitting at a bus stop a few yards further down the road.

"Hey, babe," Breezy says, jogging over to her.

Susan's an immigrant. She was born in rural Kenya and has stunning high cheekbones that cause her smiles to light up like fireworks. This evening, though, she's distracted. She's looking down at her phone. That's no surprise, but the intensity of her focus is unusual, especially as she was waiting for Breezy. She's changed out of her medical uniform. Tight jeans accentuate her curves, while a loose top hides her bust. Her frizzy, curly hair has been tied down into cornrows forming neat lines on her scalp.

Susan looks up at Breezy. Tears line her cheeks. The street lighting is poor. Her skin is as dark as the night. The bright blue/white light from her phone illuminates her face from beneath, casting long shadows and washing out her face.

"Breeze," she says, springing to her feet and throwing her arms around Breezy's neck.

"It's okay. I'm okay," Breezy says, returning the hug and patting her back.

Susan leans back, still embracing her while looking her in the eyes. "I—I'm confused. I didn't know what to think."

"About what?" Breezy asks.

Susan's arms fall to her sides. "I can't even..."

"Can't what?"

"It's not true, right?" Susan asks, holding her phone up so Breezy can see the screen. "Tell me it's not true."

It's been several hours since the robbery. The text of a news article unfolds before Breezy. She has no idea what she needs to read, but the image tells her all she needs to know. Arms protrude from behind a set of shelving. To one side, boxes of hair dye have been neatly arranged on a shelf, being stacked in order from lightest to darkest. They've been lined up with the front edge of the shelf, setting them in stark contrast to the chaos that lies beyond them. A dark patch has formed on the carpet, spilling out into a broad puddle soaking into the synthetic fibers. The dead man is lying on his back. Both hands are open. Fingers curl toward the ceiling. It's what's missing that's alarming. There's no gun lying nearby. The caption reads: *Summary execution in an armed robbery. In Washington, D.C., there's no need for a judge and jury, just an undertaker.*

"He was armed," Breezy says, realizing this is the guy at the front of the store, the robber watching the main door. "He had a Glock. I saw it tumble from his hand."

"There's video, Breezy. They've got you on video!"

"What?" she says. "No, that's not possible. The police wouldn't have released the footage. Not yet. It's too soon. I—I was just up there with them in the precinct. They're still processing this."

Susan sniffs. "I want to believe you. I do. It's just. The video."

Susan scrolls back to the top of the article and hits play, turning her phone sideways so the image increases in size. Breezy takes hold of the phone. She doesn't need to. Susan's holding it still and it's easy enough to see, but Breezy *needs* to take control. It's not like it makes any difference but she feels compelled to take the phone from her girlfriend. It's as though the act of holding the phone will somehow change its contents.

There's no audio. The image is in color but the harsh white lights within the drug store leave the colors washed out. The camera is positioned behind the counter, looking down along the central aisle at the front door. This is a different angle to the photograph. The robber is standing side-on. He's pacing. He's nervous, looking out the window. His left hand hangs by his side. His right arm isn't in view. The resolution of the video camera is probably quite good, but someone zooms in, focusing on his upper torso and it goes grainy. This isn't the original footage. Although it may be unaltered, by zooming in the perspective changes. The periphery is lost. His arms are in the shot, but not his hands. It's only for a split second, but it's enough that a slight glimpse of his right hand appears as a blur when he turns around. It's impossible to tell if he has anything in his hands. The camera zooms out slightly, taking in his legs again. Someone's messed with the raw footage, trying to better frame the action.

The young man steps forward, passing slightly behind the shelving. He's still visible, but only just. Then, in utter silence, his head lashes back. Blood splashes across the window behind him. His body collapses to the floor. A dark puddle forms behind his head. His hands lie upturned with his fingers catching the light. He twitches and falls still.

"He dropped the gun," Breezy says, pointing at the shelving on the edge of the image.

"He didn't drop anything," Susan says, "I've watched this a dozen times. There was nothing in his hand."

Breezy is defensive. "Are you calling me a liar?"

"No," Susan says. "It's not like that. I just didn't see it. No one did."

"They didn't have my angle. They couldn't see him from my vantage point."

"What did you see?" Susan asks. "From where you were, did you see a gun?"

"He had a gun. I know he had a gun."

"Did you see it?" Susan asks. "Did he point a gun at you?"

"I—I was looking down the barrel of my gun, looking along the sights. All I could see was his head and shoulders."

"So you didn't see a gun?"

"He had a gun!" Breezy says, frustrated by the argument. She's looking intently at the screen. The freeze-frame captures the moment of grief. Dead eyes stare at the ceiling tiles. He's fallen across the aisle. If there was a gun, it's fallen four or five feet to his right and been hidden by the shelving. Breezy doubts herself.

Susan leans in close to look at the image again. "Did—you—see it?"

"I saw something drop from his hand."

"Did you?" Susan asks. "Or did you see what you wanted to see?"

"I don't know, goddamn it," Breezy snaps, yelling at Susan as strangers walk past on the street. "I saw him. I saw his face. There was no time to second-guess. I knew I had to shoot. He had a gun. A Glock. So did the other guy."

Susan hangs her head.

"What?" Breezy asks.

"They only recovered two guns, Breeze. Two. Only two. The shotgun from behind the counter and the Glock. The one you fired."

"No," Breezy says, feeling her hands tremble. "No, it can't be. The lookouts. They both had guns."

She scrolls down and sees another image. This one is from the front of the store looking back toward the counter. The fire door is visible on the edge of the frame. A body lies sprawled out before a terrified woman crouching in front of the counter. Her presence in the photo gives Breezy a sense of the timing. This is before the police entered the building. There's no gun. Breezy saw him holding a gun. Or did she? She saw a shadow—a blur. She was peering between items on the shelves. He was crouching. She assumed he was preparing to fire at her but he could have been hiding out of fear.

No, she saw a gun tumble into the aisle. She knows she did. Or did she? What the hell was it that fell from the shelves?

One aspect overlooked by the news article is the state of the young man's jeans. They're pale, being made from stonewashed denim. Although he's lying face down on the carpet, there's a dark patch running down one leg. People will shit and piss themselves at the point they die, that's no surprise to Breezy, but the angle's all wrong. He pissed himself while he was crouching—before she shot him. That's the only possible explanation for the stain reaching down his leg. It only extends to his

78

knee, but that wouldn't have happened after he was lying flat on the floor. If he was kneeling, that's as far as it would go.

"He was fifteen, Breezy. He was a child."

"I—I."

It's only now Breezy realizes he was terrified. He'd inflicted terror on her and the old women, but for him, it was a silly game. Then shots were fired. He panicked. He hid behind those far shelves. He wasn't threatening anyone anymore.

"I—I don't understand," she says, desperate to recall not only the moment she pulled the trigger but the aftermath. Breezy stood not more than ten feet from his body, collecting her phone and ID, and yet she didn't look at him. She couldn't. From memory, there was no gun at that point. She assumed it had been collected as evidence. The cops wouldn't leave a loaded weapon lying beside a dead body. Or would they wait for the forensic team to come along with their flags and plastic counters? Would they wait for photographs to be taken of each scene before disturbing it? Or would gun safety be more important?

The lead investigator told her not to worry. Is this what he was talking about? Was he already thinking about damage control for potentially unlawful killings?

Wait.

What was it Director Johnson said? He told Breezy he was going to have her discredited. He wanted to build an effective cover story for her to infiltrate the clowns. Is this part of that? Has his sting already swung into effect? No, it's too quick. How the hell did the news media get these images and this video footage? Who leaked them? Who even had access to them?

Susan snaps her back to reality, saying, "I can't do this, Breanna. Not anymore."

Her use of the name Breanna is alarming. No one calls Breezy Breanna. It's her name, but it's not even on her birth certificate. When Breezy was born, some clueless clerk made a mistake at the Pennsylvania Department of Health and Breanne was entered into the system instead of Breanna. It was several months before Breezy's parents realized what had happened. Only a single letter was out of place in a hideously complex document, but the government refused to change it without going through a formal process the family couldn't afford. Growing up, she became Breanne, legally and socially. In high school, the nickname Breezy stuck and Breanne became her formal name. Breanna was lost to obscurity. Breezy only ever told a few people about her real name. From memory, she only told Susan once while having dinner in a fancy seafood restaurant a few years ago.

Susan's using Breanna on purpose. The context has changed. She's no longer talking about what happened in the drug store. She's using the name Breanna to grab her attention and shift the focus.

"We need to talk."

"Come," Breezy says, leading Susan into a bar next to the precinct. To call it a cop bar is an understatement. The walls are lined with images of police officers in action or being awarded medals. A shot-up patrol car door hangs from the ceiling. Bullet holes have peppered the paintwork, leaving the metal around them bare. A bunch of signed pictures and a framed description on the wall identifies it as a relic from a shootout in Rock Creek.

Breezy and Susan slip into a booth by the window looking out across the street.

"What can I getcha?" a waiter asks.

Breezy takes the lead as she so often does in their relationship. "Two Coors Light. And a bowl of french fries, please. No sauce."

As soon as the waiter leaves, Susan clutches her hands together on the table. "This is what I'm talking about."

"What are you talking about?" a bewildered Breezy asks.

"This!"

"I don't understand."

"Can I have my phone back?"

Breezy looks down at the phone in her hand. She didn't even realize she still had it. Sheepishly, she hands it to Susan saying, "Uh, sure."

"I tried, Breeze. I really did."

Susan's the only one that can get away with calling her Breeze instead of Breezy. It's another ploy, leaning on their emotional connection.

Breezy says, "Tried? As in past tense?"

"I can't go on like this."

"You're leaving me?" Breezy asks, leaning forward on the table.

"You're impossible," Susan says, breaking eye contact. "We're... we're just not—"

"We're not what?" Breezy snaps.

"See?" Susan says, gesturing with her arms wide. "This is what I mean. This is what I have to deal with. I can't even finish a sentence without you interrupting."

"No, go ahead," Breezy says. Her eyes fall toward the water stains on the old, varnished wooden table.

"I can't go ahead," Susan says. "Don't you understand? You *need* to be in control. You need to control everything. Life isn't a light switch, Breeze. There's no pause and rewind button. I can't just go back to that sentence and continue as though nothing happened in between. You've pushed me on and now we're here."

"And where is here?"

"You—can't—control—everything," Susan says, leaning across the table. She's getting frustrated. "I know you think you can, but you can't. It's a lie."

"I don't—"

"Oh, no," Susan says, interrupting her. "You're not rewriting this. Not this time. You snatched my phone. You dragged me in here. You ordered for me. You cut me off. Listen, Breezy. Just listen."

Breezy clenches her teeth. The veins in her neck go taut. She clenches her fists beneath the table.

Susan lets out a sigh. "Just sit back and listen."

"I'm listening."

"See?" Susan says, pointing at her. "You had to tell me that. You couldn't just listen. You know people listen with their ears, right? Not their mouths."

Breezy tightens her lips.

The waiter returns with two beers and a bowl of french fries. He places them on the table and leaves. Neither woman touches either their food or their drinks.

"We come from different worlds," Susan says. "I thought we could make it work. I really did. I've tried. For years, I've tried, but the song remains the same. It's always about you. It's always your training, your work, your duty, your career."

Breezy is a blubbering mess. Tears run down her cheeks. She blurts out, "I was trying to be nice. I was trying to bring you dinner."

"I know," Susan says, reaching across the table and taking hold of her wrist. It's telling that she doesn't hold her hand. She wants to touch Breezy. She wants to reassure her, but she doesn't want to be intimate. "You brought me dinner. You. You. You did. I was fine. I didn't *need* anything."

"It's not my fault," Breezy says with quivering lips. "I went in there for a Coke. They did it. They shot him—the security guard."

Susan says, "And you did what you were trained to do. You took them down."

Breezy hangs her head. Susan's right. Even her choice of terms is telling—*trained to do, took them down.* Susan's using her terminology. She's avoiding the cold, harsh truth. She could have said, "*You killed them.*" She'd be right, but she's speaking to gain agreement. She's not trying to fire up an argument regardless of how Breezy may react.

"We see the world in a different light," Susan says in a kind voice. "We see through a different lens."

"How?" Breezy asks, struggling with just that one word. She feels as though her world is falling apart.

"Look at them," Susan says, gesturing to the window. "What do you see?"

Outside, a protest marches down the street. Forty to fifty people are walking along, chanting in unison. They're mostly on the sidewalk but some of them spill onto the road. A few of the protesters are dressed up as clowns. They're carrying placards.

Demand change!

Stop and think for yourself.

Speak truth to power. Don't compromise!

Think we're a joke? Look at the government!

Parrot or Patriot. You choose.

Who do you trust? Why?

"Those idiots?" Breezy asks, on the verge of laughing through her tears. "Seriously?"

"Do you know what I see?" Susan asks. "Do you even care what I see?"

"What do you see?" Breezy asks, picking up her beer and taking a swig. She needs to do something to keep herself grounded and her beer is the only thing at hand.

"People that care."

"What?"

"People that want change."

"Susan, I—"

"You can't see it, can you?" Susan says. "And this is the problem. You can't see what's right in front of you."

"What is there to see?" Breezy asks, looking at the crowd. "A bunch of weirdos dressed up as clowns?"

Susan says, "Every generation has fought their parents for change. How is this any different? The hippies in the '60s. The anti-war protests. The Civil Rights movement. Greenpeace in the '80s. Occupy Wall Street. Climate activists. Black Lives Matter. Me Too."

"And you think this is—what? The next revolution? You think clowns hold the answer?"

"No," Susan says. "I think they're looking for answers. We should all be looking for answers. We shouldn't just accept things the way they are. We can change this world if we want to, but it takes all of us, Breezy."

"Where has this come from?" Breezy asks. She can't believe what she's hearing from her partner. "Are you... Are you listening to them?"

Several more clowns walk past. They're dressed in baggy clothing with rainbow-colored Afro wigs on their heads and the classic red nose. One of them holds an old-style bicycle horn aloft. He squeezes the black, rubber bulb and the polished brass nozzle sounds off with a familiar blast echoing into the night.

Hooooonk-key!

Honk-key! Honk-key! Honk-key!

The clowns are carrying placards. Although most of them have a slogan, several are abstract paintings. One is a tie-dye pattern. Another is nothing more than pink polka dots on a white background. There's even one with zebra stripes set on an angle. To Breezy's mind, they're absurd. What the hell are these fools protesting about? Their lack of fashion sense? Those with words, though, are unmistakable.

You can't have justice in an unjust society.

We can't throw away lives like they're garbage.

Justice should not be the end of someone's life.

Carrot & Stick: We need rewards, not just punishment.

Justice needs to care.

85

"What is justice?" Susan asks, looking at the signs and ignoring Breezy's question. "What does it mean to you?"

Breezy laughs. She doesn't reply. She simply shakes her head and takes another swig of her beer.

"What are you afraid of, Breeze?"

"Me? I'm not afraid of anything."

"Then what is it? What is justice?"

"Okay. I'll play along with your little clown routine," Breezy says, setting her beer down. "Justice is the mechanism by which laws are enacted and enforced in society to ensure just outcomes. There! Happy? It's Congress. It's judges. It's lawyers for the prosecution *and* the defense. It's juries. It's police officers keeping the peace."

"It's a myth," Susan says.

"What?"

"Justice is an illusion. You know that. Justice is about keeping up appearances. Look at me. Look at the color of my skin. What kind of justice do you think I'll get if I so much as put a foot wrong? Do you think I'll get the same treatment as a pretty white girl?"

"It's not like that," Breezy says.

Susan cocks her head sideways, staring at Breezy with an annoyed look on her face.

She says, "Honey, you know it's all for show. There are two types of justice in this country. Rich and white—and then every other sucker. Ain't nothing changed. And you. A Hispanic woman. Shooting three white boys. How do you think that is going to play before a judge?"

"I'm with the Secret Service."

"Oh, you think that's gonna be your little *get-out-of-jail-free* card? They are gunning for you, Breezy. This article is just the start. The right-wing media. They're going to come after you. Now if you were a white man shooting a bunch of black teens during a robbery, it would be different. Hell, you'd barely make the news." She taps the window, adding, "Can't you see? We talk a big game, but we're playing in the little league. We talk about justice and equality but we let shit slide all the damn time. But them! Those fools out there. Those clowns you despise. They're trying to make a difference. They want real change."

Breezy says, "They can't change anything by walking down a street."

Someone marches past with another placard.

Justice is more than enforcing the law.

"You don't get it, do you?" Susan says. "Our whole notion of justice is backward. For us, justice exists as a reaction to injustice. Doesn't that strike you as shortsighted? It's the cart leading the horse."

"What are you talking about?" Breezy says. "Society needs laws."

Susan says, "Society needs to have a heart."

One of the protesters taps the window, but he's not being aggressive or belligerent. He smiles and waves a friendly hello as he walks on.

Susan has a sense of admiration in her eyes.

Breezy shakes her head. To her, protesting at night is dumb. Protesting at night on the weekend is even dumber. Who's watching them? What are these clowns expecting? It's performance art, but for whom? On Saturday night, no one cares. All the politicians have gone away for the weekend, running off to their holiday homes on the Chesapeake Bay or in Ocean City. They'll be sipping a glass of fine wine, looking out over the Atlantic. By now, all the lobbyists will have nestled away for the night in their fancy mansions in Mount Vernon. They're not thinking about change. They're thinking about nine holes at Fort Belvoir tomorrow morning followed by lunch in the clubhouse. They're thinking about trading in for a new Caddie. They're thinking about spending winter in Florida.

"These guys are wasting their time," Breezy says.

"These guys," Susan counters, "are trying to stop the train before it reaches the end of the track."

"Well, it ain't gonna work."

"I'm a doctor, Breezy. If you fall off a riverbank and break your leg I can help. I can set it in a cast and get you walking again. That's good, right?"

"Right."

"But do you know what's better? Not—*breaking*—your leg!"

"I don't get it," Breezy says, grabbing a handful of french fries and stuffing them in her mouth.

"The solution isn't to have more hospitals with more doctors and nurses setting more and more broken legs in casts. The solution is to put up a handrail along the river. The solution is to put up a sign warning people about the sudden drop."

"And how does that relate to justice?"

Susan says, "Our judicial system is a *reaction* to society's problems. It's not a *solution* for them. It'll always be one step behind us."

"So what is the solution?" Breezy asks.

Susan points at the window.

Breezy is on the verge of spitting out her beer. "Clowns? You cannot be serious."

"We need change. We need to care for each other. We need to build a society where the judicial system is the *last* resort, not the first."

"You're being naive," Breezy says.

"Am I?" Susan asks. "If we keep doing the same thing, nothing changes. Nothing gets better."

Breezy is blunt. "Things can get worse."

"Things can get better," Susan says, fidgeting in her seat. "Don't you see that? Can't you feel it? We need this, Breeze. We need change. All of us. You. Me. Alice."

Breezy snaps. "Don't you bring her into this!"

"Why?" Susan asks, leaning forward on the table and inviting a response. "She's not a kid anymore. You can't keep treating her like a child."

"She's my child," Breezy says, feeling defensive.

"She's turning eighteen next month," Susan says.

"And what? You think she's going to move out? She's not going anywhere."

"Breeze," Susan says, sitting back and breathing deeply. She looks into Breezy's eyes. There's sympathy there. Compassion. "You can't be afraid of change. Life is change. It can be scary, but it doesn't have to be."

"I'm not afraid."

"You know what I mean," Susan says. "I know you. Five years, babe. I know you're not afraid of anything in this world. Bullets, bombs, bad guys—you eat them for breakfast. But this is different. You can't fight this. Breeze, honey, it's okay to feel unsure about the future. You can't control—"

"Her?" Breezy asks, raising her eyebrows and cutting Susan off.

"Everything," Susan says. "That's what I was going to say. Don't you see? This is the problem. You want to control everything, regardless of what it is, but you can't. At a certain point, you have to let go."

"Of you?" Breezy asks with quivering lips.

"Of me. Of Alice. Of everything. You can't hold back the tide."

Breezy hangs her head.

Susan says, "I'll always be there for you and Alice."

"But not as my partner?"

"As your friend."

"You think you understand me, but you don't," Breezy says. "You're a doctor. You fix people. It shapes the way you see the world. But me? I protect people. That's what I do. I look for threats. I assess the danger. I take action. I keep people safe."

Susan says, "To a man with a hammer, everything's a nail. You can't live like that, Breeze. You have to see the world in a new light. You need to trust others. You need to trust *me* when I tell you I see something different. Not everyone is out to get you. People aren't either good or bad. We're all just dumb old humans. We need to work together to change our world for the better."

Breezy is unmoved. "People are sheep."

"Breeze, that's not a healthy outlook."

Breezy doesn't care. "Sheep need a shepherd to protect them from the wolves. Because it is a wilderness out there. There are people out there that would tear you to pieces in a heartbeat. Now, you can hold to your hippie *change-is-coming* mentality all you want but make no mistake: it's a luxury. It's a privilege people like me have to fight to defend."

"We're not sheep," Susan says. "Don't you get it? I'm not mindlessly following along. That's the whole point of wanting change."

Breezy is undeterred. "We all want a world full of unicorns and rainbows, puppy dogs and flowers, but that's not reality. Eighty-one people were executed in Saudi Arabia last week. Eighty-one on a single day. And why? Because they wanted free speech. Because they spoke to the Western media. Because they were forced to confess to crimes they never committed."

"Why would they confess to something they never did?" Susan asks.

Breezy replies, "You'll confess to anything once they start ripping your teeth out. Can't you see? This is the world we live in. It's a mess."

Susan doesn't blink. She seems lost in thought. As horrific as this is for her, she senses something deeper. She takes Breezy by surprise, asking, "And what did you do about it?"

"What do you mean?"

"You," Susan says calmly. "You're a shepherd, right? What did you do to protect the sheep?"

Breezy is flustered. "Ah, I didn't do anything. This was in Saudi Arabia."

"So?" Susan says, shrugging. "Don't you see the problem? You're outraged by this. And so you should be. I am too. But outrage isn't enough. What should we do when faced with barbaric acts like these? Get angry? Yell at the TV? Complain about injustice while drinking in a bar? That's not good enough."

"So what would you do?" Breezy asks.

"Push for change. I want change. I want it here *and* there! But it has to happen here before it'll happen there. Turning a blind eye to what happens here doesn't help anyone over there."

"And you think the clowns will give you this?" Breezy asks, incredulous.

"I think we have to start somewhere," Susan replies. "We can't continue on as we have."

Breezy isn't impressed. "And I think you're naive. There are no fairy tale endings. Freedom comes with a price tag. The freedom we have here cost us something. It needs to be defended."

"And that's the difference between us," Susan says. "You think people are helpless. You see kindness as weakness. You think *you* need to protect us. You don't. You can't control everything. And when you do...."

"When I do, what?" Breezy asks, indignant.

Susan looks her in the eye and says, "People die."

COPS

Olivia sits on the side of the main road beside her aging Volvo. She sobs into her shaking hands. She's still holding the tire iron but can't bring herself to change the tire. For now, it's enough just to simply breathe. Headlights sweep across her as a car pulls in behind her. She squints, looking into the bright lights, accepting her fate. Car doors slam. One, then another. She drops the tire iron.

A flashlight is shone in her eyes even though she's already bathed in the headlights of the vehicle. Through the haze, she sees a man in uniform standing before her with his hand on a holster set firmly on his hip.

"Hey? Are you okay?"

Olivia nods, aware another officer is flanking her, standing slightly out of sight to one side.

"What happened?"

"Flat tire," Olivia says, gesturing to the side of the Volvo even though it's obvious. The second officer is a woman. She shines her light in the rear of the Volvo and then the front, looking at the seats and in the footwells. As the driver's window is open, she leans in, taking a good look.

"And that's all?" the first officer says. He's easily six foot four, with a bazillion pounds of iron-pumping muscle that barely fits into a blue uniform.

Olivia nods.

"Let's get you to your feet," he says, although he doesn't offer her his hand. Instead, he steps back, watching as she grabs the bumper of the Volvo and gets up. "Have you got your driver's license on you?"

"It's in my purse," she says, gesturing to the front of the car.

"Have you been drinking?"

"No."

"Doing any drugs?"

"No."

Olivia keeps her hands in front of her, resting them in plain sight on the lid of the trunk. The cop seems relaxed, but Olivia's aware he could change in an instant with the wrong move from her.

"I'm going to search you for concealed weapons," the officer says. Concealed? The only thing she's concealing is the silicone in her breasts, but she's pretty sure the officer already knows that.

"Keep your hands where they are. Legs apart."

Although she's wearing a t-shirt and tight jeans, the officer treats her as though she were wearing a baggy trench coat. He runs his hands over her shoulders and along her biceps, squeezing tightly. He sweeps his gloved fingers under her armpits, and—there it is—his hands reach around her chest, squeezing her breasts. His fingers follow the contour of her bra.

Bastard.

He continues on, moving down to her hips. Olivia locks eyes with the female officer, who shrugs. Before working his way down her thighs, he reaches between her legs and grabs her crotch from behind.

Asshole.

For the sake of appearances, he continues down to each ankle before stepping back and saying, "Turn around."

The officer has a chest-mounted camera, but there's no way to know whether it's recording. Regardless, it wouldn't have caught him groping her.

"Have you called anyone to come and help you?" he asks as though he hasn't just sexually assaulted her.

"No," Olivia replies, playing the game.

"Where are you coming from? Where are you going to?"

"I just finished work. I'm heading home."

No sooner has she said that than Olivia regrets her choice of words. If she weren't so freaked out by what just happened, she would have spun a believable lie. Being vague with cops is never smart, but the male officer knows he's caught her reeling from being groped and accepts that.

The female officer asks, "And the donuts on the backseat."

"They're old," Olivia says.

"Open the box for me."

"Sure."

Olivia moves slowly, keeping her hands in sight. She opens the back door, asking, "Do you want one?"

"Bribing an officer with a donut," the male cop says, laughing, "You realize that's a felony?"

Oh, that's not the only thing that's a felony.

Olivia forces a smile. As she leans in the back of the vehicle, she's aware the female officer is flashing her light over her ass. It seems they're both happy to play around.

Creeps.

Olivia leaves the lid open, but she can't help herself. A tear rolls down her cheek. Three donuts sit bumper to bumper, dripping with glaze and sprinkles, in a box designed for nine. That seems to satisfy the cops. At this point, Olivia realizes they've probably accepted her as a damsel in distress they can shakedown for a bit of fun on an otherwise dull patrol. There's no insistence on seeing her license. They've probably already run her plates. As the car is registered in her sister's name, they probably assume she's Janet.

"Why the tears?" the female officer asks as if she doesn't know. Olivia hates playing games. Nothing is going right. Tomorrow, when the body of the prostitute is discovered less than a mile from here, this particular stop-and-search is going to seem all too relevant. She only hopes it's considered coincidental. Given that she really does have a flat tire, it's plausible.

"It's—been a long day."

Sometimes the best lies are the ones grounded in truth. The officer nods.

"Well," the male officer says. "You better get that fixed and get on your way."

The female officer slaps him on the shoulder, saying, "You fix it."

"Me?"

"Come on, Mr. knight-in-shining-armor. You're the one that wanted to pull over."

"It's fine," Olivia says, waving them away, but after squeezing her breasts and her crotch, it seems the male officer wants to show her he's a good guy.

"All right," he says, slipping the jack under the rear of the Volvo.

To Olivia's utter dismay, the female officer stands back, talking casually with her while Officer Roaming Hands changes the tire. Olivia doesn't say much beyond *um,* and *yeah,* as the female officer talks about the weather and the surf out at Ocean City.

Once the tire is changed, the officers excuse themselves, wishing her a good night. The disconnect is profound. Somewhat in shock, Olivia says, "Thanks."

They drive off as though nothing happened, leaving her to put the jack, the tire iron and the blown tire in the trunk. Red and blue lights flash over the trees on the side of the road as the police car loops back in the other direction, but only for a second. They're letting her know they've seen her pulling back out on the road. At a guess, this is their idea of being friendly.

Olivia drives toward her home in Fairfax, just outside DC, but her hands are still shaking. Cops notwithstanding, someone wants her dead. No, that's not quite it. Someone already thinks she's dead. By morning, that illusion will be shattered. She's got to get home and warn Janet. It's time for the two of them to take a long vacation. They could head north to cooler weather. There are dozens of small towns in upstate New York just shy of the Canadian border where the cops are sleepy, and a girl can disappear for a couple of months.

On turning into her street, she sees a paramedic pushing a gurney with a sheet pulled over a body. He wheels it to the back of an ambulance and slams the doors shut. Olivia slows but doesn't stop. Tears stream down her cheeks as she drives past. Cops trample the thin strip of grass in front of her home. A small crowd has gathered on the pavement, but in the darkness, she goes unnoticed.

Feeling numb, she drives on. Eventually, she pulls into a McDonald's parking lot and wanders inside in a daze.

"Can I help you?" a teenage girl asks, pointing at a self-help ordering screen where Olivia can help herself. She orders coffee. As she goes to sit in a booth, she pulls her phone from her back pocket. A business card falls to the ground. It's blank. She turns it over, expecting to see contact details for the juggler at the mall. There's no phone number, no email address, no Twitter handle or Instagram profile, no physical address or post box, just a single word.

—Clowns—

CLOWNS

Olivia doesn't know what to do.

Although it's the middle of the night, the lights in McDonald's are as bright as the noonday sun. Plastic tables. Plastic cutlery. Hard plastic seats. Nothing's real. Everything around her has been fabricated. It's been molded to suit the business, not the people. Olivia shakes her head. The damn clowns are wearing off on her. Next, she'll be painting her face and joining a protest rally on the National Mall. Unlike most fringe groups, the clowns don't have a single agenda. They want it all: *voting rights, women's rights, climate change, gun control, judicial reform, health care, equality for minorities, immigration reform, national education standards*. The list is exhausting.

Olivia stirs creamer in her coffee.

She's numb. What does it matter? What does anything matter anymore? Her sister is dead. And for what? For twenty grand she never got. For twenty grand that always sounded too good to be true. Her lips tremble but she doesn't cry. She's beyond that now. If there are five stages of grief, then all of them are *shock*. Nothing is real. Not the polish on her nails. Not the rings on her fingers. Not the stupid-ass dumb business card in her hand.

> *—Clowns—*

There's no phone number, no address, no email—nothing.

Olivia doesn't know who she can turn to. She wonders about the others involved in the blackmail shoot.

Ordinarily, Snow White contacts her via a dead drop. Once a week, on either Friday, Saturday or Sunday, Olivia walks around Lake Thoreau for exercise. She never goes on the same day or at the same time from one week to the next. Once she's walked around the water's edge, she sits on a seat looking out over the lake before returning to her car. Sometimes she takes stale bread to feed the ducks even though she's heard it's not good for them. If there's a fresh *Don't Litter* sticker on the side of the garbage can, she reaches under the seat and pulls off an envelope taped beneath the wooden slats. Then she places a *Climate Emergency* sticker over at least one corner of the *Don't Litter* sticker to let Snow know she got the message. At some point over the next couple of days, Snow will peel both of them off, and the communique is complete.

Work is sporadic. Sometimes Olivia will get three gigs in three weeks; then she'll go three months without anything. She doesn't mind. She enjoys walking around the lake. In between, she picks up work stocking shelves at the local grocery store. It's not as high-paying as fucking a stranger, but there's less risk of everything: being beaten, being robbed, being shortchanged, being infected with some god-awful disease. She's got a few regulars that pay well, but even they can disappear for a couple of months. At around the four-month mark, if she hasn't heard from Snow, she'll take some impromptu porno work, but she doesn't like to rely on it. There are too many creeps in the industry. Olivia's been bashed too many times.

If there's a letter waiting for her beneath the seat, Olivia won't open it until she's back home. Normally, it contains little more than an address and a contract amount along with a date and time range for the shoot, like between 1 and 3 pm. Sometimes there are special instructions: get a Brazilian, color your hair pink, wear a lace bra or don't wear a bra at all that day. Once there was a Christmas card and a gift voucher. That was nice.

The problem now is, Olivia's got no way of getting hold of Snow. She considers driving to the lake in the middle of the night and trying the reverse strategy. She could put one of her *Climate Emergency* stickers on the bin and stick a note beneath the seat telling Snow what happened. Nah, it wouldn't work. Snow wouldn't know to check. Besides, even if she saw the sticker as she walked past, she might think of it as a coincidence. Snow probably wouldn't check beneath the seat until she's got another job lined up.

Fuck.

Olivia picks at her fake nails.

Someone's trying to erase this particular deep fake before it even comes to light. Was Snow in on the hit? Is Snow even alive? Olivia's a bit player. She doesn't know anyone inside the operation—by design. That way, she can't go blabbing to the cops. And it goes two ways. The arrangement is supposed to protect both of them. It means no actual identities are known. Olivia met Snow through a dark web porno ad offering a little extra cash on the side. They've both been careful to keep their distance from each other, although Olivia hates the whole *pick-a-name-from-a-fairytale* thing. Snow gets to keep her name from one gig to another, but she insists on Olivia jumping from Alice to Belle to Minnie to whoever. The issue is, she only responds to Olive, Ollies or Olivia.

Olivia flicks the clown's business card over in her hand. There's still nothing on the back, but it doesn't matter. That's not the point. She's lost in thought. If these assholes went after her, they would have gone hard on Snow and the others. The only clue Olivia has is that they didn't hit them at the house. They waited until afterward. That tells her there's something important about that place.

Olivia tries to recall as much detail as she can about the home. As she was in the back of a van and came in from the garage shared with the property next door, she never saw the front of the house. Even so, she's confident she could figure it out from Google Maps based on the wall she climbed at the back of the garden and the path along the river.

The house was beautiful, but it lacked something. It didn't feel like a home. There were no pictures of any family. Oh, the paintings were stunning. The marble floors looked immaculate. The kitchen was spacious, while the gardens were beautifully maintained. For all that, it felt like a display house rather than a home.

Air conditioning spills out of the vent above Olivia, chilling her even though it's warm outside. She cups her hands around her coffee. Vapor drifts from the cup.

Olivia feels lost. This morning, she was in control of her life. She was confident—strident. Now, her world has been shattered. Her sister is dead—murdered by what's known in the trade as a cleaning crew. It was probably the same team that thought she was in Arlington cemetery. Like her, they wouldn't know who they're working for. Everyone's a patsy in this game. It seems whoever was the target of the deep fake got wind of the job and decided to close it down before it could be complete.

Olivia looks up from her coffee. The streetlight is out on the corner, but lights on the other side of the road illuminate a solitary figure in silhouette. He's facing the restaurant, holding a helium balloon on a string.

"That's some freaky Pennywise shit," she mumbles, sipping her coffee. "Ain't no way—"

She looks down at the card on the table.

—*Clowns*—

"No. It can't be," she says, looking up.

The man is gone.

Olivia gets up, putting the card in her purse. She hoists the strap of her purse over her shoulder and walks out into the night, taking a wad of napkins with her. She stuffs them into the side pouch of her purse. The staff don't care. They're teens working crazy hours to make enough to buy the latest dumbass smartphone or to pay for a ski trip to Colorado. No one looks up as she leaves.

Olivia grips her keys in her palm, positioning the brass tips outward between her fingers, forming a knuckleduster. She's never had to strike someone with her *wolverine* claws, and they're a helluva lot shorter than the *adamantium* version in the movies, but she's confident they'll send a message if needed. If anything, that they barely protrude beyond her knuckles is a plus. They'll go unnoticed in the dark. Even a glancing blow is going to get an attacker to think twice.

Once blood is drawn, the game is over. Oh, men might get pissy and violent, but even a musclebound creep will think twice with blood dripping from the side of his face. In her experience, men who hit women are cowards. Draw a little blood in reply, and they'll curse and swear and sulk away, throwing around hollow threats and lame insults.

As a prostitute, Olivia has had to defend herself. In her experience, broken glass is the best weapon. Glass is everywhere, so it's always accessible. Smashing a window serves two purposes: it gets attention, and it gives her a fighting chance. Grab a broken shard of glass along with even something as seemingly useless as a dishcloth, and the two combine to form a knife that's as effective as a switchblade. It's homemade but it'll cut like a razor. A glancing blow is enough to rip someone open. A six-inch gash makes most men melt even if the cut's not that deep.

Olivia keeps her right hand out of sight in the shadows. She doesn't like the dark. She's not afraid of the dark as such. Experience has taught her it's a great place to hide, but it's also taught her it provides an easy platform for muggers.

Olivia's already evaluating where she can get some glass if her key trick doesn't work. In a nightclub, it's bottles and drinking glasses that come readily to hand. The broken stem of a wine glass is better than a pickax. Out here on the street, it's store windows. Part of an old wooden crate lies in the gutter ahead. It's been broken up as vehicles have driven over it. Hurling a bit of that through the abandoned storefront will wake the dead. If the keys don't work, the napkins will allow her to grab some glass. They'll protect her hands for a couple of strikes at least.

She crosses the parking lot, being wary of attack as she steps behind parked cars.

The streetlights ahead go out. One of them flickers. The others are dead. She walks out onto the street. It's empty.

A voice speaks from a darkened doorway. "You're pretty. You should be a performer."

"On Broadway or in a circus?" she replies.

A man steps forward.

"Anywhere other than on a sex tape."

"Who are you?" she asks, surprised by his lack of height.

The man seems to realize she's taken back by his size. Far from being imposing, he's physically a joke—or so it seems at first appearance. Olivia doesn't feel threatened by him in the slightest.

She asks, "Are you a clown?"

In the blink of an eye, he dives into a somersault, resulting in a forward roll on the concrete pavement. He curls over on his shoulder and bounces up in front of her with a fake bouquet of flowers springing from his hand. Olivia stands there stunned. One moment, he was over there in the shadows. She barely had time to breathe before he sprung up in front of her with a smile lighting up his face.

"Aren't we all?"

"I—um," she says, unsure whether she should reach for the flowers. As her keys are in her right hand, still locked between her knuckles, she reaches out with her left hand to take them. Before she can react, he waves his hands in front of each other, rolling them together. The flowers disappear and are replaced by a white dove.

"W—What?" she says, astonished to see the bird cupped in his outstretched hands. The stunned creature turns its head, looking every bit as bewildered as she is. It coos softly. He gives it a slight lift, raising his hands toward the dark of night and opening them wide. The dove unfolds its wings and takes flight. Olivia steps back as the bird beats at the air in front of her. Feathers brush against her hair as the dove soars into the darkness.

"And these," he says, holding her keys up and letting them jingle from his hand. "You won't need these to protect you—not from me."

Olivia looks down at her empty hands in astonishment. Her palms are open and upturned. The strange man drops her keys back into her hand.

"Who are you?" she asks, slipping her keys into her purse and zipping it closed.

"A friend."

He starts walking, heading up the road away from the McDonald's. He's walking into a poorly lit industrial area.

"Are you coming?" he asks, turning back toward her.

"Yes," she says, feeling enchanted rather than afraid. "What's your name?"

"Buster."

"I'm—"

"Olivia," he says, frowning. "I know. I'm sorry about your sister."

"You knew?" she says, lifting her purse higher on her shoulder so the strap doesn't slip. "How did you know?"

"You attracted a lot of attention at the mall."

"I did."

"When people attract attention, we pay attention."

"Who's after me?" she asks, not caring where they're going.

"Who isn't would be a shorter list."

"Really?"

"We spotted agents from the FBI, NSA and Secret Service at the mall, not to mention local police and a few private eyes."

"But... why?"

"It's not you," Buster says. "It's who you were playing in the deep fake."

"I don't understand. There is no deep fake—not yet. We only just recorded it. These things take time. Post-production can take weeks."

"It doesn't matter," he says. "They knew the game was on."

Olivia's lips tremble. She struggles to speak. "W—Who was it? Who killed my sister?"

"An ex-Navy SEAL who goes by the name Johnny Ringo. His real name is Jonathan Rheims, but he's a pawn. And he's already been removed from the board. Right about now, he's floating face down in the Potomac."

"I don't understand."

"You really don't know what's going on, do you?" Buster says.

"No."

"The first rule of assassinations is: *kill the assassin.*"

"Assassin? But I'm not—"

"You're part of a coup to replace the President of the United States. Oh, it's elaborate. No one will see it coming, but it's unfolding like a game of chess. The bishop is in position. The rook is covering the exits. The knight is now in play. All they need is patience."

"And me?"

Buster says, "You're a pawn. You're expendable. The only reason you're still alive is they think you're dead. Tomorrow, all that changes."

"But why kill my sister?"

"They couldn't take any chances. They couldn't risk you telling her something that might leak out. Pawns can become queens."

A solitary tear rolls down Olivia's cheek.

"How?" she asks, trying to compose herself as she walks along with him. "How can a deep fake roll the President of the United States?"

"The guy you were fucking."

"Dopey?"

"Remove a couple of moles and tweak just four facial points by less than 10% each and he's a dead ringer for the Vice President. And you. They made sure they only got you facing away from the camera."

"They're going to blackmail him?"

Buster says, "He has a mistress. They meet twice a week at various spots around the city, including that home. Only he's careful. Each house gets swept by security for bugs."

"So they had to fake it," Olivia says. "They had to get him to think they missed a camera."

"Yes."

"He's Catholic, a family man," she says, recalling what little she knows about the Vice President.

"That's what makes him vulnerable. He wants to protect his image. He's concerned about his legacy. He'll resign for *health* reasons or they'll go public."

"Huh," she says, recalling how the camera operator watched his light meter before the shoot. She says, "He won't even realize it's fake."

"Nope," Buster says.

Olivia mumbles, "They probably only need to show him a few seconds."

Buster nods, saying, "You were performing for an audience of one."

"Okay, so he resigns and then what? Who's going to take his place?"

"I don't know. Yet. I'm still trying to figure out who's behind this and why."

"But doesn't the President pick the replacement?"

"He'll be pressured by hardliners into the right choice."

Olivia says, "This doesn't sound good, but it's hardly overthrowing the government. The President is still the President. While the Vice President is largely symbolic."

"But," Buster says.

"But?" Olivia repeats back at him, still not seeing this as anything other than an oddity.

"That replacement is a heartbeat away from the presidency. One well-placed bullet changes everything."

"Fuck," she says.

Buster laughs. He raises an eyebrow, looking sideways at her as he says, "Well, to be fair, that is what started all this."

"And you?" she asks. "Why are you helping me? I mean, you're a clown, right?"

"Don't let the name fool you," he says, pointing at the darkened fairgrounds looming at the top of the hill. "Clowns are no joke."

The familiar shape of a Big Top rises in the distance. One side of the tent has collapsed. Instead of three central poles holding the canvas aloft, there are two. Circus rides are visible in silhouette against the night sky. Thin tracks and rickety scaffolding mark a long-abandoned rollercoaster. A Ferris wheel looms over the trees. One of its vast steel support rings has collapsed, falling in against the other. Twisted seats hang from the ruins, the relics of some forgotten storm that ravaged the ride. Flags flutter in the breeze. Their ends are frayed.

"Why are you getting involved?"

Buster comes to a halt, turning to face her. "That's the question no one asks."

He walks on. Olivia rushes to keep up.

"But I asked."

"You did," he says, maintaining his pace up the hill.

"And the answer is?"

"Because this changes the shape of our world. And we should all care about that."

"I don't care," Olivia says, being brutally honest. "Why should I? It's either one rich entitled prick in that office or another. Regardless of their political leaning, they're the elite. They don't care about you or me."

"They care about something," Buster says. "Sometimes it's ideology. Sometimes it's money or power."

"They're selfish," Olivia says.

"Everyone's self-centered," Buster replies. "But that doesn't mean everyone's selfish. We're all stuck in one place, looking at one moment in time. We all need to see the big picture."

"So you're *woke*?" she asks.

"What's the alternative?" he asks. "Being asleep?"

"You know what I mean."

"Woke. Awake. Aware," Buster replies, smiling. "*Woke* isn't the slur people think it is. It's like treating the terms *honesty* or *compassion* as though they were somehow tainted."

Buster sweeps his hand to one side, waving out across the Potomac toward the lights of Washington. With the industrial area behind them, they're walking toward the crest of the hill and the fairgrounds. Long grass rises from abandoned lots. An old farmhouse has collapsed to one side. What's left of the roof struggles to reach waist height. Signs warn of the danger beyond as the hillside falls away sharply toward the river.

"You need to see more than just what's in front of you," he says, coming to a halt before a long, overgrown driveway. "Can you see that? The lights stretching out to the horizon?"

"Sure," she says.

Buster points at the heart of the capital several miles away.

At night, DC is a breathtaking kaleidoscope of color. Spotlights illuminate the lily-white Maryland marble that forms the buildings of the US government. The dome on Capitol Hill is visible, as is the Washington Monument. The streetlights are yellow, setting up a nice contrast with the pale white landmarks. The Potomac winds before them, curling through D.C. Lights reflect off the water, adding a blurred impression of the city's foreshore.

"Look at the horizon. You can see it, and yet you can't. Because it's not there. There is no horizon. Go to that point. Go and stand on that distant building and ask yourself, *where is it now*? It's moved. Only it hasn't. It was never there to begin with. The horizon exists only because of *you*. The horizon is found only in the limits of your own mind."

Olivia's not sure what to make of his comment.

Buster explains. "As wonderful as this view is, it exists only *behind* your eyes. Oh, the buildings are real. The roads and bridges are all there, along with the parks and monuments, but this...." He shakes his finger at the distant city. "This view only exists because you're standing here now! Stand anywhere else and you'll see something different. You're framing reality. Your position in life determines what you see."

"And what do I see?" she asks, looking at him rather than at the river.

"You're an American. You see yourself in the mirror and no one else. And this is the problem. If you were born in Ethiopia or Afghanistan, you'd still be you, you'd still have the same conscious awareness, but you'd see the world in a different light."

"You really are strange," Olivia says. "I heard you guys were some kind of cult."

"Cult? No. You heard what they wanted you to hear. That's the oldest trick in the book. If you can't counteract an argument, discredit it. It's lazy rather than logical, but it works."

"And we're just dumb enough to fall for it," she says, accepting his point.

"Not dumb," Buster says, walking toward the fairgrounds. "Smart."

They cross a desolate road. The concrete slabs are uneven. Weeds grow up through the cracks. There's a gravel parking lot outside the gates of the fairground. Beyond that, there are several empty fields. Aging signs with fading arrows direct traffic to an overflow parking lot that no longer exists. Olivia rushes to keep up with Buster.

"Smart?" she asks, confused by his logic.

"Would you like to know a secret?" he asks, standing before a gate topped with barbed wire. Heavy chains hold the gate shut. The chains are linked together by a rusted padlock. Buster runs his fingers over the lock. In the darkness, she can't quite make out what he's doing. He's got his back to her. The chains fall open.

"Um, sure," she says, feeling a little uneasy entering an abandoned fairground with a stranger in the dead of night.

"Smart people are the easiest to fool."

"Wait," she says, walking through the gates with him. "That doesn't make any sense."

"They don't see it coming," he says, closing the gate behind her. He reaches through the handles, slipping the lock back in place on the chains. Buster taps his temple. "They're too smart. It makes them an easy mark."

"Hang on. I've heard of *Dunning-Kruger*," Olivia says. "People who are too dumb to realize they're wrong, but that doesn't apply to intelligent people."

"Doesn't it?"

"No. By definition, smart people aren't dumb."

"It's not that they're dumb," Buster says, repeating his earlier point. "It's that they're arrogant. There's a difference. Smart people are easily distracted. They're intelligent. That makes them confident, which is only one step away from being overconfident. It's easy to overlook the obvious. I mean, look at you."

"Me?" she asks, pointing at herself in surprise.

Buster gestures at the distant lights visible through the chainlink fence. A large **M** glows at the end of a forty-foot black steel pole. They've walked easily half a mile from the McDonald's restaurant to the fairgrounds. "You're smart. You were down there. Now you're here."

Olivia grabs the chainlink fence, suddenly realizing the gate is locked. Her fingers pull at the wire. Frustration ripples out from her clenched fists, reverberating through the wire links, chiming like a crash cymbal being struck on a drum set.

"You were free and now you're not," Buster says. "Whether you like it or not, your life will never be the same."

DIRECTOR JOHNSON

Nobody walks alone at night in downtown Washington. Breezy is beyond caring. She needs time to get her head together. Besides, she's in no rush to get back to her car. The longer it takes, the later it will be when she gets home.

Susan's gone home to pack some clothes. At some point, she will return and spend the night at the serviced apartments across from the hospital. They're used by doctors and nurses pulling 12-16 hr shifts when the health system goes into overdrive. As heartbreaking as it is, it's better if Breezy gives Susan some distance. If Breezy were there, her presence would aggravate things. Yelling at each other won't help. As difficult as it is, Breezy has to give her some breathing space.

Accepting criticism is never easy. Although she doesn't want to admit it, Susan's right. Breezy can be overwhelming. Even when she tries not to interfere, she invariably says something controlling. It's not malicious. Often it's innocuous. *"Where are you going?"* or *"What time will you be back?*" From her perspective, these are practical questions. They're curiosities. If Susan's going to the mall, Breezy might ask her to pick up something. '*Might,*' being the opportune word. She never does. As for asking when she'll be back, it helps planning things like cooking meals. Breezy likes to be there when Susan gets home from work. It's important to her. She doesn't mean to smother her.

The problem is, Breezy has a teenage daughter. Alice is seventeen. Susan's twenty-five. Breezy's thirty-five. Susan and Alice get along like sisters. At first, that seemed like a plus, but the age difference between all of them hasn't helped. Susan and Alice are closer in age. They're part of the same generation. They have the same likes, the same interests, and the same attitudes toward the world. Breezy feels as though she's ancient. To them, she's a matriarch. Susan shouldn't have to tell Breezy not to treat her like a teenager. Breezy doesn't want to, but she can't help herself.

Walking along the uneven pavement past closed car dealerships gives Breezy a rare moment of clarity. She's afraid. She's scared of losing them both.

"Too late," she mumbles to herself as her boots crumple weeds growing up between the cracks in the concrete.

Breezy tried to hold onto them, to care for them, to protect them, but each act has only driven them further from her. She couldn't see that she was pushing them away.

Susan wants a lover, not a mother. Being an intern in her first year of residency as a doctor, she's ahead of almost everyone else in her field. She's making life and death decisions every day, and Breezy's worried about when she will get home?

Breezy scolds herself. "Fucking stupid!"

Susan's leaving. Alice won't be far behind her when she hits eighteen. Hell, they'll probably move in together. They're great friends. Perhaps that's why Breezy feels as though there's a dagger plunging through her chest and into her heart. It didn't have to be this way. She's done this to herself.

"But clowns? Really?" she asks no one, kicking an empty soda can and watching it skid across a side road. Cars rush past on the main road, ignoring her. There are people in the shadows, sheltering from the light rain that's begun falling. Breezy's not worried about them. Homeless folk aren't demons. They're inconvenient. They're an embarrassment. Not to her. To society. To a society that's failed them. Like the cars driving past, tossing trash out the window, it's too easy to ignore them.

"Hah," she says, laughing at the thoughts rattling around her head. "I'm starting to sound like a goddamn clown."

Although she couldn't admit it to Susan, Breezy understands their passion, if not their arguments. Who doesn't want the world to change for the better? No one wants polluted rivers or trash washing out to the sea. Looking away isn't a solution, but it sure is easy. Getting caught up in the melodrama of work or paying off a mortgage is a nice distraction.

The rain gets heavier, soaking her clothing, but as it's hot, humid and sticky, it's welcome. Besides, it hides the odd tear that runs down her cheek as she pities herself. Come on, Breezy. It's not the end of the world. Susan just needs some space. Yeah, as in light-years of dark, cold, empty space.

She walks past a bar. A couple of drunks are holding up a lamppost. They watch her walk past with idle curiosity. They're no threat. See, that's the problem, Breezy. The whole world is interpreted using a threat matrix. Risk profiling might help keep the President safe, but it has no place on a rainy, wet Saturday evening.

Breezy walks past without looking. Usually, she'd be observing changes in posture, looking for ways in which weapons could be concealed and thinking about strategies, but Susan's right: if a man has a hammer, everything's a nail. Can't a couple of buddies hang out and chat after a long, hot week? As it is, they head back inside. They were smoking, but the rain put an end to that.

"My mind is fucked," she says, looking at the fall of her boots in the puddles forming on the concrete. All situational awareness is gone. That she's even aware of that lack is sad. It's only now that she realizes how her job has molded her, shaping her personality and thinking processes. Forget taking a bullet for the President—this is the real sacrifice.

Cars drive past, hugging the curb and sending water splashing over her legs. Who fucking cares?

Her phone rings. Before she can respond to the call, the voice on the other end says, "Breezy?"

"Director Johnson?"

The director sounds panicked. He's speaking in hushed tones but in a series of rapid-fire comments that barely make sense.

"They're here. They're inside. I can hear them. They're downstairs. I'm alone. I need help."

"Call the cops," she says. It's an instinctive reaction. As soon as a 911 operator identifies the call as coming from the home of a senior government official, he'll get every patrol car within ten miles parked outside.

"I did. They laughed."

"What? I don't understand."

"Clowns, Breezy. They intercepted my call. I need you."

Breezy's already running down the street toward the hospital where her car is parked. She can see the neon cross in the distance. A helicopter takes off from the roof with navigation lights flashing. She switches her phone to speaker so she can talk while she runs.

"Where are you?"

"Apartment three. 5541 St Jude Ave. Fairmount Heights. Third floor."

"I'm ten to fifteen minutes away," she yells, pumping her arms and jumping the curb as she runs across a side street. "Barricade yourself in the bathroom. If you have a steel bathtub, get in it. Lie down. Stay low. Tiles, steel, ceramics—they'll fragment small arms fire."

"Okay. Oh—" he says, and with that, the call is cut.

"Fuck, fuck, fuck," Breezy yells, pumping her hands. "Hey Siri, call John Alexander on speaker."

"Calling John Alexander."

Breezy pumps her legs, driving them harder. Her boots pound on the concrete, hurting her knees. Her lungs are burning. The phone rings, but there's no answer.

"Jesus, John. Pick up, goddamn it!"

The call goes to voicemail. She hangs up.

"Hey Siri, call John Alexander," she yells, barely able to speak between breaths. Her change purse is in her back pocket. She can feel it working loose as she runs and has to grab it before it sprawls out on the concrete.

"Calling John Alexander."

A grumpy voice answers. "Fuck off, Breezy."

"Director Johnson," she says, vaulting a low brick wall as she reaches the hospital parking lot. She's out of breath and in pain.

"Call someone else," he says. "I've got the Vice President tomorrow. I need my sleep."

"Johnson's being attacked at home," she says. Her lungs feel as though they're going to explode. "Get a team over there. I'm—I'm five to ten away."

"What?" he says with a distinct change of tone in his voice. "Shit. Okay. On it."

He must be able to hear the sounds around her: the rain falling, the cars driving past, her boots slapping at the pavement, puddles splashing, her heavy breathing. This clearly isn't a prank call.

"Putting you on hold," he says. "Setting up a conference call."

Breezy and John went through training together. He ended up on the close-support team for the Vice President while she was assigned to the outer perimeter of crowd control. They're the most unlikely friends. They couldn't be more different. John's in his twenties and has a stomach like an ironing board. During basic, he'd do one-arm pushups while she struggled on her knees using both hands. While on grueling 15-mile training runs, he'd hang back with her, encouraging her to keep going. The only area where she excelled beyond him was marksmanship. Even then, it was close. For the most part, the guys and gals on their rotation stuck together in cliques, but not John. He had a soft spot for Breezy. Perhaps it was that he could see how hard it was for her. He was always there to help.

Breezy jumps across the hood of a nearby car, sliding on the wet sheet metal and landing in front of her car door. She's got her keys in her other hand. The indicators on her car flash as she reaches for the handle. Within seconds, she's inside and starting the engine. Her phone connects to the car's stereo as she reverses out of her parking spot. She bites her parking ticket and searches through her purse for her credit card.

Breezy pays fifty-five dollars at the exit. She's triggered an overstay fee.

"Son of bitch!"

As the boom gate rises, she hits a couple of buttons on the stereo console and the call is transferred. She can hear muffled talking. She's no longer on a separate line.

"Talk to me."

"Police are en route. I've got air assets with eyes on the property. SWAT is being mobilized."

"Good. Good."

"Hold on for a moment," he says. She can hear him talking to someone else on another phone.

Breezy accelerates down the road, hitting seventy-five miles an hour in a matter of seconds. There aren't too many cars on the street. She plays slalom with them, weaving in and out of the light traffic.

As part of the Secret Service, Breezy has to be evasion-rated every twelve months. Racing a black armored SUV around the track at Langley can only be described as fun, especially when random cars pop out from behind trees and the dozens of signs set around the track. Her instructors loved those sessions. They'd hang out of the windows firing paintballs at them to simulate an attack. If they could, the instructors would even try to ram the principal. No one ever thinks they'll actually be the only agent to spring to the aid of the President or a member of Congress, but everyone has to be ready just in case. Breezy might be on the outer pedestrian/crowd detail, but she's got to be able to pivot to getting the VP out of town in a hurry or rescuing members from the House of Representatives if needed. That training is kicking in now.

There's a red light ahead, but she knows exactly what to do. She already has her hazard lights on, warning other cars she's about to do something stupid. On reaching the intersection, she slows to thirty and flashes her headlights. She also hits her horn. Bewildered vehicles crossing in front of her come to a halt. They honk back. From their perspective, she's annoying. From her perspective, she knows she's been seen and avoided. The combination of noise and light maximizes her presence on the road. It's not just cars she needs to dodge. When cutting the lights, there's a real danger of hitting a pedestrian. In the dark, they're difficult to see. Lights and sound give them the best warning she can offer, but she's not stopping for anyone.

In the background, Breezy can hear John talking on the other call. He's running it through another speaker. From what she can tell, he's established a conference call. A familiar chime announces other people joining the call, but they're all on mute. Breezy remains quiet, knowing there's more for her to learn than contribute.

"Agent De la Cruz is en route to the director along with local law enforcement. She's on the call and listening in. I've alerted Colonel McMasters at Joint Base Anacostia-Bolling. He's activated Delta Force and is ready to swing into action if this is a broader attack on the government. The White House is in lockdown. Until we understand the scope of the attack, we will continue operating a Code Black. No decision has been made on moving *The Bear*. I'm handing over coordination to the Secret Service office in the West Wing. Principle Agent Glenn Rogers is taking the lead."

The Bear is the President. John's gone hard. He's a good man. He's not playing games. He's making sure everyone's in the loop. It would be a mistake to assume an attack on the director of the Secret Service isn't part of a broader assault about to unfold at multiple locations.

"Thank you, John," Rogers says. "As a precaution, the Vice President is being evac'd from the Naval Observatory to Camp David. The Speaker of the House is currently in New York. He's being moved to a secure location in Manhattan with local police being placed on high alert. I've got...."

Breezy tunes out the rest. She needs to focus on the road. The rain has made the concrete slippery. Her old Toyota fishtails around the corner. The suspension is spongy. It's not designed for high-speed maneuvers. As she turns into a T-junction, a police car comes tearing along the main road. Its lights are blazing. Its siren screams into the night.

The patrol car races up behind her aging Toyota but holds off at a distance of three car lengths. Her flashing hazard lights must be enough to tell them she's not joyriding. Hopefully, someone back at dispatch is thinking on their feet. The police command center would be a hive of activity after John called in the attack on the director. They've got to be connecting the dots. The cops behind her are probably still running her plates. Will her name be enough to identify her as a Secret Service agent? Probably not, but dispatch should have her name. John would have passed it along. He would have told them she was on her way to the location. They must be on the lookout for unmarked cars moving in support toward Fairmount Heights. In a crisis, not everyone's a bad guy.

"Breezy," John says, distracting her as she races past an empty mall. "We've got reports of semi-automatic fire from a 911 operator talking to one of the neighbors."

"Copy that," she says, mumbling, "Not good."

Her knuckles go white as she grips the steering wheel.

The police car pulls out onto the other side of the road. If the cop wants to stop her, this is the place to do it as there are barely any other cars on the four-lane highway. A slight nudge on her rear bumper and her Toyota will go into a tailspin that'll bring her to a screeching halt within about a hundred yards. The cop car's 3.6-liter v6 engine roars as it overtakes her tiny four-cylinder 1.6-liter shopping cart. The Ford Interceptor races up the outside, flying past her. The cop pulls in several car lengths ahead of her. Okay, they got the memo. He's leading her on and clearing the road for her. If anything, she's slowing him down as she simply cannot take corners at high speed without flipping her car on its roof. Once her Toyota loses its momentum, Breezy has to thrash the engine into a frenzy on the next straight. She feels like she's whipping a dead horse on a racetrack.

Breezy's Toyota is an automatic. She flicks the shifter back and forth to keep the engine revs high. At five and a half thousand revolutions per minute, she's in danger of blowing the engine. The damn thing sounds like a sewing machine.

Breezy slides around the corner and sideswipes a parked car. The sheet metal panels on her passenger door crumple like paper-mâché.

"Oops."

If the cop ahead of her notices in his rearview mirror, he doesn't care. He slows a little to let her catch up and then continues down the next boulevard. It takes another five minutes to reach Fairmount Heights.

Ahead, police cars block the road. They've turned sideways. Their lights are flashing, but there are no sirens. Red and blue lights flicker over the buildings. Breezy slows. The patrol car in front of her pulls to one side, letting her go through. Although it's after eleven at night, a crowd has formed behind the police line. The director lives in a high-rise opposite a strip mall with fast food outlets and a bar.

An ambulance drives slowly down the street beyond the police line. Black-clad SWAT officers crowd the entrance to the building. They're armed with AR-15s, shotguns and tactical shields, but they've been stood down—that much is evident from the way they're milling around.

Breezy brings her car to a halt in front of a police officer waving her to one side.

"US Secret Service," she says, winding her window down and showing him her ID. "I'm on point for the agency."

The cop checks her ID, flashing a penlight on it as he reads the details. "This way, Agent De la Cruz. We've been expecting you."

Breezy parks in the middle of the lane, kills the engine and leans over, unlocking her glovebox. Her Glock is in a leather holster. Three extra magazines are mounted in another leather pouch. She leaves them, taking only the Glock. She slips the holster into the small of her back. Breezy flips her ID over, tucking the leather back into the front of her jeans. Her ID faces forward. No one will be able to read it without kneeling, but it's a symbolic gesture. Without anything else to identify her, the various officers securing the scene will realize she's cleared to be there.

The police officer leads her over to a detective standing beside a police cruiser and introduces her. He leads her down the road on foot.

Breezy's still on the conference call. There hasn't been much discussion over the past few minutes. The squealing of her tires and the crunch of her Toyota slamming into a parked car probably got a little too much attention.

"John, are you still there."

"I'm here," he says. "We're all listening in."

Breezy turns to the detective as they cross the road. "What can you tell me?"

The detective seems to understand there are a helluva lot of important people on the other end of her phone. He speaks clearly, without any emotion. He could be reciting a shopping list. Breezy's not ready for what comes next. In her mind, she and the team have done everything right. They've reacted quickly. They've marshaled resources across multiple authorities to respond to an unforeseen critical incident. These are the key points for success. This is where all the discipline and training are supposed to pay off.

"Officers Greene and Thomas were first on the scene, arriving within four minutes of the call. They found the director on the steps outside. They rendered assistance, but he was gone before EMS arrived."

Breezy is holding her phone up so the microphone faces the sky, wanting to make sure no words are missed by those on the call. Her fingers go limp. She's on the verge of dropping the phone.

"What?"

"I'm sorry. He's dead."

"Suspects?" she says, grasping at any loose threads. She's in shock, but she's aware she has a role to fill. She needs answers, and not just for herself. "Do you have anyone in custody?"

The detective shakes his head.

A body is rolled over to the waiting ambulance. A sheet may hide the identity but the blood soaking through the white material leaves nothing to the imagination. There are multiple gunshot wounds to the torso, legs and arms. The blood streaking the steps leaves no doubt he crawled down three flights of stairs.

Breezy activates the camera on her phone, asking John, "Can you see this?"

"Yes."

The gurney is pushed into the back of the ambulance. The doors are shut. Breezy stands there for a moment. Her mind is rebooting. Meaning is lost. The prospect of bringing the killers to justice might appeal to the living, but it's pointless to the dead. Lives cannot be replaced. The score can never be equaled. She breathes. She doesn't want to. That semi-autonomous urge drives her on. Breezy lowers her head out of both sorrow and respect. The police detective waits patiently beside the stairs. Red and blue lights wash across the white sandstone building.

"What are they waiting around for?" Breezy asks, turning away from the entrance and looking across the four-lane road at the crowd on the far pavement. There's no hustle or bustle. No one's trying to push past the police. It's raining. Why are they still standing there silently in the dark? What is there to see?

"We get this a lot," the detective says. "I know it's strange. For you, this is personal. For them, it's a spectacle."

The word *spectacle* breaks like thunder overhead. She turns to him. Her eyes go wide. She's on the verge of grabbing him by the throat and throttling him. It takes all her willpower to keep her clenched fist by her side. Her fingers grip the phone, squeezing it against her palm. She has no idea what the phone's pointing at. For all she knows, John's staring off into the distance at some crazy angle, but she can't help it. It's *The Spectacle* that gets her. Buster bragged about this in the interrogation cell, but that can't be what the detective means. He looks at her bewildered, seeing the fire behind her eyes.

"They're ghouls," he says, defending a point he doesn't fully understand. He seems to sense she needs more. He laughs, adding, "I don't think even they know what they're waiting for. Something. Nothing. Ah, don't worry about them. They'll get bored and wander off."

The ambulance leaves, driving slowly through the rain.

"Can I see the crime scene?" she asks, composing herself and raising the phone to steady the image. John is conspicuously quiet.

The detective says, "Just don't touch anything."

Crime scene investigators move around in white disposable suits. They're carrying sample collection kits and cameras. Flashes go off as photos are taken. The detective hands her a pair of disposable covers for her boots so she doesn't leave any tracks. She slips them on, followed by a pair of disposable gloves, all the while juggling with her phone. They walk up the outside of the stairs, avoiding the blood streaks on the tiles.

The detective stops on the second landing and points at a bloody mark on one of the doors.

"He tried to get help, but no one answered."

He crouches, tapping a pen against the wall. "See how the blood's smeared here but dropped there on the floor. It's at this point he went from crouching to lying on his chest, pulling himself on."

Breezy nods but doesn't say anything. She sweeps around with the camera on her phone so John and anyone else watching can take in the scene.

The detective leads her to the third-floor apartment. The steel door has been bashed in. A fine white powder coats the handle. Someone's looking for fingerprints. Breezy's more interested in the damage to the door. From the circular imprint, it's clear the attackers have used a steel battering ram to knock the door off its hinges. It's standard SWAT gear, but it would be difficult for a civilian to pick up without leaving a paper trail. It would be easy enough to fabricate one in a workshop but would require testing and refinement. It's not as simple as a weighted bar. It needs to be balanced and have shock-absorbing handholds to allow for multiple strikes. Breezy makes a mental note to get someone from the service to run a check with suppliers.

The detective notices her lingering.

"We've got overlapping trails at this point. Three strikes for entry. That's ten to twenty seconds to breach."

"And once they were inside?" Breezy asks, staying next to the wall as she walks down the entry hall. Bootprints cover the floor. Blood has smeared over them, but a few clear prints have been dusted and photographed.

The detective points. "Broken vase. He threw this at them, buying himself some time while going for his gun."

"Did he get to it?"

"I think so," the detective says, using his pen to tap at a couple of fine holes near the ceiling. "They were using AK-47s. These holes are too small and in the wrong direction. They've been fired high and wide. They look like defensive fire."

"I spoke to him on the phone," she says.

The detective leads her into the bedroom. "We found the phone here."

A cellphone lies face-up on the carpet. The glass is smashed. Someone's slammed a boot down on it, crushing the electronics.

"Butt of a rifle," the detective says, seemingly reading her mind. He crouches nearby. "See the dull, rounded point of impact on the glass? It's too focused for a boot."

"Ah."

"This is where he made a stand," the detective says, moving around the edge of the bedroom. "Behind us, there are impacts from defensive shots."

"He had a service-issue Glock," Breezy says, examining one of the bullet holes in the edge of the doorframe.

Clothing lies scattered on the floor in the walk-in closet leading to the bathroom. The door is peppered with holes. They've splintered the wood. The door's open, but it's clear it was closed and locked.

"Automatic fire," she says.

"At least forty rounds," the detective says. "It's surprising he lived as long as he did."

Within the bathroom, broken tiles lie scattered across the floor.

"They were standing, firing down on an angle," the detective says.

The bath is made of steel and has been inset in a tiled frame. Bullet holes have punched through, but not every round penetrated the steel. Several have been deflected. The bottom of the bath is stained in rich, red blood.

"How many assailants?" she asks.

"Three," he says. "One with the ram. The other two with AKs."

The detective draws her attention to the upper hinge on the bathroom door. "We think they fired first then reverted to the ram."

"It doesn't make sense," Breezy says.

"What doesn't make sense?"

"Why use AK-47s? An AR-15 is far more accurate. AR-15s are a dime-a-dozen. They're lightweight. They don't jam. An AK-47 is a poor choice in a confined space. And it's going to be easier to trace."

The detective is quiet.

"This," she says, turning and pointing at the blood trail. "This is personal. This isn't a hit. It's a message."

"I don't understand," the detective says.

"Are you still there, John?" she asks, raising her phone.

"Yes. What are you thinking, Breezy?"

"This is a statement—a public execution. Nothing about this is haphazard or accidental. They're saying, *we can strike you when you least expect it*. We'll wait until you're vulnerable and use overwhelming force."

"Why?" the detective asks.

"That's the question," Breezy says. "This marks a change in tactics. They're not going after the public face of the government. They're going after human infrastructure. They're hitting the wheels that would grind them into dust."

The detective asks. "Who is?"

"The clowns."

"Clowns?"

"Are you sure about that?" John asks over the speakerphone. "They're idiots. They're a radical, fringe group, but they've never advocated violence."

"Not openly," Breezy says, conceding that point.

"They're not even on our threat radar," John says.

"They should be," she says, turning over a copy of Time Magazine on the coffee table and looking at the cover. There's a picture of Buster standing in front of thirty or forty people in clown makeup, forming a triangle stretching out behind him. They're wearing all types of clothing, representing police officers, nurses, office staff, construction workers, and grocery store clerks. Most of them have traditional clown makeup on, but some have disruptive patterns—it's the kind of thing that would confuse facial recognition. They have their arms folded across their chests. The lede for the article says, "*No one's laughing now*."

Breezy taps the cover. Someone's circled Buster's face with a sharpie. "They were on his radar. That's what made him a target."

"Let's not jump to conclusions," the detective says. "We've got a helluva lot of evidence to process here. Rushing to finger someone isn't going to help. It could send us down a rabbit hole."

Breezy asks, "What security surveillance is there?"

"There's a camera on the main door and at least one external camera on the bar across the road. If they knew what they were doing, though, they'd have scouted those and will have obscured their identity. Our best strategy is to go wide and catch them on cameras they're not aware of—traffic cams, mall cams, dash cams. It will take time to gather these together, but they should give us some leads."

"What are you thinking?" John asks over the phone when Breezy fails to respond to the detective. "Why clowns? Is there something you know that we don't?"

"No, no," she says, following the detective out of the apartment. "It's just...."

"It's hitting us all hard," John says. "Detective Summers is right. We need to step back and let the investigation play out. It's been a long day. Get some rest."

"Okay," she says reluctantly, heading back down the stairs. Breezy's frustrated. She's angry. She's helpless. She's been defeated without a fight. It's not fair. All of this combines to leave her feeling unsettled.

"What's next?" John asks. His voice breaks up slightly over the phone.

"I'm going after these guys," Breezy says. "We need to match fire with fire."

"Let me know what level of operational support you need and I'll get it done."

"Thanks," Breezy says.

"Okay. I'm dropping off the call now," John says. "I need to brief Sec Homeland Security. I'm going to tell him there are no immediate leads but we're pursuing loose ends. I'll tell him we need to increase security around director-level intelligence assets and remain on high alert."

"Understood," Breezy says, hanging up the call. She slips her phone into her back pocket.

Outside, the rain has stopped. Police lights reflect off the wet road. The crowd has thinned, but it hasn't gone.

"If there's anything else you need," the detective says, seeing Breezy's somewhat absentminded.

"No, thanks," she says, waving a friendly gesture to him as he returns to the apartment. Babysitting duty is over. For him, it's back to work. She may get to go home. He'll be here till dawn.

Breezy walks across the empty street, flanked by stationary police cars blocking the road some fifty feet away on either side of her.

She hears a woman's voice drifting on the wind.

"Breezy."

At first, she ignores it. In her mind, it's Susan. She's so damn tired she's having an audible hallucination. She may not want to go to sleep, but she's not going to have a choice in the matter. Her body is demanding rest from her.

"Breanne," the woman yells, and she turns, looking to the police line. A thin strip of yellow tape stretches between a lamppost and a few bushes on the edge of the mall parking lot. A solitary cop stands there with his back to her.

It's then she sees her. A woman runs behind the bushes, waving her hand over them, trying to get Breezy's attention. She's come from somewhere to the right and looks out of breath.

"Breanna, please," the woman says, stopping behind the yellow tape. That name gets Breezy's attention. How does she know Breezy's real name?

Breezy changes angle, marching over to the cordon.

"Is everything okay?" the police officer asks as she approaches.

"Fine," Breezy says, crouching under the tape and stepping between the bushes. On the other side of the thin grassy strip, there's a cinderblock wall and a drop of a couple of feet to the parking lot. The woman down there leans forward, clutching her knees and sucking in air. She's not a runner.

"Can I help you?" Breezy asks, standing beside one of the bushes, more curious than anything. How did this woman identify her? And how did she know her actual birth name?

"It wasn't them," the woman says, but Breezy's distracted. She's too busy taking mental notes for a sketch artist if needed. The woman's five feet six inches with an hourglass figure. Blonde hair—natural blonde, not peroxide. Slight wave on her right, but the rain has matted that down. Her complexion is flawless even though she's not wearing makeup. She could be an actress—no, a model. Her hair is ruffled, but it's been styled. It's not messy so much as tossed and caught by the wind and rain.

"Who are you?"

"Doesn't matter," the woman says, straightening up and looking around to see if anyone's joining Breezy. "They told me to tell you it wasn't them."

"Wasn't who?"

134

"The clowns."

With that, Breezy jumps down into the parking lot, drawing her Glock. She doesn't point it at the woman. She keeps the barrel directed down at the concrete at an angle where an errant shot won't deflect. She's ready to go hot if need be. There's a van parked over by the back door to the bar. It's the only angle of approach that has limited visibility. If someone intends on jumping her, that's where they'll come from, and that's where they'll die.

"Please, don't," the woman says, backing away from Breezy with her hands out in front of her. "I'm not armed."

"I asked you who you are?"

"Olivia."

"Olivia with no surname?"

The stranger asks, "Did you believe the first name?"

"No."

"Then what does it matter? Call me Jane Doe if it helps."

"No ID, huh?" Breezy asks.

"Nope," Olivia says, backing away from the road and keeping her hands in sight.

Breezy advances slowly, wanting to keep the distance between them to about fifteen feet. She's close enough to chat, not so close she's in any danger.

"And the clowns sent you?" Breezy asks.

"They saw what happened," Olivia says.

"That quick, huh?" she says. "And you believe them?"

"I don't have to," Olivia says. "That's your problem, not mine. Believe what you want. Believe what you need to. I'm just delivering a message."

"You've seen them—the clowns. You know Buster."

Olivia nods.

"Where is he?"

"I don't know."

"You're lying."

"Am I?" Olivia replies. "I know where he was. I have no idea where he is. He could be anywhere by now."

"Where was he?"

"Oxon Hill. At the old fairgrounds overlooking the river."

"And you're just going to give him up?" Breezy asks. "Just like that?"

"Too easy, huh?"

"Way too easy," Breezy replies. "So it's a trap?"

"No. I don't think so. Not that I know."

"Now that," Breezy says, pointing at Olivia with her left hand. "That's honest. Why are you doing this?"

"I have no choice," Olivia says. "I—I'm trapped."

"I can help you. I can protect you from the clowns."

"You don't understand. You have no idea what's going on, do you?" Olivia lets out a solitary laugh. She points at the apartment across the road. "You can't protect me any more than you could protect him."

"I can help," Breezy says, ignoring the hurt caused by that last comment.

"You don't get it," Olivia says. "It's not the clowns that want me dead."

"Then who?"

"I wish I knew."

DECISIONS

Breezy's tired. Physically, she's exhausted. Emotionally, she's a wreck, but she can't turn back. Not now. She walks along the backroad toward the rundown circus, avoiding the streetlights. As they're only on one side of the road, their pale, yellow glow casts long shadows. Graffiti adorns the roller doors of a motorcycle garage and a chop shop where stolen cars are stripped to the bone. By day, they bustle with activity. At night, they're as quiet as the grave.

In the distance, at the top of a quarter-mile gentle slope, sits the old county fairgrounds. They've been abandoned for over a decade. The factory next door contaminated the groundwater, making the land unusable. Toxins seeped through the grass, turning the fields into a sewer. Oh, anyone wearing shoes would be fine, but kids stick their hands everywhere—and then they stick them in their mouths. The government closed the fairgrounds, and the circus went bankrupt. Now, most of the fields are overrun with sapling trees.

A homeless vet sits in the doorway of a closed cafe. Fresh urine streaks the pavement nearby, but he doesn't care. He cradles a bottle of wine. Grease stains cover his jacket. A bunched-up sleeping bag rests by his boots. As Breezy walks past, there's movement in the shadows. A dog sits up, watching her with more interest than the veteran. It remains by his side. Like the army vet, grey whiskers droop from its face.

"You lost?" the vet asks. He's not even looking at her. Perhaps he's blind and simply heard the fall of her boots as she approached.

Breezy walks on. She wants to quicken her pace but doesn't. Her training tells her she needs to focus on situational awareness. The constant change around her is unnerving. A burned-out car sits on the side of the road. Soot stains the concrete. Thick oil has run along the gutter for several yards, turning it black. Beyond that, there's a van blocking her view. Someone could be hiding in front of it, and she wouldn't know until she walked past. To the right, there's a dark alleyway. Steel bars protect the next store from break-ins but not from broken windows. Glass lies scattered on the concrete. Weeds grow out of the cracks in the alley. The stench from the dumpster is rancid.

Breezy's so focused on threat detection that she doesn't reply to the vet.

"Stuck-up bitch!" he mumbles, returning to his bottle.

There's movement in the alley. Newspapers tumble in the wind, catching on a chainlink fence. A guard dog growls, pulling its chain taut.

Breezy could have driven up to the gates of the fairground, but she wants the element of surprise. She considered taking an Uber to the hilltop, but she needs to reduce her electronic footprint in case they're monitoring the approaches. Even if she paid cash for a taxi, there would be a trail. Cabs have GPS trackers. Dispatch records can be correlated. She wants to keep this quiet. If things go nasty, she needs to be able to withdraw without anyone even noticing she was ever there. The taxi driver's phone will ping off cell towers, allowing her location to be triangulated. As it is, she's pulled the battery from her phone. If Breezy wants to take the clowns by surprise, she's got to go old school. The ever-changing landscape within the industrial district keeps her on edge.

A couple of teens spot her from across the street. They've been hanging out in front of a biker bar.

"Hey, babe," one of them calls out.

She keeps walking.

"Wait a minute," he yells, crossing the street behind her with some of his buddies. Reluctantly, Breezy quickens her pace. She might not know what she's walking into, but she knows what she's walking away from.

The abandoned circus is dead-ahead, but she turns the corner, wanting to lose her harassers. There's another rundown bar further along on the other side of the crossroad. A neon glow advertises beers, wines and spirits to an empty street. She makes as if that's where she's going, wanting to lose her tail. Out of the corner of her eye, she can see a couple of the teens have already dropped away.

"Come on, babe," one of the more persistent teens says, jogging up alongside her. "We just want to talk, that's all."

He's muscular, confident. His hair is shaved on one side, forming a mop on top that lops over onto the far side of his head. At a guess, his heritage is Eastern European as he has a slight accent, smooth complexion and jet-black hair.

Another teen loops around to her right, cutting her off. He hangs back a little, which makes Breezy uneasy. She'd rather have both of them squarely in front of her.

Breezy pushes forward past the teen with the fancy hair. She steps to one side, wanting to slide past next to a shuttered storefront. An arm cuts off her escape. A hand slams the steel roller door, rattling it.

141

"What's the rush?"

"You don't want to do this," Breezy says. "Believe me. You really don't want to do this."

"Don't want to do what?' the first guy asks.

"We just want to talk," the second guy says, but he remains stubbornly out of sight behind her. Breezy takes a quick glance, but she doesn't want to turn away from the main asshole.

At a guess, these guys are eighteen or nineteen years old. The tattoos on the back of their hands identify them as members of the White Lords street gang.

"Why don't we go somewhere we can talk?" the first guy says. "In private."

Breezy steps in close, moving into his personal space. She gets close enough to whisper in his ear.

"I'm not your type."

With that, she draws the Glock from the small of her back and presses the barrel into the guy's crotch. She positions her gun so it's pushing hard against his groin.

She looks into his eyes, saying, "You understand."

"Oh, wow," he says, stepping back with his hands well away from the gun. "Damn, girl. That's some serious foreplay."

Breezy's so focused on him that she loses track of the second guy. He was on her right, about two feet back. Now, he's directly behind her. Asshole number one is the distraction. Asshole number two is the hitman. It's the eyes of the first jerk that give it away. He's smiling, ignoring the gun. He looks over her shoulder. At a guess, he's waiting for his buddy to reach around her neck, probably with a knife pressed hard against her throat.

Breezy's being outplayed. It's one thing to be a crack shot on the range. Up close, she's too damn small to be a threat. Physically, she's too easy to overpower. Jujutsu is great in the dojo. When everyone's wearing loose, baggy clothing, there are plenty of holds available. The lighting's good. There's a soft mat. Opponents come with predictable timing and from set angles. In the dojo, attackers follow a script of sorts, working through well-rehearsed routines. On the street, that doesn't mean shit. Make a mistake in there, and she gets to review what went wrong and then bow, out of respect for her instructor, and try again. Out here, it'll cost her either her life or a brutal rape.

A hand grabs her shoulder from behind, pinning her in place. The sharp tip of a knife pushes through her shirt and into her lower back. It's positioned off to one side, lining up nicely with her kidney. The blade punctures her skin, drawing a little blood, but it's just a warning. It's a message—*don't do anything stupid, bitch!*

Time is not on her side. Even if she could call in the nearest backup, they'd never get here in time. Breezy's got a fraction of a second to decide what to do. The gun should have been enough to scare these creeps. A warning shot is going to wake the neighbors. A kill shot will draw in the cops, but worse than that, she can't shoot them both—not with that damn knife already pressing on her skin. These assholes are playing high-stakes roulette. If she squeezes the trigger, she's going to end up with a knife plunged into her back and through to her abdomen, probably followed by a few quick strikes to the side of her neck—and all that before she can wheel around for a second shot. She'll bleed out before paramedics arrive. They know that. They're counting on that to get her to back down.

"Hey," she says, raising the barrel of the gun toward the eves of the storefront and ejecting the magazine. "I think we got off to the wrong start here, fellas."

The magazine slides from the pistol grip and falls to the ground. It clatters on the pavement. It's more symbolic than anything as there's still a round chambered and they know that.

The creep in front of her gestures with his hand, wanting her to surrender the gun. He's grinning. He won't be for long. Breezy isn't defusing the situation so much as lining up her ducks. Already, the hand on her shoulder has relaxed. The knife has been withdrawn. It's still there somewhere behind her, hovering near her spine, but she's learned something important about her attackers. The guy behind her is left-handed. Given the option of targeting either kidney, he pressed his knife into her left side. It's his right hand on her shoulder. This tells her she needs to break to the right to avoid his dominant hand. That'll buy her some time.

At this point, Breezy's concerned but not worried. Although the Secret Service normally has the odds in their favor, relying on their massive superiority in surveillance, coordination and firepower, they're trained as underdogs. Training, by definition, implies the repetition of well-understood routines and procedures, but the emphasis in the Secret Service has always been on taking the initiative. Being predictable leaves an opening for terrorists and assassins. Being disciplined and yet flexible shifts the odds. Breezy has never needed that kind of thinking more than she does right now.

Breezy tosses the Glock slightly in the air, turning it around and catching it by the barrel. She holds the gun with the pistol grip facing asshole number one. She's inviting him to grab it. That one round in the chamber worries her, but she's got to deal with the guy with the knife first, and that means distracting the asshole in front of her while she goes for number two.

The asshole with a wide grin and the mop of hair reaches for the gun just as she lets go of the barrel, allowing it to fall. The average human reaction time when taken by surprise is 250 milliseconds. That's an entire quarter of a second in which she's in control and they're not. He grabs at thin air as the Glock drops away from his fingers. His hand closes, but the gun is gone. It plummets to the ground, leaving him grasping at the air. The asshole behind her, though, doesn't know that. All he saw was her handing his buddy the gun.

Breezy turns, twisting to the right, knowing she's moving away from the knife and onto the clumsier, weaker, less-coordinated side of this guy's body. She reaches up, taking hold of his hand still resting on her shoulder. This allows her to control his position. While asshole number one is fumbling for a Glock bouncing across the pavement, she's getting her first good look at the six-foot-four bean pole behind her. It's no wonder they were so confident. This guy is an entire foot taller than she is! He would have been towering over her as she faced the other guy.

He's taken by surprise. She twists his wrist around, forcing him to roll his shoulder and drop in height. Although he's still got the knife, he's off-balance and she's well away from the glistening blade.

Breezy performs a jump kick. Ordinarily, back in her dojo, she'd use this to strike up around the head, but she's not going to make it that high, not on this guy, even with him leaning forward. She leads with her left foot, jumping and raising it up. While she's in mid-air, she swings with her right foot. The arch on top of her boot lines up perfectly with his crotch. She strikes so hard she launches him into the air. It's probably a combination of the strength in her thighs and his reaction, but he's going to be talking in falsetto for at least a month. His balls are now firmly embedded in his throat.

The knife spirals through the air.

Breezy grabs it as the first guy reaches for the Glock lying on the ground. She steps on the gun, covering it with her boot, and lunges at him with the knife.

Ah, decisions, decisions, decisions.

As this guy is bent over, going for the Glock, she's got multiple targets: face, neck, throat. An overhand strike behind the shoulder blades would probably puncture the back of his lung. It's a question of how much damage she wants to inflict and whether she wants it to be lethal. He's right-handed. As he's facing her, she has to stab across to her left if she wants to hit his dominant arm. The jugular is a better target, but Breezy just wants to be left alone. She doesn't want to kill anyone. Not again. She plunges the knife into his right shoulder, driving hard.

Being a switchblade, the knife is short. It's designed for stabbing, allowing for a quick strike and withdrawal. She hits hard. The blade sinks in up to the hilt. Within a fraction of a second, she's already pulled it back and is ready for a second strike. Breezy's never stabbed anyone before. Oh, she's stabbed watermelons during training sessions, but it's not the same. Perhaps they're a better analog for a stomach wound than thick muscle. The dense tissue in this guy's shoulder and the bones beneath his skin, forming the joint, make the motion more like stabbing bark on a tree.

She steps back, sliding the gun away with her boot. It skitters across the pavement and into the gutter.

"You *fucking* bitch," the first asshole says, not appreciating the fact he's still alive. He clutches his shoulder. Blood surges between his fingers.

"Get the fuck out of here," she snarls, wielding the knife before her and threatening a second lunge.

The tall guy is still doubled over. He's already on the move, heading back across the road. He's running with a lope, trying to reduce the sheer amount of pain he's in. He clutches his groin with both hands, moaning. Asshole number one joins his buddy, still gripping his right shoulder.

"You'll pay for this, you goddamn witch."

Breezy waves. "Say hi to your Mom for me."

His arm hangs limp. She didn't hit an artery, but she messed up something deep inside. That dude needs surgery, which will make for an awkward conversation. Any half-decent doctor is going to report the injury to the police.

Breezy drops the knife into a drain. She listens as it plops into the dark water. With the magazine back in her Glock, she doubles back and continues down a side alley toward the hill in the distance. The abandoned fairgrounds are old and dimly lit. Moonlight catches the side of a Ferris wheel. Several carts hang down beside the ride, having come loose from their supports over time.

"Why the fuck did they stick a circus here?" she asks the quiet night, but she knows the answer: cheap land.

She jogs. Time is of the essence. Those two gang members are going to go crawling back to their den. Once the rest of the White Lords find out what happened, they'll hit the streets looking for her.

Breezy quickens her pace.

HOUSE OF HORRORS

Breezy reaches the top of the rise. Behind her, the sound of motorcycles cuts through the night. She looks down the street. Six bikes roar up the road with headlights blazing.

The fairgrounds are surrounded by a chainlink fence topped with barbed wire. Beyond the fence, there are several open fields that were once used for parking, with the circus being located at the rear of the sprawling property. With the White Lords approaching, Breezy has to find cover. Rather than sneaking into the fairgrounds, she goes around them, working her way along the edge of the abandoned factory next door.

Breezy follows a brick wall running along the boundary, creeping through the darkness above an open sewer. Oil swirls on the surface of the water. Ivy clings to the bricks. She keeps her back to the wall, feeling her way in the dark, being careful not to step on twigs or branches. The sound of dry, cracking wood will give away her position.

Once they're at the top of the rise, the motorcycles fan out, turning in both directions. Their throaty roars shake the quiet of the night. Headlights break through the trees, casting long shadows. At one point, a brilliant white light passes over her. Breezy freezes, standing perfectly still. As she's wearing dark clothing, she should blend in with the shadows. The light moves on as the rider parks his bike, leaving the engine to idle. Through the trees, she can see the White Lords gathering in the gravel parking lot outside the fairgrounds.

"Where did she go?"

"She went in there."

"I'm not going in there."

"What are you afraid of?" a gruff man with a full beard says.

"Nothing," someone replies.

"I don't see you going in there," another man says. He's wearing a leather vest with chrome studs on the shoulder boards. From the way the others defer to him, he must be the leader.

"Haha," they all laugh in response to him.

"If she's gone in there, she's as good as dead," the leader says, revving the engine on his bike. He's got his legs out on either side of the gas tank. His boots rest in the dust.

"Shame," another man says.

"Let's go."

With a roar like thunder breaking overhead, the gang departs. Several riders perform donuts in the gravel parking lot, kicking up dirt and stones before following the others. Once they're out of sight and the roar of their engines is a distant hum, Breezy emerges from beside the factory.

The chainlink fence surrounding the fairgrounds is new. The steel hasn't weathered yet. It's clearly not part of the original design. The concrete footings are pristine. They've been set in front of a low wooden farm fence running along the front of the property.

Breezy walks along the road, staying in the shadow of trees as she surveys the perimeter. Even though it's topped with barbed wire, she could climb the fence in seconds. All she needs to do is wrap her jacket around her forearms to prevent the barbs from sinking in. Then it's a matter of flipping over the edge and landing in the grass. For Breezy, though, this is a chance to learn more about the site.

Tall weeds grow beyond the fence, covering a stretch of ground several acres in size. Once, this would have been the main parking lot for cars and vans, with the gravel area outside being used for heavy vehicles, like delivery trucks and animal floats. The fairgrounds themselves are set back well beyond the road, sloping down toward the river. As this was a permanent fixture, neon signs rise over the distant buildings. They're set in rows. When all the lights were on, it would have looked spectacular.

"Huh," she mumbles, realizing how easy it was for the clowns to arise in such an environment. For them, the glitz and glamor was only ever fake. Stepping from here into the world at large, it was easy for them to project their own cynical views onto things like social media, politics and religion. For them, *The Spectacle* was once good business.

Breezy slips along the far edge of the fairgrounds. There's a horse track on the other side of the fence with a grandstand backing onto the carnival row. Although it looks as though it could be used for races, it's not big enough to be a racetrack as such. As everything within the circus, it's for show. This is probably where various live animal acts were performed, along with stunt car tricks and parades.

Further along, there's a gap in the chainlink fence. Someone has cut the wire and pulled the fence open. As the gap is only a few feet high, it must have been kids. Breezy pulls on the links. She clips a loose bit of wire further back on the fence, holding it up. Against her better judgment, she crawls through on her hands and knees, emerging behind the stables.

In the distance, there's laughter. It floats on the wind, being indistinct, not giving her any idea of its direction. Someone's watching her, taunting her. For the first time, Breezy feels afraid. It's the uncertainty, the lack of control. When all hell broke loose in that drug store, she knew what she was doing. When those teenage thugs hassled her, she felt on edge but not afraid. At no point did she doubt herself. She knew she might come out of it bloodied and bruised, but she was confident she would come out the other side. Breezy's not a fighter as such, not in the sense of having a black belt in a martial art. Oh, she knows a few different fighting styles, but in the heat of the moment, there's no one form she draws upon. Breezy's a brawler. Punch her in the face, split her lip open, jab at her eye, and she won't care. She'll keep swinging. It won't enrage her so much as cause her to focus. She'll lower her head, keep dancing from side to side, and look for an opening to strike back. She'll lock eyes with her opponent and wait for them to blink. A little bit of pain allows her to zero in on what needs to be done. This, though, is different. She's rattled. It's the unknown. What the hell lies out there in the darkness?

Breezy pushes her shoulder up against the stable wall, reducing her profile from the side. She reaches around, touching the Glock in the small of her back. She knows it's there. She can feel it against her skin. She knows it hasn't slipped out while she ducked through the fence, and yet she needs to be sure. There's something in the act of reaching that reinforces the need for caution. She's rehearsing a draw. Usually, she keeps her t-shirt draped loosely over her gun to hide it from view. Not here. Not in a darkened, abandoned fairground. Breezy tucks the shirt behind the Glock, making sure she can grab the pistol grip with ease.

She creeps along in the shadows, watching the way the moonlight falls. Looking around, she plans a path through the darkness. If she keeps to the service alley, she can reach the main concourse. From there, a set of bleachers form a grandstand overlooking the racetrack. They'll provide her with cover as she moves toward the circus tent. Several support poles have fallen within the big top, but the main arena is still standing.

A pair of eyes peer out of the darkness just a few feet ahead. Her heart races. A cat scurries away, darting across the pavement. It runs through the weeds growing up out of the cracks.

Laughter floats on the breeze.

"This ain't no joke," she mumbles, coming up behind a dumpster and peering out across the fairgrounds. To get to the main circus tent, Breezy has to head down the sideshow alley. That means exposing herself to the moonlight. She takes a single step forward, preparing to run for cover on the other side of the alley, but in that exact instant, the lights come on. The fairgrounds come to life with a cacophony of colored lights and noise, startling her.

A merry-go-round starts turning. Plastic horses move up and down their poles as the base turns slowly. Music plays. Notes are struck on an old-time piano, filling the air with joy. Lights reflect off the mirrors at the heart of the ride. The bulbs have yellowed with age. Roughly half of them no longer work, but those that do shine like the sun, destroying her night vision.

Within the sideshow, dozens of mechanical clown heads turn in unison to face her. They have their mouths open, awaiting a ping pong ball to be dropped into a steel maze. They swing back and forth within the sideshow game, laughing as they turn.

"Test your strength. Don't be afraid. Take a swing," a recorded voice says from an aging speaker beside a steel tower. The bell at the top beckons. The voice has a metallic sound. The words sound as though they're spoken by a robot. A large wooden mallet leans against the tower, enticing invisible patrons to take a swing.

Breezy steps out into the middle of the walkway. All pretense is gone. She'd hoped for the element of surprise, but the clowns know she's here. The White Lords made too much damn noise. She pulls the Glock from the small of her back and walks along with it hanging by her side. Her fingers flex around the pistol grip. If they want to send a message by turning on the power, she's happy to reply in her own way.

Sawdust covers the ground. It's dank and smells of rotting wood.

The silhouette of distant ducks rolls past at the back of one of the stalls. They've been painted white. The metal has been dented by hundreds of shots over the years, scraping away the paint. Several BB guns lie in a row, tempting her to take a shot.

"Show us your skill," a voice says. "Win a stuffed bear and a whole lot of love. Five shots for five dollars. What have you got to lose?"

Breezy puts her Glock on the counter, leaving it facing toward the back of the stall. She picks up a rifle with her left hand, leaving her right hand free to grab the Glock. A steel chain keeps the air rifle from being turned away from the counter while a plastic tube feeds up into the action, acting as a magazine. Breezy, though, isn't interested in winning a prize. She wants to take a glance back behind her. By turning side-on, she gets to see if anyone's following her by checking her peripheral vision. Rather than leaning down and resting her elbows on the counter, she stands, holding the children's rifle with one hand. She fires five shots in rapid succession, only she isn't looking at the targets drifting by on the steel chain at the back of the stall. She's looking around at the lights, the torn speaker, the prizes, and the cotton candy cart next door. It's the narrow access walkway behind the stall that interests her most. She's thinking about how she'd handle this environment. If this was her home ground, what advantages would she exploit? She'd distract her opponent out here while sneaking by back there.

Turning on the power within the sideshow alley was smart. It robs her of sight and sound. The chaos of flashing lights, moving rides and good old ragtime music is disruptive. Her primary senses are confused. It makes threat detection nigh on impossible. They're making a point. If they wanted to kill her, she'd be dead already.

Breezy's sure the walkway behind the stalls is '*in play,*' to use surveillance terminology. That's the route she would use if she were stalking someone in the fairgrounds. By laying her Glock on the wooden counter, she's tempting the clowns to show themselves, making it seem as though this is an opportune time to strike. In reality, she's milliseconds away from a crack shot at anyone creeping through the shadows back there.

Breezy's five shots with the air rifle hit five ducks in rapid succession, causing them to fall backward with a distinctly metallic *plink!*

"Congratulations. You've won!" the voice says from the speaker. Okay, so this isn't mindless tracks playing on a loop. Someone somewhere is watching her as she advances down the sideshow alley. "Pick your prize from our astonishing range of identical teddy bears!"

Breezy grabs a pink stuffed bear, holding it in her left hand as she picks up the Glock with her right hand.

She walks on, aware the clowns are channeling her toward the circus tent at the end of the alley. She's walking into a trap, but the Glock hanging from her fingers is comforting. It's a known among the unknowns that surround her. A coward's shot might take her, being fired from the shadows, but that's not their style. From what she understands, they prefer terror to a clean kill. They could have shot the director in the head as soon as he got out of his car. Busting into his home and firing AK-47s was intentionally chaotic. They went loud for a reason.

Oh, Olivia and John might not think the clowns were involved. Breezy's not convinced—not after seeing the way Buster dismantled those two detectives in the interrogation room. It was like watching a cat torment a mouse. For now, though, it seems they're as keen to meet her as she is to face them.

If it comes to a one-on-one fight, Breezy's happy to back herself and her Glock. Breezy's not afraid of dying. Everyone dies. In the grand scheme of 13.8 billion years—of which Earth waited some 4.6 billion years for humanity to arise—the difference between living for forty years or eighty is trivial. Either way, it's a spit in the ocean. Breezy's in no rush to die, but she's not naive enough to ignore death and pretend she'll live forever. Besides, she'd rather go out fighting than shitting the bed.

There's movement ahead. A rollercoaster starts up. Empty carts roll along the tracks. They click and clatter as they're drawn up a steep slope. One by one, they roll away, circling around tight corners and curling along steep bends. There are even fake screams of delight timed with each corner to encourage ride-goers to let loose. The pandemonium is infuriating. The cracks and strains of noise coming from the metal frame jam her radar. She can't help but focus on the rollercoaster, but that was always their intent. It takes a deliberate effort for her to look away.

Lights run in patterns around the edge of a rundown old Ferris wheel. Even though the ride is broken, the music still plays.

Behind her, various sections of the sideshow fall idle. They power down, slipping back into darkness now that she's moved on, boxing her in a region of chaotic sights and sounds while allowing the clowns freedom of movement around her. Clever.

"This is too goddamn elaborate," she mumbles to herself. Her knuckles go white as she grips the Glock, but she keeps it facing the ground. The clowns know who she is. They know why she's here. They're putting on a show for a reason. They want her to feel uncomfortable. And they know she's not a cop, not in the traditional sense of the word.

Fingers appear around the edge of a nearby doorway. Breezy makes as though she hasn't noticed, keeping her head facing forward. She glances to her right, turning away from the makeshift building at a hotdog stand on the other side of the alley. Out of the corner of her eye, she keeps her focus on the door. The sign reads:

Crazy House of Horrors

"Well, that figures," she whispers. Once she's level with the building, she darts sideways up a set of temporary aluminum stairs. The fingers are gone, but someone's in there.

Breezy nudges the door open with the barrel of her Glock. She adopts a two-hand hold, with her left hand under her right. By locking her elbows, she's effectively giving her pistol grip the accuracy of a rifle. As she's still holding the pink bear, it hangs beneath the gun, flopping around as she turns. That cute, cuddly toy will be a pleasant surprise for anyone at the other end of her barrel. It may even give her a few milliseconds advantage as it will confuse the shit out of them.

Breezy creeps forward. The floor beneath her shifts from side to side. It's part of the attraction, trying to unsettle patrons. For Breezy, it's annoying.

"Where are you?" she whispers, keeping her gun low, ready to bring it to bear.

"What do you want?" an electronic voice asks as she steps into a room with a long, spinning cylinder wrapping around the ceiling and floor. A raised walkway allows her to continue on above the blue cylinder as it turns, but the motion is disturbing. Although she tries to walk straight, the movement of the cylinder creates an optical illusion. She feels as though she's falling to one side. By compensating, she ends up bumping into the rails on the walkway. Breezy pushes on regardless, keeping her eyes on the end of the elongated room.

A laughing voice booms around her. "What are you looking for?"

"I'm looking for you, asshole," she yells. Her motive is to get answers. That and to avoid ending up faceless in the Potomac. Even if Olivia is right and the clowns aren't involved in the director's death, there's something sinister about them. They're not just some pop-culture phenomenon. No one lights up an amusement park for a Secret Service agent just for kicks. Why were they so quick to distance themselves from the director's death? Were they listening in on her conversation with the detective? Did anyone check the apartment for bugs? Given the blood and carnage strewn along the hall, a microphone hidden behind a picture would go unnoticed for days.

What about the agent sent to infiltrate them? Someone ripped out his teeth. That didn't happen by accident.

As it is, any prospect of her slipping into the cult as a mole died along with the director.

Breezy creeps forward, minimizing the soft squelch of her shoes on the linoleum. The portable building rocks slightly on its raised legs. It's impossible to tell if that's because of someone moving around or the crazy contraptions within the ride. Doors slide open and shut. The floor rocks from side to side on actuators instead of shuffling back and forth as it did near the entrance. Like everything in here, it's designed to disorient her.

The next room is a maze of mirrors. Everywhere she looks, she sees herself. Instead of being arranged in sets of four, giving her predictable angles of 90 degrees to work with, each section is divided by sets of six, seven or eight floor-to-ceiling mirrors roughly two-feet wide. The angles make it impossible to know if she's continuing straight ahead or doubling back on herself. She reaches out with her hand, pushing against the glass, unsure of herself as she tries to find a path through the maze.

A clown appears in front of her. Dozens of reflections bounce around her. Which one is real?

"Don't move," Breezy says, training her gun on the clown, but she could be pointing at a mirror.

A white face stares back at her with dark eyes. A blob of deep red paint marks the nose, but it's been applied without any care, being more of a smudge than deliberate makeup. The woman standing before Breezy smiles, revealing jagged teeth like those of an animal. Her hair is unkempt and straggly. It's oily. It hasn't been washed in days, if not weeks. Her clothing is baggy. Once, the colors would have appeared playful. Now her clothing is torn and stained.

"What do you neeeeeeed?" the woman asks, on the verge of growling with her words.

"Stay where you are," Breezy says, reaching out with her left arm next to her gun, trying to feel for the clown. "Don't move!"

"Or what?"

Breezy rushes forward.

The clown steps to one side, disappearing from view. On reaching where it stood, Breezy realizes she only ever saw a reflection of a reflection. She turns, wanting to figure out where the image came from. Mirrors surround her. She's walked into a dead end. She pounds on one of the mirrors. It flexes but doesn't break.

Breezy turns. Behind her, another mirror has slid in place, trapping her in an area no more than four-foot square. She twists around. Seven mirrors. Or is it eight? She looks down at her boots, wanting to gauge the size and shape of this mirrored trap.

"Everyone wants something," the voice says, echoing around her. "What do you want with us?"

"I want to know who you are," she says. "I want to know what you want." But she's lying. She came here for revenge. She came here to find a killer.

"You don't want that," the woman's voice says, calling her bluff.

The voice seems to come from behind her. Breezy turns, wanting to face the clown, but all she sees is herself in the mirrors. The location of the woman's voice changes yet again, always coming from the other side of the mirrored cell. "Others may want that. What do you want?"

Breezy wasn't expecting this. She turns, searching for a gap in the mirrors. She presses on the edges, trying to force them open.

"I want to get out of here," she says. "I want to talk to you."

"Wants are simple," the woman says. "Wants focus on what we need."

"I don't need anything."

"You need air."

It's at that moment, Breezy realizes she's growing lightheaded. She stumbles, trips and collides with one of the mirrors. A quick look up and she sees a vent on the ceiling. A fine mist cascades over her, dissipating as it reaches her shoulders.

Dots appear before her eyes. Breezy is losing consciousness. Her fingers go numb. Her thinking is dull. She tries to lift her arms, wanting to bang on the glass, but her muscles feel like lead weights.

"No," she yells. Her voice sounds strangely different. The atmospheric density has changed, altering the pitch of her speech. "Can't... Breathe...."

The world around her narrows. Her inner ear spins, causing her to lose her balance. She collapses, sliding to the floor. Within a matter of seconds, her life is ebbing away. Her muscles are unresponsive, but she manages to push the barrel of the Glock against the glass and squeeze the trigger.

In the confined space within the mirrored trap, the shot breaks like a thunderclap. The pressure of the shot swells around her, causing her ears to pop. The bullet tears through the glass, punching a hole in the mirror. Cracks splinter outward, but the glass holds.

Breezy shoves her mouth over the hole. The glass is sharp but doesn't cut her lips. She sucks, breathing in through her mouth and out through her nose, drawing in as much precious oxygen as she can get. There's not enough air coming through the tiny hole, but she's alive. With the butt of her gun, Breezy hacks at the shattered glass around the hole. She dares not remove her lips from the broken mirror. She needs that oxygen. With a few strikes beside her face, the glass gives and the hole widens.

The mirrors are made from reinforced glass. They're designed to fracture rather than break, remaining in one piece as jagged lines run in splinters, expanding as they move away from the hole. Breezy pokes her gun barrel through a weak spot and pries the glass away, allowing whatever gas displaced the breathable air to dissipate. The mirror has some kind of plastic laminate as a backing. It's stubborn, refusing her efforts. It takes all her strength to rip the sheets of broken mirror fragments away.

"Oh, that's seven years of bad luck," the voice says, laughing. Initially, it was a woman tormenting her. Now, it's a man.

161

They've switched.

Why?

They're setting her up again.

She's going from one trap into another. As there's a slightly tinny ring to each word, it seems the voice has been electronically altered to obscure the identity of the speaker.

"You bastard!"

The clown is undeterred. "Be honest with me, and I'll be honest with you."

Breezy regains strength in her arms. She cups the palms of her hands under the cuffs of her jacket and tears the glass pane apart, being careful not to cut her hands.

"You tried to kill me," she says, pushing herself through the broken glass and rolling into another section of the mirrored maze. She shoves her Glock ahead of her, inching it along the ground as she pulls her legs through the gap behind her. The gun slides across the floor as she crawls on her hands and knees. The lights flicker, threatening to plunge the room into darkness.

"Incapacitate," the hidden clown says. "I sought to disarm and defuse a human time bomb—and without recourse to violence. Clowns are jokers, not fighters."

"That," Breezy says, crawling forward on her hands and knees. "That felt pretty damn violent to me."

She's dizzy. She gets back to her feet, but she has to lean against a mirror to stand. Breezy reaches over, picking her Glock up from the concrete. She grabs the pink teddy bear for no other reason than it's hers, goddamn it! Her hands are shaking, but she maintains her trigger discipline, keeping her index finger running along the outside of the trigger guard.

Shadows move around her. The lights overhead flicker, threatening to plunge the maze into darkness. In the kaleidoscope of reflections around her, she sees someone crouching. They dart away from her. Breezy finds her reserves of strength. She gives chase. Her shoulder collides with various mirrors. She bounces through the maze like a pinball.

"Face me, you coward!"

The clown replies, "Find me, you fool!"

She runs into a dead-end and has to backtrack.

The view of shattered glass reflecting in the mirrors around her gives her a point of reference, allowing her to weave through the maze. The bullet she fired embedded itself in the floor. If it had soared through the mirrors around her, it would have given her a straight line to work with. Instead, she has to weave in and out of dead ends toward the end of the maze.

Breezy reaches a set of stairs leading up to the next level within the crazy house. There's an emergency exit at the foot of the stairs. The door is ajar. Breezy edges it open with her boot, leading with her gun and getting a good look at what lies beyond the steel door before venturing out.

She emerges in a maintenance area. Ropes lie coiled on the concrete. Dirt clogs the fibers, marking their age. An oil can lies in the grass. Scaffolding holds torn sacking, forming a barrier separating this area from the sideshow concourse. There are fresh footprints in the mud. They lead toward the circus tent.

"I've got you," Breezy says, but she doesn't rush forward. She doesn't want to run into another trap.

Grass has grown up beneath the chassis of an abandoned flatbed truck. The tires are flat. Rust is eating through the bottom of the doors.

Now that she's away from the main strip, the lighting is poor. Out in the alley, lights flash as rollercoasters run empty, click-clacking their way around the track. Synthesized music plays through metal speakers. It's a distraction, something she needs to shut out as she moves into the animal holding area. This is the backstage setting for the circus proper.

Breezy creeps past a makeup station. Lights wind around half a dozen mirrors set in front of solitary chairs, but these lights are off. Dressing gowns hang from coatracks. They're old and worn.

Breezy moves with caution, unsure of herself. Her heart is pounding in her chest. Rather than walking down the middle of the tent, she keeps to one side, over by a series of darkened, empty animal cages. They've been rolled into place beneath the edge of the support tent, being part of a train of cages mounted on trailers. To move between sites, the carnies probably lower the canvas sides and haul these behind a semi-truck.

There's movement in the shadows beside her. Breezy's confused. The circus has been abandoned for over a decade. There aren't any animals in here—there can't be. Something scurries at the back of the cage, kicking up rotten straw. There's a musty smell. It's pungent. Putrid. It reeks of decaying flesh.

As much as she doesn't want to, Breezy takes her eyes off the muddy path ahead.

Is that a rat in there?

It's too damn big to be a rodent.

Teeth appear, catching what little light there is in the darkened cage. Long incisors snarl. A primate rushes her, screeching and screaming.

Breezy jumps back. Thin arms reach for her. Claws push through the bars of the cage, trying to grab her. Motley patches of fur cling to thin bones. Tendons flex.

Breezy points her Glock at the creature. The teddy bear is snatched from her fingers and torn to shreds. Bits of pink fluff and stuffing fall to the mud.

A baboon presses its face against the bars, baring its teeth, only it's not alive. It can't be. On one arm, the flesh is almost entirely missing, exposing the upper bones in the elbow and forearm. Strips of dead muscle hang down from the animal's shoulder. Claws clutch at the air, wanting to grab her. Dark eyes peer at her. The baboon's cheeks rise as it snarls, but the fur on its head is emaciated and patchy. The animal's ribcage is exposed. There's no heart. No lungs. Nothing.

"What the fresh hell?"

The rest of the cages around her roar into life.

Monkeys jump onto the bars, shaking them, desperate to escape. They shriek and call to each other in a pitch that causes her to cringe. Several of them climb upside down in their cages, shouting at each other. But they're dead. Like the baboon, the thin bones in their arms are visible. One of them has lost all the hair on its head, leaving only a skull. Far from being the white, pristine bone of a museum exhibit, its skull is covered in scraps of skin and flesh. With no lips, the dead animal's teeth are imposing. It opens its jaw wide, but no sound comes out.

Breezy points with her Glock, turning from cage to cage, trying to make sense of what she's seeing. Her legs shake but she pushes on.

A tiger stalks her, pacing within its cage, watching her as she creeps past. Its trailer rocks with its shifting weight. Its eyes are hollow sockets. The big cat snarls, baring its canine teeth. Fur hangs from its ribcage. Its hips and hind legs are nothing but bone. Its massive paws scrape at the rotten straw in its cage. Maggots drop from its rotting carcass.

"H—How is this possible?"

Breezy quickens her pace. The tiger circles around to the back of the cage and rushes her, charging at her. It leaps, rising on its hind legs and slamming its front paws into the door of the cage, rattling the steel. The bolt holding the door closed shakes, working loose. There's no lock.

Breezy keeps her gun aimed at the tiger, not that it would do any good. Even against a live tiger, a 9mm round is going to do little more than piss it off. A dead zombified tiger is her worst nightmare brought to life.

The tiger roars, warning her of its hunger. The hairs on her arms stand on end. She backs up, leaving the screeching dead animals behind her and pushes through a heavy curtain. Breezy's shaking like a leaf in a storm. She has no idea what's beyond the curtain. Right now, it doesn't matter. Nothing could be more terrifying than what she's witnessed.

Her boots kick at the edge of a plywood ramp. She turns, keeping her gun out in front of her trembling arms as she walks into the darkened big top tent. Her trigger discipline is gone. Her finger is on the goddamn curved metal, already flexing against the spring. Sweat drips from her forehead, running into her eyes, but she won't wipe it away. She can't.

Breezy walks into the circus. The far side of the tent has collapsed. Poles and canvas lie on the bleachers, burying them.

A brilliant white light illuminates a single figure standing in the middle of the darkened central ring.

A clown.

WELCOME TO THE CIRCUS

"Don't move," Breezy says, walking slowly into the big top. She places one boot in front of the other, stepping forward carefully. It's as though she's walking through a minefield.

The clown laughs. He's mic'd up. His voice booms from a series of metal speakers set on poles around the tent. They're the old-fashioned kind used for public announcements.

"Me?" the clown says, pretending to raise his hands. "You make it sound like I'm the one that's walked into a trap."

"What is all this?" she asks, ignoring him. Hiding behind a gun no longer has her feeling brave.

Damp sawdust sticks to the soles of her boots. Breezy does her best to take in the tent. It's too easy to focus on him alone, but that's the intent behind the placement of the spotlight—to stop her from being aware of her surroundings. She's got to fight the temptation to become fixated on him. She needs to remain circumspect.

"What was that? Back there? The animals? They're dead, right?"

"Aren't we all," the clown asks, giggling, slapping his thighs and dancing on the spot.

Breezy wants to run from the tent. Nothing about this is right. Hell, nothing she's seen so far comes close to being sane. Her nerves are electrified with fear. Reason is gone. Forget about fight or flight. The only sensible course of action is to back out of here slowly and knock back a few shots of whiskey with her new buddies, the White Lords, but she can't turn away. She *needs* answers.

Wooden bleachers surround two of the three rings at the heart of the circus tent. The third ring is partially covered by the fallen canvas. Thin steel scaffolding rises above the entertainment area, providing rigging for the lights. A solitary spotlight directly above the clown is the only source of illumination in the darkness. Around her, the shadows move.

"What is this place?" she asks.

"A circus!"

"Yeah, that's not helpful," she replies, still reeling from the horrors she walked past in the animal enclosures.

Breezy stays out wide, wanting to make her way to one of the aisles between the bleachers. She's already thinking about an exit strategy. If those fucking zombie animals get in here, she's going to have to move fast. She reviews the mental map she's created of the fairgrounds. Immediately beyond the nearest exit is the sideshow alley. From there, it's fifty yards to the racetrack. If she takes a hard left at the ticket booth, it's another forty to fifty yards to the fence beyond the stables. At a full sprint, that's eighteen seconds to the boundary. Given the sheer amount of adrenaline coursing through her veins, she figures she can vault the fence even though it's seven-feet high and topped with barbed wire. At the moment, escaping with only a few deep, bloody scratches on her arms would be a win. Rather than clambering over the barbed wire, she imagines a flip where she somersaults over into the grass. She knows she won't stick the landing, and she's liable to bust an ankle, but at least she'll be on the other side of the fence. From there, she can make it to the road.

"Who are you?" she asks.

The clown laughs, throwing his head back. He refuses to look at her as she works her way around in front of him, choosing to address the imaginary audience instead. The spotlight is so bright it casts long shadows down his face, hiding his features. Specks of dust drift through the beam of light, giving it a ghostly, surreal appearance. It's as though some monster is being conjured from the deep.

"Me? I'm but a lowly clown. This place, though," he says, before bellowing, "*Welcome! To the greatest show on Earth!*"

He's wearing a tiny hat perched on a fake rainbow-colored afro wig. This clown's got the classic white face with a bright red nose. This isn't the woman Breezy saw earlier. Where the hell is she? It seems her job was to lead Breezy here, but why? For all Breezy knows, she could be flanking her or blocking the closest exit or watching her from a distance, staring down the sights of a rifle.

Breezy steps around the guy wires holding the steel scaffolding in place. Although she's keeping her gun on the clown, she's aware she may need to swivel in several other directions if additional threats arise. Her training kicks in. She prepares herself to face any rush of noise, dropping into a kneeling stance to steady the aim of her trembling hands. There will be no warning offered. If anything rushes her out here, it's going to be greeted with at least one 9mm jacketed hollow-point round coming in at a thousand feet per second. Let's see you dodge that, you goddamn crazy dead baboons, or whatever the hell you are. Undead or not, bullets will shatter bones.

"Talk to me," Breezy says.

"Why did you come here?" the clown asks, giggling like a child. "What do you want?"

"Answers," she says. "Did you kill the director?"

"We've already told you," the clown says, shuffling his oversized red shoes in the sawdust. He kicks up dirt as he dances on the spot. "You didn't believe us then. Why would you believe us now?"

Breezy walks around the ring. "This place is a madhouse. Those animals. Those creatures back there."

"You like my petsssssss?" the clown asks, accentuating the s and drawing it out like a snake hissing in the grass.

Breezy comes to a halt in front of him. She aims her gun at him, keeping his center of mass down the sights of her Glock the whole time. The tension's so great, she's not sure if she's blinked in over a minute. She needn't have bothered with such intense focus. Once she's square on, she gets a good look at him. The left side of his face is largely missing. Skin hangs from the bone on his jaw. His teeth are visible, as is his cheekbone. Seeing the molars at the back of his mouth is disturbing. He's only got one eye. The other is little more than a dark pit in his head.

The dead clown's wearing a baggy shirt and oversized pants. They're held up with suspenders clipped onto a hula-hoop sewn into his polka dot trousers. His clown shoes, with their bulbous ends, look playful enough were it not for the bones extending into them instead of legs. He's wearing white gloves, but the tips on one hand are stained with what looks like blood. Whatever it is, it's still wet. Dark red drips fall to the sawdust. There's a gap between his sleeves and his gloves, revealing the bones in his wrist.

"You knew I'd come, didn't you?" she says. "You knew I couldn't resist."

"You are predictable," the clown says.

"This is madness," she replies, lowering her gun. It's pointless keeping up a facade. If the clowns wanted her dead, she wouldn't have made it more than a few feet into the fairgrounds—that much is obvious. If all they wanted was to put on a show and freak her out, they've succeeded. The whole undead routine is working a little too goddamn well for her, leaving her feeling like death itself. It's all she can do to quell her anxiety and avoid vomiting on the sawdust.

She asks, "Who the hell are you?"

"Wrong question," the clown replies at a distance of twenty feet. He dances on the spot again, bouncing around with glee and playing the fool.

"What are you?"

"That," he says, giggling and coming to a halt and raising a single finger into the light. "That's the right question."

A white bone pokes through a tear in his glove. He looks at the missing fingertip and bursts into laughter.

Breezy drops onto her haunches. Nothing she's ever faced has prepared her for this. Emotionally, she's spent. It's not that she's out of her depth. It's more like there's nothing beneath her. She feels as though she's been dropped into the middle of the Atlantic and told to swim to shore. Anything and everything is futile.

"Popcorn?" a friendly voice says from beside her and she just about dies from fright.

An attendant holds out a tray containing caramel popcorn, what she assumes is either Coke or Pepsi in disposable cups and a few old-fashioned ice cream cones.

Breezy scrambles to her feet, backing away from the attendant. Even though he's dead, she points her gun at the center of his chest. He's wearing a neat, navy blue uniform with gold trim and a hat. His eyes are sunken, but at least he has both of them. His lips are blue while his cheeks are gaunt, pulling tight against his cheekbones. His hands, though, are nothing more than spindly bones, gripping the tray as it hangs around his neck. He leans forward, wanting her to take something.

"It's okay," he says.

"No," Breezy says. "No, it's not."

"The popcorn is fresh."

"I'm fine," she says, raising a distinctly intact hand and gesturing for him to hold still where he is as her right index finger tightens on the trigger of her gun. The attendant lowers his head and turns away. He looks dejected—disappointed. He shuffles rather than walks, disappearing into the shadows.

Breezy turns back to the clown. He's juggling five red balls. He looks up as they soar through the air. His feet shuffle through the sawdust. He repositions himself, frantically working with his gloved hands to keep the balls in motion.

"I'm hallucinating. I must be. You've drawn me into a trap."

"You came here of your own free will," the clown says, juggling. "You're free to go."

"What if I don't believe you?"

"It's quaint that you think beliefs actually matter."

"None of this is real," she mumbles.

"Oh, it's real," he says, sending each ball up high into the air at the end of his act. The balls disappear beyond the spotlights, never to fall back down. "Ask yourself: what is reality?"

"None of this," Breezy says, taking a seat in the front row. She leans forward with her arms on her knees. The Glock hangs from her fingertips.

"On the contrary," the clown says. "What you think of as reality is an illusion. Your world, your life, your job—none of it is real. Not in any meaningful sense. Not on a cosmic scale. It's fleeting. It barely registers in the history of life on Earth. America is an artificial construct, a mirage, a magic trick, a rabbit conjured from a hat. What you think of as established is fleeting. It is but the flash of lightning on the horizon. There's the rumble of noise, but in a heartbeat, it's gone."

"You're insane," she says. "What am I saying? I'm insane. I'm talking to a dead clown!"

"Maybe, but I'm alive with ideas," he says, squeezing a plastic bulb in the palm of his hand. A thin stream of water squirts from a fake flower on the lapel of his jacket. It curls forward, catching the light briefly as it falls to the sawdust. "You think this is a circus? The real clowns are out there on Capitol Hill and over in the White House. Those that wear their neatly pressed suits and sit in their fancy swiveling chairs behind solid oak desks—they think they're in command of this world. They're not. They make fools of us all."

Breezy asks, "How is any of this real?"

The clown makes wild gestures with his arms as he speaks. He sounds like a game show host charged with enthusiasm, appealing to the crowd, wanting to get them pumped.

"What do you want? Manicured lawns! White picket fences! An old colonial home in the suburbs! A job in a skyscraper, any skyscraper will do, it doesn't matter so long as it has a view of the next concrete monstrosity! A nice, shiny new car! A steady job with health insurance! Don't you see? It's all a distraction. It keeps you busy. It keeps you from thinking, from seeing reality. Oh, everyone wants that lifestyle, only there's no style at all. It's a lie. You're living in *The Spectacle!*"

"And this *Spectacle?*" Breezy asks, appealing to the clown's own logic. "You're the ones that'll bring it to an end?"

The clown takes off his tiny hat, holding it in one hand as he bows before her. He extends his right leg behind himself. He takes his time, exaggerating his motion before returning upright and placing the hat back on his head.

"You jest, for sure," he says. "Perhaps, you should be a clown?"

"Me?" she says, faking a sense of flattery. "But I'm not real, remember?"

"Reality is that which persists regardless of us and all we do," he says. "Reality isn't manufactured. Reality isn't forced or fabricated. Post a picture on Instagram, and what are you doing? You're creating a narrative that didn't exist. For better or worse, you're curating your life for others. You're telling them what they should and shouldn't see. And then you feed off their likes. You spend your life longing for reality while accepting a fake!"

He points at her and asks, "Go for a walk in nature and what do you walk upon?"

"A path," she replies.

"A path *through* the wilderness. You never actually walk in the forest—you walk *through* it on gravel paths or along wooden bridges or on concrete paving stones. Even when you '*get-back-to-nature,*' you never really get anywhere at all. You're stuck!"

"In *The Spectacle?*" she asks, playing the game, wanting to make sense of the madness before her.

The clown rolls up his sleeves, pushing them back to his elbows, only instead of revealing his arms and showing her he has nothing to hide, he exposes raw bone.

"All of life is theater," he says, pulling a bouquet of flowers out of thin air. With just the flick of his wrist and a wave of his gloved hands, a bunch of red carnations appears wrapped in cellophane. "You're either playing to the crowd, or you are the crowd. No one is exempt."

"So you admit it," she says. "You're no different."

He smiles, saying, "Some of us laugh at the insanity. Some of us want to be seen for who we are. We choose to be clowns. Rather than play along, we mock *The Spectacle*."

He walks forward, offering her the flowers, holding them out with filthy gloved hands. Breezy's unsure of herself. She's not afraid. Not any more. She's way beyond fear. Alice has fallen down the rabbit hole and landed squarely on her ass in Bizarro Wonderland. She's curious. She reaches out, accepting the offer.

The flowers are real, which surprises her. Usually, this kind of trick is done using fake flowers compressed into a small space so they can be concealed until needed. These, though, have green stems and leaves beneath the tight folds of the carnations. She sniffs them. They smell nice. She can't identify the exact scent, but it's pleasant. Although she doesn't count them, there are easily eight flowers. The stems form a solid bunch in her hands. A rubber band holds the cellophane in place.

Breezy can't help herself. She smiles in delight. She's been transported back to her childhood with the novelty of a magic act—only it's been performed by a dead clown in the dark of night. She's too damn tired. For a moment, though, she's at peace, which is a peculiar feeling following the rush of fear and adrenaline. She rests the flowers on the seat beside her. The Glock, though, never leaves her right hand.

"Why clowns?" she asks, realizing they're a front, but for what?

"Clowns are honest," he replies, skipping away from her playfully. The clown circles around the edge of the ring before returning to the center. The spotlight follows his every move. "Clowns offer relief from a world that takes itself far too seriously."

"Why dead clowns?" she asks, knowing this cannot be real. There has to be something else at play beyond the supernatural.

The spotlight returns to its original position, highlighting the center of the ring. The clown, though, stands slightly behind it, making him difficult to see. He holds up a skull, raising it at an angle and standing in side-profile as he addresses it with a thick British accent. The clown speaks with clarity, avoiding the temptation to rush these few sentences, giving them feeling. It's as though he's lived them, but that's impossible.

"Alas, poor Yorick!

I knew him, Horatio:

a fellow of infinite jest, of most excellent fancy:

he hath borne me on his back a thousand times;

and now,

how abhorred in my imagination he is!"

"You're mad," she says, unable to reconcile her conversation with a corpse.

"Madness is a legitimate point of view," he says, tossing the skull aside and stepping into the light. Breezy watches it tumble through the darkness, anticipating its trajectory. It should land nearby, out in the shadows, but it disappears in midair.

The clown stands beneath the spotlight, holding his arms wide as he says, "Madness defies all we call sane. It asks questions too uncomfortable to consider. It challenges our assumptions. It demands we step outside the theater of life, even if only for a moment."

He spins around with his arms outstretched. Glitter falls from the spotlight above him, swirling around him as he cries aloud, "We're living in *The Spectacle!* We're held spellbound by *The Dazzle!* Like a moth circling a flame, we're caught in the lights of Broadway. We seek the shiny and new. We crave release from the drudgery of each day. We want to be free but not to escape. We want things to change, but not too much. We want to be free to live in *The Spectacle*. We're caged birds too scared to venture out of an open door."

"What—are—you?" Breezy asks, wanting to break the spell. "I mean, you're not even alive."

"Not a single atom anywhere in the universe can ever be described as alive of itself—and yet here you are! What is life?" the dead clown asks, holding his chin with one hand and making as though he were posing a philosophical idea. "Life is not a thing. It's an event. It's both nothing and everything at the same time."

He moves his hands in an arc, leading them from one side to another, raising his gloved hands high over his head as he does so. Glitter falls around him. It glistens in the light.

"A rainbow is beautiful, but not because of the light refracting through millions of tiny water droplets. It's beautiful because we see it. It's beautiful because of what it gives us—hope!"

Breezy says, "But a rainbow's not... I can't believe I'm having this conversation."

"But what?" the clown asks. "It's not alive?"

"No."

"But you are? You're alive?"

"Yes."

"And yet, just like a rainbow, you're made of water. Everything that gives you life is found in a waterfall, in a river, in the ocean, and even in a rainbow. Your brain, as marvelous as you think it is, is almost three-quarters water. All those hundreds of billions of neurons are nothing without that rainbow. They're nothing outside of a muddy stream. At what point does a rainbow die so you can come to life?"

"I—I don't know," Breezy says, deflecting. She feels uncomfortable discussing her own mortality. She's so used to rushing on through life that she ignores reality. She's special, unique, or so she'd like to think, and yet the elements that make up her body are ordinary. They're exceptional only in that they're hers. She lashes out with, "You're being silly."

"Of course I am," he replies. He raises a single finger on his white-gloved hand to his lips, making as though he's telling her a secret. "I'm a clown."

Breezy says, "You're weird."

Her mind is spinning. She shouldn't be here. She shouldn't be having this conversation. On the other side of that chainlink fence, everything seemed so clear. In here, nothing is what it seems.

"Why so sad?" the clown asks, turning his head to one side and exaggerating his motion. He runs his finger down his face, mimicking the way a tear would roll down someone's cheek.

"He was my friend—my mentor."

"Director Johnson?"

Breezy nods. What is she doing? This is crazy. She's confiding in a clown. She's holding a conversation with a corpse. How is any of this possible? Has she lost her mind? It's all too much for her. Perhaps she's far more frail and vulnerable than she thinks. With everything that's happened today, the drug store robbery, losing Susan, and the director's brutal murder, she's unraveling. Is she hallucinating? Is all of this playing out in her own mind? Is she so sleep-deprived and stressed that she's conjuring up nightmarish visions of clowns? Is she imagining everything she fears? Is this a nightmare? That would explain the zombie animals in the cages.

"Why?" she asks. "Why kill him?"

"That is the wrong question," the clown replies, toying with her.

"Okay. I'll play your game," Breezy says, fighting back tears. "Who killed him?"

"Not me," the clown says, turning his oversized red shoes outward as he points at his chest with both hands, trying to look innocent.

"You're lying."

"And you're talking to a dead clown."

He holds his hands out in front of him, touching his boney wrists together as though he's waiting for someone to slap on a pair of handcuffs. "If you think I broke the law, what are you waiting for? *Arrest me, officer! I wanna speak to my lawyer!*"

"I don't know what all this is," Breezy says, waving her gun around as though it were a pointer rather than a firearm. "I don't know what kind of animatronics or puppetry you're playing with. I don't get why you've gone so heavy on the theatrics, but I know when someone's not telling the truth."

"And yet you're still here," the clown says, laughing and clapping as he turns in a tight circle, swinging back around to face her again. His large shoes cause him to waddle as he walks.

"Tell me," the clown says. "What's your safe word? Oh, no," he laughs, holding his hand to his mouth and squatting slightly, faking a sense of amusement. "Don't tell me. That would ruin everything, wouldn't it?"

Breezy laughs. Whoever's behind all this, they're damn good.

The clown points to one side, saying, "There are four vans parked a couple of blocks east of here. Their engines are running. I make eight SWAT members in each. ETA 90 seconds. But the police chopper will get here in under a minute. Do you think FLIR is going to allow them to see me?"

He frowns. "I'm not sure infrared will work with my pale complexion. It was smart, though, having the helicopter circling downwind so the sound of its rotors doesn't reach us."

"I want answers," Breezy says.

"I've given you answers," the clown says. "But you don't want to hear how your world is fueled by vanity."

Breezy is blunt. "Look. I've enjoyed the show. It's all very interesting, but it's fake. It has to be."

"Does it?" the clown asks. He raises his elbows level with his shoulders and folds his hands under his chin, pretending to rest his head on his gloves. "I expected more from you. I really thought you were going to understand."

That Breezy doesn't reply straight away is probably a little too telling on her part.

"We'll find you," she says. "You know that, right? You can't hide forever. You might play your silly little games with me. You might be able to hide behind this particular *spectacle*, but someone will figure out who you are. Someone's going to expose your organization, and when they do,

I'll be there. I'll be the one to slap the cuffs on you. I'm going to take you down. You, Buster and the whole gang."

The clown laughs.

A helicopter roars overhead, circling low above the tent.

The spotlight within the big top goes out but not before the powerful search beam on the police helicopter illuminates the tent from the outside. *'We'll find you,'* was the trigger for her hidden support teams to swing into action. They moved into position independently of her almost an hour ago, hoping to avoid surveillance, but the clowns weren't fooled. The rest of her threats were to buy some time for the teams to get on the move before anyone here realized what was happening.

She can hear engines roaring down the street outside. A police armored personnel carrier smashes through the chainlink fence, opening the road for the other vehicles behind it.

Breezy walks forward with her gun outstretched. She can see the silhouette of the clown standing inert before her even though the lights are off. The helicopter circles the big top. Its spotlight runs over the grounds outside before flickering back across the canvas. Shadows move about her. As Breezy gets close, the clown lunges at her. Gloved hands reach for her. Teeth as sharp as daggers glisten in the half-light. She fires. The gun recoils in her palm, but there's no deafening boom. Laughter cackles around her.

"What the hell?" she says.

The clown retreats into the darkness. Outside, the helicopter swings around again. Its spotlight dances across the canvas. A black stick protrudes from the barrel of Breezy's Glock. A red flag has unfurled with a single word proudly displayed on it.

Bang!

The clown giggles.

"The other clown. The girl. The one in the maze," Breezy mutters, realizing she must have switched Glocks while Breezy was disoriented. There was a moment as Breezy crawled through the broken mirrors. The lights flickered. She was pushing the Glock ahead of her across the floor. The other clown must have swapped them at that point.

"Bye-bye," the clown says, waving fondly and blowing her a kiss.

Outside, several vans pull up. They slide to a halt on the gravel in the sideshow alley. Boots thump on the raised wooden walkway leading into the tent. Armed police charge into the big top, coming in through multiple entrances at once. They're shouting. Spotlights flicker over the inside of the tent. Police in SWAT uniforms run between the bleachers with tactical shields in front of them.

Breezy drops to her knees. The toy Glock lands on the sawdust a few feet away from her. The red flag crumples. She puts her hands on her head, interlocking her fingers. Now is not the time for a case of mistaken identity.

"Breanne De la Cruz," she yells in the darkness. "US Secret Service!"

She remains perfectly still as thin Maglite beams illuminate her and the damp sawdust around her. She knows they're slung beneath the barrel of various snub-nose MP5 submachine guns. She has no desire to feel half a dozen bullets tear through her back because someone got nervous.

As SWAT members run past, she calls out, "He went through the back of the tent. Be careful with the animal cages. They're boobytrapped."

Boobytrapped might not be the best description of what she witnessed, but it'll ensure caution and avoid confusion—for now. In a hostile situation, being concise is more important than being accurate. A long-winded explanation could get someone killed.

One of the SWAT team members peels a gas mask from his head. Sweat mats down his hair.

"You okay?"

"I'm good," she says as he offers her a hand and helps her to her feet.

Each team leader sounds off over the radio clipped to the commander's tactical vest.

"*Alpha on the perimeter: clear!*"

"*Beta in the staging area: clear!*"

"*Charlie backstage: clear!*"

"*Delta in the alley: clear!*"

"No, no, no," Breezy says. "He was here. They were all here—just seconds ago."

"Who was here?"

"You heard him, right? The clown? The dead clown?"

"You're not making any sense," the commander says, crouching and picking up her Glock. "We didn't hear anyone in here other than you."

"What?" Breezy says, confused.

The commander ejects the magazine and checks the chamber to ensure her gun's not loaded. A bullet drops into his hand. He slips it into the magazine and hands her both the Glock and the magazine separately. It's a simple enough act, but Breezy is speechless. She stares at her own gun with utter disbelief.

"What happened in here?" he asks. He sounds confused. "Why did you call us in?"

"You didn't hear him talking to me?" Breezy says, walking over toward the animal cages. Someone has pulled back the heavy curtains, tying them off to one side. Flashlights ripple over the bars, revealing empty cages. One of the SWAT team members crouches, shining a light beneath the trailers. He illuminates long grass, flat tires and rusting axles.

"We heard you," the commander says. "And only you."

"Just me?" Breezy replies.

"Yes. You were talking to yourself."

"No," she says, distracted by the empty holding area. Breezy walks over to the tiger's cage. Her fingers reach out, touching the scratched steel.

"You were coming in clear," the commander says. "We had you on your chest mic as well as the long-range directional mic from the hide across the river. We heard everything you said, but it didn't make any sense. It was as though you were talking to someone on a phone."

"That's not possible," she says. "They were here. The clowns. I saw them."

"We've got a cold site," the commander says. "There's no one here. Our perimeter surveillance team hasn't detected anyone fleeing the area. We've got two drones and the water police covering the river. I'm sorry, but we never detected anyone in here other than you."

Breezy looks at the tracks leading from the crazy house of mirrors. The SWAT team hasn't ventured that far. Their concern has been on securing the big top. She crouches, running her fingers through the crushed grass, looking at the imprints in the mud and sawdust. There is only one set of prints: hers.

QUESTIONS

Olivia wakes to the sound of a horse neighing outside. Her mind is hazy. She feels as though she's been drugged and slept for days. She sits up and looks around, unsure where she is. A glass of water sits on a bedside counter. A bottle of Xanax has spilled open. Several pills lie on the rough wooden surface.

"Should've stuck to one," she mumbles, ruffling her hair.

Sunlight streams in through the curtains of an old wooden, horse-drawn caravan. Her fingers reach out, touching the polished interior. Thin slats run horizontally, forming the walls and a curved roof. This isn't decades old. It's got to be closer to a century. The basin opposite her narrow bunk is made from enamel-coated metal. The edge is chipped and scratched, while the white has yellowed with age. The faucets are ornate. Faucets? Plural? Her eyes focus on a blue **(C)** and a red **(H)** on the cap donning each of the taps. Olivia's never seen a bathroom basin without a single mixer. What do you do if the water from the hot water tap is too damn hot? Mix it in the sink? Seriously? You could burn your hand!

She blinks, rubbing her eyes. Polished brass pipes disappear beneath the aging floorboards. There's a toilet next to the basin, but there's no privacy shield or curtain. Anyone could walk in through the narrow door at the end of the caravan at any moment. That they haven't done that in hours doesn't register in her thinking. It's the possibility that disturbs her. She can't go *number one* on a wooden toilet seat in full view of anyone wandering in. Actually, she can. Her bladder tells her it's happening, and it's happening now.

Olivia relieves herself and washes her hands. Both taps deliver equally cold water.

"Huh?" she says, a little disappointed.

There's a single light within the caravan, but it's not wired into the wall. It hangs from a screw-hook with a black extension cable running between hooks along the ceiling. The cable disappears around the edge of the door.

Olivia walks the length of the caravan. It's narrow and rocks slightly as she moves. If she reaches out with her hands, she can touch both walls at once. Further along, there's a bench seat, a small table and a tiny bar fridge, along with a washing basket overflowing with dirty clothes. Her shoes are by the door. She sits and puts them on, noting the soles are muddy.

Before leaving the caravan, Olivia pulls back the curtains and peers out the window. To her surprise, she can see wooden wheels rising on the side of the cart. They're old-fashioned spoked wheels with metal around the rim. A thin coat of what she assumes is black rubber is a poor substitute for actual tires. Sitting inside this thing while it's on the move would be torture.

"At least they won't go flat," she mumbles.

Olivia rests her hand on the round doorknob. It strikes her as profound that she's only ever used levers or handles to open doors. Never, in her entire life, has she twisted a clunky old brass knob before. It rattles in her hand.

"Which century am I in?" she asks no one but the wind slipping through gaps in a few of the slats. She pushes the door open.

Olivia peers out through the crack. An elderly woman is washing clothing in a metal tub resting on the stump of an old tree. She scrubs a pair of jeans against a corrugated sheet of iron, lathering soap and working it into the material. Children play on the grassy slope leading down to the river. They're naked. They can't be more than five or six years old. Buster walks past, smoking a pipe. He's barefoot and wearing a pair of jeans with suspenders leading up over his shoulders. His jeans are too long for him, so he's rolled up the bottom of each leg. He's not wearing a shirt. His physique is impressive, but his body has been horribly injured at some point in the remote past. His body is lean. Lines of scar tissue run over his muscles. At a guess, he's been lashed by horsewhips.

Olivia pushes the door wider. It squeaks on old hinges. Buster turns and sees her.

"Good afternoon."

"Afternoon?" she says, stepping out onto a small wooden porch in front of the quaint old caravan. A wooden stepladder leads down to the lush green grass.

Olivia laughs.

Buster asks, "What's so funny?"

She throws her arms wide. "This! All this! Oh, the madness! I'm surrounded by relics from the past, and the only question I have is—*what time is it?*"

"Two in the afternoon," he says, checking a pocket watch on a chain. To her, it looks like a boy scout compass. The silver cover snaps shut. He slips it back into his baggy jeans.

"Where am I?" she asks.

"Hmm," he says, holding onto the rounded end of his pipe as it hangs from his mouth. "It depends."

"It depends?" Olivia asks, flabbergasted by his response. From the expression on his face, she can see he's trying to be lighthearted, but to her, this is a serious question. She drops herself down on the steps, sitting on the second wooden plank. Her shoes sink into the long grass. "On what?"

"Why, your point of reference, of course."

"My what?"

"You're sitting in front of a caravan. Yes, I'm sure of it," he says, pointing with the end of his pipe. "That's exactly where you are."

"Really?" she says, being sarcastic.

"Yep," he replies, grinning from behind the pipe clenched between his teeth.

"Where am I?" she asks, shaking her head in disbelief, still trying to throw off the lethargy of sleep.

"Earth," he says, throwing his arms wide and turning through 360 degrees, taking in the entire vista around him. The old woman laughs. The kids chase a dog across the meadow. They're trying to retrieve a ball from its mouth, but it's tormenting them, retreating a few feet from them as they laugh.

"Okay, wise guy. Where on Earth?"

"Washington, D.C.," he says, shrugging. "Where did you think you were?"

Olivia walks out on the grass to get a better look around.

There are four aging caravans lined up on the meadow next to each other. Several acres of uncut grass and a chainlink fence separates the meadow from the sagging big top and the decrepit circus rides. The fairgrounds are at the top of the rise on the neighboring lot. There's an old wooden barn off to one side that's in desperate need of paint. The Potomac curls in front of her, cutting through the landscape. Trees along the bank obscure her view of the far side, but if she focuses, she can see fancy mansions on the other side of the vast, muddy stretch of water. At a guess, she's not that far from the house where she fucked Dopey. It looks like she might be a little further up the river on the other side.

"Mount Vernon," she says, pointing.

Buster nods.

"And this is your land?" she asks, pointing at the green grass beneath her feet. "You own this?"

"I do."

"You know you're sitting on prime riverside real estate here, right?" she says. "You could do so much with this place."

"I like it just the way it is," he says.

"I mean, it's worth millions—tens of millions. How big is this place? There's got to be at least twenty acres if you include those woods. You could be set up for life."

"I'm set up to live," he says, turning her point around on her. "This land is worth more than mere money."

Olivia won't let go of the point. She gestures to the old woman, saying, "You could buy her a washing machine."

Buster laughs.

"It is a life I love," the woman says, smiling, revealing uneven teeth.

189

Olivia raises her eyebrows at that response, mumbling, "I need to take you to a mall."

"Hungry?" Buster asks. He tosses her an apple.

"So this is it?" Olivia says, looking around at the decrepit sideshow rides and the partially collapsed big top. The circus seems sad. It should be bustling with people. Seeing a rusted cart sitting idle on a rollercoaster track seems wrong.

"This is it," Buster says, beaming with pride.

"This?" Olivia says. "This is clown HQ? I mean, I've got to say, for an underground counter-culture quasi-religious cult wanting to overthrow modern political life, I was expecting more of a high-tech evil underground lair. You know, like with Blofeld and his white cat. You've got henchmen, though, right?"

"We're not the bad guys, Olivia."

"Who or what are you?" she asks.

Buster gestures to a wrought-iron bench seat overlooking the grassy meadow leading down to the river. She sits next to him, but she's careful not to get too close.

"Am I your captive? Your slave?"

"You're free," he says. "No one forced you to come back here. That was your choice."

"Yeah, but with a bunch of thugs out to kill me, what choice do I really have?"

"There's always a choice," Buster says. "We may not choose our lot in life, but we can choose what we do with it."

Olivia says, "For me, there was no choice. The only reason I'm alive is because of an accident. I got a flat. If I hadn't broken down on the side of the road, I'd be dead."

"It was no accident," Buster says, and Olivia sits bolt upright. "After the mall, we ran the numbers. We didn't know what was going down, but the odds were you were driving into a trap."

"You followed me?"

"We stopped you."

"H—How?"

"A subsonic dart fired from a stealth drone following you at a thousand feet. If you'd gone back about fifty yards, you would have seen the steel tip lying on the road." He holds his fingers a couple of inches apart, indicating the size. "It looks like a tiny arrow."

"But the others? My sister? The prostitute in the car? Snow White and the rest of the team?"

"We were running a probability routine. We didn't know what you were mixed up in or how deep it went, but from the activity at the mall, we knew something was going down. When you headed toward the cemetery, we figured they were digging a grave for you. We knew that if you died, any evidence you had would die with you."

"So you used me?" she asks. "You only saved me because I had value to you?"

"We knew someone was *willing* to kill you to cover their tracks. We could have just followed them. Well, we did follow them, but we chose to save you—not merely for information. We saved you because we could."

"And the cop from last night?" Olivia asks. "Did she come here?"

"Special Agent De la Cruz? Yes. She arrived about an hour after you."

"Why? What did you want with her?"

"It's not what I wanted. It's what she wanted."

"And what did she want?" Olivia asks.

"Answers."

"And did you give them to her?"

"You gave them to her—back in the parking lot, opposite the apartment complex."

"But she didn't believe me, right?"

"No," he says, puffing on his pipe.

"So why bring her here? I mean, if this is your secret base, why invite her in?" Olivia pivots, turning around and looking back at the fairgrounds on the hill behind her. "You know this is a really bad spot for a super-secret spy base, right? Clowns and circuses kind of go together. It's a little obvious."

"We have nothing to hide."

"Really?" she says, looking sideways at him. "Agent De la Cruz didn't think so."

"We're misunderstood," Buster says. "We're simple people. All we want is to strip away the facades, that's all."

"You know what the US does to people like you, right? You know what it does to anyone that stands in its way? Like Saddam, Bin Laden."

"We've done nothing wrong," he says.

"Neither had most of the chumps we rounded up in Guantánamo. A bunch of Blackhawk helicopters could be on their way here right now. They could be just about to come over those trees."

Buster smiles. "You have a very active imagination."

"And Uncle Sam plays hardball."

"We have nothing to fear."

"One thing I don't understand," Olivia says, shaking her head slightly. "You're clowns. You're trying to overthrow the government. Why does a coup even bother you? Is it just that someone else thought of it first?"

"Oh, no," Buster says. "We want to overturn the government, not overthrow it—there's a difference."

Olivia lowers her forehead, glaring at him. To her, that's semantics.

"An overthrow is violent. It's brutal, reckless."

"And you're not?" she says, raising an eyebrow.

"We want to overturn the government. We want the existing structures examined, reviewed and changed. We don't seek chaos. We want reason to prevail over money."

Olivia leans toward him, saying, "Don't take offense at this, but you know you guys are kind of weird, right? That's not news to you or anything, is it?"

Buster laughs.

"Why clowns?" she asks. "Why are you pushing this crazy narrative on the world?"

"It's the world that's pushing the narrative," he says. "Society tells us we're not pretty enough, or we're too fat, or that we need the latest sunglasses or smartphone or a flashy new car. We're constantly told we're not good enough as we are. And why? So we buy more shit. Humans are lumps of coal being shoved into the furnace that is capitalism."

"But not you, huh?" she says.

"There's nothing wrong with a nice smile or fancy clothing, but they're used to create avatars. They become substitutes for us. They're masks behind which we hide."

"Says the guy that dresses up like a clown at a kid's party."

Buster doesn't bite. "We have a little fun along the way."

"You want to see the real me, huh?"

"No," Buster says. "I want *you* to see the real you."

Olivia bites into her apple. She feels a little awkward.

Buster says, "Think about kings and queens, presidents and prime ministers. They surround themselves with the trappings of office. Their men wear uniforms or suits and fancy ties. Their women wear diamonds and designer dresses. They drive in lavish cars or fly in prestigious planes and private helicopters.

"They make a spectacle of power, be that a glistening crown or an oval office. And they're not content with their country's flag—they need something more. They need a seal of office. Why? Because they know the secret. They know that without *The Spectacle*, they're nothing.

"And it has been this way for thousands of years. From the pharaohs of Egypt to the President of the United States. We're so caught up in the spectacle of life we're blind to it."

"Like Adam and Eve in the garden," Olivia says, looking at the half-eaten apple in her hand. "They were happy, but only while they were naked. Once they were clothed, they were miserable."

"Yes, yes," Buster says. "Whether you believe it or not, that story speaks loudly about our heritage. It has influenced us for untold generations. Our myths are far more revealing than we intend. Ask yourself this—what caused their downfall?"

"It wasn't an apple, right?" she says.

"No, it was knowledge," he replies.

Olivia nods. "The knowledge of good and evil."

Buster says, "Think about how crazy that is. How could knowledge be our undoing? An origin story like this tells you something profound about us as a species—we're happiest when we're ignorant."

"That's kind of sad," she says.

"It is," he replies. "Learn a little bit about who we really are, look at both the good and the bad throughout history—"

"And you're ashamed," she says, cutting him off. "Just like Adam and Eve."

"We flatter ourselves," Buster says. "We like to think of ourselves as an intelligent species, but we're not. We're emotional. Pride is more important than reason. Anger shapes our logic."

"We really are selfish," she says. "Oh, my god. Listen to me. I'm turning into a clown!"

Buster laughs.

She grabs his arm. "I don't have to wear gaudy makeup, do I?"

"No," he says. "That's just for show. It's to get attention, to get people to listen to our message."

Olivia smiles. "Good. I'd look awful in a clown suit." She pauses. "I saw a bunch of your clowns at the mall. Why do they wear makeup and masks?"

"We all wear masks," Buster replies. "Some are just more colorful than others."

Olivia looks down at the apple core in her hand. "This isn't drugged, right? You're not getting me high or anything."

"No," he says, puffing on his pipe. "But I'm smoking weed. Do you want some?"

"Oh, no," she says, waving him away.

Buster draws in on his pipe. He's considerate. He's careful to blow the smoke so it catches in the breeze and drifts from her. Olivia enjoys talking with him. She used to spitball like this with the girls in her sorority. On Friday nights, they'd brainstorm half-drunk. They thought they were going to graduate and save the world!

"What would you do differently?" she asks, enjoying the warmth of the sun on her skin and looking out across the grassy meadow at the trees running along the riverbank. "If you could tell *everyone* in the world just one thing that would change their lives, what would it be?"

"I wouldn't say anything," Buster replies, "There's nothing I could say that hasn't already been said. There's nothing they don't already know."

"What?" she asks, surprised by his response. It's not just that she's surprised he doesn't have an answer prepared and ready to go, but that he doesn't want to answer. In her experience, ego is one helluva drug. Most of the men she's known through the years would jump at the chance to explain things to her and spell out their solutions to the world's problems as though she were a child.

"You must have something," she says, insisting on an answer.

"Our world has no lack of prophets," he says. "Take your pick: Moses, Christ, Buddha, Mohammad, Gandhi, Dr. King. Hell, pick Kant or Descartes if you want. They're all far more eloquent than me. And they all say the same thing."

"I don't understand," she says.

"We don't suffer from a lack of ideals. Our problem is: we bury them. What do you want me to say? *Love your neighbor as yourself? If you love yourself, you could never hurt another?* Or, *hate cannot drive out hate—only love can do that?* These phrases are both absolutely true and utterly worthless at the same time. They've become clichés. I'm not

196

telling anyone anything they don't already know. They've heard it all before. They've already plastered it on a t-shirt, or it's hanging on the kitchen wall."

"So what do you want from them?" she asks, turning toward him with a sense of fascination.

"I want people to think for themselves. I want people to arrive at these conclusions for themselves—on their own. Life is not a game of Trivial Pursuit. Facts are dangerous. Quotes are meaningless. Even the best of ideals can be toxic."

"I don't get it. How can these things be bad?"

"Because they're passive," Buster says. "They require no depth of thought. And without that, there can be no action. I need people to think, not parrot. Ideals are a poor substitute for reason."

"And being a clown does that?" Olivia asks, making her skepticism known.

"We're all fools," Buster says. "Only some of us are willing to admit it."

Olivia laughs. "Okay, you've got me on that one."

"In medieval times, in the courts of France, Germany and England, there was one person that could confront the king: the court jester. But why? Why did the kings and queens and princes and emperors allow such insolence?"

Olivia smiles. "Because everyone else was sucking up to them."

Buster snaps his finger. "Exactly. As much as they hated it, they needed someone to be honest. They needed someone to poke fun at their stupidity."

"And you think you can change the world?" she asks.

"I think we need clowns to show us our blind spots," he replies. "Our problem is we give away our allegiance too easily. No one buys snake oil for the taste. They buy it because of the smile. They buy it for the hype. They buy it because, deep down, they want it to be true. All it takes to get followers is passion. You don't even have to be right, just zealous."

"Huh?" Olivia says. "So to counter conspiracies, you've come up with your own conspiracy."

Buster smiles.

"To catch a fish, you must bait the hook," he says, "but it's not the bait that's the problem—it's the hook hidden from sight. Tell someone their freedoms are under threat or that their rights are at stake, and you'll get their blood boiling. That's the bait. It's what draws them in. But it's the hook that's the problem, not the bait. They bite on conspiracy and lose what little freedom they have. They surrender their reason to the herd. No crowd is formed from individuals—only clones."

"But you?" Olivia asks, fascinated by the discussion.

"We catch and release," Buster says, grinning. "There's bait. There's no hook."

She laughs. "I find it hard to believe you're not tempted by power."

"Me?" Buster asks, pointing at himself and chuckling. He shakes his head. "No. Hell, no. Have you ever thought about why people cling to power? It's a good question. Look at Congress. Look at the Senate. Look at the Pope or the archbishops. Look at all those elderly folk. They're ten to twenty years past retirement age, and they're still there! Why? Why not hand the reins to the next generation? Hell, hand them down two or three generations! These fools are shaping a world they'll never enjoy. They should be sitting on the porch with a glass of whiskey, watching the sunset as their grandkids play in the yard."

"But?" Olivia says.

"But they can't step aside for one simple reason: they can't accept who they are. They look in the mirror and they see something else, something different. They're addicted to *The Spectacle*. They see what they imagine themselves to be, not reality. They're old and frail, but their ego demands more. They brush their hair and wear a fancy suit or a pretty dress. They slap on some lipstick or a bit of aftershave, and they push on. If they stopped and thought about it, even for a moment, their world would collapse. Power isn't an aphrodisiac—it's a narcotic, an opiate."

"But you?" Olivia asks. "You're a clown. You wear makeup, right?"

"In defiance, not compliance."

"You're a rebel."

"This world belongs to all of us, but tomorrow belongs to the youth of today, not the older generations. They've had their time in the sun. They've forgotten how once they protested in the streets. The temptation is to spit on those that want a better future because today is just fine—for them, at least. Change, Olivia. Never underestimate the importance of change. It's all that separates us from the Stone Age."

The old woman comes over carrying two glasses of ice tea. She hands them out.

"Thank you," Olivia says.

Buster nods, thanking the woman with a smile.

He takes a sip, saying, "Come with me."

"What?" Olivia asks. "Where?"

"I've got some errands to run. Come with me into town. We'll take the clown car."

"There's a clown car?" she asks, almost jumping out of her seat. "Like the Batmobile?"

"I'm kidding," he says. "I just wanted to see the look on your face."

Olivia laughs. She likes Buster. He's different. He's unlike anyone she's ever met. And he hasn't hit on her. His eyes haven't strayed to her breasts. As they talked, his eyes have bounced between her lips and her eyes but never any lower. Most men will sneak a glimpse at her ample bosom. She doesn't mind. She gets it. Although no one wants to admit it, humans are sexual beings. It's how one generation leads to another. Heterosexual men have an almost primeval fascination with a woman's breasts. Olivia thinks it's the contrast that sets it up. Slim arms and legs, tight waist, big tits. She might as well be wearing a billboard. Buster, though, sees her, and not just her body.

"Sure," she says.

"Great," Buster says, slapping his hands on his thighs and getting to his feet. The two of them walk up the grassy slope toward the big top. Old-fashioned wooden pegs extend beyond the canvas, but there are shiny new aluminum extenders keeping the ropes taut. They've got large handles mounted on ratchets and look as though they're regularly pulled to keep the tension on the remaining two sections.

They walk behind a bunch of empty animal cages. To Olivia's surprise, though, there are fresh scratches on the bars. The cages have been painted recently, and that's been scraped away. She looks around. There are no animals anywhere.

"Here she is," Buster says. "My pride and joy."

Water has pooled in an old canvas car cover, causing it to dip in the middle. Olivia's surprised by the vehicle's length and width. Whatever lies beneath the cover, it isn't a Japanese car or something like an Audi. It's got the layout of an oversized surfboard.

Buster unclips a few buckles on the old canvas car cover. Rather than pulling it off, he has to fold the cover over to avoid the water running into the open cabin. Rainwater spills over the grass. Buster stands back, dumping the last of the cover on the ground.

"What do you think?"

"What do I think?" Olivia asks, looking at the convertible. "It's a car. I'm not sure what I'm supposed to think beyond that?" She runs her fingers over the cracked leather upholstery. "It's old. Does that help?"

Buster laughs. "It's a classic. A 1990 Jaguar XJS convertible. Three-hundred-and-sixty-five cubic inches of naturally aspirated madness! Over three-hundred brake horsepower! This thing is a beast!"

Olivia sets her hands on her hips. "You know women aren't impressed by phallic symbols, right?"

"Oh, you," Buster says, grinning. He shakes his finger at her. "You really are a clown!"

"Hey, that's my line, remember?"

Buster opens the door and climbs in, tossing a leather satchel on the backseat. Olivia can't resist. The temptation is too great. She sits on the open side and swivels with her hips, lifting her feet and dropping into the passenger's seat without opening the door.

"I knew you'd like it," Buster says, turning a key already sitting in the ignition. The engine roars to life. Olivia smiles. For an eccentric cult leader, Buster's not afraid to show his childlike love of the simple pleasures in life.

He revs the engine, keeping the Jaguar in neutral. Each time he pumps the gas, the chassis rocks from side to side, twisting in response to the engine torque. "Can you feel that?"

"I can feel it," she assures him. He really is a kid. For Olivia, this is a profound moment. His guard is down. This is the real Buster. He's not afraid to let her see him enjoying himself. There's no pretense.

"V12 engine," Buster says as if that means something to her.

"Let me guess—you get 15 gallons to the mile."

"Hah," he says. "You jest, but fifteen miles to the gallon is economical for this old thing. Put your foot down, and you can watch the fuel gauge drop as you accelerate!"

"How is this thing even legal?" she asks.

Buster shrugs. "Who says it is?"

He puts his foot on the brake, slips the car into drive and eases on the accelerator. For all his bravado, there are no crazy squealing wheels or donuts on the grass. Buster drives at a considered pace around the big top and over onto one of the gravel roads in the middle of the next field. They could walk faster, but he doesn't seem to care.

"Music?" he asks.

"Sure. What have you got?"

"A band from California," Buster says. "*Heaven & Earth.*"

He reaches out and pushes a button on the stereo. The volume is on full. Olivia is overwhelmed by a wall of sound screaming out of the speakers in the car door. Drums pound like thunder. A guitar lick cuts through the air like lightning crackling overhead. A voice belts out an anthem, singing, "*Drive, baby, drive!*"

"Ah, maybe a little softer," she says, reaching over and turning the volume way down. "I don't think all of Washington, D.C. needs to hear us coming."

Buster winks at her. "Don't they?"

Olivia shakes her head.

JAGUAR

"This isn't a grocery run, is it?" Olivia asks as they drive around the park in Washington Circle. It's a beautiful Sunday afternoon. People are sitting on the grass, enjoying the warmth of the summer sun. Through the trees, a bronze statue depicts George Washington on horseback. The car turns onto Pennsylvania Avenue, heading toward the White House.

"No," Buster replies.

Well, at least he's not lying.

"And me?" she asks. "I'm not along for the kicks, am I?"

"No."

"I'm the eye-candy, right?"

Buster doesn't reply immediately. He grins, keeping his eyes on the road ahead. "You're evidence."

"But pretty evidence," Olivia says, putting on an air of fake disgust at being used. She has her arm up on the door, enjoying the wind rushing past, catching her hair. "And you're going to just waltz in there, acting like you own the place?"

They come to a halt at a pedestrian crossing further down the street. A young couple pushes a stroller across in front of them.

Olivia says, "I thought they were looking for you."

"They are," he says, continuing down the avenue. "Sometimes, the easiest place to hide is in plain sight."

"There is no way they're letting you into the White House," Olivia says.

"Why?" Buster asks.

"Why? Do you really have to ask why? Ah, for starters, you look like a hillbilly. You're not wearing a shirt or any shoes. And those rainbow-colored suspenders make you look like *Mork from Ork*."

Buster grins. "Never underestimate the value of a good distraction."

They slow as they cross the intersection on 17th St. The road ahead is blocked by raised bollards. Thick steel poles reach up to knee height, preventing vehicles from passing in front of the White House. A police car has been parked at an angle next to a security checkpoint. An officer sees them approaching and flags them to one side in front of the first set of bollards.

"Can I help you?"

Buster hands two plastic ID cards to the officer saying, "We're here to see the Vice President. He's expecting us."

"Just one moment," the officer says, returning to the hut.

"Smile for the cameras," Buster says. "They're running facial recognition."

"Won't they catch us?"

"No, we've hacked their image-recognition database."

"Should I wave?" Olivia says, smiling.

"Sure," he says. "Oh, and if anyone mentions Lisa Mirowski, remember, that's you."

"Lisa's such a nice name."

The bollards in front of them lower in response to a mechanism activated within the guardhouse. The officer returns to the driver's side of the car and signals for them to continue forward. He has them stop before they reach the second set of bollards. The first bollards rise behind them, trapping their vehicle in place.

"Remain in the car," the officer says—there's no '*please.*' He adds, "Keep the engine running but put the vehicle in park."

"Sure," Buster says.

Several other officers approach the car. One of them has a mirror attached to what looks like a selfie stick. He uses it to examine the underside of the vehicle as he walks around them, looking for anything suspicious on the chassis.

"Could you pop the hood and the trunk?" the officer asks.

A dog sniffs around the car, checking for explosives. The handler taps the door slightly behind Olivia. A pair of paws appear on the paintwork. A moist nose sniffs at the back seat. The handler opens the leather satchel and peers inside, moving a few papers around. The dog looks friendly, but Olivia resists the temptation to pet the animal. Officers check the trunk and look around inside the hood of the Jaguar. They close them, satisfied with what they've seen.

"Nice set of wheels," the lead officer says, handing back their IDs. "You're all clear. This is Agent John Alexander. He'll escort you to the Vice President's office. Take the first right onto Executive Avenue. You can't miss the covered entrance. It's about halfway down."

"Thank you," Buster says as the bollards in front of them lower.

"This way," Agent Alexander says, walking ahead of them.

Buster puts the Jaguar into gear and trundles along beside the agent. The V12 engine splutters. It's on the verge of stalling. The engine's running with a rough idle. Buster has to touch lightly on the brakes to keep from overtaking the agent. He keeps them roughly five feet behind the agent and off to one side. The speedometer doesn't register. According to the needle, they're stationary.

Olivia says, "And the Vice President's expecting us?"

"Oh, he's a big fan of classic cars, especially convertibles. He paid five million dollars for Joe Biden's old 1967 Chevrolet Corvette Stingray at a charity auction."

"Wasn't Biden a Democrat?" Olivia asks.

"It doesn't matter when you're talking muscle cars."

Agent Alexander talks with the Marines on the corner of Executive Ave. They take their duty seriously, guarding the approach to the West Wing. After checking with a superior over the radio, they raise a barrier, allowing them to proceed.

"You wanna jump in?" Buster asks the agent, pulling alongside him.

"No."

John Alexander is the archetype Secret Service agent. He's beefy with crewcut hair and clean looks. His chiseled jaw wouldn't be out of place on a Greek statue. A transparent cord winds from his ear to a radio hidden within his suit. The padding on either side of his jacket suggests he's packing more than one gun. It's a hot day to be wearing body armor beneath a suit.

The Vice President stands beside the entrance to the West Wing, roughly a hundred yards away.

"Come on," Buster says, waving with his arm for the agent to jump in. "Slide over the back seat. You know you want to."

"I'm fine," the agent says.

"Look," Buster says, pointing at the Vice President up ahead. He's picked up on Buster's gesture and is copying him, signaling for the agent to live a little. He points, curling his hand over toward the back seat.

"All right," the agent says.

Buster brings the Jaguar to a halt. The agent positions his butt on the side, level with the rear seats, and swings his legs over. Rather than sitting down, he keeps his feet on the seat, riding high on the panel hiding the soft top.

"Now, we're cruising," Buster says, slowly creeping forward through the parking lot leading to the West Wing. The Vice President is clapping. He knows this is a victory of sorts. Having a little fun while serving the country isn't a crime.

"How long have you worked for him?" Olivia asks.

Alexander says, "Since his days as Senate Minority Leader."

"Nice," Buster says with his arm resting on the door. "He's a good man."

Buster's in no rush, which Olivia finds peculiar. She made small talk with the agent to settle her nerves, but he's genuinely relaxed.

"He sure is," Alexander says as they approach the West Wing.

The Vice President has his phone out, holding it sideways and taking photos of them as they approach. He has a grin on his face.

"I could hear you guys a mile away," he calls out as tiny bits of grit crunch beneath the wheels of the Jaguar. "That beast sounds like thunder rolling in the distance!"

"She's a beauty," Buster says, pulling up, putting the car in park and turning off the ignition.

Agent Alexander swings his legs out of the vehicle and drops to the concrete.

"Enjoy your ride?" the Vice President asks.

"It's smooth," the agent says.

"And this is it?" the Vice President asks Buster. "It's the real deal?"

"Yes, sir," Buster says, getting out. He grabs his leather satchel from the back seat and hands the Vice President a laminated sheet of paper, saying, "Here's the certificate of authenticity. This Jaguar was owned by Reagan for about two years before it was passed down to his son and then later sold to the Auto Museum in Detroit. I picked it up off them at a fire sale about three years ago. Reagan bought it after he left office. He wasn't much of a collector. He didn't make a big deal out of it but from all accounts, he liked it."

"He bought it to drive," the Vice President says. "Not admire."

"Absolutely."

"This is marvelous," the Vice President says, walking around the car. Agent Alexander stands back, keeping everyone in sight. He's enjoying himself, but he's not lowering his guard.

Olivia is impressed. The Vice President is ignoring them. He really does love a classic. She gets out and stands back in the shade as Buster and the Vice President talk about the car. The agent stands to one side, listening intently.

"And she's all original?" the Vice President asks.

"I've had the cylinders rebored and a new muffler fitted. Beyond that and the battery, everything else is as she rolled off the factory floor."

Buster drops the keys in the Vice President's hand.

"I really appreciate you selling me this," the Vice President says. "I'm gonna take good care of her and maybe, just maybe, they'll let me take her out for a spin in the Appalachians."

"Not a chance," Agent Alexander says, smiling. "But I'll drive!"

The Vice President chuckles.

Buster says, "The handling is incredible. She sticks to the road. You get the sun on your face, the wind in your hair and the cares of the world just melt away."

"Come into my office," the Vice President says, gesturing to the side door to the West Wing. "Let's talk some more."

"Oh, I didn't think we were allowed inside," Buster says. "Your secretary said—"

"Never mind what she said. Come in. There was a bit of a security scare yesterday, so I can't take you on a tour of the West Wing, but I can show you my office. It's the least I can do."

A Marine Corps soldier in parade dress opens the door.

"I'm not really dressed for it," Buster says, looking down at his scruffy jeans, "but thank you." He gestures for Olivia to walk ahead of him. She's all but invisible. Agent Alexander follows them, talking discreetly into his collar mic.

The entranceway inside the door is covered in thick, lush carpet. A security guard at the desk eyes them warily.

"It's okay, Phil. They're with me. Just taking them to my office."

"Sir, I should really—"

"Nonsense. A glass of scotch, and they'll be on their way."

"Yes, sir."

Agent Alexander says, "I need to escort them, sir."

"Wait here," the Vice President says. "I'll be fine. Honest."

Agent Alexander does not look impressed. He stands back, whispering into his collar.

The Vice President's West Wing office is immediately inside the entrance. His secretary's desk flanks the door, but as it's Sunday, the filing trays are empty. The walnut finish has been freshly polished in preparation for the week ahead.

"Do you drink scotch?" he asks, closing the door behind them.

"Sure," Buster says.

The Vice President walks over to a drinks cabinet and pulls out three glasses, setting them on a tray. He unscrews the top of a bottle of scotch and pours a tiny slither into each glass.

"It's fake," Buster says. The Vice President turns to face him. His jaw drops. Buster clarifies. "Not the car. The video."

"What?" he asks. The bottle trembles in his hand.

"You've seen it, right?"

The Vice President rests the bottle on his desk. He leans against the polished wooden surface, trying to settle himself.

"I don't know what you're talking about."

"The sex tape," Buster says.

"I don't know who you think you are or what you think you're doing," the Vice President says, pointing at the door. "But you need to leave. Now!"

"It's not real," Buster says. "They're blackmailing you with a fake—and I can prove it."

"I—I don't understand."

"Lisa was the woman in the tape."

For once, Olivia remembers her fake name. Even though she's wearing jeans and not a dress, she curtseys but doesn't add anything. This is Buster's show.

The Vice President works his way around the edge of his desk, holding onto the polished wood. He slumps in his chair.

"Don't hit the panic button," Buster says. "We're not part of this. We're here to help. We don't want anything from you. No money. No ties. No tricks. This is not a play at blackmail. That's what I'm trying to stop."

The Vice President rests his hands on the desk. He spreads his fingers wide. Without saying as much, he's showing them he trusts them.

"How?" he asks.

Olivia says, "I was hired to do a porno at a mansion in Mount Vernon."

The Vice President says, "You make it sound—"

"—like fun?" Olivia asks. "It was, but it was also obvious to me we were filming a deep fake. It was too rigid. Too structured. Everything had to be perfect."

"How did you know?"

"Fixed camera angles. Strict instructions on what to do, where to move, things like that. Oh, and they were particular about the timing of the shot."

"Late afternoon," the Vice President mumbles. "Just before sunset."

"They want you to resign," Buster says. "They want to replace you."

"So the President is in on this?"

"No."

"I don't understand," the Vice President says. "Who would want me gone? Why? For what political purpose?"

"You're a heartbeat away from the presidency," Buster says.

The Vice President mumbles, "Senator Langford."

"I don't know," Buster says. "I think so, but I need more information."

The Vice President looks lost. "He's been a little too nice lately, offering a few too many concessions in the Senate. He's been too interested in the administration's upcoming budget."

Buster nods.

The Vice President sets his elbows on the table and buries his head in his hands. "It doesn't matter."

"What doesn't?" Buster asks.

"You coming here—warning me. Don't you see? I believe you, but no one else will. They'll see the video, and it'll be over. It's too convincing. They'll look at my travel logs. They'll figure out Justine's schedule. They'll know we were there. I'm finished. Even if I tell them it's fake, they'll believe what they want to believe."

"I'll testify," Olivia says as Buster rummages around in his satchel.

"It'll be too late. The damage will have already been done."

"I have an ace up my sleeve," Buster says, handing over a wad of paper to the Vice President. There are easily twenty to thirty sheets of paper covered in numbers lined up in neat rows. Timestamps run down one side of the page, while at the top, there's a list of locations.

"I don't understand. What is this?" the Vice President asks.

"Proof the video is fake," Buster says. "But you can't show this to anyone until the video goes public."

"How will this help?" the Vice President asks.

Buster gestures at the Vice President's laptop computer screen and his coffee maker. "Electricity isn't what it seems. We think we're getting a steady 120 volts at 60 hertz, but we're not. There are slight changes depending on the load in a particular location, along with fluctuations in supply. It's imperceptible to us, but the rate flickers slightly, wavering back and forth from moment to moment."

"Go on," the Vice President says, intrigued by what he's hearing.

"It's random. Unique. And it's captured in multiple log files. It can be verified from numerous sources."

"A timestamp," the Vice President says, looking at the printout. "Like a fingerprint?"

"Yes."

"I don't understand," Olivia says.

The Vice President flicks through the pages, looking at the locations at the top and the various timestamps. The hertz reading is to four decimal places.

$$5{:}34{:}00 - 60.0021$$
$$5{:}34{:}05 - 59.9785$$
$$5{:}34{:}10 - 60.0239$$

Buster looks at Olivia, saying, "The affair happened on Thursday. Your video was made yesterday—on Saturday."

"They'll change the meta-data on the video," Olivia says. "They'll make it read as though it was created on Thursday."

"And that'll only confirm that it's fake," Buster says.

"How?" Olivia asks.

"They can fake the time of day in the file, but they can't fake the background electrical hum. There are subtle oscillations matching the frequencies on those pages. It's imperceptible to the human eye but easily verifiable by anyone with a video editing suite. The flicker of a lightbulb, the slight hum from nearby electrical equipment, the imperceptible buzz of the recording itself—it'll all say Saturday, not Thursday. It'll expose your video as fake."

"This could work," the Vice President says.

"It will work," Olivia says, realizing the importance of those seemingly cryptic numbers.

"But you need to sit on this," Buster says. "You can't play this card until they've shown their hand. Once the video is in the public domain, you can lay this down. Until then, they have to think you're scared. They've got to think you're worried. You can't give them any hint of the ace up your sleeve."

"I understand," he says, opening a briefcase and shoving the loose pages into a folder, hiding them behind a bunch of other papers. He closes the briefcase and changes the numbers on the lock. "How can I thank you for this?"

"Remember us," Buster says. "That's all I ask."

"Who are you?"

"We're clowns," Olivia says, beaming with pride.

"I'm going to need some time to process this," the Vice President says, shaking his head as he walks toward the door.

"I understand," Buster says, "but remember, you're excited about the car."

"Yes, yes," the Vice President says, laughing. "It's such a beautiful car. And it's real, right? It's not fake."

"It's real," Buster replies as they step out into the lobby. Agent Alexander whispers into his microphone. The four of them walk out of the West Wing. The agent stays slightly behind the Vice President.

"I guess we're gonna have to call an Uber," Olivia says, squinting as she walks out into the bright sunlight.

She blinks and everything changes. Agent Alexander grabs the Vice President, hurling him to one side, sending the 67-year-old man crashing into the bushes beside the door.

"Wh—" she says, unable to complete that single word with the chaos unfolding around her. She's confused. Why is a Secret Service agent attacking the Vice President? It takes her a fraction of a second to realize Agent Alexander is removing him from them, separating him from what he perceives as an immediate threat. Several other agents appear from the far side of the Jaguar, where they've been crouching out of sight. They have their guns drawn.

"Don't move," a woman yells. Olivia recognizes her. It's Breanne— the agent she met last night. There's a glimmer of recognition in her eyes, but it's not one of friendship. Olivia raises her hands.

Buster's distracted. He's not looking at the agents pointing their guns at him. He's concerned about the Vice President being dragged into the bushes.

Olivia's mind is racing at a million miles an hour. She wants to nudge Buster. Her hands are up but not his. This is the White House. If anyone's grabbing the Vice President, it's the good guys. Buster doesn't think of himself as the bad guy, but in their minds, he's a terrorist. Olivia

215

wants to grab him and shake him. She wants to yell at him to stop, but everything is happening so goddamn quickly that her thoughts can't materialize into actions. Buster steps away from her, making for the shrubs. He's trying to rescue the Vice President.

Olivia doesn't hear the shot that kills Buster. She knows there must have been a deafening boom as she sees the recoil of the gun and the involuntary grimace of the agents around the shooter. In her mind, though, there's utter silence. As Buster's in motion, the bullet clips the back of his head, cracking open his skull. His brain seems to explode. Fragments of bone and grey matter spray out across the wall of the West Wing. A smattering of blood splashes over the bushes. A red mist hangs in the air, lingering for a moment as his body slumps to the grass beside the path.

Buster's eyes stare blindly at the wheels of the Jaguar. His hand twitches, but his legs never move. It's as though they were never alive to begin with. They lie there like granite. What's left of his brain oozes out onto the grass. Blood stains the concrete rim around the edge of the garden bed.

Several Secret Service agents rush the Vice President away from the area. One of them holds his head low while the others hoist his arms over their shoulders, running him down the street away from the entrance. For his part, he's passive. He doesn't even try to resist their efforts.

Olivia sinks to her knees.

Secret Service agents surround her. They shout at her, screaming at her to get down on the ground, but she can't. She takes hold of Buster's hand. His fingers are warm but limp. Tears stream down her cheeks. Half a dozen barrels point at her.

Breanne yells, "Down! Down! Down!" But Olivia is in shock. At this point, she has no rational control over her actions. Oh, she's conscious, but she's running on emotion, not logic. If crouching here beside him means dying by his side, so be it. She can't let go of his hand. Her fingers shake. Her hair hangs down over her face, obscuring her trembling lips. Saliva runs down her chin as she sobs. The sheer speed and overwhelming violence leave her feeling hollow. Buster was alive just seconds ago. Step back a few feet, rewind the video, and he's laughing and joking with the Vice President. Now, he's dead.

The agents keep their distance. It seems no one wants to approach her. Are they afraid of her? Why? She's nothing. She's unarmed. She's no threat. She should be dead. She would have been if not for Buster. He saved her. He gave her refuge. He showed her that kindness is more than words. He treated her with respect. She can't let go of his hand even though she knows he's dead. Her fingers play with his, searching for a response that will never come.

"Please," she whispers. "Don't leave me."

But those are words he'll never hear.

FAST PACE

Breezy doesn't move. She watches as the body crumples to the concrete, sprawling across the nearby grass. It's a body, not a human, not a person. It's a corpse. That's the only way she can reconcile what's just happened.

Her hand clings to the Glock in her outstretched arms. She's still on target. Her index finger is still wrapped around the trigger, pulling it tight against the inside of the guard. She breathes, relaxing her grip. She's alive.

The act of shooting someone at barely fifteen yards was trivial. Even with his sideways motion, Breezy could pull that shot off with ease dozens of times in a row with barely the bat of an eyelid. This shot, though, leaves her feeling sick. Death comes too damn easy these days. She was doing her duty, and duty is not to be questioned, and yet she feels sullied. She's dirty, grimy, filthy, unclean. She wants nothing more than a hot shower to wash away the disgust she feels, but she knows she can never be clean. Very few people have ever killed someone. Those that have know they can justify the act all they want. It'll never feel right. This is her fourth kill in two days. Fuck! Her stomach churns. It's all she can do not to lean forward and vomit. She pushes herself on. Her training is all that's keeping her sane.

Breezy's running on instinct, albeit one that's been honed by hundreds of hours of training. No thought was given beyond neutralizing the target. As soon as Buster stepped toward the grass, he was dead. The act of aiming and pulling the trigger was a mere formality. As the seconds pass, reality hits. Her partner Susan was right. She's a killer.

Blood splatter has sprayed across the building, forming an arc leading to the bushes. The bullet embedded itself in the rendered brickwork behind Buster, narrowly missing a window frame. Bits of brains and shattered bone lie strung out on the concrete. Blood soaks into the grass.

The snatch team has the Vice President. They run him down the road. The clowns have been neutralized. She's done her job. And yet the look in Olivia's eyes will haunt her for years to come. The sheer terror that woman feels transcends mere words.

Olivia falls to her knees. Her hands are obscured by the Jaguar. She could be going for a gun or something like a knife strapped to her ankle. It's not likely, but Breezy's training demands a response.

Breezy jumps, sliding across the hood of the car, yelling, "Down! Down! Down!"

Olivia ignores her. For once in her life, Breezy feels powerless. Given the circumstances and the power imbalance between them, it's strange to feel as though it's she that's been stripped bare. Breezy killed Buster. She did that. She was in control, and yet now she has no control over Olivia. The woman's not armed, but she's not complying either. She should be on the ground, but her defiance is profound. She's neither fighting nor fleeing. She's holding Buster's hand. For Breezy, it's disarming to see such an utterly human response to the tragedy of death.

One of the other agents steps beside Breezy, ready to grab Olivia. Breezy holds out her hand, wanting him to wait. She doesn't say anything. The weight of the loss bears down on her. Perhaps she's getting soft. Perhaps she should have never allowed herself to become so goddamn hardened to begin with.

Olivia weeps. She's no threat. She's grieving. Another agent approaches from in front, having come around the hood of the vehicle. Breezy understands his intent. Their training says they need to isolate combatants. They need to check for weapons on both the living and the dead, but this is different. Act swiftly. Be decisive. Offer no quarter. Yeah, Breezy knows all that and yet the shattered skull of the man lying before her is unlike anything in the training manual.

The agent makes eye contact. Breezy shakes her head. He steps back, keeping his gun on Olivia. Several Marines come running over with their AR-15s raised.

Breezy crouches beside Olivia. She rests her elbows against her knees. The Glock hangs from her fingers. The pungent smell of burned gunpowder fills the air.

"Please," Olivia whispers to Buster. "Don't leave me."

"Come with me," Breezy says, holstering her gun and putting her hand over Olivia's shoulder. Even though she's the killer, the distraught woman turns and sobs into Breezy's neck. Slowly, they stand.

For all the training she's received, Breezy realizes there was only ever one goal: to divorce her from reality. The intent was to have her act as a machine. She's supposed to follow a script, but she can't. She has too much goddamn blood on her hands.

As they walk away, she hears the agents behind her searching the body.

"No gun. No concealed weapons."

Her heart sinks.

Death is cruel in ways most people can't imagine. The sun still shines. Birds still soar through the air. The wind blows through the trees, rustling leaves. Life goes on for all but one. It's at that point the bitter reality sinks in. She didn't have to kill him. But she didn't know that at the time. She couldn't know that. She had to do her duty.

The agents at the gate searched the car, but he could have had a ghost gun made from plastics, evading metal detectors with all but a few critical parts. It could have been taped out of sight and been missed during the inspection. They should have never let him drive up to the West Wing. But a Secret Service agent was with the two of them at all times. An agent she trusts.

Hindsight is cruel. She'll go before a board of review. She'll face an investigation into a shooting on the White House grounds. They'll analyze everything that occurred in meticulous detail, but they can't replicate reality. Breezy didn't have the luxury of debating her options. Breezy did what she had to in the moment. She hates herself for it, but with what she understood in that split second, she took the only action she could.

Johnson was going to have her stood down after the shooting in the drug store. She only wishes he'd lived long enough to do that. If he had, some other agent might have rushed Buster and wrestled him to the ground instead of firing at him.

The Secret Service is frugal in assigning blame. If the shot is deemed to be justified, she'll be quietly commended and reassigned. If it's considered a mistake, she'll be quietly reassigned. The difference is in the stares she'll get from her fellow agents and the whispers in the locker room.

Goddamn it, Johnson. Where the hell are you? Breezy needs her mentor now more than ever. If he hadn't been brutally murdered, if she hadn't been at the circus last night, everything would be different. She would have had her finger resting along the outside of the trigger guard instead of against the curved steel. She would have given herself a few more milliseconds to make a clear decision. Buster would be in custody instead of sprawled out on the pavement.

It's the clowns who are at fault, she decides. They killed the director. Denying it doesn't change reality. If they didn't kill Director Johnson, then who did? Someone wanted him out of the way.

In that moment, as her finger tightened on the trigger, there was a maelstrom of conflicting emotions clouding her thinking. Revenge was part of the equation, but more than that, she was afraid Buster would *walk* again. She saw what happened at the precinct. Buster was untouchable. What would the future look like if the clowns continue to mock the rule of law? They're a joke. They're not a political party or government agency. They have no democratic authority. No right to interfere in society.

Several SUVs pull up with lights flashing. Agents pile out. Someone runs over to Breezy, asking, "Is she injured?"

"No," Breezy says, withdrawing her arm from Olivia. "Take her into custody."

"Understood."

Olivia never raises her eyes from the concrete passing beneath her feet. Her hands are handcuffed and she's bundled into an SUV.

Breezy is still trying to take stock of what happened. She was in the USSS briefing room on the first floor of the Executive Office opposite the

West Wing when the call came through. Facial recognition had failed to get a match, but someone spotted Olivia in the Jaguar convertible. They'd been shadowing the FBI detail sent to intercept her at the mall yesterday. They still had a mugshot print. When Breezy saw it and heard the description of the driver, she knew it was Buster. It was the scars that convinced her. The officer by the gate said he'd never seen someone with so many scars.

She walks down the road toward the Vice President, composing herself. Even though the threat has been neutralized, the Secret Service agents have him standing behind an armored SUV. They're ready to whisk him away if needed.

The Vice President is distraught. "What have you done?" he asks, looking at the body sprawled on the concrete.

"My job," she replies, but doubts are sliding through. Her words lack conviction.

"They're not the enemy."

"What do you mean?" she says, squinting as she stares at him in the harsh sunlight. "They're clowns."

"I know."

There's clapping behind her. It's slow. A familiar voice says, "Well done, Breezy."

She turns, seeing a ghost walking toward her in the bright sunlight. Director Johnson is casual and relaxed in his demeanor. He's smiling. Her knees go weak. The tips of her fingers go numb. A cold realization washes over her. She may not understand all the details, she might not know the intricacies of how and why, but she's been played. She's been betrayed.

"Wait. What?" she says, feeling her head starting to spin. She points at him. "You're dead. You. I saw your apartment. I saw them wheel your body away."

"You saw what we wanted you to see," the director says. "What you *needed* to see to get close to them."

"I don't understand," Breezy says, gesturing to Buster's lifeless body.

"What the hell is going on?" the Vice President asks.

The director says, "This is part of a larger national security operation against the clowns."

"You used me?" Breezy asks, feeling sick. Her knees feel as though they're going to buckle beneath her.

"I didn't intend this," the director says, pointing at Buster's lifeless body. "It... complicates things, but we can adapt."

"I want a full report," the Vice President says, but to Breezy at least, he doesn't seem as strident as he could or should be. He's shaken, and not just by what happened. Something else is bothering him, that much is obvious from the way he looks around. He's nervous, but why? He's surrounded by the Secret Service. He growls, "I want it on my desk by Monday morning. Understood?" But he's not convincing, not to Breezy. It's as though he's putting on a show.

"Yes, sir," the director says, lowering his head in deference to the Vice President's authority.

"I need to talk to the President."

"He's locked-down in the Oval Office."

The Vice President storms off flanked by secret service agents. He heads along a path in front of the West Wing.

225

"Come with me," the director says to Breezy, turning toward the Executive Office Building.

"What's going on?" she asks, following the director across the parking lot. Veins pulse in her neck. Her head feels as though it's going to split open.

"We need to talk," he says. "But not here. We need to go somewhere secure."

Breezy follows him into the building. Something's horribly wrong. Goosebumps rise on her skin but not from the chill of the air conditioning. They walk down a narrow set of internal stairs and into the basement. Pipes crisscross the ceiling. Labels indicate whether they carry freshwater, sewage, or steam for heating in winter. The two of them walk down an unfinished concrete corridor flanked by more pipes and thick wiring looms.

Breezy wants to talk. The knot churning within her stomach demands answers. "Why did you fake your death? Why would you do that? To me of all people?"

The director doesn't respond. His dress shoes make a distinctly hollow clomp on the concrete. The echo is disturbing. The lighting is poor. At the far end of the corridor, there's a dimly lit steel door.

Far from being relieved he's alive, she's angry at being misled. If that wasn't his body, then whose was it?

Her mind is reeling from the implications of being deceived. The director used her to get to the Clowns—only they didn't play ball. As far as she knows, she spoke to a ghost or a ghoul or the undead or some hideous damn thing. Whatever it was, it sure as hell wasn't human. Then the SWAT teams rolled in, and the clowns disappeared into thin air.

What the *fuck* is going on?

What should she do?

For the first time in her life, Breezy's unsure of herself. What action should she take? What's the right thing to do? The right thing? Really? Now, she's worried about doing the right thing? She willfully suspended her moral compass for this guy and the institution he represents. It's too late to think about doing the right thing. She did the only thing she could when pulling that trigger on Buster. Even now, she's doing the only thing she can by following the director's lead. Without her own core values, she's at the mercy of his every whim. What the hell is he playing at?

"This isn't a game, sir," she says. But her use of the term 'sir' is telling. As much as she wants to be strident, she remains submissive to the chain of command. Her voice reverberates down the concrete tunnel but the director ignores her. He keeps walking. She's hoping there's an explanation that resolves all this. But she's lying to herself and she knows it. What justification could there be?

Breezy isn't entirely sure, but based on the turns they've made and the distance they've walked, she suspects they're no longer under the Executive Office building. They've gone too far. She rests her hand on the concrete wall. There's a slight rumble as a truck drives along above them.

"We're beneath the street," she says.

"Beneath 17th Street, to be precise," the director says, walking on toward the door. "You always were sharp, Breezy."

Oh, she's sharp enough to know when she's being conveniently ignored. Breezy's sharp enough to know when she's being used. The director's not the only one that can play stupid games. If he's going to be aloof, she'll pretend to be compliant—just a good, old, loyal lapdog.

"Why so low tech?" she asks, having been in dozens of secure rooms over the years. Usually there are all kinds of scans and shielding in place. "Why are we in a tunnel?"

"Do you know what the problem is with all forms of security?"

"No," she says, trying to peer past him, wondering if there's facial recognition or an access card point or perhaps a keypad on the door ahead of them. If there are cameras watching, she can't spot them.

"The very notion is a contradiction. Security needs to keep some people out while simultaneously allowing others in, and therein lies its flaw. You can never keep everyone out."

"Okay, sure."

"Security is complex. It's tough, so we outsource it. But that makes the problem worse as the risk is spread wider. We give it to guards, or we rely on video surveillance, or we use software to provide electronic identification."

"But?" she asks, knowing there's more to his argument.

"But all that does is introduce more layers—more weakness. It shifts the risk. It doesn't remove it."

"So, what's the answer?"

"Need-to-know," the director says, reaching for the door. "Only involve those you trust. Keep it small. Keep it close."

He opens the door and walks down a set of steel stairs. A pump hums somewhere nearby. At the bottom of the stairs, he removes his shoes and his belt, placing them on a rusting shelf.

"You'll need to leave your phone and gun here, along with your shoes. Oh, and your bra."

"My bra?" Breezy asks, astonished by the audacity of his request.

"No unshielded metal inside," he says, pointing at the wooden door in front of them.

"I don't get it," she says. "If this is top secret, surely you have guards and stuff."

"We need to keep this op quiet," he says. "You've already walked through four checkpoints. Your cellphone lost coverage before we left the building. As far as anyone knows, you're still on the other side of the street."

Breezy slips off her bra, working it beneath her shirt. She folds it, placing it on the next empty shelf, saying, "And all this is because...."

"We're facing an enemy unlike anything we've ever seen before—anywhere on Earth."

He opens the door and walks inside.

To Breezy's surprise, they're in a broad, open basement flooded with light. They must be somewhere beneath one of the other government buildings surrounding the White House. The basement looks like an abandoned parking level. Prefabricated, demountable offices the size and shape of a shipping container have been set on large metal springs, only the office walls are made entirely of glass. Each supporting spring is the size of a desk. The steel coils are as thick as her arms. Rubber mats separate the springs from the offices. As the various walls of the offices are made from glass, she can see joins between them, allowing staff to walk around. Everything inside appears a deep shade of green. They've used thick ballistic glass. None of the offices touch either the walls or the ceiling within the basement. There are desks and computers, whiteboards and meeting tables. It all looks rather standard, even if it is clandestine.

"What is this place?"

"Secure," is all the director will say. He walks up a short set of stairs in his socks. The top stair, though, doesn't touch the office. There's a gap of less than a foot, forcing him to open a glass door before he steps up into the network of offices.

Breezy follows him. Stepping across that final gap leaves her feeling as though she's passing from one world into another.

"And now we can talk," the director says, closing the door. He taps the glass, saying, "Triple glazed bulletproof glass with a near-vacuum in between the layers. Nothing gets in or out of here."

"Oooo—kaaaay," she says, noting that the carpet beneath her feet has a thick underlay, absorbing her footsteps. It's like walking on foam.

They walk down a corridor and into a boardroom. There are several screens on stands, but they're displaying a meaningless array of numbers. At a glance, it's mainly zeros with the odd one, two or three clustered together at various points. It's a graph of some sort, or perhaps a matrix of possibilities as there's an x and y-axis surrounding the numbers.

The various meeting participants are huddled in groups, talking with each other. No one pays any attention to them as they take their seats.

"Have they responded?" the director asks, and the discussions around the room come to an end.

John says, "We're seeing activity over Sør Rondane. There's at least one i-class shuttle inbound. Heading toward the Southern Atlantic Ocean."

Like the others, John's wearing a name tag, but there's no surname, no designation of his rank or whether he's in the Armed Services. His manner gives Breezy the impression that he's in the air force.

As John continues, the director whispers, "Antarctica," for her benefit.

"How long until they reach the US?" someone asks from the far end of the table.

"Eighteen to twenty hours," John replies. "Assuming they don't have any assets already off the coast of Nova Scotia, they're going to trace the Mid-Atlantic Ridge at subsonic speeds, avoiding shipping."

"Well, that buys us some time," the director says.

"Social media is going nuts," John says. "There hasn't been a formal announcement about Buster's death, but the clowns are already mobilizing on several continents. It seems they've got their own version of Defcon."

A woman at the far end of the table says, "They're leaking this to control the narrative."

The director says, "We need to send a message of our own. We did not initiate this escalation. They did. They crossed the line. They should have never come to the White House. This isn't our fault. It's theirs."

"How?" John asks. "We don't have any open dialogue with them."

"We have to frame this as an attack on us, not on them."

"We just cut the head off the snake," John says. "They're not going to see this as anything other than a hostile act."

The director says, "We need the President to move us to *Fast Pace*."

"Defcon Two?" John asks. "We haven't been there since the Gulf War in the '90s, and before that, the Cuban Missile Crisis."

"You're talking about mobilizing half a million men and women across the Army, Navy and Air Force within six hours," a woman named Suzanne says. "That will cause utter chaos. We're supposed to be in the shadows. This turns on the spotlight."

"The media will go nuts," John says.

"The media are already going nuts," the director counters. "And they're monitoring it. We need to use that to send a message of our own.

We need to frame this in the right way. We say, '*The Vice President was attacked on the grounds of The White House.*' We get the President to go on national television and state that we believe a foreign adversary was behind the attack."

Suzanne says, "The Russians and the Chinese will *freak-the-fuck-out!*"

"I know. I know," the director says, "But our friends need to understand we did not attack them. We defended ourselves."

"Friends?" Breezy says, confused.

"What does she know?" someone named Melvin asks, peering down the polished table at her.

"Nothing," the director says.

John is flabbergasted. "Nothing? She pulled the goddamn trigger and she doesn't know?"

"I—um," Breezy says, unsure of herself. "We're talking about the clowns, right?"

"Jesus," Suzanne says, burying her head in her hands. "We're fucked!"

"We can manage this," the director says. "We just need them to understand it was an accident. We were defending ourselves. We didn't assassinate him. He threatened us. He was off-limits. He should have never been on The White House grounds, let alone in the West Wing with the Vice President."

"They're just clowns," Breezy says, shaking her head, confused by the discussion.

Suzanne glares at her from across the table. "They're the spearhead of an extraterrestrial expeditionary force surveying planet Earth. Does that spell it out clearly enough for you? Try to keep up, sweetie."

Breezy struggles to swallow the lump welling up in her throat as the discussion races on.

John says, "If this escalates, we could find ourselves in open warfare."

"Defcon Two prepares us for that," the director says. "They'll know we're serious."

"They'll wipe us out," Suzanne says.

"Not over one death," the director says. "Not over an accident."

"I hope you're right."

Breezy shrinks in her chair.

"And the President?" Melvin asks.

The director is blunt. "We keep him in the dark."

"Wait," Breezy says, astonished by what she's hearing. "The President doesn't know about this? Any of this? The President of the goddamn United States of America doesn't know?"

"This President?" the director says. "Hell, no. Besides, a four-year term is too short. Eight years isn't even enough. This will stretch into generations. We can't risk any leaks."

Breezy shakes her head. "Where's the oversight? Where does the money come from?"

"We're the Secret Service, Breezy. So long as everyone's safe, no one asks what we do with our money."

"Can you take this off-line?" John says, annoyed by the interruption.

"Yes. Of course," the director says.

"I think he's right," Suzanne says. "We don't have a lot of options. We've got hostile craft inbound. We have to go loud. We have to go *Fast*

Pace. It's the only way we have of sending them a clear message through open channels. They'll see it. They'll understand we're moving to a war footing."

John says, "There's a danger this will continue to escalate."

"We'll have to accept that," the director says.

THE COLD WAR

"The world is in chaos," a reporter says, standing outside the gates of the White House. "Two attacks in two days!"

The reporter's knuckles go white as she grips the microphone in front of her.

"Key members of the Gardner Administration have been targeted, including Vice President Langdon. America is once again under attack, only this time there's confusion about where the attack is coming from. Some blame the clowns, an alt-culture group set on radical political reform. Others say it's a proxy attack by a foreign intelligence service trying to destabilize the US. Either way, America is on the warpath.

"As troops are called up all across the country, we're expecting the President to address the nation, but so far, there's silence from the Oval Office. America is ready to retaliate—but against who? That's the question on everyone's lips. It's a question only the President can answer, but he seems in no rush to come forward. For now, this is Jillian Foster, in Washington, for the BBC World News Service."

Breezy's fingers are clammy. A cold sweat runs down her brow. She leans forward, dry-heaving into a trash can. With one hand, she holds her hair back, keeping it from falling across her face. Bits of spittle and sick hang from her lips. She takes a sip of water and spits it into the basin in the break room. As there are glass walls everywhere, including the bathroom, people notice. They pretend they don't, but the sideways glances say otherwise.

Cool air spills out of a vent above her. She squeezes her eyes shut, trying to center herself.

It's been ten minutes since Breezy emptied her stomach in a bathroom stall. The privacy shields in there only reach from knee to chest height.

Susan was right. Breezy doesn't want to admit that to herself, but the conclusion is inescapable. She's a cog in the machine. She might think she's acting out of honor, she might pretend loyalty is the highest virtue, she might dedicate herself to her duty, but it's facile. Hollow. And now, she may have started an interstellar war. People are going to die—a lot of innocent people.

Her fingers tremble.

The seats within the break room are made out of plastic. They're designed for brief respite with a gentle reminder not to get too comfortable built into the polycarbonate finish. They look good, but like everything in her life, they're for show. She should go back into the bathroom. At least there, she had a semblance of privacy. In there, she can dry retch without people seeing anything beyond her genuflecting in front of the most holy, sacred toilet bowl.

The news, though, keeps her grounded. Someone else is talking now. They're standing in front of the reflecting pool with the Washington Monument rising behind them.

"Behind me, you can hear the roar of fight jets circling the Capitol. These aircraft are a visible reminder of America's strength. As they did in the wake of 9/11, they're prowling the skies over most major US cities. They're sending a message, but is it empty comfort? Surely, they can't be used here in America."

The director is several glass partitions away from her, leaning over a computer screen. Although it makes her sick, she needs to know what's happening. The news is both alarming and reassuring. War hasn't broken out yet.

"We're crossing live to our correspondent in Munich," the news anchor says.

"Protests are breaking out in the UK, France, Spain and Italy," a reporter says, standing on the steps of an old building. Behind her, hundreds of thousands of people are marching, carrying hastily made banners. "The clowns have galvanized public opinion in a way that hasn't been seen since the 1960s. Rather than focusing on one cause, like climate change, equality, #MeToo or Black Lives Matter, they appeal to all groups—effectively uniting them. Their message is simple: *change cannot wait*. And that message resonates with both young and old. With the death of their charismatic leader, Buster Al-Hashimi, there's renewed vigor in the movement.

"Here in Berlin, we're seeing hundreds of dome tents set up in front of the Bundestag, the German federal parliament. The message is clear: *We're not going anywhere. The time for talking is over. Change must come, and it must come now.*"

Breezy can't look at the screen. She stares at the spit in the bottom of the trash can. Her stomach muscles cramp, but she resists the need to retch again.

"Here in the US, the White House is calling for calm while the army mobilizes," the anchor says. "In Portland, protesters have clashed with right-wing extremists resulting in at least two deaths. Meanwhile, in Dallas, shots have been fired into a crowd gathering outside the state capitol. Riot police have declared the assembly unlawful, but that hasn't deterred protesters. In Birmingham, Alabama, protesters have sat down, blocking the streets around the central business district in scenes reminiscent of Martin Luther King, Jr. and the civil rights movement. The governor has called in the National Guard, but for now, they're being used to keep white supremacist groups from reaching the town center and clashing with protesters."

"Are you okay?" the director asks, leaning into the break room.

Breezy wipes the back of her wrist across her lips. "I'll be fine."

"It's a lot to take in."

"It sure is."

"I still don't understand why you faked your death."

The director sits on one of the chairs opposite her.

"Without sonar, how can you spot a submarine? How do you get close to a stealth aircraft that can evade radar? How do you protect yourself against a sniper lying in wait in camouflage? You can't. You've got to provoke them into making a mistake. We had to get the aliens to think they were going to be blamed for the actions of someone else. Who did they think ordered the hit? Organized crime? Perhaps some covert Russian espionage that went bad? I don't know. It doesn't matter who they thought it was, only that they thought *we* might pin it on them. That's the only way we could stir them into action. We needed them to reach out to you and protest their innocence."

"But why?"

"So we could track them, or at least, try to track them."

Breezy's head is swirling. "How did you even learn about them in the first place?"

"We came across them by accident," he says. "Way back in 2013. Hell, we didn't know what we were dealing with for about three years. At first, we thought they were a highly-sophisticated foreign intelligence surveillance team operating on US soil. We just didn't know which country they were from. You can imagine our surprise when we stopped thinking countries and started thinking star systems."

"They've been here since Obama was in office?" she asks, surprised by the notion.

"Probably longer. We're not sure."

"What are they doing? Watching? Waiting? For what?"

The director rests his elbows on his knees. He leans forward, pressing his fingers together in earnest. His suit jacket pulls tight across his shoulders. "They have an agenda, but it's not an invasion. About four years ago, they moved from passive to active."

"The clowns."

"It's a front. It lets them mingle with us humans. It lets them try out new ideas. Probe our reactions and response times. They seem particularly interested in social media and provoking different sectors of society."

"So Buster was one of them?" Breezy asks. "An alien?"

"No. We don't think so. He was the frontman. Like the lead singer in a band."

"And the girl?"

"Olivia?" the director asks. "We're not sure what her role was. She says she's not involved, but he took her to the West Wing. That's a damn big play for a nobody."

"And all this?" Breezy asks, gesturing around her.

"We're flying blind. We can't involve other agencies. We got close to them a few times, and they shut us down."

"They shut you down?" she says, surprised by the notion.

"Oh, they're masterful at manipulating humans. They know how to play the game. We had a few high-tech surveillance programs running and they got wind of them. Suddenly, there would be a swing in the senate or an investigation or a court ruling. Sometimes people would be paid off. Sometimes they just disappeared. Sometimes they betrayed us. Sometimes they died."

"So, which was it?" Breezy asks.

"Which was what?" the director asks, confused.

"FBI Special Agent Philip Zambarrow. The guy they found floating in the Potomac. You know, no face, no fingerprints. Did they kill him? Or did we?"

The director laughs. It's not malicious. Breezy knows him well enough to realize he's reacting to her abrasive personality. He must have known she'd bring this up. He just didn't know when and didn't expect it so soon. "He got too close."

"He started to believe," she says.

The director looks at her for a moment without saying anything. He weighs his words. She'd like to hear more, but he's under no obligation to provide her with an explanation. Something went wrong and he figured he'd cover it up and blame Buster. Even though she knows it's a brutal, bloody business, it's difficult for her to accept the agent's death without knowing all the details.

Director Johnson says, "It's cat and mouse—only this cat comes from another planet around some other star and has an array of technology we cannot even begin to fathom."

"Not looking good for the mouse, huh?"

"No."

"So that's why we're down here?" she asks.

"Yes. There's a helluva lot of rock and concrete between us and the outside world. Everything in here is shielded. There are no connections with the Internet—nothing beyond our own internal network. No wifi. No Bluetooth. No USB ports. Hell, we're still running Windows NT down here."

"And that's bad?" Breezy asks.

"They tell me it's like wearing a bulletproof vest made out of tissue boxes, but it was coded before the aliens began poking around so we know it's not compromised. So long as we're isolated, it'll work. It's more important we stay the hell off the net than up to date."

"So the aliens don't know about you?" she asks.

"They know someone's watching, but they don't know who we are or what we can see. Like the Allies working with the Enigma code in World War II, we're careful about information leakage as we don't want to tip our hand. But then again, so are they. For all I know, we're fooling ourselves and everything we're doing is completely transparent to them. It's impossible to know for sure. I suspect we have at least some secrecy— perhaps not as much as we think or we'd like, but we've been careful to cover our tracks."

"But going to Defcon Two," Breezy says. "That puts us on a war footing."

"As bad as it is, going to Defcon Two and calling on the President is better than the alternative. If they find us, they'll kill us. We're at war, Breezy. It's a cold war, but it's a war nonetheless."

Breezy nods.

"And you can track them?" she asks, recalling the point about spacecraft over Antarctica.

"We can track the atmospheric disturbance of their shuttles," he says. "It's not precise and it's not real-time, but it's something, at least. It lags by about five to ten minutes, but it's enough for us to know a little about their movements."

Breezy shakes her head, astonished by all she's heard.

"I need you, Breezy. I don't know what comes next, but you've seen them. You know what we're up against."

"I don't know what the hell I saw," Breezy says. "I mean, they were dead. All of them. The animals. The clowns."

"It's a ruse," the director says. "It's a strategy of misdirection. They know how superstitious we get. They understand our tendency to jump to conclusions. Fear is a powerful emotion. Fear creates illusions. And they play to that, wanting to mislead us."

"So that—in the circus—that wasn't real?"

"Oh, it was real. But you weren't talking to a ghost or a zombie. They animate these things as a way of hiding in plain sight. It keeps the locals as scared as hell."

"I bet."

"You've got to remember what we're dealing with," the director says. "Imagine if you traveled back in time, just a few hundred years. A smartphone would be magic. A lighter would give you near-supernatural

242

control of fire. Even in the age of muskets and cannons, a Glock would be sheer wizardry."

"So it's a diversion."

"Yes. If anyone gets too close, they send them rushing off in the wrong direction. But I'm curious why they spoke to you. I want to know what they saw in you. They're normally reserved about their theatrics. What did they tell you?"

"I—I don't know," Breezy says, and she's being honest. She doesn't remember any specifics. Her head is still spinning from the pace of events around her. "They went on about *The Spectacle*. I mean, it sounded like dogma to me—psychobabble."

"Think, Breezy. Did they tell you anything significant? Did they want you to do anything for them? Did they mention their plans?"

"No. I don't think so."

"Did they say anything about the President or the Vice President?"

"No."

The director sits back. He looks disappointed. He purses his lips. He's on the verge of speaking but seems to be measuring his words, being careful with what he says to her.

"Olivia is being questioned at Sibley Memorial."

"At a hospital?" Breezy asks, surprised by that.

"We have her in an MRI. We need to see what's going on inside her head, to see if there's anything unusual. We can't hold her for long. They won't let us. They'll muster an army of lawyers if need be. They're smart. They know how to play along with us here on Earth."

"Like back in the precinct?"

"Yes. I need you to go there and observe. I need you to be my eyes and ears. If you see anything strange, if there's anything out of the ordinary, no matter how trivial it might seem, I need you to tell me."

"Understood."

"I need to know what they were doing in the Vice President's office."

Breezy nods. She should acknowledge his last point by saying '*Yes*' or '*Understood*' or something along those lines, but she doesn't. On each earlier point, she's acknowledged him, but on this one, she leaves him hanging. It strikes her as strange that the director needs this extracted from Olivia. Couldn't he simply ask the Vice President himself? Isn't he a more reliable witness? She keeps that thought to herself.

The director's hiding something. She can't trust him anymore, not after all the shit he's put her through. Breezy can't pretend the whole elaborate apartment assault didn't happen. She gets that they're dealing with aliens, but there's still been no credible explanation as to why he had to fake his own death. Why was that so elaborate? What was he looking for from the clowns? Everyone else might be focusing on some goddamn UFO flying up from Antarctica or down from Nova Scotia, but not Breezy. Something else is going down. Now that she's had time to gather her thoughts, she smells a rat.

INTERROGATION

It's night. Olivia is led into a nearby hospital through a back entrance. The door's locked but the Secret Service agents have a key. Inside, all the lights are on, but there's no one in this wing as there's no movement anywhere. The rooms are empty. The nursing stations are devoid of clutter. The corridors are quiet. This place hasn't been operational for a while.

One agent leads the way. Two other agents hold her by her upper arms. They're on the verge of lifting her off the ground as they push her on. There are at least another two agents behind her.

"Where are you taking me?" she asks, even though she saw the signs directing paramedics where to go as they drove in. She knows precisely where she is. No one answers. "I want to speak to my lawyer."

Fat chance.

Olivia doesn't have a lawyer, but they don't know that.

"Hey, I'm talking to you," she says as she's bundled into an elevator. "Why am I in a hospital? I have a right to know what you're doing."

The doors open on the next floor and she's marched out. Olivia looks around for signs on the walls, wanting to understand where she is within the hospital and where they're taking her. The rooms on this floor have their lights off. The doors are closed, but she can see in through the observation windows. They're empty.

"Hey," she yells, leaning back with her head, on the verge of screaming. "Is there anyone out there? Hello? Help!"

There's no reply beyond the slight echo of her voice bouncing off the harsh linoleum floor stretching along the empty corridor. The agents don't react.

Radiography

"What's that?" she asks, trying to pull away as they lead her into a sterile room. "Radio what? What are you going to do to me?"

A plexiglass shield separates a complex control panel from a series of machines set within the room. The only one she recognizes is the massive donut-shaped MRI scanner.

"What are you going to do with that?" she asks, seeing them power it up. The machine hums.

Olivia is laid on a gurney.

"I know my rights," she says to the agent removing her cuffs. He ignores her. He uses a pair of plastic zip-ties to hold her wrists in place on the gurney. It's only *after* they're tightened that the idea of escape registers in her mind, even though it's hopeless, given she's facing five armed agents. Olivia twists on the narrow mattress, but that only serves as a reminder that her legs need to be restrained as well.

"Great. That's just great," she says as zip-ties reach around her ankles, pulling on her legs. "I don't know what you think you're going to find inside my head, but my high school teacher Mrs. Jay would tell you you're wasting your time."

An alcohol swab is rubbed in the crook of her arm.

"What's that for?" Olivia asks, leaning forward and trying to sit up. She wants to see what's going on. "What are you doing?"

One of the agents prepares a syringe. He lowers it toward her arm, saying, "Just relax."

"Relax?" she cries aloud. "Let me stick that fucking thing up your ass. Let's see you relax."

Olivia squirms, trying to delay the inevitable. Another agent pins her upper arm in place. The needle pierces her skin, punching through into a vein. Cold fluid runs into her arm.

"Fuck. Fuck. Fuck," she mumbles, pushing her head back and looking at the ceiling. The needle is withdrawn. Pressure is applied. Olivia can breathe again. Then a second needle punctures her arm.

"You motherfuckers," she yells as another cocktail of drugs swirls within her bloodstream. Her vision blurs. She blinks rapidly. The slightest turn of her head has her on the verge of being sick.

"Ooooh. This is not good."

The MRI is activated. A sculptured foam pillow is placed around her head, ensuring she stares up at the ceiling. She's rolled into place beneath the thick ring. Ordinarily, she'd hate this as the curve of the sensor is uncomfortably close to her forehead, but the drugs coursing through her veins leave her feeling dazed.

"Who are you working for?"

"Hang on, that's my line?" she says, struggling not to slur her words. "Are you guys really the Secret Service? You don't seem very secretive to me. I've seen your faces. The secret's out now. Haha!"

They ignore her, saying, "You're a prostitute. A porn star. What were you doing at the White House with Buster?"

"Well," she replies, "I wasn't offering blow jobs—if that's what you were wondering. Although, if you send that tall blonde guy over, I'll reconsider." She leans to one side, trying to make eye contact with him and adding, "Hey, cutie!"

"Tell us what we want to know," another voice says.

"I gotta say," Olivia replies. "When you pumped me full of juice, I was a little scared. But, honestly, this is some good shit. I mean, I've had high-class drugs before, but this is top shelf. My compliments to the chef!"

One of the agents talks discreetly into a radio. He seems panicked, which Olivia finds paradoxical. She's the one that should be panicking, but at the moment, she just doesn't care about anything. The tall, handsome blonde agent signals to several of the others and heads toward the door.

"You're leaving me?" Olivia says, compressing the foam as she leans to one side, wanting to see them. "So soon? Can I come too?"

Four of the agents leave. Only one remains—a woman in her fifties.

"You're a goddamn whore," the woman says, scolding her. "What were you doing working for the clowns? Are you part of a honey pot operation? Were you blackmailing the Vice President?"

"Me? Noooo," Olivia says, feeling strangely compelled to tell the truth. "We're all whores, you know. We all sell ourselves for a lousy buck. The only difference between the two of us is, I know who's fucking me. You... you poor dumb bitch... you get fucked over, and you don't even know why. I mean, look at you. You think you're in charge. You think you're in control. You can't even control your bladder for more than a couple of hours. Jesus, listen to me. I sound like a fucking clown. Hey, maybe that's it. Maybe I am. I'm a clown. And all this, it's just a bad joke. I've been good. Can I go now?"

The door behind the agents opens.

"Oh, hey, Breanne. Fancy seeing you here. You want some drugs?" Olivia asks. She follows up with a fake whisper, making as though she's revealing a secret, "These guys are giving out drugs for free—and they're really good."

"What do you know about the threat to the Vice President," Breanne asks.

"The Vice President? Oh, no, no, no," Olivia says. "It's not him. It's the President. They're after him."

"Who's after him?"

Olivia shrugs.

"The clowns?" Breanne asks.

"Nope," Olivia says, fighting against her restraints. "We were trying to warn him. We told the Vice President."

"Told the Vice President what?" Breanne asks.

"About electricity. You'd be surprised. Electricity is like a fingerprint. You know, those squiggly swirls on the soft part of your finger."

"She's not making any sense," the other woman says.

"What did you give her?" Breanne asks.

"Sodium Pentothal and ethyl alcohol. She's so pumped full of truth serum she should be singing like a canary."

"You got her drunk," Breanne says. "You realize that, right? That's all you've done."

"But I am telling the truth," Olivia says, trying to be helpful. "It's the electrical fingers that prove it! The answers you need are all there in the numbers! Lots of numbers. Oh, there were so many numbers. I've never been good at numbers. But the numbers don't lie. I hated Math in high school. What about you, Breanne? Did you hate Math too? I think you did."

"Get her out of there," Breanne says.

"I'm going home?" Olivia asks innocently.

"Uh, wait," the other woman says. "Where's the rest of the team?"

"They were recalled."

"On who's authority?"

"You ask too many questions," Breanne says. There's a scuffle. Olivia tries to see what's happening, but her field of view is narrow. Punches are thrown. Desks slide. A gun clatters across the floor. There's grunting. A chair topples.

"Umm," Olivia says, trying to raise her hand to interject. She pushes against the straps but she's only able to flex her wrist and lift a finger. "I don't mean to interrupt or anything, but—oh, never mind."

A dark patch appears around the crotch of her jeans. Urine soaks the white sheets on the gurney. Drips fall to the linoleum.

"It's okay. Don't worry about me. I don't need to go anymore."

There's kicking and punching, but it's out of sight. The gurney shakes. Boots scuff the floor. After a few seconds, there's silence.

"Hello?" Olivia asks, confused by what's unfolded. "Is that you, Bre—"

"I'm Breezy," the woman says, using a pair of scissors to cut the zip-ties around Olivia's ankles.

"It was you," Olivia says, frowning. "You're the one that pulled the trigger."

"I know."

"He was a good man," she says as Breezy cuts the ties holding her hands to the gurney. "He didn't deserve that."

"I know."

"You can't undo it, you know. In the movies and video games, you can, but not here in real life."

"I know."

"You know a lot," Olivia says, rubbing the red marks on her wrist as she sits up. "But you should know better."

"We need to move," Breezy says.

"I miss him," Olivia says.

"I can't undo the past," Breezy says, "But I can change the future."

Blood drips from her hairline, trickling down the side of her face.

Olivia turns sideways on the gurney, swinging her legs over the edge, saying, "You're hurt."

"I'll be fine."

Breezy grabs Olivia by the upper arm, marching her toward the door. The other agent lies on the ground. Her legs and hands have been hogtied behind her using a combination of plastic zip-ties. A roll of bandages has been wrapped around her face, forming a gag over her mouth. For now, she's unconscious.

"Are you a clown?" Olivia asks.

"No," Breezy says, peering both ways down the corridor. "Come."

They rush toward a fire exit overlooking the parking lot at the far end of the empty ward.

"They gave me a truth serum."

"I know," Breezy says, pushing the crash bar on the fireproof steel door. The two of them slip into the concrete stairwell. It's unfinished and dusty.

"You can ask me anything, you know," Olivia says, stumbling down the stairs beside Breezy.

"Just—watch your step."

"I can't lie."

"It doesn't work like that," Breezy says as they round the stairs, heading toward the main door.

"Ask me about God, and I'll tell you. I'll tell you everything." Olivia's eyes go wild and wide. "No, ask me something cool. Ask me about aliens. Or ghosts! Or about quantum motors! Yeah."

"Mechanics," Breezy says, peering out through a window at the empty parking lot. "It's quantum mechanics."

"That's it," Olivia says, raising a triumphant finger. "Just ask me, and I'll tell you the truth about quantum mechanics."

"That's not how it works," Breezy says. "First, you have to know something about quantum mechanics."

"Ohhhh," Olivia says, disappointed in herself.

Breezy opens the door and crouches. "Stay with me."

They run toward an old beat-up Toyota. Rust has eaten through the bottom of the doors. It's missing a hub cap.

"This is it?" Olivia asks as Breezy fumbles with her key fob, pushing one of the buttons over and over. "This is our grand escape? This piece of shit?"

The lock clicks. Breezy opens the door and shoves Olivia into the passenger's seat, pushing her head down and rushing her inside.

"This piece of shit is about to save your life."

"Okay," Olivia says, shrugging. She puts on her seatbelt.

Breezy jumps in and starts the engine. She throws the car into reverse and backs out into the parking lot.

"You should put your seatbelt on," Olivia says. "Seatbelts save lives."

Breezy snaps. "Not now."

"It's true, you know," Olivia replies, slurring her words. "I can't lie."

"I know, I know," Breezy says as they roar out onto the main road and turn south. She fumbles with her seatbelt, dragging it across her chest and plugging it into the anchor point. "Are you this annoying when you're sober?"

"I don't know," Olivia says, thinking deeply about the question.

The streets are wet. Even in her old Toyota, Breezy's able to slide around corners. It's bald tires rather than the superb handling of her car that makes it work.

"Whatever happens," she says, keeping her eyes on the road. "Trust no one."

"Listen," Olivia says. "I'm drunk or drugged or both, but even I know that makes no sense."

"What do you mean?"

Olivia slurs her words slightly. "When someone says, trust no one, what they're really saying is, trust me and me alone—and no one else."

"Yes," Breezy says. "That's exactly what I'm saying. Right now, neither of us can trust anyone else. Just us. We trust each other, right?"

"Ohhh," Olivia says. "I thought you meant, trust no one, including you."

"Why would I say that?" Breezy asks, getting frustrated with how the truth serum has scrambled Olivia's thinking.

Olivia tries to be helpful. She points back over her shoulder as they whip down the road. "That was a red light."

"Just. Let. Me. Drive."

"Okay."

A radio crackles. The run of words is too fast for Olivia to catch. Several people are talking, coordinating their efforts. They know Olivia escaped but don't know how, or where she's going.

Breezy raises the radio handset, saying, "Arc Four in pursuit of a black Buick, registered here in DC. Run the plates on WZ 1515. Heading north on Wisconsin toward Bethesda."

She lets go of the transmit button but doesn't return the handset to its cradle.

Olivia points at a street sign ahead. She's trying to be helpful. "We're going south."

"I know we're going south," Breezy says, exasperating. "That's the point. I need to send them in the opposite direction."

"Oh," Olivia says. "And the black Buick?"

"It's sitting in the parking lot back there."

"Ah!"

There are several more rapid-fire comments over the radio. Olivia catches terms like *aerial units* and *intercept,* but the other terms are cryptic. Breezy turns on her stereo. A familiar radio station plays. She twists the knob until static hisses from the speakers. Then talks into the radio handset again.

"Arc Four in the ahhhh... can you ahhh... need immediate ummm... blocked... being blocked. They're jamming us."

She keeps one finger on the transmit button while raising the other to her lips, gesturing for Olivia to be quiet. Olivia nods and smiles.

A few seconds later, Breezy says, "You're breaking up... east toward Silver Springs... Silver... On a back road... Springs... Shots fired... Need support."

For the next five minutes, they drive in the relative silence of radio static. Other police and security units try to talk on the channel, but they have to fight the static to be heard. Breezy turns off the freeway and onto a side street. She switches off both her radio and the stereo.

"Where are we going?" Olivia asks.

"Back to the circus. I need to talk to them."

"To who?"

"The clowns."

"Oh, okay," Olivia says, trying to shake the lethargy from her mind. She's gone from feeling doped to fighting a thumping headache, but her thinking is becoming more lucid.

Breezy drives slowly along the main road. She passes the McDonald's where Olivia's car still sits in the parking lot. Olivia's tempted to say something, but she's aware she's got no advice to offer. Without Buster, she's as good as dead. If Buster's right and there's a conspiracy to change the government, then someone would have tracked

255

down her car by now. It's probably got a GPS beacon stuck on it somewhere. Even in her drunken state, she knows driving it would be a mistake. Besides, she doesn't have her keys. They're in her handbag, which is probably still in that tiny wooden wagon behind the circus tent.

In the distance, sirens sound. That's not unusual for Washington, D.C., but the growing chorus is unmistakable. Normally, sirens come from one direction. Sometimes, there will be several sirens in sequence as EMS vehicles race to an accident. This is different. The sirens are converging.

"We need a distraction," Breezy says, pulling over in front of a biker bar. It's early evening. The bay windows are open, allowing a breeze to flow. Inside, most of the patrons are grey-haired with gang patches more for looks than allegiance, but there are some hard-core bikers. Three white, overlapping triangles distinguish the White Lords from the others with a not-so-subtle reference to the KKK. Denial is a powerful ally. The symbols are cones, or so they say—pyramids. No one is fooled. Hell, their intent is right there in the name.

Breezy crosses onto the wrong side of the road, lining her old Toyota up with the row of motorcycles lined up out the front of the bar. A neon sign glows, attracting customers from afar. One glance inside, though, and they'll probably walk on.

Olivia's been around plenty of motorcycles over the years. She understands there are two types of bikers: commuters and riders. Her brother used an old Yamaha 850cc to get to work. He had to weave in and out of traffic on the 395 cutting through the heart of DC. It was one helluva commute during rush hour, but he never considered himself a rider. His best friend, though, worships the chrome on his Harley Davidson. His Fat Boy was never left out in the rain. He'll work oils and creams into the leather at least once a month. Olivia saw him tinkering with his bike constantly. She only ever saw him ride it once—and only with a sense of reverence. These guys might be bikers, but like cowboys in the old wild west, they love their rides. Streetlights reflect off polished chrome. Leather saddlebags hang from immaculate seats. The various teardrop fuel tanks have been painted with everything from a bald eagle to the Stars and Stripes.

"Hey, assholes," Breezy yells, rolling down her window. "Remember me?"

To Olivia's horror, Breezy nudges the front bike with her bumper. It lifts, rocking off its stand, and falls onto the next bike, setting off a row of dominos falling to the concrete.

"You *fucking* bitch!"

"You're dead! You're so fucking dead!"

Cans bounce off the thin sheet metal roof of the Toyota. Beer sprays through the air. Breezy pulls out onto the road, but only half of the bikes have fallen. She steers into the rest, making sure they all fall. The front wheel of her car rides over one of the bikes. Someone sprints after her, waving a crowbar and yelling as she accelerates down the road.

"That was not a good idea," Olivia says, looking back at the bikers righting their motorcycles and starting their engines. Deep, chesty roars fill the night, competing with the sound of sirens closing in. There are gunshots, but nothing strikes the car.

"Bikers, I can handle," Breezy says. "The US Government, not so much."

THE FAIRGROUNDS

The tiny engine in the old Toyota screams as they race up the road. The big top comes into view. The gates are still open. Gravel kicks up from their wheels. A dust cloud follows them as they swerve through the old parking lot and head down the carnival alley. Olivia vomits into the footwell of the car.

"Sorry."

She feels like shit.

Behind them, bikers race toward the big top. Police vehicles and unmarked SUVs converge, arriving moments later. There's confusion. The bikers react, revving their engines and pulling donuts on the dirt as they realize they've been drawn into a trap. The cops and the Secret Service agents, though, are equally confused by their presence. Far from wanting to apprehend them, they try to ignore them but can't. There's mayhem as the police try to stop the bikers and question them, but the White Lords are convinced they're being set up. Shots are fired. The bikers evade the police cruisers, leaving the police second-guessing what they should be focusing on, which buys Olivia and Breezy time to get into the big top.

Breezy runs along the wooden walkway above the mud. Olivia staggers behind her, still trying to clear her head. She grabs at the railings, pulling herself on.

Outside, the sun is setting. Golden yellows and pinks light up the canvas, seeping in through tears and around openings for the tent poles. Triangular portions of the canvas roof have been replaced with plastic insets, but the difference in tension and strength makes these sections weak. Water drips from the seams as rain begins falling outside.

"Now what?" Olivia asks.

"You're asking me?" Breezy says, turning around on the damp sawdust. She has her gun out, but she's not pointing it anywhere other than at the ground. "Call them."

"Call who?"

"The clowns."

"The clowns?"

"You're a clown, right? Call them out. We need them."

"What are you talking about?" Olivia says, frustrated.

"You told me you were a clown!"

"I *never* told you I was a clown!" Olivia yells, pushing off a tent pole. She's fighting a numb feeling in her legs. Olivia staggers into the central ring.

"What? But you were there with Buster at the White House."

"Still not a clown," Olivia says, shaking her head. "I'm a high-class hooker. I was on a porno shoot, but it was a trap. They were setting up the Vice President with a deep fake. They want him to resign. That's it. That's all I know."

"What?" Breezy says. Disbelief lines her weary face.

"This is what I've been trying to tell you," Olivia says, holding her hands out, feeling exasperated. "This is bigger than us. They're trying to roll the Veep *and* the President. They want to replace them. Both of them."

"Who?" Breezy asks, shaking her head. "The clowns?"

"God, you are so dumb," Olivia yells, swinging her numb arms down in front of her. She half-crouches, locking her knees together so she doesn't fall. It's all she can do not to collapse on the muddy ground. "The clowns aren't the enemy. They were trying to stop it!"

"Fuck," Breezy says. "Fuck. Fuck. Fuck!"

"And you killed him. You killed Buster."

"I know. I fucking know that, okay?" Breezy yells at her, exasperated. She's trying to do the right thing. She's trying to correct her mistake, but nothing is working. Olivia feels for her. They're both trapped, and not just physically. Circumstances have conspired against them.

Outside, a bullhorn sounds. "Come out, Breezy. We know you're in there. You're surrounded. Bring the call girl out with you. No one has to get hurt. This doesn't have to end in tragedy."

"Fucking Johnson. It's all a lie," she says to Olivia. "He's the one behind all this. He bitched about *this* President. He's the one that wants to get rid of them. And he's played me for a goddamn fool."

"Who's Johnson?" Olivia asks.

"He's the director of the Secret Service. He kept all this from the President, and now he wants to replace him."

"Kept what from him?" Olivia asks as flashlights illuminate various spots around the tent canvas.

"The aliens."

"What aliens?" Olivia asks, screwing up her face. "You mean the clowns?"

Breezy says, "Not so fucking dumb now, am I?"

"Oh," Olivia says, raising her hand to her forehead and pressing hard, wanting to block out her pounding headache. "We're dead. We're so dead."

"Yep." Breezy walks toward the back of the tent. "But the asshole out there lied. He wants us to feel helpless, but we're not. We're not surrounded."

"How do you know?"

"Because they're not going to shoot themselves. They'll set up a field of fire facing us. They want all the bullets going one way. That will force them to leave the rear without effective cover fire. They'll rely on helicopters to track us as we pull back." Breezy points at the back of the tent. "What's out there?"

"Ah, there are a bunch of circus trailers—the old wooden horse-drawn kind. They're in a meadow that leads down to trees by the river."

"Good, good," Breezy says, pulling back the heavy canvas and staring into the long shadows being cast by the setting sun. Rain comes down in waves. Thunder rumbles overhead. A helicopter circles above the tent. Its harsh searchlight illuminates the opening, forcing Breezy back.

"What's the plan?" Olivia asks.

"Stay alive," Breezy replies. "Make contact with the clowns."

"I don't understand," Olivia says. "Why did you rescue me? Why are you even in here with me? You shot Buster! You're one of them! You should be out there. What changed?"

"This is not about taking sides," Breezy says. "That's our problem: our undying loyalty to the tribe. No one wants to admit a mistake, but—*fuck*—this could cost us the goddamn planet!"

"So fuck the tribe," Olivia says.

"Fuck the tribe," Breezy says. "We've got to do what's right."

Outside, headlights wash across the canvas. From their size and spacing, they're either trucks or large SUVs. Red and blue emergency lights ripple back and forth over the vast empty tent, causing a confusing kaleidoscope of color within the big top. Breezy finds a power board by a control desk for the circus. There are a bunch of circuit breakers with labels.

"Oh, I recognize these," she says, which confuses Olivia.

Shooting Gallery

Balloon Pop

Laughing Clowns

Rollercoaster

House of Horrors

Lucky Bingo

Ring the Bell

Carousel

"Let's light things up," she says, flicking the various switches. The spotlight within the big top comes on, but it's the sideshow alley that erupts with colors and noise. Music begins blaring from the speakers. Carefully choreographed sequences of lights sparkle, bringing the old fairgrounds to life. A prerecorded voice bellows into the night.

"Step right up! Step right up! This is the greatest show on Earth!"

"Confusion is good," Breezy says to Olivia. "It'll make them nervous—keep them guessing."

Olivia asks, "And us?"

"We need time and space. We need to get out of here and figure out our next steps. I sure could use a few dead clowns about now."

"Dead ones?"

"Never mind."

From behind them, someone yells, "Drop the gun!"

Breezy turns, firing at a flashlight in the aisle between the bleachers. The shot is deafening within the confines of the tent. Olivia doesn't know if Breezy hit anyone—she's too busy crouching and covering her ears. There are several more shots, but they seem to come from different angles. It's the slight variation in the bone-shaking boom that has Olivia drop to her knees. She bends over, making herself as small as possible, crouching by one of the metal tent poles.

Breezy's hit!

Red mist sprays out from her shoulder. Bits of torn flesh scatter across the sawdust. Her left arm hangs limp. She returns fire, crouching on one knee, but when she turns one way, someone shoots from the other direction. Blood explodes from the top of her thigh, causing her to fall sideways. She screams, collapsing on the sawdust. Olivia clings to the pole between the two center rings, trying to hide behind it as she kneels in the dirt.

Outside, the storm grows. The canvas flexes, surging in and out. It's as though the tent is alive—it's breathing with the changing air pressure. The poles around the edge of the tent lift. They sway in the wind, being held down only by loose ropes and straining wires. The thick aluminum poles at the heart of the big top shake. Loose tent flaps swing back and forth, slapping the sides of the tent.

Ropes come loose. The whole tent begins to rock in time with the surge of the wind howling overhead. The power goes out, plunging them into darkness. Lightning crackles through the sky, illuminating the night.

Breezy is lying on her back with her good arm stretched out over her head. She fires upside down, which is perplexing to Olivia. A body falls between the gaps in the bleachers.

Another shot from another angle blows out her right knee cap as she lies on her back with one leg slightly raised. Blood and bone spray across Olivia, catching her hair and staining her face. She screams. Breezy returns fire, but she's rolling in agony, shooting blindly at the bleachers. She's swearing. There's a near-constant stream of expletives as she doubles over in pain on the sawdust.

Breezy drops the gun, leaving it lying in the bloody mud. With her good hand, she tries to stem the flow of blood from her leg. She's in excruciating pain.

Olivia rushes to her. She grabs an old bandana from where it's been shoved between the ropes running up the central pole. It's greasy, but it's all she's got. She tries to apply pressure to the leg wound, but Breezy's knee is a mess of shattered bone, torn tendons and blood-soaked muscle. Olivia presses hard, wanting to stem the flow of the bleeding. Breezy joins her, pushing her hands hard against Olivia's and fighting the blood loss from a severed artery. It's futile. Blood oozes between both of their fingers.

"This is it. It's over," Breezy says through gritted teeth, but something's wrong. The storm rages outside. The gods are angry. Lighting flashes in staccato. Thunder rumbles through the air, but there's no more gunfire. No one's rushing them.

There's movement in the shadows. In the half-light, Olivia sees something unnatural. Something rushes along the bleachers, but it's not human. The curve of its back, the motion of its legs, the lope and gait— it's a primate, but which species? It's too small to be a gorilla, too big to be a monkey.

"What the hell?" Olivia mumbles. The creature jumps, leaping effortlessly for twenty feet before coming down on a cop. There's screaming and gunfire, but it's not directed at the two of them. It's coming from outside the tent.

"Pull back. Fall back," is yelled. The silhouette of a tiger is visible on the hood of one of the patrol cars outside. The headlights of a distant truck illuminate the animal as it leaps. The big cat pounces, landing on someone sheltering by a van and drags them into the darkness.

One by one, the lights on the various police vehicles go out, sweeping from her left to right, moving up toward the entrance on the brow of the hill. There's screaming. A body is thrown into the outside of the canvas. The shape is unmistakable, having landed sideways. It slides to the ground and is pulled away.

Gunfire competes with the thunder, but it loses the battle, slowly falling silent.

Around the edge of the tent, poles lift off the ground. Ropes snap. Support wires break. They ping and twang, causing metallic sounds to resonate through the central metal poles. Olivia looks up. The storm ravages the big top. The canvas tears. Rain pours in, drenching her clothes.

Olivia crouches, leaning over Breezy, trying to shelter her as she bleeds out. The wind howls around them. One moment, they're inside a massive tent. The next, it's gone. In the blink of an eye, the big top is ripped from the ground and sent tumbling into the distance, catching in the trees.

The sideshow alley is in chaos. The rollercoaster has collapsed. The roof on the House of Horrors has been peeled off by the storm. Signs lie scattered on the grass. Several police vehicles have been flipped on their sides, tossed by the storm swirling around them. Trees have snapped in half. It looks like a tornado hit the fairgrounds.

Rain lashes Olivia's face. Mud soaks into her jeans. She can barely see, but she has to look. She has to understand what's happening. Bodies lie strewn in the fields.

A solitary figure walks toward her. Olivia keeps her trembling hands on Breezy's shattered knee. She wants to run. She wants to spring to her feet and sprint toward the forest, but she can't. It's not fear that keeps her there. Whether she likes it or not, she can't abandon Breezy. If Olivia is going to die, so be it, but it won't be due to cowardice.

"I'm not scared of you," she yells into the storm, but it's a lie. She's terrified. She's calling out in a futile effort to instill bravery into her trembling hands.

A clown steps forward with jagged teeth.

"You should be."

Rain sweeps over his dark hair. His face is pale. Blood drips from his mouth. Although he's wearing white gloves, the bones in his forearms are visible. There's no skin. No muscle. Bullet holes pepper his chest, but there's no bleeding.

Breezy is either unconscious or dead. Her eyes have rolled into the back of her head. Her body is limp.

267

Olivia's never been brave. She's never stood for anything other than her bank balance. From her late teens onward, her ethics were defined by pretty clothes and sparkling jewelry. Buster changed that—and yet he didn't. The change was always there, waiting beneath the surface, longing for the real her to awake. Buster knew that. He believed in her, and now she believes in herself—not her looks or her ego. Buster was right. She's more than a facade, more than pretty clothes and youthful looks. She's human.

The clown asks Olivia, "What do you want?"

"Answers."

On either side of the clown, there are circus animals, only like him, they're dead. Their fur is motley. The skull of one of them is visible in the crack of lightning rushing through the clouds. Blood drips from the canine incisors of a baboon.

"Help us," she says.

Another clown walks up behind the first one. Her eyes are different colors. She holds her fingers to her lips, saying, "Ssss-shush!"

"Why?" Olivia asks. The rain hides her tears.

"Can't you hear it?" the dead clown asks.

Olivia looks up. The clouds above her swirl with the formation of a tornado. Dark funnel clouds reach down from the storm. A vortex engulfs the fairgrounds. Bits of timber and broken branches fly past, circling out beyond them.

"Can't you see it?" the female clown asks.

"Yes," Olivia says, feeling her heart beating out of her chest.

Black metal breaks through the cloud cover. It's smooth. There are no angles or edges, no rivets or panels. The storm rolls around the alien spacecraft, consuming it. The underside is as black as obsidian glass.

Fallen poles lift off the ground. Loose ropes rise like streamers. Cages roll across the field, joining the chorus of debris swirling around them. Clumps of sawdust, bits of grass and straw rise with the two women.

Olivia feels herself being drawn toward a single point of light amid the darkness. It shines like a star. Earth drops away. The trees swaying in the forest slip below her. Olivia holds Breezy to keep her from drifting away. The lights of Washington, D.C. are visible through the driving rain. The Potomac winds through the landscape beneath them.

A helicopter races along, staying low over the river. Red and white navigation lights reveal its path as it traces the Potomac. The chopper banks. Its rotors barely miss the treetops. Already, Olivia and Breezy are high above it, looking down on the craft as its spotlight comes on. Vast swaths of the fairgrounds are illuminated. The spotlight sweeps over dozens of bodies and several overturned police vehicles.

The clowns smile.

REVENGE

The blinding light around Breezy forces her to open her eyes.

"You're awake," Olivia says, seeing her move and rushing to her side.

Breezy squints, trying to take in where she is but the brilliant white light reflecting around her makes it impossible to focus. There's no respite from the light. Every surface is akin to a spotlight. The floor, the walls, the ceiling—if there even is a floor, wall or ceiling—are as white as the driven snow.

"Where am I?" she asks. Her throat is dry. She puts her hand out, pushing against what feels like a bunch of pillows. There are no rigid, hard surfaces. Everything's elastic. It's as though she's in a gigantic foam pit. She sits up, and the foam behind her inflates, responding to her motion and keeping her upright.

"Trippy, huh?" Olivia says, dropping down on her knees. White foam surrounds her legs. "It's like walking on marshmallows in here."

"Where are we?"

271

"Dunno," Olivia says, "but look at your knee."

It's only then Breezy realizes she's not in pain.

"What the...?"

The blood that soaked into her jeans has dried. Torn threads lead down to clean, clear skin. She reaches out, taking hold of her leg, suddenly realizing her left shoulder has also been healed.

"How did they?" Breezy asks, still shielding her eyes with one hand. She squints, struggling to make out Olivia's pale form in the saturated white light.

"I don't know," Olivia says. She's squinting as well, but she's not covering her eyes. "You were like that when I woke."

"We were out cold? For how long?"

"How would I know? Your guys took my phone. It could have been hours, minutes, days, seconds. Hell, it could have been months. I dunno."

"I don't understand," Breezy says. "You're not a clown, right?"

"No."

"So what do they want with you? Why did they rescue us? Just because we were there in the tent?"

The light around them fades. As darkness descends, the material they're sitting on becomes transparent, allowing them to see the lights of Washington stretching out below them. It's as though they're floating on a cloud. From the layout of the buildings and the grids marked out by streetlights, they've got to be at least ten thousand feet up above the city. Breezy's flown in and out of Ronald Reagan Airport on the south side enough times to recognize Joint Base Anacostia-Bolling from the air at night.

The dome of the nation's Capitol building is visible to the northeast, with the National Mall stretching out before it. The

Washington Monument looks small at this altitude. It rises over the grass parklands around the mall. The Lincoln Memorial at the far end of the mall is illuminated with spotlights. They're several miles south of the White House, but it's clear that's where they're heading. Arlington drifts by beneath them.

"How are they not seeing this?" Breezy asks. "We should be lighting up on radar."

In the distance, a flight of six F-35 Lightning fighters soars over the city. Like the UFO, they remain below the cloud cover. There are four of them in formation, with two hanging back a few hundred yards. Their afterburners make for a deliberate show of force. If they were on a combat patrol, they'd be separated by several miles and flying at entirely different altitudes in stealth mode. The Pentagon wants them to be seen, but that presents Breezy with a problem. They're not aware of the spacecraft closing in on the White House. If they were, they'd be engaging the UFO. Either that or running.

Above her, a black tube descends from the darkness. Olivia sees it first.

"Umm."

She points as hundreds of tentacles wrap around Breezy's head, neck and shoulders. They're thin, barely the width of a pencil. Suckers attach to her skin. Most of them focus on her temple and forehead.

Breezy screams, but it doesn't hurt. The tentacles holding her head and shoulder stiffen, keeping her still. She calms herself, breathing deeply.

"What are you doing?"

"Look," Olivia says, seeing herself standing on the doorstep of an all-too-familiar office. Far from being thousands of feet in the air at night, they're suddenly on the ground during the day. The sky above is blue and bright. A concrete road stretches alongside the West Wing. A plastic weather shield shelters Buster and the Vice President from the harsh sun. The Secret Service agent is in the shadows. The Jaguar XJS is there, but the viewpoint is all wrong. This isn't how Olivia remembers the afternoon. She's seeing things play out from Breezy's perspective.

The reconstruction of the scene has flaws. Anything not in Breezy's immediate line of sight is missing. Olivia walks over. It seems she wants to examine herself within the hologram. The invisible foam floor shifts beneath her feet, forcing her to step carefully. She reaches out, wanting to touch herself within the vision, but the viewpoint shifts as Breezy recalls sliding across the hood toward her.

Lips move, but there's no sound. It's unnerving drifting with a fixed point of view instead of moving around. It leaves Breezy feeling helpless. At the time, she was in control of what happened. Now, she's a spectator.

Buster lies half on the concrete, half on the grass beside the garden bed. Blood, brains and bone fragments lie strewn on the wall behind him, forming an arc curling toward the bushes. Thick, red goo oozes from the leaves of a nearby plant.

"I didn't know," Breezy says, pleading with the aliens probing her mind. "You have to believe me. I didn't. If I'd known...."

Within the hologram, Olivia crouches, taking hold of Buster's hand. On the alien spacecraft, actual Olivia crouches beside the specter of herself. Tears fall from both cheeks. A hand reaches over her virtual shoulder.

The aliens freeze the image, rotating it and taking a good look at Buster's shattered skull. His mouth is open. A trickle of blood runs from his nose. Blank eyes stare into the distance. His last expression is one of disbelief and shock.

"I'm so sorry," Breezy says, sobbing. The tentacles probing her mind reposition themselves as she moves, searching for her memories. With each change, there's a slight tweak in the brightness, coloration and contrast of the hologram.

The reconstruction continues. There's talking, but the portion of her memories they're tapping into don't contain audio. To Breezy's surprise, though, it does include smell. Fresh cut grass, engine grease and the acrid bite of gunpowder reach her nose. Although it seems impossible, it's no different from the light of the hologram reaching her eyes or the heat of a sun that doesn't exist warming her cheeks.

Director Johnson leads Breezy across the parking lot and into the Executive Office building. Breezy didn't notice at the time, but she hangs back slightly rather than keeping pace with him. This means he doesn't make eye contact as he talks. Instead, his head turns sideways, looking down across his shoulder. The body language of both of them is far more telling than any words. She's subservient. He's condescending. She's a subordinate. She's not his peer.

Back then, Breezy was staring at the ground as she walked into the building so the focus of the hologram is on the fall of her feet on the polished marble. What was she feeling in that moment? Shame? Confusion? Hurt? Her emotional memories are blank. She followed him blindly—like a good soldier.

The director leads her downstairs, through a maintenance door and into the basement. There's a set of furnaces, but they're not running. Insulation lies crumpled on the concrete. Dust is everywhere, but the walkways are mostly clear. Air ducts crisscross the ceiling. Wiring looms stretch along the east wall. Pipes and conduits follow carefully choreographed paths around the building's support pillars.

"I don't understand," Breezy says, not realizing why the memory extends beyond Buster's death.

"It's you," Olivia says. "They didn't come for me. They wanted you."

"Me?" Breezy says as the view shifts. The director walks ahead of her along a dimly lit tunnel. Moisture seeps out of the concrete walls. Water runs in gutters carved into the side of the walkway.

For Breezy, there's an uneasy question plaguing her mind. "Why?"

Her holographic image walks down a set of steel stairs behind the director. Her gun and her phone are dumped into an old wooden set of shelves set to one side. The door is opened and she sees the network of glass offices set on raised springs.

"What is this place?" Olivia says, waving her hand through the hologram. People walk around desks, work away at computer screens and draw diagrams on whiteboards as they talk.

"You used me," Breezy yells. "This was never about us! It was about finding them!"

She reaches up and tears the suckers away, prying them from her skin. The hologram dissolves. They're hovering over Washington, D.C., but now they're almost directly above the White House. Still, there's no sense of recognition from the military or anyone on the ground of their presence.

Her path from the side entrance to the West Wing appears as a red line projected onto the ground. It's probably not visible to anyone other than them, but it traces her route through the access tunnel. The path leads through the Executive Office building and across the road, ending beneath one of the buildings on a side street.

"What is that building?" Olivia asks, pointing at the end of the glowing line.

"I don't know. It's trade or treasury or something like that, but all of this has been about one thing—and one thing alone."

"What?"

"Revenge," Breezy says.

Olivia asks, "That's where the director took you?"

"Yes. It's the base they're using to track the clowns."

"Damn," Olivia says.

The flight of fighter jets circling the city pull in a tight circle, arcing toward them. They've disengaged their afterburners, but they're running with their navigation lights on. They still haven't gone into stealth mode. They still don't realize the danger looming over the capital.

There's a flash of light from the rear of the lead plane. Flames trail through the air. The aircraft are a couple of miles away but moving fast. The lead jet swerves, clipping its wingman. Panels peel away from the wings of the doomed planes. One canopy pops, and then another. Ejection seats roar out into the sky, but the aircraft were tumbling as the pilots pulled on the eject ring between their legs. One seat goes sideways—the other heads down toward the ground at an angle. The seats plunge out of control. Drogue chutes stabilize them. Large white canopies appear, slowly billowing as they inflate.

The wreckage of the two planes forms a fiery meteor streaking over the city, breaking up as it loses altitude.

"They're going to kill them," Breezy says. "Make it look like an accident."

The wreckage of the lead plane strikes first, hitting the forecourt of the building on 17th St, just across from the Executive Office Building. Jet fuel streaks across the road. Flames erupt from the fuselage as it tumbles. The nosecone remains intact. It skids down the road, leaving a trail of flames.

The second plane hits the building itself. A fireball rises into the air. The aircraft catches the corner of the building, tearing through the second floor. Bricks, concrete and glass spray out across the road, covering it in burning fuel. Black smoke rises, billowing onto itself as it reaches into the night.

The front of the building collapses, falling forward into the street and crushing cars parked on the road. Part of the roof gives way, causing the floors below it to pancake. Dust billows along the street. Most of the building is still standing, but the section immediately above where Breezy once stood is buried in rubble.

"You bastards," she yells. "I'm the one that killed him, not them. They didn't want this. It was a mistake. I was too quick on the trigger. But them? They were doing what they thought was right. Don't you get it? They don't understand you. No one does. They were trying to protect us, that's all."

As those words leave her lips, she knows they're not true. Director Johnson may not have intended to drag her into Buster's interrogation, but he saw an opening when the opportunity arose. He'd lost his informant. He needed someone on the inside. He needed a patsy. He kept her in the dark. He knew the clowns could see her on the far side of that one-way mirror in the interrogation room. He faked his death knowing she'd go ballistic. He knew she'd go to the circus and confront the clowns. He wanted her conflicted. His previous mole had failed. The clowns knew that but what if he sent someone they didn't trust? What if they saw her as someone they might be able to turn given time? He was using her to deceive them. Only the clowns were playing her as well. They saw an opening to rid themselves of the surveillance team. Both of them treated her as a useful idiot. They both despised her, only for the aliens, it was with good reason—she killed Buster.

Breezy hangs her head.

It's Sunday evening down there. She's not sure how many people were on duty, but they were no doubt watching what was unfolding at the circus. Did the impact kill the director? She doubts it. Director Johnson's a control freak like her. He wouldn't have been onsite at the circus, but he would have been nearby, setting up a command post. He wouldn't be content to watch from the basement. Did those in the underground base have any warning? Regardless, all of their surveillance has been lost. Burning jet fuel and falling concrete have a way of destroying records, irrespective of whether they're electronic or not. Did they have offsite backups? Would they risk that? Probably not. They've lost years of effort in a matter of seconds.

The aliens have won—and they've won without laying their cards on the table.

The lights of Washington recede below them.

The UFO races into the sky with a burst of acceleration. Olivia collapses, rolling on her back. Breezy wants to watch the planet fall away beneath her. She stiffens her arms, leaning forward with her knees in front of her center of mass, but even if she locks her elbows, she can't hold her weight. Breezy collapses face-first into the transparent sponge-like pillows. Her cheeks feel as though they're peeling off her face by the relentless drag as the ship accelerates. This can't be normal. They're punishing them.

The crush of acceleration is as though someone's piling sandbags on top of her, weighing her down. She blinks, but her blinks become longer and longer. She can no longer move her head. Her eyes peer to one side, seeing the curve of Earth extending beneath her. There's a faint glow on the horizon.

Sunlight blinds her. One moment, there's darkness. The next, she's staring into what could be a spotlight held inches from her face. She knows it's the sun, but she's never seen it so bright. Breezy squeezes her

279

eyes shut. The sun, though, continues to torment her, turning the inside of her eyelids bright red. Veins stretch across her vision. She's lightheaded. Dots appear before her closed eyes. Her lips feel swollen. When darkness finally descends, it's because she's unconscious.

DESERT

Grit sticks to the side of Breezy's face, clinging to her cheeks, lips and chin as she pushes herself off the ground. Dirt blows in her eyes. She's lying on hard, flat bedrock. Breezy blinks, trying to take in her surroundings. Sharp stones litter the desert around her. She presses her arms against the rock, trying to lift herself but her muscles are weak. Instead, she rolls over on her back. The harsh sun lashes her eyes. She squints, covering her face with her hand.

Olivia is lying facedown a few feet from the edge of a water reservoir.

"Hey," Breezy says, glad she's not alone. She reaches out and touches Olivia's shoulder. Even though the sun is hot, Olivia's clothing is icy cold. It's at that point, Breezy touches her own shirt. It's cold, but more than that, there's a light coating of frost clinging to the front of her jeans.

Olivia doesn't open her eyes. She mumbles, "Let's not do that again, okay?"

"Do what again?" Breezy asks.

"The whole dead-clown-spacecraft thing. That was insane."

Olivia sits up on the flat rock. Waves lap softly at the shore not more than ten feet away, but something's wrong.

"Where are we?" Olivia asks.

"I don't know," Breezy replies, looking around them. They're in a depression spanning several miles. The lake seems to stretch on forever, with no shore on the far horizon. The water's dark, bordering on black. Behind her, there's a rocky plateau reaching toward a distant mountain range. A barren desert stretches away from her.

"Are we on another planet?" Olivia asks, although she seems to second guess herself. "That's not a dumb question, right? We were just in an alien spacecraft. We could be anywhere. If this were America, we'd see clouds, contrails from aircraft, birds, stuff like that. Are we even on Earth?"

"I'm pretty sure we're still on Earth," Breezy says, sniffing the air.

"Why?"

"Blue skies. Breathable air. If this is another planet, it's not one in our solar system. I mean, we're not on Mars."

Olivia says, "Mars would be red, huh?"

Breezy shrugs. "I guess."

"Maybe they took us to their homeworld," Olivia says.

"Wouldn't that take years?" Breezy asks. "The stars are a long way away. Besides, if this is their world, why drop us here in the middle of nowhere? Wouldn't they have buildings and bases and stuff?"

"*In the middle of nowhere,*" Olivia says absentmindedly, repeating Breezy's point as she gets to her feet and dusts herself off. "Yeah. They could have dropped us anywhere. Hell, if they wanted to get rid of us, we'd be sucking on the vacuum of space. So why drop us here? That's the question."

"It is," Breezy says, getting up a little slower than Olivia. Her joints ache. Her muscles feel as though they've been sucked dry.

"At least we've got water."

"I wouldn't drink that," Breezy says. "Look at what's missing. No grass. No trees or bushes. No life. Whatever that is, it's not healthy."

"Ah, yeah, I guess," Olivia says, nodding as she looks at the dark, murky lake. "It kinda stinks, huh?"

"So," Breezy says, rubbing her hands together to loosen the tiny stones embedded in her palms. "Which way?"

"That way," Olivia says, pointing directly away from the vast lake.

"Not around the edge of the lake or off toward the mountains?"

"Nope. That way."

"It's uphill."

"I know," Olivia says with surprising confidence.

"Why?" Breezy asks, not seeing any rationale for going in any particular direction.

"Dust cloud," Olivia replies.

Breezy squints. "Can't see it."

"Over there. It's not from a storm. It might be from a vehicle."

"Well, you're optimistic. I can't make it out, but okay. It's as good a reason as any."

The two women walk along the bedrock, following the edge of a shallow, washed-out river. Heat mirages shimmer in the distance. At the top of the rise, they turn and survey the lake from a distance. There's no sign of life anywhere. Reluctantly, they turn and walk on under the hot sun. After a couple of hours, they come across a small cliff rising over a bend in the dried-up river.

"Look," Breezy says with excitement. She points at the cliff.

"What am I looking at," a dehydrated Olivia says, hobbling along on sore feet. Her lips are cracked, while her cheeks are gaunt.

"Shade," Breezy says.

"Oh, yes."

The two women slide down the shale on the edge of the riverbed. Loose rocks slip beneath them. Dust swirls around them. The riverbed is almost fifty yards wide. It's bone dry, but the temperature is several degrees cooler in the shade.

"I vote we walk at night," Olivia says, plunking herself down on the sand and leaning against a rock.

"Sounds good to me," Breezy says, joining her in the shade.

"Why didn't they drop us back in DC?" Olivia asks. "Dumping us in a desert to die of thirst makes no sense."

"No, it doesn't," Breezy says, but she's distracted. For the last few miles, she's been quietly reliving the events of the past few days. Nothing makes sense. Buster. The clowns. Director Johnson. The alien spacecraft. In her mind, they're disjointed.

Out of nowhere, Olivia says, "Feet are ugly. Do you ever think about that?"

"What?" Breezy says, screwing up her face and adding, "No!" It's only then that she realizes Olivia has been walking around with bare feet. For whatever reason, the Secret Service removed her shoes back at the hospital. It probably wasn't out of spite so much as a practical decision. Maybe they thought they contained metal and would interfere with the

MRI. Regardless, she's wandering around the desert without anything to protect her feet.

Olivia flexes her dusty feet. "You don't look down and think, damn, I've got short, stubby, disfigured fingers for toes? I mean, they're nasty! I'm telling you. It doesn't matter how beautiful you think you are. It doesn't matter if you're Brad Pitt or Taylor Swift. Your toes are an abomination unto the Lord."

Breezy shakes her head, trying not to laugh.

"Have you got family?" Olivia asks, followed closely by, "Of course, you have a family. Everyone does, right?"

"I have a daughter," Breezy says, avoiding any talk of her parents or her ex-partner.

"You?" Olivia says, lowering her eyes and staring at her.

"Me. Is that so surprising?"

"Ah, I guess not. It's just...."

"It's just what?"

"You don't seem like the maternal type."

Breezy laughs. "You think Secret Service agents don't have a life?"

"No," Olivia says, being blunt. "Not an ordinary one."

"Oh, it's not ordinary," Breezy says, laughing. "I wish it was. My daughter and I...."

Olivia raises her eyebrows, curious, wanting her to continue.

"Jesus, what am I doing here?" Breezy says, leaning forward with her elbows on her knees and burying her head in her hands.

"It's okay."

"Is it?" Breezy asks, turning to look at her. "Really? Because, last time I looked, we were dying of thirst in some godforsaken desert."

"Tell me about your daughter," Olivia says. For a high-class whore, she's got some heart. Breezy understands what she's doing. When people panic, a clever distraction is the key to stopping them from falling into a downward spiral. Whatever misgivings Breezy had of Olivia evaporate like the sweat from her arms. She's okay.

Breezy sighs. "Alice is seventeen going on twenty-one. She's nothing like me. She's tall and pretty and has a dashing personality, the kind that lights up a room."

"Oh, you light up a room," Olivia says. "With bullets, bombs and explosions."

Breezy offers a wry smile and a slight tilt of her head at that comment. Olivia smiles back. Fake innocence lights up her face. It seems she too needs a distraction. Dark humor has a way of cutting through the gloom.

"Alice and Sue—my ex, my very recent ex—get along so well. Sue's an ER doctor. Alice wants to go into medical research. Me? I'm the odd one out. I send people to the ER. When I didn't come home last night, Alice would have called Sue." Breezy shakes her head, thinking about what would have unfolded. She tries not to cry. "Sue's staying in the short-term apartments across from the hospital. They're used for doctors and nurses pulling crazy hours. I bet Sue nabbed a nursing pass and gave it to Alice. She probably has her wearing scrubs. Alice will think it's a great adventure."

"See," Olivia says. "Nothing to worry about."

"And you?" Breezy asks, feeling uncomfortable and wanting to move the conversation beyond her own personal dramas.

"Oh, everyone gets us prostitutes wrong. People think it's all about blowing rock stars and snorting cocaine off a mirror."

"I—I didn't think that at all," Breezy says, shocked by Olivia's blunt comment. "But it certainly paints a vivid mind picture."

Olivia says, "Sex work is dirty—only it ain't. Sex is normal. It's natural. Enjoying it is natural. We're providing a service."

"A service?"

"Yes," Olivia says. "Me? I don't work the streets anymore, but I've got my regulars. There's Candy Andy, Mark the Shark, Joe the Dildo."

"Joe the Dildo?" Breezy says, bursting out laughing. "Oh, this I have got to hear."

"They're silly names I make up for them," Olivia says. "Although, Joe is well hung. He runs a fancy waterfront restaurant in Georgetown. He's married to his five million dollar bank loan. Works crazy hours. Out of the blue, he'll text me at two in the morning: *you awake?* I am now. Ten minutes later, we're pounding the mattress. The guy has more testosterone than an NFL linebacker. Doesn't want any strings attached. Just a good time. I go down there on Sundays, and he treats me like royalty. Snaps his fingers. Scolds the waiters if they turn their back on me for a moment. Won't let me pay. I tell him, *it's okay. I'd like to. Oh, no,* he says. And then later that night, *Bing!* There goes my phone again."

Breezy smiles, shaking her head. Olivia's describing a world she can barely imagine.

"Then there's Johnny No Marbles."

"No Marbles?"

"He was in a motorcycle accident about five years ago. Lost his—"

"Okay," Breezy says, holding out her hand, not needing any more detail on that point.

"He had it all. Quarterback at college. His girlfriend was a beauty queen. He's shown me some photos. That girl could turn heads a mile away. The accident really messed him up. He was in traction for a couple of months. Still walks with a limp. It cracked open his skull. Left him with a steel plate stretching from his forehead to behind his ear. It's covered in skin, but his hair doesn't grow there anymore, so he keeps his head shaved. It makes him look like a '70s punk rocker. I guess it's easier. Avoids questions: *why do you only have hair on one side of your head?* He's got a big old ugly scar running down his cheek and along his jaw. He went from having everything to nothing in a heartbeat on that cold, wet night. And it wasn't just physical scars. He's got mental ones. Emotional ones."

"And the beauty queen left him, huh?" Breezy says.

"Yep. And he jokes about it. He says he'd leave too if he could."

"And you?" Breezy says.

"I tell him he doesn't have to leave. I tell him he doesn't have to go anywhere. I tell him he's wonderful just as he is. Suicide's always sad. I think I'm the only one that's talked openly with him about it. He told me he sat in his garage with the engine running. He'd brought a length of plastic pipe. He was going to connect the exhaust to his window. He just couldn't see any way out. His phone chimed with a notification from his mother, asking him to pick up some milk on the way over for dinner that night. It snapped him out of it, but he never told her. He couldn't. Me, he can tell. Why? I'm a stranger. No strings attached. No judgment. No shame. I told him, the world would be a colder place without him."

Breezy's quiet.

"He picked the name, you know. Johnny No Marbles. I told him it doesn't matter. He's no less of a man... He cries afterwards. Sometimes it's just a tear in the corner of his eye. Other times, he'll sob into my neck. I wish other women could see beyond his scars. He's a good man."

Breezy nods. "And the whole fake name thing?"

"It makes things easier. No ties. I think that's what they like about the arrangement. Even Joe the Dildo likes his anonymity. Oh, it wouldn't be hard to figure out his real name, but I don't go there. That's private. It's his life. I respect that boundary."

Breezy shakes her head in disbelief, astonished by what she's hearing.

"Neil the Eel brings me gifts."

"Neil the Eel," Breezy says, sniggering. "Ah, do I want to know? I don't know that I want to know. Yes. I want to know. Tell me about Neil the Eel."

"Okay, so Neil the Eel. Drop-dead gorgeous. I mean, blonde hair, blue eyes, long, dark lashes. Curly hair that sits just off his shoulders. The guy's got barely an ounce of fat on him, huge chest, pumped biceps, chiseled abs and a set of butt-cheeks that could crack a walnut!"

Breezy bursts out laughing.

"First time he came to the apartment he was carrying ten red roses in a bouquet. I ask him if he's lost. I say, *Are you sure you're in the right place?* He fumbles with his wallet, stammering as he talks. It's full of cash. *Okay, come on in.* He sits on the bed. I sit behind him and run my nails across his chest. Hell, I'd do that for free. But he only wants to talk. So there I am, sitting cross-legged on the duvet in a beautiful silk negligee, and we talk. Two hours later, he gets up and kisses me on the cheek."

"And that's it?" Breezy asks.

"That's it," Olivia says. "Next week, he arrives with a white box complete with a red bow. It's lingerie. He's got my size right. Damn good guess. I slip out of my clothes and dress in front of him as we chat. He's talking about his dad's mechanical workshop as I'm trying on this lacy bra with a silk butterfly bow in the middle. Still, no sex."

Breezy shakes her head, repeating that point. "Still, no sex?"

"None. So next week, I have candles burning, the lights down low, some Sade playing in the background, and he arrives with this summer dress in a beautiful gift box. It's winter. It's like ten degrees outside. I try it on, flirt with him for a while, and we talk. By this time, I'm getting worried. It's not the drunk assholes that dump you in a ditch; it's the ones with the nice smiles that end up being the psychos."

"But Neil the Eel?" Breezy asks.

"Neil the Eel has a stutter. He tells me he lacks confidence. I don't get it. He's never stuttered with me. He's cheerful and confident when he's in the apartment. Then I remember that first time with the roses. He stammered. *Neil, honey,* I say, reaching over and using a finger to pull his hair away from his face, looping it over his ear. *Am I your therapist?* He nods but can't make eye contact. It's the first time he's been quiet. It's as though he's being told off. Now, I don't know what therapists charge, but whatever. *As your therapist,* I say, *there's something very important we need to do. This is going to help you. Okay?* He nods, and I say, *Think of it as therapy with benefits.*"

"Hah, I love it," Breezy says, forgetting that she's sitting in a dry riverbed in the sweltering heat. "And next week?" she asks as though she's getting updates on a sitcom.

"From there, it varied from therapy one week to benefits the next. Now, he's the Chief Operating Officer of some investment think tank. Makes several hundred thousand dollars a year. He's got a girlfriend, but he still comes around for a chat now and then."

"So just therapy."

"Yep."

"He found his confidence."

"He did."

"Nice."

"And then there's Snow White," Olivia says. "She was my side-hustle. She would set me up with porno shoots and deep fakes."

"Ah. Let me guess," Breezy says. "She's got a bunch of short men working for her?"

"She's dead," Olivia says, killing the conversation for a moment before adding, "I think."

"Oh."

"Our last job was faking the Vice President in an affair. The affair was real, but they didn't catch it on camera. They called us in to recreate it."

Breezy hangs her head. She knows how this story ends.

Olivia wipes a tear. "And then they started killing everyone. Snow. My sister. Me. Only the clowns got to me first."

"That's how you met Buster, huh?"

"Yeah. I—Wait. What the hell is that?" Olivia points out into the middle of the dry riverbed. A black tar-like substance oozes around the bend. It moves like lava, piling up on itself and easing forward, slowly consuming rocks and stones. Its motion is hypnotic, being unlike anything Breezy's ever seen. She and Olivia get to their feet.

"I don't know," Breezy says, walking forward with no sense of fear. She's curious about this treacle-like substance moving slowly over the dusty ground. The two women stand there, watching as grains of sand, grit and dirt swirl on the smooth, flat surface.

"Is this what the clowns wanted us to find?" Olivia asks.

"I don't think so."

By walking away from the cliff, they get a good view along the riverbed. Black tar winds through the canyon, reaching both walls, but it's low. It's no more than a few inches deep.

"Is that a tree branch?" Olivia asks, pointing at a thin, skeleton-like structure caught in the flow.

"Or a tumbleweed?" Breezy says, stepping back, staying four or five feet beyond the leading edge. Neither woman feels in any danger.

"What do you think this is?"

A rumble echoes down the riverbed.

Olivia starts to speak, saying, "I don't think we should be...." But she doesn't finish her sentence. The rest is obvious. Roughly two hundred yards away, white water smashes into the wall of the riverbed. Waves splash over boulders, causing them to tumble forward. Part of the bank collapses, falling into the raging floodwaters.

"Run!" Breezy yells. She sprints, running for the far side of the broad riverbed. The cliff they were sheltering beneath offers no means of escape. They've got to cover thirty yards before they reach the far bank. From there, it's another ten to fifteen yards uphill before they're back on the plateau.

Olivia's not as quick.

Murky, dark water surges around them, washing up over their legs. In the distance, white spray hangs in the air. Waves crash against the rocks. Breezy reaches the bank. Already, the lower section is a muddy quagmire. She pushes hard with her thighs, grabbing at rocks and boulders before her. The roar of the floodwaters is overwhelming. Water swirls in eddies. The flood is upon them. Dry dirt slips beneath her wet shoes. Her jeans are soaked up to her thighs, making them sodden and heavy. Breezy pushes on. Her lungs are burning, but she's learned to ignore her body in a crisis.

A cry for help reaches her ears. It's faint, almost lost in the thunder of the flash flood roaring by just a few yards beneath her boots. Were she to slip, she would be swept away. Breezy ignores the cry. She needs to get to safety. Self-preservation demands she pushes on. She has to make it back to civilization—for Alice, for Susan. There's so much she needs to say. So much she has to change.

"Please!"

Breezy turns her back toward the flood. She can hear it. She knows it's still growing, swelling within the riverbed, but she can't abandon her friend. Olivia clings to a boulder. The fury of the water whips her legs behind her, trying to drag her under. Her fingers cling to the rock. The water rises, submerging her hands. Waves wash over her. She struggles to breathe.

Breezy assesses the situation. The bank between them is made from loose shale, dirt, rocks and sand. Once the water hits it, it's going to be mud. She can get down there quickly, sliding with the debris. She can halt herself on top of the boulder. She can reach Olivia. But she can't get back. Not quickly enough. The river is rising too fast. Go down there and they both die.

Fuck!

Breezy slides down, anchoring her back leg and leading with the front, surfing on the loose shale. Already, the boulder is underwater. A hand reaches out of the torrent. Fingers reach for help.

Breezy lands in the dark water rushing over the boulder. It's less than a foot deep but almost sweeps her off her feet. She reaches out with one hand, holding onto the riverbank, trying to steady herself as she grabs Olivia. She doesn't make the mistake of grabbing her hand. Fingers make for a lousy hold. She reaches a little further, grabbing her wrist. That gives her far more control.

293

Breezy leans back as she pulls against the current. In any other context, she'd flop on her back, but this allows her to anchor her feet and tug Olivia toward the bank.

Olivia is drenched, and that makes her heavy. She splutters, coughing up water. She's disoriented. She's in no shape to climb the bank.

Already, the water is up to Breezy's knees. She can feel the boulder starting to move with the current. She pulls Olivia in close, dragging her right on top of her.

"Hold on," she yells over the crash of waves spraying her with water. Olivia wraps her arms around Breezy's neck and her legs around her waist, still struggling to get her breath. Breezy might be small. She might be slight. Her oversized thighs might be the laugh of the team during training sessions, but today they're going to get her out of trouble. She steps off the boulder into the soft, crumbling muddy bank and pumps her legs. Having Olivia in front of her and needing to go up a slope makes it almost impossible to gain momentum, but her legs refuse to stop. She drives herself upward, dragging mud with her. Breezy's hands guide her. She feels for rocks and pulls on them. Her legs push hard. With each step, she slides back a little. Within a minute, she's cleared the lower, unstable region. She hasn't reached the rim yet, but the rocks here are larger. They give her more to work with.

Olivia climbs down, almost falling from her as she lies on the bank.

"We can't stop yet," Breezy says between breaths.

"I," Olivia says, vomiting. Black water sprays out across the rocks. She spits, clearing the gunk from her mouth. "Know. I know."

Breezy hoists Olivia's arm over her back and drags her on.

They reach the rim and collapse. Below them, the flood races past, washing down toward the lake barely visible several miles in the distance. Waves splash over the rocks, further eroding the bank.

Olivia turns to Breezy, still lying next to her on the rocky ground and says, "I *fucking* hate clowns."

NIGHTFALL

It's late afternoon. Neither of them is in a rush to start walking again. Olivia's in bare feet. Breezy's jeans are caked in mud. They sit on the side of the bank, tossing stones in the river. The water is muddy. Occasionally, a branch or some other piece of debris whips past, revealing how fast the current is moving out in the middle of the river.

Breezy pulls off her shoes and socks and dries them on the rocks. As the sun descends toward the horizon, she hands Olivia the socks, saying, "Put these on."

"Won't you get blisters?"

"Dunno. Maybe." She ties her shoes, pulling the laces tight. "We're not going to get far if you can't walk."

"Thanks," Olivia says, slipping on the socks.

The two women get to their feet. From where they are, the plateau continues to slope upwards. The whole region has the topology of a snooker table with a lean. Dunes have formed on the bedrock, but close to the river, there's only the occasional sandy patch on the ground. The wind seems to prevent dunes from forming near the gullies.

"What's that?" Olivia asks, pointing upriver. In the distance, a thin line runs across the swollen floodwaters. It wasn't apparent during the day, but with the sun setting in the distance, the contrast of colors makes it obvious.

"Is that a bridge?" Olivia asks.

"I think so," Breezy says, getting excited.

They make their way along the riverbank, staying well away from the crumbling edge. The bridge is roughly a mile away. By the time they reach it, darkness looms overhead. Thin clouds high in the stratosphere catch the last rays of the dying sun, lighting up the sky with hints of yellow and red.

"This is good, right?" Olivia says. "I mean, bridges are built for a reason. People want to get from one side to the other. Someone's got to come along here at some point.

Breezy crouches, looking at the track leading to the bridge. It's not a road in the American sense of the word. A single lane of crushed rock stretches in a straight line, disappearing into the desert. It's difficult to see, but vehicle tracks follow the crushed stone. The dunes sweep across the road at points. Fresh tracks on the shallow dunes give Breezy hope. Those couldn't be more than a day old.

The bridge has concrete buttresses on either bank, but it's been built out of railway ties, with the steel railway tracks placed beneath the wooden ties to support them. It's as though someone flipped a section of the railway, but only over the river. Water swells just a few feet below the bridge.

"Someone's got to come along soon," Olivia says, looking around, apparently expecting the cavalry to arrive at any moment.

"Not at night," Breezy replies. "They probably avoid traveling at night as it would be too easy to miss the track in the darkness or drive into a ravine."

Stars appear. At first, there are only a few crystal clear white pinpricks of light. As the darkness grows, there are hundreds and then thousands of stars stretching across the sky.

"Beautiful, huh?" Olivia says, hugging herself against the cold descending on the desert.

"They look different."

"They do," Olivia says. "They're the same, and yet they're not. Yesterday, they were distant suns. They were a mere curiosity. Pretty but nothing more."

"But now," Breezy says, feeling the same sense of awe.

"Now, they're full of life."

Neither woman talks for a few minutes. They're content to sit there under the stars. A cool breeze descends on the desert.

"Where are you from?" Breezy asks.

"Poland."

"Poland?" Breezy says, surprised by her answer.

"My dad was stationed there with the air force. He fell in love with a cute blonde Polish girl, and the rest is history."

"You don't sound—"

"Polish?" Olivia says. "Oh, I've worked hard on shedding my accent. Teens can be cruel. I was ten or eleven when we moved to Arizona. I got teased relentlessly, but *Stajesz się tym, z kim się zaprzyjaźniasz..*"

"What does that mean?"

"It's a polish proverb. *You become your friends.*"

"Oh."

"I so wanted to be accepted, I lost sight of who I really was."

"*The Spectacle*, huh?"

"Yep. Life's easier if you step out on stage and play your part." Olivia points at the brightest star. "What about them? What's life like on their homeworld? Where do you think they come from? I can't help but wonder which star is theirs."

"Dunno."

"But it's got to be close, right? Like you said, space is big."

"It is," Breezy replies. "We see so much and yet so little."

Olivia laughs. "Are you sure you're not a clown?"

"Damn, it's cold," Breezy says, rubbing her arms with both hands. "Just a few hours ago, I'd have done anything to cool down. Now, I'm freezing."

"Yeah, the desert can be like that," Olivia says. "We lived just outside of Palm Springs for a few years. Dad would take us camping in the Mojave. It was about as far removed from Poland as I could imagine. It would get stupidly hot during the day and then stupidly cold at night. I could never get a suntan. I just turned pink and then red like a tomato."

Breezy laughs at that.

"I swore I'd never go back into the desert," Olivia says.

"And here you are," Breezy says.

"Here I am."

Out on the edge of the horizon, where the dark of night gives way to the pitch-black desert, there's a thin beam of light.

"Now that," Breezy says, "is not a star."

Slowly, that single light resolves into several lights darting between the dunes.

"Yes!" Olivia says. "Finally, we can get the hell out of wherever we are. Civilization, here I come."

Breezy says, "I'd sure feel better if I had a gun."

"A gun?" Olivia says. "Are you kidding me? We need transport, not weapons."

"Two women alone in the desert?" Breezy says. "I could do with a bit of insurance."

"We need to hitch a ride," Olivia says. "We can't stay here."

"As much as I hate to admit it, you're right," Breezy replies. "But every instinct I have says hide."

"And you said no one would be out here at night," Olivia says.

"Which raises the question, why are they out here at night? Why risk running off the road at night when it's safer to travel during the day."

"You're overthinking this," Olivia says. "Maybe they don't have a/c. Maybe it's too damn hot. Maybe they prefer to drive around in the cool of night?"

"Maybe."

"Well," Olivia says. "At least we know where we are?"

"Where?" Breezy asks.

"Earth."

Breezy's not impressed. "Okay, I thought that was a given, but all right. We're on Earth. Time to find out where on Earth."

As the lights approach, it becomes clear there are several vehicles in a convoy.

The sound of an old diesel engine drifts on the wind. As the vehicle approaches, Olivia waves her hands over her head. Breezy stands reluctantly to one side. She wants a good look past the lead truck, down the length of the convoy. There are three trucks and an SUV. Beyond that, there's a pickup. There's something on the back of its flatbed, some kind of large metal contraption. A steel barrel points at the stars.

"Anti-aircraft," she mutters, realizing this is why they're traveling at night. "This is not good."

If she could, she'd drag Olivia down the bank or into the dunes, but it's too late. The driver of the truck has seen them. He pulls to one side, allowing the truck behind him to come up beside him. It's a classic roadside military tactic. Vehicles in a line suffer from a lack of visibility. Any firepower further down the line can't be brought to bear on a target. Sure enough, just as Breezy expected, the second truck pulls to the other side of the road, allowing the third truck to come up level with the first two. These guys know their shit. They're now three trucks abreast. That's six headlights on high beam, blinding the two of them. Not only does this illuminate an area the size of a football field, it gives the rest of the team the opportunity to flank them. The SUV has got to be the command vehicle, with the pickup being for defense. They're clearly coordinating over the radio. If Breezy were in that SUV, she'd have a ground unit heading to the top of the nearby dune with a rifle, ready to snipe. If gunfire breaks out, it'll be directed at the trucks, allowing the wide unit to pick off attackers from the side. Her night vision is gone, but she makes out a couple of guys running up a nearby dune. It's poor consolation, but she's not wrong about their tactics.

"Fuck," she mumbles, holding her hands up in surrender.

Olivia has no situational awareness. She's further forward and hasn't seen Breezy raise her arms.

"Hey," Olivia calls out, waving cheerfully. Breezy can't believe how naive she is. She's going to get them killed.

"Get your hands up," Breezy calls out, not wanting to watch Olivia being gunned down by what she assumes are tribal rebels.

"What?" Olivia says, turning to see Breezy standing motionless with her arms high above her. "Oh." She turns back, lifting her hands.

On either side of each of the three trucks, soldiers level AK-47s at them. It took Breezy a few seconds to be able to spot them in the bright lights. They're a little too far forward. She can see the barrels. If she were training this crew, she'd scold them for that mistake. Not only does it make them visible, it reduces their night vision. Just one step back, and they retain considerably more tactical advantage. But, hey, they're up against two unarmed women in the desert.

That no one speaks is telling. Both Breezy and Olivia have spoken in English. They may not have been shouting, but their voices would have carried over the idling diesel engines. These guys either don't speak English or they're disciplined, waiting for their commander. Hah, she thinks. They don't speak English.

The two guys on the dune have continued past them, reaching the riverbank. They're now out of sight. Breezy's not happy.

"*Dyzyňyzda! Dyzyňyzda!*"

Olivia steps back, wanting to get closer to Breezy while still facing forward with her arms raised.

"What's going on?" she asks.

"Stand still and remain quiet," Breezy says, fighting a sick feeling welling up in her stomach.

"*Düşmek! Downere aşak!*"

A lack of compliance is never smart when someone's got their finger on the trigger of a gun. Breezy has no idea what instruction they're being given, but it sounds a lot like '*down,*' and that makes sense given they're clearly being taken into custody.

In a calm, quiet voice, she says to Olivia. "Keep your hands up. Go down on one knee and then the other. Then lie flat on the ground. Keep your hands in sight at all times. When you lie down, keep your arms out in front of you."

"*Onerde ýa-da ot açýarys!*"

"Nice and slow," Breezy says, lowering herself to one knee. She's deliberately slower than Olivia, trying to replicate her compliance while also learning as much as she can about these guys. Olivia's on both knees; Breezy's on one, which leaves her mobile.

Pebbles crunch softly behind her. The wide team has circled around behind them just as she expected. They're going for an active take-down. That means they feel threatened. As two unarmed women in the middle of the desert represent precisely zero threat, these guys are either running drugs or weapons. Either way, they're militia rather than military.

Fuck. Fuck. Fuck.

"American," she says. "We're Americans! Do you speak English?"

"*Amerikaly?*"

It's a bluff on both their parts. These guys would have had their suspicions when they didn't respond in the local language. As for Breezy, she's trying to buy herself a little time by introducing some uncertainty.

Breezy pushes her mind to focus. It's the only weapon she's got.

People underestimate the value of sound. Sight is the primary sense, but Breezy's been trained to use her ears effectively. The subtle

304

difference in the sound of rocks shifting beneath heavy boots is as good as sight. There's an asshole ten to twelve feet back, roughly two feet to her right. He's more concerned about getting directly behind her than he is about getting too close. That's good. It means he's an amateur. The guys in front of her aren't going to shoot one of their own. If he's coming up behind her, he's in the line of fire. She can use that to her advantage.

The soft squelch of sand reveals the second guy. They've both approached. Anyone with any decent training would hold back rather than following along into the danger zone. Asshole number two should be providing cover for asshole number one. That gives Breezy a reasonably good idea how she can escape.

If she lets him get within five feet, he'll be too far away to strike her while being too close to use a long arm like an AK-47. If he's switched to a sidearm, he'll have shouldered the AK-47. That gives him an imbalance. It'll slow his reaction time as the straps on those things are as lousy as their aim. They're designed for parades, not combat. They're loose. They slip off the shoulder too damn easily, and compensating for that will slow down his reaction time.

Breezy visualizes her escape. He's off to her right. If she breaks slightly left, she'll force him to change his point of aim. She'll have her arms down, ready to push any sidearm he has at the ground. He'll fire. He'll hit the dirt, but the confusion will buy her milliseconds. By going left, asshole number two is going to have an obstructed view. That'll stop him from firing. The shooters by the trucks are going to watch this play out. They're not going to fire as they're not under attack and, for at least a fraction of a second, there's uncertainty about what's happening. They're not going to want to risk hitting their guy. Besides, guys are bigger than gals. They'll see this as a mismatched fight. They'll assume he's going to trounce her. Big mistake.

After striking down to disrupt his aim, Breezy's going to rush him, raising her elbow into his throat. Even a casual knock to the windpipe is enough to send most people into a panic. It's the fear of suffocating. He'll react. He'll take a couple of staggering steps and fall into asshole number two. From there, she'll dart past both of them, moving on an angle, using them for cover as she makes for the riverbank.

In her mind, Breezy figures she'll hit the edge of the river in less than a second. She'll be behind all that wonderful, thick, heavy rock and dirt in just over a second. If the guys by the truck do open fire, she's got good cover. From there, it's less than ten feet to the water's edge. The current will pull her out of sight within ten seconds, especially in the low light.

"*Amerikaly, bolýan ýeriňde gal!*"

Olivia is lying prone on the gravel. She's got her arms out. Breezy feels her heart sink. She can't do this to her. She can't abandon her. Breezy's of no use to Olivia if she gets caught as well, but the thought of fleeing eats at her heart. Breezy can't run. A couple of days ago, she wouldn't have hesitated. The rationale is simple: she's of more use to Olivia on the run than as another captive. In reality, once she's in that river, she's not coming back, not without a squad of Marines in support.

Breezy lowers her other leg, kneeling on the rocks with her hands still high above her head. Her ability to react quicker than someone's trigger finger is now gone. Fuck.

Is she getting soft? Has Susan got to her? Running would at least give her a chance at getting back to Susan and Alice alive. Who is she kidding? Even at night, these guys could probably track her down. Or she could drown. Or she could be injured as she's swept down the river, and end up dying from sepsis before she reaches civilization. Or she could die from dehydration in a couple of days after wandering aimlessly in the desert. If she's going to die, it'll be with Olivia by her side. She won't abandon a friend.

From somewhere beyond the lights of the trucks, her nemesis calls out, "*Amerikaly, näme üçin bärde?*"

Breezy doesn't even try to respond. She lowers herself to the ground. There's a rustle behind her. Those two assholes by the river are growing in confidence. At the moment, the best she can hope for is to avoid being struck on the back of the head. Life isn't a movie. There's no such thing as a clean blow to the skull that knocks someone out. It's a myth. The brain is a delicate organ. There's an important evolutionary reason it's surrounded by bone: the skull is nature's version of armor plating. From behind, though, all those nerve connections coming up through the spine are exposed. If she gets struck there, it could kill her or leave her paralyzed as much as unconscious. She rushes, wanting to get down before those two assholes get to her.

Breezy's barely an inch from the crushed rock and gravel when the wooden butt of an AK-47 catches her behind the ear. In that fraction of a second, she's thankful it's a glancing blow. Her forehead, though, smacks into the rocks and she loses consciousness.

Blood oozes on the ground.

DIFFERENT JOBS

Breezy lies on a stiff wooden bench. No mattress. No pillows. No sheets or blankets. Saliva drips from her lips, sticking to the hard, unforgiving plank beneath her. Blood trickles from a cut behind her ear, running down around her neck. It drips through the gaps in the boards, splashing on the muddy floor.

Her eyes flicker.

Stone walls surround her. The smell of rancid shit and stale piss lashes at her nostrils like smelling salts, forcing her awake.

A single light bulb hangs from the ceiling. It's feeble, casting more of a glow than any actual light. Her vision is blurry. Her body aches. The muscles in her neck have seized. They refuse to move. She stretches, opening her mouth and working her jaw loose. With her tongue, she can feel her molars wobble. The gentlest touch against those teeth sends pain shooting through her skull.

Breezy grimaces as she tries to sit up.

Olivia's kneeling in front of the bars of the cell door. She turns slightly to acknowledge Breezy's awake, but she keeps her back to her. Olivia's got her hands up on either side of her face. Her fingers are in motion. Her head rolls from one side to the other. Breezy's confused. Why is she on her knees in the mud by the bars of the jail door?

Breezy blinks, trying to clear her vision and peer out into the corridor. There's groaning, but it's not coming from Olivia.

It takes considerable effort, but Breezy swings her legs down from the bench and pushes her back against the stone wall, sitting upright.

Olivia ignores her. She twists her head slightly, working her face against the bars. It's then Breezy sees the guard. He's standing in the hallway outside. His hairy knuckles grip the rusting bars of their cell. His head rolls back. He looks at the ceiling and moans. His boots shuffle slightly on the dirty, concrete floor. Spasms run down his arms.

"*Ohhhh.*"

Olivia leans back. The guard's belt hangs loose. His trousers are open. He shoves his penis back inside his underwear, laughing. Semen drips from the bars. The guard leans forward. He reaches through the bars, grabbing Olivia's face by the jaw, but not in anger. His fingers are enormous. They touch lightly at her cheeks.

"*Örän gowy, Amerikaly. Gaty gowy.*"

Olivia pulls away, falling back on her butt on the dirty floor. He laughs, slaps the bars and walks off. The guard whistles as he saunters into the distance, cinching his belt tight.

Breezy whispers, "What just happened?"

Olivia holds out an open palm, wanting her to be quiet for a moment. She gets up and leans over a broken sink and spits. Brown water runs from the tap. She scoops some into her mouth and rinses, spitting several times.

"What do you think you're doing?" Breezy whispers in disbelief.

Olivia wipes her mouth with the back of her hand. She creeps over and sits beside Breezy, replying in a whisper. "My job." She holds up a set of keys attached to a ring, but she's careful, holding them so they don't clink together. "I've gotten us out of this fucking cell. Now, you need to do your job and get us the hell out of this godforsaken country."

"Jesus," Breezy says, shaking her head in astonishment.

Olivia doesn't care. "He's going to be asleep in about five minutes. That's when we make our move."

"Five minutes?" Breezy says. "How could you possibly know that?"

"You really don't understand men, do you?" Olivia says, laughing softly. "That guy is an easy mark." She holds up one hand, wriggling her fingers slightly as she adds, "The secret is to tickle th—"

Breezy is swift, cutting her off. "I don't want to know." She stutters. "That. That. That was..."

Olivia completes her sentence. "That was gross, but if it's between that and rotting in some stinking jail cell for the next twenty years, I'll take a blowjob any day."

"Twenty years?" Breezy asks, still trying to catch up to reality.

Olivia says, "Look, I don't speak *wherever-the-fuck-istan,* but there's one word they've thrown around that's all too clear."

"Which is?"

"Spy."

"Oh, fuck."

"Oh, yeah," Olivia says. "Now, if you don't mind, I'd like to get the hell out of Dodge. From what I can tell, they're going to ship us somewhere else tomorrow. A small-town jail like this is one thing; a big city prison is another. Look at me. I'm a busty blonde American babe. I'm a trophy to these guys. I do not want every clown from here to Teheran tapping my ass for the next decade. We need to escape—now! It's now or never."

"Yes, yes. Of course," Breezy says, pushing through the fog in her mind. "Okay. Options. What options do we have?"

Outside, a diesel generator rumbles in the night. Fumes waft in through the window. Breezy stands on the bench, peering into the darkness. The glass is frosted, but it's broken. She reaches through the bars and pulls at the fractured shards. After working a section loose, she gets a good look outside. The trucks from the convoy are parked on the other side of a broad, dusty road. There's a bar over there, complete with lots of talking and yelling. Light spills out onto the gravel road.

"Okay, the bar is good news," she says as Olivia joins her, standing on the bench seat beside her. "It'll cover any noise, and it means your friend is probably the only one on duty. Everyone else is getting drunk. I doubt they get Coors out here. They're probably drinking something that borders on unrefined aviation fuel, and that gives us a tactical advantage."

"An advantage?"

"They ain't gonna be able to shoot straight."

"Well, that's good to know."

"Look at how they've parked their trucks," Breezy says, pointing between the bars. "They've come into town the wrong way—from the wrong direction."

"So?"

"So they're facing the wrong way down the street. They've crossed onto the other side."

"I don't see how that helps us," Olivia says.

"Fuel tanks," Breezy says, pointing. "See how the fuel tanks are facing us. They can't see them from the bar."

"And?"

"And that means we can unscrew the caps and pour some dirt in. That'll fuck up any pursuit."

"Don't the engines have filters to stop that kind of thing?" Olivia asks.

"Yes, but they're designed to stop small bits of grit. We'll clog them up and grind them to a halt."

"Nice," Olivia says. "And then what? Hotwire the SUV?"

"Oh, no. It's going to get some dirt as well. We're taking the flatbed."

"The one with the gun?"

"That pickup is a Russian Gaz 4x4. It'll drive over anything. Hell, the engine is so old and antiquated, it'll keep running with a dozen bullet holes in the block."

"And you know this how?" Olivia asks.

"My first ex, Alice's dad, is a Navy SEAL. He loves all this nostalgic Russian shit. If we get back to the US, he's going to want to know everything—every last detail." She points further down the road. "That thing on the back. That's a Soviet-era twin-barreled anti-aircraft cannon. It'll fire something like a 20mm or a 25mm round."

"And that's big?" Olivia asks.

To be fair, to the uninitiated, 25mm sounds small. Breezy, though, is excited. She says, "Big enough to bring down an elephant. I dare those bastards to follow us. Dear God, I'd love to fire that thing. Anything smaller than a tank is going to be turned into a steaming hot pile of fresh camel dung."

"Okay, so we've got a plan," Olivia says. "I'll drive, and you pick off anyone dumb enough to follow us."

Breezy smiles. "We can only hope."

"You really want to fire that thing, don't you?"

"So badly. So, so badly," Breezy says, chuckling. "You have no idea."

She hops down with the shard of glass still in her hand.

"And what about Dopey?" Olivia asks.

"I'm going to need one of those socks back."

Olivia pulls a sock off her foot and hands it to Breezy. She wraps it around the glass, allowing her to hold it in her palm like a knife.

"You're going to kill him?"

"Well, I wasn't going to kiss him," Breezy says. She holds up her makeshift knife, saying, "If ever you need to kill someone, take a knife, a screwdriver or even a piece of glass and strike at the carotid artery in the side of the neck. There's one on either side of the windpipe. Puncture that, and he's unconscious inside five seconds. Dead within ten."

Olivia reaches through the bars of the door and fiddles with the keys, quietly inserting the biggest one into the old, rusted lock. "I think I'll stick to blow jobs."

"I won't kill him if I don't have to," Breezy says, peering along the corridor at an angle as Olivia works with the key.

"So you do have a heart."

"Not quite," Breezy replies. "Leaving a trail of dead bodies is a surefire way of pissing people off. And that'll make them more determined to chase us. If he's asleep, we'll sneak past."

The lock clicks. Olivia winds the key. The bolt within the lock turns. She opens the door. It squeaks on its hinges. The two women slip through and into the corridor. The lighting is dim. At the end of the hallway, the guard is leaning back in his chair with his boots up on the desk. A television is playing. There's laughter, but the dialog isn't in English.

Breezy whispers. "Lock the door."

"What?" Olivia whispers, unsure of herself.

Breezy points at the guard. "We'll leave the keys on the desk."

"Why?" Olivia asks, pulling the door closed and locking it again. It must seem stupid to risk more unnecessary creaks and groans coming from their jail cell, but Breezy has her reasons.

"Confusion is our ally. Uncertainty is our friend."

Olivia shrugs, not understanding.

Breezy creeps along the hallway, whispering, "Anything that confuses these guys will delay them, and that buys us time. This will leave them scratching their heads as to how we escaped."

Olivia nods.

They work their way along the far side of the hallway, keeping to the shadows. The guard snores. Breezy keeps her glass shiv at the ready. Olivia steps forward beside the officer. To Breezy's horror, Olivia wants to replace the keys on his belt. Breezy's already standing by the door. She shakes her head and waves her arms, wanting to shout at Olivia. Her fingers tighten on the shiv. The sharp edge of the glass cuts through the cotton sock.

Olivia crouches beside the guard. She hangs the keys back on a leather loop on his belt. It needs to be fastened by clipping two studs together. Undoing it took some work, but it must have come apart without too much movement as he didn't notice. Snapping it closed, though, seems impossible.

Breezy slides her boots across the floor, edging closer to Olivia. She wants to grab her and drag her out of the door. She's holding the shiv like a dagger, ready to plunge it into his neck if he so much as rocks in his chair.

Olivia sees her. She holds out her hand, gesturing for patience. Olivia positions the studs on top of each other and squeezes them together, slowly building pressure. There's a slight *snap,* but it's no louder than the chatter on the black and white television.

Olivia stays low, backing away from the guard. She reaches up on his desk, taking his coffee mug. Breezy wants to scold her. She can hardly wait until they reach the road. The two women slip out through a swinging door and into the dusty street.

"What are you thinking?" Breezy asks. "You're taking souvenirs? Really?"

"No," Olivia says, bending and scooping up the grit from the roadside. "It's for the fuel tanks."

Breezy shakes her head, smiling. She's misread Olivia one too many times. They might be from different worlds, but she's smart. It seems courage isn't confined to wielding a Glock.

"You're all right," she says, smiling and squeezing her shoulder.

"I know."

Breezy whispers, "Okay. We need dirt. We want something that's going to dissolve. Sand's okay as the fine grit will dissolve. Dirt is better. Stones won't do anything."

"Okay."

Now they're outside, the two of them get their first good look at the town. At a guess, it would have under a thousand inhabitants. The street is broad, being set on the outskirts of an industrial area. Lights dot the hillside where rundown shacks double as houses. Unfinished cinderblock walls support rusting corrugated iron roofs. There are no windows as such, just square holes in the brickwork. A few of the homes have glass. Most use curtains instead.

Behind the jail, there's nothing but the vast, flat, featureless plain of the desert. For all appearances, it looks as though the town was built here simply because there happened to be a hill in the middle of nowhere. Breezy realizes it probably stemmed from a more practical decision, like access to water or being on a trade route, but life here looks bleak.

The road is wide enough for several vehicles to drive abreast in either direction, but it's doubtful there's ever that much traffic. There's no concrete, just more of the same crushed gravel they saw out by the bridge. No street markings. No street lights or street signs. The bar on the other side of the road is the only place that's open. Shadows move in the pale light. Laughter fills the air.

Breezy walks across the road toward the trucks without a care in the world. Olivia hurries beside her.

"Shouldn't we be crouching or something?"

Breezy says, "If we don't look out of place, we're not. Act natural. People ignore what they expect to see."

Olivia doesn't sound convinced. "Ooooh-kay."

They cross behind the cab of the first truck. The diesel fuel tank is located beside the steps leading to the door of the cab. There's a lock on the cap. Breezy is undeterred. She twists, expecting the lock to catch, but the cap comes away in her hand. The lock is broken. Security tends to take a back seat to convenience. Someone got sick of climbing back into the cab for the keys. She looks at the lock. They've hacked at it with a crowbar. They probably lost the gas key.

Olivia sorts through the cup full of dirt and rocks, saying, "I think we're good."

Breezy cups her hand around the metal tube leading down into the tank. Olivia pours, shaking the cup gently. Fine grains of sand and grit run over Breezy's fingers. They'll have all sorts of dust and dirt clinging to them.

"I still don't get it," Olivia says. "Why send us here? Why did the clowns drop us in the middle of this fucking desert?"

"I don't know," she says, replacing the cap.

"They could have dropped us anywhere," Olivia mumbles as she crosses the road to get some more dirt and sand from the far gutter. "Paris would have been nice. Venice. Tokyo. Hell, I'd settle for Baltimore."

Breezy moves on to the second truck. The cap on the diesel tank is stiff, but it too has a broken lock. Behind her, in the bar, there's a ruckus of noise. Someone's celebrating something. Over the banter, Breezy hears a loud clicking, only it's from the other side of the road. She looks up. Olivia's snapping her fingers and pointing at the first truck. Someone's standing by the rear wheels. Urine hits the tires. Steam rises into the cool air.

Breezy freaks out. They've been busted. She's got her glass shiv in her back pocket, but this guy is easily twenty feet away. From his silhouette, it's clear he's got an AK-47 shouldered. Even if she could get to him before he slipped that down, he's going to squeal like a pig once his throat's been slit. If he's got a handgun, she won't get close enough to use her makeshift knife.

Fuck. Fuck. Fuck!

318

He calls out, *"Goý, şol derýa aksyn!"* But there's something in the way he's speaking that transcends mere language. He's not yelling *at* her. This isn't a cry of alarm. It's banter. He's being friendly. He thinks she's pissing on a tire as well.

Breezy turns her shoulder away from him slightly, not wanting the outline of her figure and especially her breasts to give her away. She leans back, holding her hands in front of her groin in mimicry of him and laughs out loud. She keeps her chin low near her chest, trying to hit a few deep, masculine notes. To her, it's not convincing.

He wanders back between the trucks, saying, *"Içýäris. Biz jyns edýäris. Ertir bolsa söweşeris."*

Breezy grunts, hoping at least tacit acknowledgment is enough. She adds a couple of laughs for good measure.

Olivia comes running up beside her, whispering, "What the hell are you doing?"

"Pissing like a man," Breezy says. "Like an extremely drunk tribesman!"

"We need to get the fuck out of here!"

"No shit," she replies, taking the cup from Olivia and tipping it into the tank.

There's a metal toolkit mounted on the side of the truck beside the fuel tank. Olivia rummages around within it, pulling out a screwdriver. She continues to the third truck as Breezy replaces the fuel cap.

"What are you doing?"

Olivia fiddles with the side of the tank. "Improvising."

She uses the screwdriver to loosen a clamp on a rubber hose. Diesel begins leaking onto the road.

"I like it," Breezy says, moving on to the SUV. She grabs a length of 2x4 wood from the back of the last truck. As there are several bits of wood all roughly the same length, it looks like they're used for leveling loads. She works it up beneath the wheel guard on the SUV, shoving it hard against the tire. Breezy jams the wood into the front support struts. It's out of sight from the road. Although it would be visible in the daylight, someone would need to crouch to spot it in the dark.

"That should at least cause some steering problems."

Olivia jogs past, heading for the pickup. Quietly, she climbs into the unlocked passenger's seat and slides across in front of the steering wheel.

Breezy opens the glovebox and starts shuffling through papers. "Look for a spare key."

"Way ahead of you, champ," Olivia says. She stabs the screwdriver into the ignition and turns it. The diesel engine splutters into life. "Where to?"

"Ah," Breezy says, freezing for a second. She hadn't thought about where they were going. Anywhere other than here sounds good. Getting this far was a victory in itself. She assumes they're facing in the direction of travel, meaning they came from somewhere behind them, but the convoy could have driven around the side of the town. It's rare for Breezy to get flustered, but getting to the end of a sequence of events, she arrives at a blank. She can't just say *anywhere*. They need to maximize their escape. They need to be heading in the right direction, but what is the right direction? Fuck.

Olivia looks nervous. She points at the bar. A couple of men stand out the front, holding bottles in their hands. They're looking right at them. Whether they can see them or not is debatable as they don't seem alarmed. In the low light, they probably can't see Olivia within the cab, but they can hear another diesel engine beyond the generator.

"We need to go. Now," Olivia says.

Breezy finds a map in the glovebox. She stretches it out on the seat, trying to make sense of it. She turns it one way and then another. There are no obvious features, like the lake where they were abandoned by the clowns. Lines crisscross the desert, converging on a few points. Those must be towns.

One of the men calls out, "*Haý, sen! Näme edýärsiň?*"

"I think we're here," Breezy says, pointing at the map. She's thinking tactically but now is not the time. Her training, though, demands precision. She's been taught to avoid reacting, as that can make things worse. Smart moves are planned moves—that was the mantra at the academy. She fusses with the map, frustrated by the lack of landmarks and the foreign notations.

"Get in," Olivia says, putting the pickup in gear. "I don't care where we are. Right now, we need to be anywhere other than here."

"Fair point."

Breezy jumps on the back of the pickup with the map. She clambers into the seat of the anti-aircraft cannon for no other reason than it's got padded cushions. Olivia pulls a u-turn and then turns again at the first intersection. Breezy looks back as they go around the corner. The two men are still standing there talking. They don't seem bothered by what they've seen. Perhaps they're not part of the convoy.

Olivia is relaxed. She's not in a rush, which is good. She's not drawing attention to them. She pulls open a sliding window at the back of the cab, allowing them to talk.

"See that sign?" she says, pointing as they drive through the slums.

Breezy looks over her shoulder. There are a bunch of unusual characters. They're neither English nor Arabic.

"Yeah," Breezy says, trying to match the symbols with something on the map, but the light is too dim.

"I'm going to head toward that. Maybe it's a city."

"Umm. Okay," Breezy says, folding away the map. Her teeth hurt. Her ear throbs. She can't think straight. Heading toward a city might be a good idea; it might be a terrible idea. She isn't sure. She needs time to settle herself.

Once they're out of the town and well clear of any danger, they can stop and examine the map using the headlights. Until then, she needs to quell her OCD. She busies herself, examining the anti-aircraft gun. Firing it seems easy enough as there's a big ass trigger inside the handle, but she's not sure how to cock it or how to reposition the barrel. There's a two-handed lever that winds, lowering the gun. She works it with her arms, but that only translates to a slight movement. Either she's doing something wrong, or this thing is next to useless against a moving target. She's got to be doing something wrong. A Glock is much simpler.

They drive past a few well-lit areas within the town. There's a gas station and what looks like a convenience store.

Olivia throws on the brakes. The pickup slides to a halt on the gravel. Breezy is thrown back in her chair.

"What's wrong?" she says, twisting around to face Olivia.

"Buster?"

"What?" Breezy asks. "What are you talking about?"

"I just saw Buster. Back there. In the forecourt of the gas station."

"Not possible."

"I'm telling you, it's him. Short and stocky. Hairy chest. Scars all over his arms. Rainbow-colored suspenders."

Olivia swings the pickup around. She drives into a dark alley beside the gas station. Breezy stands up on the back of the flatbed. She leans over the cab, trying to get a good look at the guy rushing along the alley ahead of them.

"Buster?" she calls out, seeing someone familiar in the headlights.

Buster turns and looks at them as though he's seen a ghost.

BUSTER

Buster runs.

What is he thinking? They're in a truck. He can't outrun them—not in a straight line. He sprints down the alley, pumping his arms.

"Stay with him," Breezy yells. "If he goes over a fence, you stay with the pickup. I'll follow on foot."

"You got it," Olivia says, accelerating down the narrow dirt road. She rolls her window down, coming up behind him. "Buster. It's me. Olivia."

Buster breaks to the right, cutting down a narrow gap between the houses within the slums. Breezy jumps from the back of the pickup. All the pain is gone. Adrenaline overrides every nerve cell in her body. She runs after him.

Wooden planks link together, providing a walkway over a drainage ditch. A thin trickle of water runs along the center of the open drain. From the smell, it's sewage.

The ditch isn't straight but leads roughly in one direction, winding between the huts. Worried faces appear at broken windows, watching from the shadows as they sprint past. Out here in the desert, nothing gets discarded. Anything can be building material if you try hard enough—and these people are hard. Car hoods with bullet holes form walls. A truck door hangs in the doorway of a ramshackle home. Torn sheets of plastic catch in the breeze as they rush past. Mud has been plastered inside chicken wire to form walls. A severed airplane wing forms the longest straight section of the laneway.

Buster pushes off concrete bricks as he rounds turns in the bend. His shoulder collides with sheet metal.

"Wait," Breezy yells, chasing after him.

He panicked, but why? The look in his eyes—it was as though he didn't recognize them. He was in the headlights, so he may not have been able to make them out, but he must have recognized their voices. At the very least, two American women calling out to him in English in the middle of this place must have struck a chord. Someone's after him. Someone other than them. That's the only reason he'd run. What the hell is he doing out here anyway? He's dead. He was dead. Breezy shot him. She saw the back of his head explode. Are the clowns fucking with all three of them?

Headlights move in parallel with her, trundling along the next street. Olivia's smart. Breezy likes her style. Being in the pickup, she could easily race ahead. Although she can't see Buster or Breezy, she's keeping roughly on pace with them, hedging him in. On one side is the main road. He just ran away from there. He's not going to go back that way. Breezy's behind him, so he can't double back. Olivia's on the other side. He's out of options. He can only go one way. And he can't run forever.

Breezy jumps a low wall. She's gaining on him, but he's still barely a shadow pounding on the wooden boards ahead of her.

"Buster. Stop," she yells between breaths. "We don't want to hurt you. We just want to talk."

Ahead, the slums come to an end. There's a broad, empty gravel road before the squalid homes continue on the other side. Olivia gets there slightly ahead of them. She turns, coming to a stop with the headlights of the pickup illuminating the street.

Buster stumbles. His arms go flying as he tries to keep his balance. He flails about. He's hurt. Blood drips from the side of his leg. He's caught his trousers on a nail or some of the corrugated iron in the darkened alley.

He turns and limps on, almost tripping over his own feet as he crosses the road bathed in the headlights. Olivia's out of the cab. She stands beside the hood of the vehicle.

"Buster please," she says, pleading with him.

Breezy comes to a halt on the street, giving Buster plenty of room. He's in no condition to continue running, but she doesn't want him to feel trapped.

"Buster. What's happening?"

He leans forward with his hands on his knees, sucking in air. Between breaths, he says, "Not—Buster!"

"What?" Breezy says, walking slowly across the street. As she steps into the headlights, she looks at the blood splatter on the dirt, wanting to assess how bad his injury is without seeing it. From the way he's favoring one leg over the other, she thinks he's nicked his upper right thigh. It'll hurt like fuck, but he can probably still run with a hobble. There's not enough blood loss to be problematic, but it will leave a nice trail to follow.

"If you're not Buster," she asks with her hands out wide, showing she's unarmed as she advances on him, "Who the hell are you? And why did you run?"

"Chester," he says, standing upright. "We're brothers. Twins."

Breezy and Olivia exchange looks.

"But you're one of them?" Breezy asks. "You're a clown?"

Chester laughs. "A clown? Yes. Oh, where do I start? Okay. I'm a clown. I'm a real clown. I run a circus." He points at the sky, adding, "I am—*not*—one of them!"

"We need your help," Olivia says.

"Oh, no, no, no," Chester says, waving his hands in front of him and backing up toward the shadows. "You're not dragging me into this. Get Buster. He's the one you want. Go talk to him."

"He's dead," Breezy says, feeling it's best this news comes from her.

"What?" Chester says, stumbling forward into the light. He turns his head sideways, looking at her with astonishment. He holds his hands out toward her, but it's theatrical. He's not trying to grab her. It's as though he's struggling to express words with his hands. "No, no, no. That's not possible. They won't allow it."

"He died yesterday," Olivia says.

"Oh," Chester says, coming to a halt in the middle of the gravel street. He hands his head. "Oh, no. We're fucked."

Olivia says, "Oh, yeah. We kind of figured that out for ourselves."

"If—If he's dead. It's over."

Breezy steps toward him. "What's over?"

"Everything. He was the only one holding it all together."

"Holding what together?"

Chester points at Breezy. His hands are shaking. His fingers tremble. "How did you find me?"

To Breezy, it seems obvious, but he must be assuming they flew into the country and tracked him down using the CIA or something. She's not sure how to say she was abducted by aliens. She blurts out, "They dropped us off," knowing he'll understand.

"Them?" he asks, pointing at the sky, wanting to be sure.

"Them!" Olivia says, pointing into the darkness above her.

"Where?"

"By a lake."

Chester gets angry. "Be specific, woman. *Where* by the lake? Tell me exactly what you saw. Leave nothing out. Do you understand? I need to know precisely where they put you down."

"Ah, there was nothing around us," Olivia says, shrugging, unsure what else she can say.

Breezy says, "We were dropped in the desert. We woke about ten feet from the shore of some stinking, smelly cesspool."

"Were there any plants? Any bushes? Any trees? Any grass?"

"No. Why?" Olivia asks.

Breezy says, "There was a dried-up riverbed leading down to the lake."

Chester shakes his head. He raises a clenched fist to his lips, but it's not aggressive. If anything, it's out of frustration. He mumbles something incoherent.

"What?" Breezy asks, stepping closer, and walking further into the headlights. Long shadows stretch from her legs, disappearing down the street.

Chester looks at her, saying, "It's where they crashed. That's where he first met them. Nothing grows there anymore. The fish died. The grass shriveled. But he kept going back there. He helped them. He talked to them like no one else ever could."

"We need your help," Olivia says.

Chester lowers his head, looking at his boots.

"For Buster," Breezy says.

"For Buster," he replies, limping toward the pickup. "Take me back to my car. You can follow me to the circus."

"Another circus," Olivia says, raising her eyebrows as she looks at Breezy. "Great."

"This'll be fun," Breezy says, climbing on the back of the pickup.

Chester sits in the front with Olivia. As she drives back toward the gas station, he asks, "Where did you get this?"

"We stole it."

"Oh. You know they're going to be looking for it, right?"

"We know," Breezy says. She's figured out the controls for the anti-aircraft gun. There are bicycle-like pedals that control the lateral motion from left to right, while the handles she turns with her arms determine up and down. She lowers the cannon, pointing it directly behind them, imagining the recoil when it fires. The anti-aircraft gun is mounted on the flatbed with bolts. It's probably not intended for firing while on the move. The kick is going to play havoc with the steering.

"Where are we?" Olivia asks.

"You're in *Kindzhak*."

"Ooooh-kay," Olivia says with sarcasm, trying to avoid potholes.

Chester points in various directions as they drive along the dusty road. "We're at the heart of the crossroads of Asia. This is the meeting place of many nations. The border between Turkmenistan and

Uzbekistan is about three miles that way. Just over the mountains. Afghanistan is roughly ten miles south of here. Tajikistan is maybe fifty miles east, while Iran is no more than three hundred miles southwest of us."

Olivia's chirpy. "I knew we were somewhere in the *'Stans.*"

Breezy sits sideways on her chair so she can face the cab of the truck. "What are you doing here? You're an American, right? Why are you even in this hellhole?"

"Because it is a hellhole," Chester says. He shakes his head. "You wouldn't understand."

"Try me."

He laughs, pointing down the street at a car parked in the shadows. "Pull over. Soon, you will understand. Follow me and you will understand."

Olivia pulls over and lets him out. Chester walks toward a beat-up Toyota Corolla from the 1980s. He yanks on the handle of the old rusted car door. It's on the verge of falling from its hinges. It opens and he plunks himself down in the seat in full view of their headlights. It takes him a couple of attempts to close the door properly. The window is down. He waves with his hand for them to follow him.

"Do you trust him?" Olivia asks as they pull out behind Chester.

"No."

Breezy abandons the anti-aircraft cannon. She holds onto the rim of the open cab window and slides into the front seat. They drive into the desert for several miles. There are no lights beyond their headlights. Breezy's not even sure they're following a road. The suspension in the pickup is shot so they feel every sharp rock rattling through the cab. Chester's car kicks up dust. The headlights can't penetrate the gloom, reducing their visibility to fifteen feet.

Breezy reaches under the seat, searching for anything that might be useful. She pulls out a first aid kit. It's almost empty but there are a few foil-blister packs containing tablets. At a guess, they're painkillers.

"You want some?" she asks Olivia.

"Random drugs? Nah. I'm good."

"Suit yourself," Breezy replies, slipping a few into her mouth. It's difficult to swallow without water but she gets them down.

Chester turns off what was, by comparison, a road and onto a rough, undulating dirt track. Although he rushes ahead, Olivia can't go more than 10 mph without being in danger of bouncing through the roof of the cab.

"Where the fuck is he taking us?" she asks, not that Breezy knows.

"Which country are we in?" Breezy asks her in reply, joking with her. "If we really are at the crossroads, we could have passed through several countries by now."

"No borders, huh?"

"Not beyond lines on a map."

Red brake lights appear through the dust. They pull over and stop next to a bunch of wooden trailer homes with oversized tractor tires on their wheels. Lanterns on poles mark a camp on the edge of a forest at the base of the mountains.

"Hey, I recognize those," Olivia says as the antiquated trailers are illuminated by the pickup's headlights. "Buster lived in an old trailer home like this behind the big top."

Breezy says, "If shit goes down out there, make your way back here. The first one back starts driving clockwise around this place until the other one can get to them, and then we flee. Agreed?"

"Agreed," Olivia says as they climb out of the pickup. She leaves the screwdriver/key lying on the bench seat. "But I don't think it will. I've got a good feeling about this."

A woman rushes to Chester's side as he gets out of his car. She's seen the blood soaking his jeans. They talk in the local language, with him dismissing her. The woman fetches a first aid kit, but it's white with a red crescent instead of a red cross. She stands back as he talks to them.

"You want to know why I'm here in this hellhole?"

Breezy nods, looking at the various circus vehicles. Paintings of lions jumping through fiery hoops adorn the canvas side of a large truck. Beyond that, there's a flatbed pickup with thick tent poles and piles of neatly folded canvas. Camels graze. An elephant lies on a bed of straw. It's awake and watching them but doesn't seem alarmed. A few dogs walk around. Their ribs are visible through their scrawny hides. A couple of older men sit around a fire chewing what she assumes is tobacco. There are several other vehicles in the background, but in the darkness, she can't make out too much beyond ornate letters advertising a traveling circus in a foreign language. One of them has a smiling clown face. Of course, it does.

Chester leads them to the truck with the canvas sides. He slaps the canvas, calling out, "دى ملګرى دوى زه‌راوو. ده سمه داد."

"What's that you're speaking?" Breezy asks, realizing this isn't the same language used by their captors back at the bridge.

"Pashto," he says. "It's spoken in Iran, Pakistan and Afghanistan."

"And what did you say?"

"I told them, it's okay to come out. You're friends."

A child's face appears at the edge of the canvas. Her eyes are like emeralds. Although her cheeks are grimy and her hair's straggly, there's a sublime beauty to her smile.

Chester holds his hand out, saying, "شی ودار چې نشته شی هيځ."

"And now?" Breezy asks.

He smiles, looking at her and saying, "There's nothing to fear."

The child's mother appears. She's as beautiful and radiant as her daughter.

"You're smuggling them out of the country," Olivia says.

"Out of *several* countries," Chester says. "Taking them along the Silk Road. Over the next month, we will perform shows between here and the Caspian Sea. Once there, we will hand them off to the captain of a local trawler, who will take them to Baku in Azerbaijan. From there, they can go to Armenia, Georgia or Turkey and on into Europe, where they can apply for asylum. For them, one life is coming to an end. Another is yet to begin."

"They're refugees," Breezy says as several more faces appear at the opening in the canvas. They chat happily with each other, pointing at the two American women as they hop down from the truck. They're easily excited.

One woman in particular, catches Breezy's eye. She's wearing a beautiful silk headscarf. She holds it closed with her hand up in front of her face. Her eyes peer out of the shadows.

"Tell her, it's all right," Breezy says. "Tell her, we're pleased to meet her and her friends."

Chester speaks with the young woman at length in Pashto. She's reluctant, but her head covering doesn't seem to be religious. After much nodding and encouragement from Chester, she opens the scarf. Her face is hideously scarred. The hair on her head is patchy, having been burned off. The skin on her forehead has partially melted over one eye. Her cheeks have drooped, deforming her swollen lips. She's nervous. She tries to smile, but it's lopsided. She looks away, embarrassed.

"It's okay," Breezy says, reaching out her hand and taking hold of her fingers. Chester doesn't translate. He doesn't need to. The kindness in Breezy's voice is enough. The woman makes eye contact. Breezy squeezes her hand. "No one's going to hurt you. I promise." Again, Chester is silent. The woman daubs at her eyes, but no tears fall. She nods slightly, moving out of the way so the others can climb down, but Breezy walks along with her, not wanting her to disappear into the shadows.

"Her husband," Chester says. "He threw battery acid on her."

Breezy shakes her head. Anger wells up within her.

"It's common," he says. "Men get jealous. They blame women for their failings."

Breezy grits her teeth. She's torn. Her blood is boiling with indignation at the injustice this woman has endured. Deep down, though, Breezy hurts. It's the helplessness. There's nothing she can do for this woman, and that leaves her with an ache gnawing at her heart. She desperately wants to make things right, but she can't. Her mind casts back to her conversation with Susan in the bar. Breezy was obstinate and in control, or so she thought. Susan tried to tell her that not everything could be fixed, but she didn't listen. Now, looking into this woman's eyes, Breezy understands. There's a serene sense of calm beyond those dark eyes. Regardless of any language barrier, there's intelligence in her piercing gaze.

Breezy says, "Tell her, she's brave coming here. She's brave risking her life for something better. Tell her, she's the bravest woman I know."

هغه چې ښځه زړه ټولو تر .ياست زرور تاسو ،وايي هغه" ,Chester says
".يې دلته چې وياړي دې په بايد ته چې .پوهيږی

The woman lowers her head. Her lips quiver. Gently, Breezy reaches out, wrapping her arms around her. The woman's reserved. Breezy doesn't know anything about her culture or even if touch is comforting given her horrific burns, but she wants her to know what it means to feel accepted. Breezy gives her the opportunity to pull away if she wants, but the woman reaches behind her back and buries her head in her shoulder, holding her tight.

"You're beautiful," Breezy says with tears running down her cheeks.

Chester translates. "ته ښکلې يې."

"You have a beautiful, courageous soul. Never doubt that."

"تاسو يو ښکلی، غيرتی روح لرئ. هيڅکله په دې شک مه کوئ."

The woman breathes in deeply. Breezy can feel the woman's chest swelling with the rush of emotion. She leans back, gently holding her shoulders, unsure what else she can say, but the woman beats her to it.

"Thank—you."

Her words are coarse, being spoken with a heavy accent and unsure timing. She probably only knows a few English phrases.

"You take care of yourself," Breezy says as the woman joins the others sitting on a log beneath the open sky.

Chester says, "So much is wrong. So much is broken. Women and children are treated like cattle. We do what we can to help them."

An old man smiles with missing teeth. Like the women, he's talking and pointing at them. Everyone's excited.

Chester says, "بنسخي امریکایي," in response to something said to him. He follows up by addressing Breezy and Olivia. "They've never seen American women before. They think you're pretty. They like your teeth. They say they're very straight and very white. They're asking about freedom. They've heard it's wonderful. They're grateful to have met you."

Breezy is speechless. Her knees feel weak.

Olivia reaches out and takes a little girl's hand. She crouches and introduces herself. "Hello. I'm Olivia."

The young girl is shy. She pulls away, but a smile lights up her face. She looks up at her mother, who nods in delight.

Chester asks Breezy. "Is there anything else you would like to say to them?"

Breezy has tears streaming down her cheeks. A lump rises in her throat. "I—I'm... Please tell them, we're delighted to meet them. All of them. Tell them, we're glad they've escaped."

Olivia nods, agreeing with that sentiment.

Chester speaks Pashto with the group. The women all smile and wave. Breezy is astonished by their sense of presence. They're withdrawn. Nervous is the wrong word. Modest is perhaps a better description. They seem overawed by two filthy American women in torn clothes.

There are several other women with hideously burned, scarred, melted skin. They shrink into the shadows. They don't want to make a fuss. For them, being here in the desert with Chester is liberating. They're still a long way from safety, but that doesn't seem to matter. Meeting two Americans is an unexpected delight.

Breezy feels a pain in her heart the likes of which she's never experienced before. As hard as it was breaking up with Susan, the emotions she feels in this moment are even more overwhelming. These women may not be able to speak English, but the sense of longing and compassion in their eyes transcends mere words. All they want is a chance. All they want is to live in peace.

Susan was right about justice. What justice could there ever be for these women? What prison sentence could make up for acid melting the skin from their bodies? No punishment could ever be more effective than changing the culture and killing cruel attitudes that led to these crimes. For these women, nothing will ever be the same again. No one will ever look at them as they once did. For them, there is no justice—but there can be a new beginning.

Breezy would do anything to protect these women. Beyond the President of the United States, there are very few people she'd give her life to save, but their innocence is pure. There's no guile in their eyes, only hope. She'd fight to the death to protect them, even after only knowing them for a few minutes.

She turns to Chester, saying, "We need to talk. Alone. Just you, me and Olivia. We need to understand the clowns."

"Sure," he says, turning and smiling at the others. He runs together several sentences in Pashto as well as in the local tongue. One of the women with the circus brings over a water bottle, giving it to Breezy. A man hands them both a flatbread wrap. There's some kind of crumbly goat cheese and possibly spinach leaves inside it. The bread is still warm, having been roasted over the fire.

"Come," Chester says, leading them away from the camp. He sits on a log overlooking a small stream. Water trickles over the rocks. "This is where we wash in the morning."

Olivia bites into her wrap. Breezy sips from the bottle. The water's got a muddy taste.

"Tell me about your scars," Breezy says, pointing at his arms. "Buster had the same scars, right?"

"Same torturer," Chester says, applying some ointment to the cut on his leg. "We were kids when they first got hold of us. Our dad was an Iraqi living in Iran. He loved the circus. He loved nothing more than bringing a smile to someone's face. He didn't care for politics or religion. He loved people. He couldn't stand to see them suffer."

Chester stops for a moment to apply a square bandage to his leg.

"Let me hold that," Breezy says, putting her hand on the bandage as he tears strips of medical tape with his teeth and uses them to hold it in place.

"Thanks."

Breezy nods but doesn't reply.

Olivia points at the circus vehicles, saying, "So you and Buster continued the family business."

"Something like that."

"Until?" Breezy says.

"Until we were sneaking across the border one night with a bunch of refugees fleeing the civil war, and there was a streak of light overhead. It was about three in the morning. At first, we thought it was a flare. We were expecting gunfire to follow, but the light around us faded as a meteor shot into the distance. As dawn broke, we found it."

"And it wasn't a meteorite, huh?" Olivia says.

"Nope."

"What did it look like?" Breezy asks.

"Like a big black cigar with tapered ends. It was maybe a hundred yards in length, but it was quite narrow. The skin of the craft was perfectly smooth, reflecting the desert around it. Later we learned it was one of their shuttles. The engine had malfunctioned, forcing an emergency landing."

"And that's when you met them?" Olivia asks. "The clowns?"

"Oh, no," Chester says. "They're not the clowns." He points at himself. "We're the clowns. We're the fools. We're the ones oblivious to everything around us."

"I don't understand," Breezy says, confused. "I've seen them. Dead clowns brought back to life."

Chester laughs. "The aliens didn't come up with the clowns. Buster did. They loved the idea. They gave him the tech and let him run with it."

"They *gave* it to him?" Breezy asks, astonished by the concept.

"You have to understand. It's like giving an iPad to Shakespeare. He's going to read ebooks with ease, but he's not going to be able to make more iPads."

"But why would they do that?"

"They wanted to see if he was right."

"About what?"

"Buster thought that if humanity could see itself in the mirror, it would change."

"And the clowns were that mirror?" Breezy asks.

"Yes."

Olivia asks, "So all this is an experiment?"

"It's a chance for us to prove ourselves," Chester says. "They won't interfere. They can't."

"Why can't they?" Olivia asks. "I mean, you interfere, helping these families. You see what those women are going through, and you help them escape."

Chester says, "You don't understand. First Contact isn't possible. Oh, I know. We've got our books and movies with aliens arriving in silver spaceships, but they all miss a single, crucial point."

"Which is?" Breezy asks.

"Who should they contact? You? Me? The President? Of which country? America? Why? What about the United Kingdom? Or Ireland? Or Russia? What about the Pope? What about the Chinese communists? The Germans? The French? Or the regime in Myanmar? Or Buddhist monks in Thailand? Or the Mormons of Salt Lake City? Or the remote Amazonian tribes that have fought off European contact for hundreds of years? Who, exactly, should they talk to?"

"All of them," Olivia replies.

"And say what?" Chester asks. "They can't just drop in here for the same reason the US President can't just walk around downtown Kabul. It would be like hitting a hornets' nest with a baseball bat."

Breezy shakes her head. She disagrees, but hers is an emotional reaction, not a logical response.

"We're fractured," Chester says. "We have so many conflicting, competing interests. And we lie. We lie all the damn time to get our own way. And we're cruel. And if we're not, we look the other way. We pretend there are no problems. If you were them, would you want to step into the middle of this shit show?"

Olivia shakes her head. Breezy is quiet.

"For several years after we made contact, they'd wait for us here in the Spring. We'd be sneaking across the border with a bunch of refugees and they'd rock up with lights flashing in the sky. It was comical, but this place is so remote no one noticed. They loved talking to Buster.

"I remember them asking Buster why we had warships. It confused them. We don't have any natural enemies. There's only us. We have no adversary beyond ourselves, and that just doesn't make sense. Why fight yourself? Why are we our own enemy? Think about how dumb that is. For us, it's normal to see nations fighting each other, but not for them. They see it as petty. And you want *them* to initiate First Contact with someone else?"

Breezy says, "But we need warships. We have to defend ourselves."

"Yes. We do. But we shouldn't have to. That's the point," Chester says. "The very fact we have to defend ourselves from ourselves is an admission of failure. I get that it's the reality of our world, but that doesn't make it right or normal or sane. It's sad. And seen from afar, it's mad."

Chester points at the distant sky. "Look at the beauty of the universe. Look at it and realize we're no different from anything else out there. We're all made of the same stuff. See those stars? They're not stars. They're suns like ours, with planets like ours, with life like ours."

As there are no clouds and the three of them are hundreds of miles from the light pollution of the nearest city, the stars are radiant. There's depth to them. Far from being scattered, they're clustered in bunches, on the verge of overlapping each other.

Breezy's eyes see hints of hidden wonders, millions of stars lying just off in the distance, somewhere on the edge of her vision. They tease her, telling her there's more waiting to be discovered. Like the chaos of the Grand Canyon or a rugged Alaskan forest, there's something regal about the confusion in the sky. There's no logic to the stars, no patterns. Breezy could be staring at the fabled Lion of the constellation Leo or the water bearer of Aquarius. There's no way to tell because these things don't exist. They never existed—not outside the tiny minds of ancient humans. The zodiac is a futile effort to tame the cosmos. Humanity can't accept a lack of order. The universe needs rhyme and reason even when none exists. It's a lie. The truth is there, plain for all to see—Earth is lost in this dark, stormy sea. For Breezy, there's peace in acceptance.

The distant hills form a black silhouette covering the ground, hiding the Milky Way as its vast glowing gas clouds rise slowly over the horizon.

For the first time, Breezy sees the Earth as it really is—not as a separate place but as part of the whole cosmos unfolding before her. The Earth, Sun and Moon are all part of the stunning chaos that is the universe at large.

Chester says, "We're obsessed about intelligent life in outer space, but we portray aliens as the enemy. We're paranoid. The aliens of our movies are as ruthless as a crocodile or a Great White Shark. We make them out to be space Nazis. They're going to steal our resources. They want to destroy us. And you expect these guys to just drop by the White House and say hello? How do you think that's going to play out?"

"But there has been First Contact," Olivia says. "You've had contact with them. What happened back then?"

"Oh, how I miss those days," Chester says, lost in thought. "The shuttlecraft crashed right where you landed. Black smoke guided us to the spot. We came over the horizon, and there it was, half in the water. And Buster. Oh, Buster."

He laughs, shaking his head. "We pulled up about fifty yards away on the bedrock. I thought it was an Aeroflot flight from Kabul bound for Moscow. I figured the paint had burned off. I was expecting to see bodies lying strewn everywhere. As for the wings, I assumed they'd broken off in the lake or something, but Buster knew.

"He hopped down from the truck and jogged over with a first aid kit. Me? I looked at the crater, wondering what kind of airplane forms a hole without breaking up? There was no tail fin or rudder, no rear wings. No engines. And yet the fuselage stayed intact? It didn't make sense.

"There was a crack near the nose. Black smoke rose from the rear of the craft while white steam came from the front. At that point, I'm thinking we need to call for help, but we don't use cell phones out here in the desert. The reception is too patchy. We rely on the radio, but we were in a depression. I tried to get hold of someone, but there was no reply.

"Buster climbed in the crumpled section near the nose. He dragged out the pilot—only the pilot wasn't human. He was in a spacesuit with a fishbowl helmet. He had eight arms or legs or something. I ran over. By this point, I'm not sure which way is up. Buster went back in for another one. He dragged him out. His suit was badly torn, exposing his legs, at least, I thought they were legs. And then Buster provided first aid."

"Wait a minute," Olivia says. "How do you give first aid to an alien?"

"That's what I wanted to know," Chester says. "Buster unfolded our circus first aid kit next to the wounded alien. I asked, '*What are you doing?*' Buster looked up and me and replied, '*Helping them.*'

"As for me, I was in shock. I was scared. I said, '*But you don't know what you're doing.*'

"Buster was calm. We have a high-wire act and lions in the circus. He's seen plenty of horrific injuries over the years. He said, '*The basics are the same. They have to be. Clean the wound. Stop the bleeding. Stabilize the patient.*' He squirted saline solution in the wounds to clean them. He tore open several sterile bandages and held them in place with compression wraps.

344

"The other alien with the intact suit regained consciousness. It leaned forward. All these arms started touching Buster's shoulders, but he was so focused I don't think he noticed. He was using tweezers to pick out bits of metal from a gash on the other alien. This thick white fluid wept from a long cut. He daubed at it, squirting more saline solution in to clean it, and the other alien lay back down.

"It was awake. I could see its eyes inside its fishbowl helmet. Its suit was torn just below the collar. It was subtle, barely noticeable, but when it moved you could see the creature's pale neck. It took off its helmet and lay there panting. It squinted in the sunlight. I think the light was too bright. It wanted to look around but couldn't. It closed its eyes and just lay there. Finally, Buster noticed. He scrambled up beside it, grabbed hold of the rim of the suit and said, '*Hey, everything's going to be okay. You just hang in there.*'"

Breezy asks, "Did it understand him?"

"Hell, no," Chester replies, laughing. "It was in shock. I was in shock. Everyone was in shock except Buster. '*What is wrong with you?*' I said to him. '*These things look like they're going to rise up and eat us!*'

"Their heads were the size of a basketball. They had six eyes surrounding their thick skulls, along with thin, wiry, metallic hair that caught the sunlight, refracting it like a rainbow. Man, they were ugly. I mean, they looked dead even when they were moving. White skin. Big ugly teeth. And a large red blob in the middle of each face."

Olivia butts in, "Like a clown."

"Like a clown in a crazy house of mirrors."

"Then what happened?" Breezy asks, mesmerized by his recollections.

"Buster removed the other helmet. There was no way to tell if the alien had any internal injuries. It could have been a mess beneath that silver material. Buster cracked another vial of saline solution and rubbed what I guess was its forehead. I looked at the sharp teeth and said, '*Ah, Buster. I'm not sure you should be doing that.*' And then its eyes opened—all of them at once! I stepped back. He kept stroking its head, saying, '*Everything's going to be fine. You're in good hands. We're going to take care of you. Don't you worry about a thing.*' I don't think it could believe what was happening. I know I couldn't.

"Then there was a shadow. It passed over us and I thought a storm cloud had blocked the sun. Oh, no. It was another one. There was another spacecraft, only this one was bigger. I mean, way bigger. It hovered over the lake. '*Ah, Buster,*' I said, pointing. He turned and looked, but he wasn't scared. Around us, stones and rocks lifted into the air—and I was out of there! I ran, scrambling to get away before I was dragged into the air. When I turned back, Buster and the aliens were about fifty feet up, along with a scattering of dirt and rocks. The smaller, crashed craft was gone. It had already been dragged up into the mothership. I stood there trembling and then...."

"And then," Breezy asks when Chester stalls, lost in thought.

"And then they were gone. This massive spaceship. Poof! It disappeared. It was, I don't know, a mile wide but barely a hundred yards above us. I blinked, and it was gone. Rocks and pebbles and stones fell back into the water.

"The sun had risen over the mountains. The blue sky above us was magnificent. There wasn't a cloud for miles. I'm not sure how long I stood there waiting for them to come back. It probably wasn't even an hour, but it felt like forever.

"I went back to the truck and waited. That's all I could do. I wasn't going to leave. Not without Buster. The radio crackled. Evan and the others in our troupe had stopped at *Kindzhak*. The elevation there was good. They could reach us over the radio without a booster. They asked if we had found the airplane. I said, '*Yes.*' What else was I going to say? They asked if we needed anything. I said, '*No.*' They asked me when we were coming back. '*Soon,*' I replied. One-word answers never inspire confidence. I think they knew I was lying.

"The day was long, but I couldn't leave my brother. Nightfall came. I was pissing against a boulder when the stars went black overhead. The mothership had returned. It was above the lake again. I watched as Buster glided down to the shore like Superman. I was beside myself. '*Are you okay?*' He said, '*I'm fine.*' I asked, '*Where have you been?*' And he said, '*Nowhere. We didn't go anywhere. We were up there the whole time—just above the lake.*' I told him the spaceship had disappeared. He said it never moved. And that's when it began."

Breezy asks, "When what began?"

"Our conversations. We met them by the lake each night for about three months. During the day, we'd go off to *Kindzhak,* and they'd go wherever. Hell, they could have stayed there for all I knew. But each night, we'd meet them. We used the town as a staging post for refugees anyway, so it was easy enough to run the circus there for a while. We sent Evan along the Silk Road with the women while we talked to the aliens. Buster would start a fire to ward off the cold of night, and they'd come down on a beam of stardust."

"What would you talk about?" Olivia asks.

"*The Spectacle!*"

THE SPECTACLE

"They've seen so many worlds like ours. They've seen the way we obsess over the dumbest things. They've seen how easy it is to provoke us. All we care about is our own tribe. *It's the best!* If only everyone was in our tribe and did things our way, all the world's problems would melt away, right?"

Breezy says, "They weren't impressed, huh?"

Chester laughs. "You have no idea how barbaric and behind-the-times we are. We think we're civilized. We think we're intelligent. We tell ourselves we're looking for intelligent life out there in space, but we don't stop to think about how little of it there is back here. These guys? They're not fooled. We can lie to ourselves all we want. We can blow our own horn and puff out our chests. We can stroke our egos all day long. These guys simply do—*not*—care! They see us for what we are."

Breezy asks, "Which is?"

"Apes."

"Apes?" Olivia asks in reply, feeling a little indignant at the implication of such a coarse term.

Chester says, "Yeah, like the ones in the jungle or at the zoo. We're slightly more advanced in that we build things and talk and wear clothes, but we're a species of infighting ape that's spread out of control around the planet.

"We're animals. First Contact is no more realistic for us than it is for a bunch of chimps. We think we're smart. We think we're logical. We're not. We're driven by emotion. We confuse instinct with reason. Most of our so-called reasoning is nothing more than justifying our instincts, regardless of how wacky and fucked up they may be. And we don't see it. We're blind to it!"

"Ouch," Breezy says.

"And we're selfish. Even with the advent of science, we revert to our default behaviors time and time again. Fear is more compelling than facts. And the facts never tell the whole story. To them, we're hairless chimps playing dress-up."

Olivia is offended. "Ah, I think I'd do better than a chimp at First Contact."

"You might, but everyone else out there? Not a chance. Most people don't think. They react. And just like a chimpanzee, they're going to throw shit at anything that scares them!"

Breezy leans forward, looking across at Olivia. "He's got a point."

"But they could help us get past that," Olivia says.

"Could they?" Chester asks. "Or would we draw them into the quagmire of our madness? They're not playing our silly games. They don't have to. They don't want to. As long as we screw around with conspiracy theories and dumb, selfish shit, they're taking a hard pass."

"We're not all bad," Olivia says.

"No one's all bad," Chester replies. "Those women back there. The men that beat them? That hurt them? That scarred them? They think they're right. They think they're rational. In their minds, they're not emotional. They're justified. They think those women had it coming. And this is the problem—they can't see straight. They're blinded by *The Spectacle*."

"I don't understand," Breezy says.

"We live in a spectacle of our own creation. It's an illusion of our own imagination—and it doesn't line up with reality. It's all pretense. We put on a show."

"Like a circus?" Olivia asks.

"Yes," Chester says. "We love the flashing lights. The fanfare. The rides. The sights, sounds and smells. We get bored with ordinary life. Reality is not enough. We want to spice things up. We want something more, something spectacular! We want to be dazzled. We want to be entertained. We're like crows with a shiny set of new keys.

"Our phones, our computers, our televisions, not to mention our religions, our politics, our sports, our music, and our shiny shopping malls—they're all placebos. They make us feel better, but they're hollow and empty. They're substitutes for the mundane hum of reality.

"Why can't we feel good about ourselves without them? They're not bad or evil. We're addicts. We can't leave them alone. We can't be without them. We can't stand to be alone with our own thoughts. There's always got to be something we cling to, something to keep us busy, something that enhances our world, and that's *The Spectacle!* It's what we've made of modern life."

Chester throws his arms wide in mimicry of a ringmaster. "It's *The Greatest Show on Earth!*"

He's gesturing to the barren desert beyond the stream, mocking the insanity.

Breezy says, "It's no wonder these guys love you and your circus. It's like a microcosm of the circus that is humanity."

Chester says, "*The Spectacle* is anything that becomes a substitute for us living our own lives. We're voyeurs. Everything we once lived and experienced has become a spectacle to be watched from the couch. We live our lives by proxy through someone else. Think about a movie that's set in Venice. You get to experience the waterways without getting splashed. There's no inconvenience, and you only get the highlights. Life is curated. You see perfection, not reality. You don't have to deal with crowds or the smell of pollution. It's real, and yet it's not. It's curated. It's a counterfeit experience."

"And they object to this?" Breezy asks.

"They see it as a delusion," Chester says. "We're spectators. We're no longer in the game. We think we're part of it, but we're not. The more we embrace *The Spectacle,* the more we're divorced from reality."

"I don't get it," Olivia says. "Why is that so bad?"

"Because we lose touch with what's real. We're unable to identify what's important. Think about a linebacker sacking a quarterback. To us, it's a spectacular collision. It's a rush of adrenaline that's quickly lost in the moment. To the quarterback that lives through that, it's painful. If he's injured, it's months of rehab, but we blink and look for the next hit of endorphins from the next play."

Breezy says, "So it's not sports or movies they object to—it's how they distort our view of reality?"

"Yes," Chester says. "Because that influences how we treat others around us. *The Spectacle* skews our sense of value. If something's not for sale, it's worthless. And so we give value to diamonds and gold—value

352

they don't deserve—and we miss the value of being kind and caring. We say, *oh, but gold is scarce.* Ah, yes, because in *The Spectacle,* value isn't about what you have but rather what others have and you lack. Value is found in hoarding the spectacular for yourself. It becomes a fetish driving us on. But we can't see it. Like rats in a cage, all we see is the spinning exercise wheel—the treadmill. *Run, little rat, run! Run faster! And you'll feel like you're going somewhere without going anywhere at all.*"

"Damn," Olivia says. "That's pretty bleak."

"It's honest," Chester says. "The game is rigged. This is the world in which we live. Society was once built around helping others—now it's built by helping yourself. *Don't think. Buy. Buy. Buy!* When you hear someone on the news talking about '*the market,*' or '*the economy,*' what they mean is *The Spectacle.* All must worship at its altar."

He laughs. "Good old Mick Jagger was right. Satisfaction is always out of reach in *The Spectacle.* If you're satisfied, you're not going to keep playing. And we can't have that." He pauses for a moment. "Let me ask you a question. Would a million dollars change your life?"

"Sure," Olivia says.

"You think it would, only it wouldn't. Everything scales in *The Spectacle.* Once you've got a million dollars, you'll need ten million. Get that, and you'll find you'll only be satisfied with a hundred million. And on it goes. Hell, we've got billionaires! Think of how absurd that is. Who can spend a billion dollars? I'll tell you who. No one. Oh, we have yachts worth hundreds of millions of dollars on one hand and, on the other, people struggling to survive on a few dollars a day. The difference? Luck. That's all. Oh, they'll call it '*opportunity,*' they'll brag about their intelligence and cunning, but it's a lie.

"If there's one certainty in *The Spectacle,* it's that we always want more. Those women back there in the truck. A thousand dollars would change their lives—and then it wouldn't. That's the tyranny of *The Spectacle*. We all want to get ahead, more so when we're already ahead. We're so busy faking life it passes us by without us even noticing."

"And they see all this, huh?" Olivia says, staring up into the sky, lost in his words.

"Yep," Chester says. "What's a trillion dollars to someone that can fly between stars?"

"Cruel," Breezy says.

Chester nods. He picks up a pebble and throws it into the stream. "Do you know what they call us?"

"What?" Olivia asks, curious.

"*Homo spectaculum* or Beings of *The Spectacle*. They can't bring themselves to call us *Homo sapiens*, the wisest of the hominids, and with all I've seen, I can't blame them."

"So, what's the answer?" Breezy asks, feeling humbled by the discussion. "They see us stripped of all pretense, right? So what should we be doing?"

"This," Chester says, gesturing to the cold desert before them. "Living an authentic life—unbound by *The Spectacle*."

Olivia says, "To thine own self be true."

"Yep," Chester says. "And that's the answer to your question. That's why I'm here in this hell hole. I can't turn my back on those women. I can't pretend they don't exist. The world is a mess. The best any of us can hope for in life is to bring a little light into the darkness."

Breezy leans forward, resting her elbows on her knees and burying her head in her hands. She runs her fingers up through her hair, saying, "Fuck!"

"Buster was convinced he could change the world," Chester says. "After a couple of years, he convinced them to let him try. They agreed with his idea to make fun of *The Spectacle*."

"With clowns?" Olivia asks.

"Yes. The idea was to get people to stop paying homage to the Almighty Dollar. I thought, if anyone could pull it off, it was him. I really thought he could do it—until you showed up."

Breezy swallows the lump in her throat. She tries to speak, but can't. Words won't come out. Olivia must feel the gravity of the moment. She speaks for her.

"Would you like to know how he died?"

"No," Chester snaps.

Breezy sobs. Guilt wells up in her chest. Her hands tremble.

"It's okay," Chester says, putting his arm over her shoulder. Somehow, he knows. He must be able to sense what happened from their presence here in the desert. Chester says, "He would be proud of you for making it here to be with me."

For Breezy, that's worse. Her chest heaves as she tries to speak. Snot runs from her nose. She rubs the back of her hand across her face, trying to compose herself.

"Buster knew what he was doing," Chester says. "Most people want to change the world—Buster wanted to change himself. He figured, when it came to *The Spectacle*, that was the best place to start. He knew what would happen to him. I know how he thought. If he could help just one other person, it would be worth it. All he ever wanted was to help people see *The Spectacle* for what it is—a trap!"

He rubs Breezy's back. She breathes deeply, calming herself.

No one speaks, which seems to be a rarity for Chester. After a minute or so, he gets up and walks over to a backpack resting against a boulder. He pulls out a water bottle and sits on the boulder facing them as he drinks.

Breezy massages her temples. She stares at the sharp rocks scattered across the ground. Chester's right. She's trapped in *The Spectacle*. She's got her career, her daughter, her beat-up car that keeps breaking down, her mortgage on a two-bedroom apartment just out of Georgetown. She's actually in the neighboring suburb of Palisades, but the street she's on runs into Georgetown. Her brother's in real estate. He tells her to call it Georgetown. It sounds better. It adds thirty grand to the apartment's value. From her kitchen window, she can see a thin slither of the Potomac between buildings. It's nothing, but she tells everyone she has a view. Yeah, she's bought right into *The Spectacle*.

Breezy's not a bad person. Okay, she's killed several people in the last few days, but her life isn't usually that chaotic, and they had it coming. They were all bad. Except for Buster.

Fuck.

"*The Spectacle*, huh?" she says, looking at Chester through tear-stained eyes.

"Yep. It sucks, doesn't it? You live your whole life trying to do the right thing—only you're a rat caught in a maze."

Olivia says, "We've got to get back." She wipes the tears from her eyes, saying, "*The Spectacle* is about to get a whole lot worse. Secret Service Director Johnson is preparing to roll the Vice President and then the President. We've got to warn them. The Veep knows someone is gunning for the two of them, but he doesn't know who or why."

"Why would the director do that?" Chester asks.

"He's after them—the aliens! That's his ticket out of *The Spectacle*."

"We don't even know if Johnson's alive," Olivia says. "They bombed that place. You saw them."

"We can't assume he's dead," Breezy says. "And we can't assume it's just him."

"How are we going to get back?" Olivia asks. "We've got no money. No passports. In case you haven't noticed, we're a hundred miles from nowhere in the middle of the goddamn desert."

Breezy turns to Chester. "Can you get hold of the aliens? Can you get them to come back?"

"Back?" he says, laughing. "They probably never left."

"What?" Breezy says, blinking rapidly in disbelief at his comment.

"Their spacecraft are cloaked. They're invisible, remember. They were probably hovering over the lake, wondering why you were leaving instead of staying to talk to them."

"Talk to them?" Breezy asks, almost falling off the log.

"They only talk at night. They can't handle the light. It's too bright." He shakes his head. "Weren't you listening to me?"

"They talk at night?" Breezy asks in astonishment. "As in, this night? Tonight? Like now? Right now?"

"Yes."

Breezy shakes her head in disbelief at all she and Olivia have been through. "Can you take us back there?"

"Sure."

CONTACT

Headlights flicker across the desert. They've been driving for hours. The physical and emotional toll of the last few days is wearing on Breezy. She's tired. She's sore. She's grumpy. It's got to be well after midnight.

"Are we going the right way?" Breezy asks, looking out into the darkness. "They put us down near a broad riverbed. There was a bridge and a road about four miles inland."

"Relax. We're going the right way," Chester says as they bounce on the bench seat, stretching across the front of the old pickup. The springs beneath the worn leather are old and squeak. Breezy wanted to take their Gaz 4x4, but Chester said arriving with an anti-aircraft gun on the back wasn't a good idea. His rusting flatbed is easily a decade older than their already antiquated Gaz.

"We should be seeing dunes," Breezy says, peering into the darkness. "There was a sea of dunes as we came up along the river bank."

Chester takes his eyes off the rocky ground for a moment and looks across in front of Breezy at Olivia. "Is she always this anxious?"

"Only around clowns."

"Haha. Very funny," Breezy says.

"Look," Chester says, pointing into the shadows. A dark lake looms on the edge of their vision. "See. I told you. We're coming from the side."

Breezy wrings her clammy hands together, mumbling. "Good. Good."

Chester follows the shoreline. He keeps the pickup roughly a hundred feet from the lake, tracing the sloping bedrock as it leads down to the water's edge. Countless dried-up stream beds wind their way into the lake, slowing their progress. The sand within the numerous depressions is soft. The wheels of the pickup slip and slide as they climb out of the loose rocks. Chester revs the engine madly, sending the wheels spinning and kicking up a dust storm behind them, but they clear yet another sunken creek.

"There. That's it," Olivia says, pointing at a collapsed bank caught in the headlights. The flooding has ceased, but the broad riverbed in front of them is still damp. Mud spreads out from the mouth of the river, covering the bedrock leading down to the lake.

"Yes, yes," Chester says, bringing the pickup to a halt.

They stop and get out. A cold wind sweeps in across the water. It takes a few seconds for their eyes to adjust to the darkness now that the headlights are off. Olivia walks to the edge of the lake. Breezy walks over to the riverbed. Freshly washed-up sand crumbles beneath her boots. The raging torrent has been reduced to a tiny stream trickling through the debris swept down the river.

"Where are they?" she asks, turning and looking up at the night sky. The moon has risen. The stars are visible, but they're not as crisp as they were earlier in the evening. Clouds loom over the mountains.

"Right there," Chester says, pointing above the lake.

"There's nothing out there," Olivia says.

Chester picks up a rock the size of a tennis ball and hurls it in the air. He throws it on a steep trajectory. Damn, he's got a good arm. He'd make a great baseball outfielder. The rock is going to sail easily forty to fifty feet before landing in the water. Breezy follows its path, anticipating its trajectory, but it strikes something invisible and ricochets down at a sharp angle, splashing in the lake.

There's a flash of light at the point the rock struck the spacecraft.

"Hey," Chester yells. "You guys awake?"

An eerie blue glow ripples across the ground, spreading around their legs.

"Oh, no. Not me," Chester says, dancing backward and shaking his legs as he retreats beside the pickup.

"What's happening?" Breezy asks.

"Don't fight it," Chester says.

"Ah, Breezy?" Olivia says, looking down at her feet. "This is normal, right?"

"Normal?" Breezy asks, unsure of herself. She looks at Olivia rather than at her own feet. Slowly, the two women are drawn up off the bedrock. Bits of stone and rock move with them, floating a few feet above the ground. "I hope so."

As they rise, Chester shrinks beneath them. He waves, yelling something, but Breezy can't make it out over the hum around her. Her clothing vibrates. Even from thirty feet, the terrain below takes on a different look. The world is smaller. Everything that seemed so important moments ago is suddenly insignificant. The pickup looks feeble. The river seems narrower than she remembers.

A hole in the base of the spacecraft opens. Rather than sliding to one side or swinging open like a hatch, it opens in a circular motion, growing ever larger.

"It's a smooth ride this time," Olivia says, taking Breezy's hand. Their fingers entwine. "No storm to deal with, huh?"

"No," Breezy says, desperately trying to take everything in.

The hatch closes once they're within the vessel, narrowing to a point. It's dark inside the craft. Shadows move around them. The two women stay close. Their arms rub against each other in the cool, crisp air. Already, the floor feels spongy.

An indistinct voice speaks softly, echoing around them. "You have heard it from him. You have learned from him. You have understood."

"Yes," Breezy says, not feeling any fear. She's excited. A sense of awe washes over her, causing her knees to go weak. She's talking with someone who originated on another world around some other star, and yet the tone is relaxed.

"Would you like to see?"

"Yes."

The floor dissolves. A wall of fire surrounds them, but it's hundreds of yards away, glowing on the edge of their vision. They're at the center of a ring spanning the best part of a mile. In between, there's nothing. They're suspended by the soft floor, but it is entirely transparent. The lake recedes along with Chester and his pickup. Mountain ranges shrink in the distance. A thin blue line stretches around the edge of the horizon. Over a matter of seconds, it transforms into a gentle curve. Clouds appear below them. Streetlights wind their way across the land to the south. They cluster into cities like a spider's web woven from threads of gold.

Olivia tightens her grip on Breezy's hand.

Although borders are an artificial construct, several different countries pass beneath them. They're distinguished by the density of their cities. Afghanistan is dark, with only a smattering of light in a handful of spots. Pakistan is a string of brightly lit towns and cities winding throughout the lush Indus valley. The Himalayas form a white, snowcapped barrier between India and Tibet.

Olivia stutters, "I... I."

Earth falls away beneath them. The difference between the land and the sea, as seen in the dark of night, is stark. The lights of humanity come to an abrupt end, curling around the edge of the land but venturing no further into the gloom.

Moonlight glistens off the water.

"I know," Breezy says, replying to Olivia, feeling overwhelmed by what she's witnessing.

Back in Washington, everything seemed so simple. Life was lived in black and white. There were good guys and bad guys. Unsurprisingly, Breezy was a good guy—until she pulled the trigger on Buster. When Chester described *The Spectacle*, she felt dumb. It had been there all the time, throughout her entire life, but she'd never seen it. How could she? Can an earthworm see the forest? Now, it seems so obvious. As grand and magnificent and all-consuming as life is on Earth, it's nothing. All those cities glowing in the dark. All those millions of people down there below her. They're a smudge on the side of a small, unassuming planet. Right now, they're asleep. They're oblivious to the two women staring down at them from an alien spaceship. And tomorrow, *The Spectacle* starts anew. Whatever course they're on, it'll consume them, demanding their devotion and attention. They'll rush off to work or to school or to the markets. They've got to get things done! Like green ants rushing around the entrance to a buried nest, there's too much to do. If only they could see themselves.

Earth continues to recede. The sun rises. Or Earth turns. Or the spaceship moves. Breezy's not sure which. It's probably a combination of all of them being in motion. A blinding light cuts across the gentle curve of the planet, lighting up the Bay of Bengal. The coastline of Thailand and Indonesia is visible in the distance, already enjoying the warmth that comes with the break of dawn. Sri Lanka is visible, catching the first rays of sunrise.

"Ah, where exactly are we going?" Olivia asks, falling to her knees on the soft, invisible floor.

"What do you mean?" Breezy replies, joining her on her knees.

"I mean, there's an awful lot of ocean down there. And clouds. Lots of clouds. I'm not seeing much land."

The craft turns slightly as it ascends, making it challenging to keep a familiar orientation. The west coast of Australia looms above them while Antarctica is off to one side. Massive storms swirl in the vast blue Southern Ocean. It's impossible to get a sense of direction other than that *up* is somewhere behind them.

"We're going faster," Olivia says, but Breezy doesn't feel any acceleration. She feels light. It's as though they're floating in the middle of the gigantic glowing ring.

"There's nothing to worry about," she says.

"Earth is looking small," Olivia says. "Pretty damn small. And it's only getting smaller."

To Breezy, it doesn't seem that way, but the curvature of Earth is more pronounced now. At first, they were up high somewhere over central Asia. As they drifted across India, it became apparent Earth wasn't flat, but the planet still appeared like a massive wall in front of them, dominating their entire vista. Slowly, the planet became curved before resolving into a sphere, but they couldn't see all of it at once. Now, though, Breezy can see the entire planet. It's tipped on its side, or rather, their spacecraft has rotated. Between that and the heavy cloud cover, it's challenging to distinguish landmarks.

"Is that curved section the tip of South America?" Olivia asks, turning her head to one side, trying to get it to align with north and south being her up and down. A thin strip of rocky mountains and islands curls into a brilliant blue sea.

"I think so." Breezy never was any good with geography.

"We've got a problem."

"What?" Breezy asks. Although she knows Olivia's right, she doesn't want to admit that to herself. She's overwhelmed by a sense of awe and majesty. It washes away her fears and concerns. Problems are for another Breezy in another time.

Olivia seems to sense her denial. She's sarcastic in reply. "I'm pretty sure this isn't the Red Line to DC's Metro Central. The train I used to take stopped in Bethesda."

"So, where are we going?" Breezy asks, sitting back and watching Earth recede below her.

"You're asking me?" she says, sitting back.

"Umm," Breezy says, searching for the right words, wondering how they can converse with aliens they can't see. Earth continues to shrink at an alarming rate. It gets visibly smaller as the seconds pass. Before long, it's the size of a basketball.

"They're taking us somewhere, right?"

"But not to DC," Breezy says with a quiver in her voice.

"Oh, yeah," Olivia says. "I think we can rule that out as a destination."

Olivia's already holding Breezy's hand again. She leans close, gripping her upper arm. Rather than traveling in a straight line, they're moving in an arc, circling out wide as they soar away from the planet. The effect is such that their view of Earth is constantly changing. The world slips back into the shadows. Cities in Europe appear as pinpricks of light.

"Is that the Moon?" Olivia asks as a tiny lifeless sphere of black and white shadows races past off to one side. Thousands of craters of various sizes streak by in a matter of seconds.

"I think so," Breezy replies.

"Fuck!"

"Yah think?"

Olivia asks, "Didn't it take the Apollo astronauts three days to get this far into space?"

"I guess."

Breezy regrets not paying more attention to her geeky brother growing up. He would love this. She's feeling a little nervous. Earth is smaller than a ping pong ball held at arm's length and shrinking fast. She could hold out her hand and cover it with her thumb. A shiver runs through her. It's not that she feels insignificant—it's that everything she's ever known, the permanence of everything she once thought was so important, is utterly insignificant at this distance. And this distance is nothing on a cosmic scale. The White House? Congress? Washington, D.C.? America itself? Nine *billion* people scattered around the planet? All the pomp and ceremony on TV. The self-importance of news anchors and senators with their damning takes on the politics of the moment. All the fuss over gasoline prices and trade deficits. All the aircraft carriers and submarines, the tanks and planes, the missiles and bombs, the sailors, aircrew and soldiers. All the arguments and anger as people fight to get their own way. They all look pitiful on a planet that's been reduced to the size of a marble.

"Ah, where are you taking us?" Breezy asks, leaning back and looking up at the stars on the other side of the mile-wide glowing ring of flames. "Hello?"

"Look," Olivia says, nudging Breezy and getting her to look to her right. Out across the vast flat, empty expanse inside the ring, there's a figure. Someone's approaching them. As the fiery ring is behind the being walking on darkness, it's difficult to make out much beyond a silhouette. Whoever it is, they're easily a hundred yards away. Stars shine above and below the pulsating ring. Neither of them has any sense of motion. Earth is little more than a pale bluish-white dot lost against a sea of stars. The sun is below and slightly behind them. Look in that direction even for a moment, and the stars disappear from sight.

It takes a good thirty seconds for Breezy's eyes to adjust to the darkness again and see the tens of thousands of stars scattered against the endless backdrop of the universe. As immense as it is, she knows she's only seeing a fraction of what's out there. She feels as though she's sitting on a beach in Hawaii, looking at the waves crashing on the outer reef, knowing the ocean stretches well beyond the horizon, curling around the planet beneath her. For Breezy, there's a sense of falling into eternity. The universe is without end, which is distinctly unsettling.

Until this point, she never appreciated the illusion of solid ground beneath her feet, a horizon not more than a few miles away, and the curve of the azure blue sky rolling overhead like a canopy. Earth conspired to make her feel safe in the vast, chaotic ocean that is the cosmos. As strange as it sounds, it allowed her to be centered. She was at the heart of her little world. Now, all that has been stripped away. Billions of light-years of empty space unfold before her. The odd, scattered remnants of hydrogen have fallen in together to create stars and galaxies. They taunt her with their grandeur. Reality torments her. She's outside *The Spectacle*. As hollow as it may be, she feels the loss of its comfort.

As the figure gets closer, it's apparent it's a man—a human. He's confident, walking directly toward them. Sunlight comes up from beneath his feet, casting shadows along his clothing.

"Chester?" Olivia asks, seeing grimy overalls and rainbow suspenders reaching over a scarred chest.

"Buster?" Breezy asks, feeling her heart race.

"Neither," the man says, sounding all too familiar. He sits cross-legged in front of them, asking, "Can I get you anything? Food? Water?"

"No, ah, I'm fine," Breezy says, gesturing to Olivia, not wanting to speak on her behalf.

She agrees. "No. I'm good."

"Who are you?" Breezy asks.

"Me? My name doesn't translate. It would be meaningless to you."

"Please," Breezy says.

"Grock."

"And this isn't you, right?" Breezy asks, gesturing to his stocky body.

Grock pulls at his rainbow-colored suspenders, flexing them away from his bare chest. "We felt this form would be easier for you to accept. In our experience with humans, gigantic intelligent spiders tend to elicit a flight reflex."

"Oh, yeah," Olivia says, going wide-eyed. "Good call."

Breezy asks, "How long have you been on Earth, Grock?"

"Earth," he says, chuckling.

Olivia shakes her head. "I don't get it. What's so funny about that?"

"You humans have such a narrow view of life and the cosmos. You think you see clearly, but you don't." He smiles. He's not angry. He's amused. "We first saw your world from just off the plane of your solar system. We looked up from the south and saw only ice and clouds and oceans."

"And?" Breezy asks, curious about his perspective on Earth.

"We called your world *Dieg-Jinn*. It means world of water. Our world is almost fifty light-years away. We weren't sure there was any land before we got within a few light-years. When we realized almost three-quarters of your planet was covered in water, we marveled at the name you'd given it—Earth!"

Olivia says, "When you put it like that, it does seem kinda silly, huh."

Breezy asks him, "Where are you taking us?"

"To see," he says, looking above and behind them.

"To see what?" Olivia asks.

"To see all that is yours. To see what Buster saw."

Breezy feels strangely calm given she's already well over a million miles from Earth. The sense of panic she felt has given way to a serene sense of confidence. They're not alone in any sense of the word. They're not alone on this journey or in the universe at large. They're being cared for by an intelligent species seeking to share the wonders of the universe with them personally. Three days ago, Breezy was bitching about the cost of a pastrami sandwich from her local deli. Now, she's onboard the *NCC-1701 USS Enterprise*, going boldly somewhere, exploring new worlds or something. Hey, her brother would be proud of her for remembering that meaningless collection of letters and numbers.

Breezy's given up trying to keep track of where she is in relation to Earth. For now, it's one of those dots over there. The realization that

Earth is effectively gone makes every worry she's ever had in her life utterly insignificant.

"What is it you want us to see?" she asks the alien imitating Buster.

"Words fail me," Grock says.

Olivia says, "*The Spectacle*, huh? Life has to be raw. Unfiltered."

"It's more than that," Grock replies. "There are things for which words are not enough."

"Like what?"

"Chocolate."

"Chocolate?" she replies, surprised to hear that term being raised on an alien spaceship soaring through the solar system.

Grock says, "Although there are over 300 chemical compounds in chocolate, the primary one is surprisingly simple. It's made out of carbon, hydrogen, nitrogen and oxygen—that's all. To us, it's unremarkable. Seven carbon atoms are linked to eight hydrogen atoms, four nitrogen atoms and two oxygen atoms. It's nothing special. Why all the fuss?"

"Um," Olivia says, shrugging. "It tastes nice."

"What is taste?" Grock asks. "What's nice?"

"Oh, boy," Breezy says, shaking her head.

"See?" Grock says. "There are aspects of life where words fail us. To describe what you will see would be foolish of me. Like chocolate, you must experience it for yourself."

Olivia asks, "You really don't know what chocolate tastes like?"

"No," Grock replies, "For us, human sensations are somewhat of a mystery. Our senses are not alike. We share sight and touch, but we know nothing of taste, sound or smell. For us, music is an odd arrangement of vibrations with interwoven, regular beats. For the most part, it follows natural harmonics, but how or why this is pleasing to you is something we'll never truly understand. Your obsession with tastes and smells is a novelty. You'll describe almost identical molecules as being entirely different."

Olivia is fascinated by his alien perspective. "Like what?"

"Start with a banana. Tack a few perfectly ordinary hydrocarbons on the end and you've got the scent of an orange. To us, they're seemingly identical, but humans insist on them being entirely different."

Olivia laughs.

Grock laughs as well. "This is what I'm talking about."

"Who are you? Where are you from?" Breezy asks, seeing beyond the familiar shape of Buster and realizing she's talking with an intelligence that has traversed the stars.

"Who and where are such human concepts," Grock says. "You would need when and why for such things to be meaningful in my world. Your language is limited. It's linear. You need context, but to draw on one point excludes another. Imagine looking at a flower in a field. The closer you get, the more detail you examine in each petal...."

"The less you see of the field," Olivia says, completing his sentence.

"Yes. It is the whole that concerns us, not each individual part."

"And Buster?" Olivia asks.

Breezy swallows the lump in her throat. She killed Buster. He'd accomplished the impossible. He'd made First Contact with an intelligent extraterrestrial species that otherwise would have cataloged life on Earth and then passed on to some other world where the inhabitants weren't at each other's throats all the time. He found them, helped them, and showed them kindness.

"Buster had an intelligence that is rare in this universe."

371

"How so?" Breezy asks, fighting back tears. Her lips quiver.

"Humans measure intelligence in every way except that which makes sense. You value raw knowledge. Someone recalls obscure facts, and you think they're smart. You build quiz shows around them for entertainment."

"But that's not intelligence," Olivia says.

"No," Grock replies. "Then you judge by conceptualization—the ability to perceive patterns and grasp abstract ideas in a logical manner."

"But that's not it either," Breezy says.

"No."

Olivia laughs. "You're not going to tell us, are you?"

Grock cracks a smile but he avoids saying no. Breezy feels a chill run through her bones. He tilts his head slightly, looking at her in the same manner as the dead clown back in the big top, but she gets it. This is the same technology.

She laughs. It took her a moment to realize, but she's lived this. She's seen this in Buster and Chester. It's obvious now that she thinks about it.

Breezy says, "It's how we treat each other."

Grock nods. As he's sitting in front of them, the distant fiery ring curls in an arc behind him, framing him, bathing all of them in a soft yellow light.

Breezy shakes her head. She has nothing but admiration for Grock. He could assume any form he wants, but he chose Buster. He knows she killed him. And yet he also knows she was blinded by *The Spectacle*. There's no malice, no desire for revenge. He's honoring Buster in his own way.

Olivia says, "What good are all the physics equations and startling insights if we can't help each other?"

"We have read much of your literature," Grock says. "For us, it was Gandhi who said it best: *the true measure of any society can be found in how it treats its most vulnerable.*"

Breezy laughs. "And if you're intelligent, you'll recognize that."

"Exactly."

Olivia hangs her head. "And they shot him."

"Gandhi was a threat," Grock says. "They were afraid of him. But think about what they feared. They weren't afraid of violence or war. They were afraid of peace."

He pauses. There's more to say, but it seems Grock won't force the issue. He wants the two of them to arrive at this conclusion for themselves.

"They were afraid of change," Breezy says, reluctantly completing his thought. Oh, how she wishes Susan were by her side. Susan was right. All Breezy could see in that rundown bar was the importance of now, not the hope of a brighter future.

Breezy's a history buff. She prides herself on knowing the key turning points over the last five hundred years. Nathuram Godse shot Gandhi three times in the chest. It was madness. They were both Hindu! It wasn't the Muslims. It wasn't the Christians. It was Gandhi's own people that betrayed and killed him. John Wilkes Booth shot Abraham Lincoln. He was convinced he was a patriot ridding America of a tyrant and yet he couldn't have been more wrong. James Earl Ray shot Martin Luther King, Jr.—a Catholic killing a Baptist! And for what? Because King wanted a better world? Oswald shot Kennedy. Breezy shot Buster. They all have one thing in common. They all feared change.

There's an ache in her chest, but she knows there's nothing wrong with her. It's grief. Regret is a powerful stimulus precisely because the past cannot be undone. The only option open to her, the only course of redress is *change*. No pleas for forgiveness can cleanse her soul. No penance can be done beyond changing her heart. Even then, it's a poor substitute for his life. If she could, she'd crawl away and hide, but that would be the coward's way out. There's no more fitting punishment than for her to take Buster's place.

Breezy says, "We can't stand the idea that change could be for the better, huh?"

"I get it," Olivia says, oblivious to the anguish Breezy is feeling. "Intelligence is more than knowledge. Being smart isn't enough if you're not smart enough to see the need for change."

"So this is what you're looking for?" Breezy asks. "When you visit different worlds? Intelligence without fear? Without selfishness? Without ego?"

"Yes."

"And Buster had that, huh?"

"Yes."

Olivia says, "What I don't get is why you can't show up at the UN building in New York and talk to our ambassadors? You could explain all this to them just like you have to us."

Grock says, "The only possible outcome would be violence."

"Why? How can you say that?"

Grock is brutal in his assessment. "By our calculations, after running numerous scenarios looking at a variety of First Contact possibilities, the loss of life on Earth would range from half a billion to four billion lives over a decade."

"W—What?" Olivia says. Her eyes go wide. "I don't understand. Why? How?"

Breezy knows. "Because truth is the first casualty in war."

"But we wouldn't be at war," Olivia says.

"Wouldn't we?" Breezy asks, looking at her with raised eyebrows. She understands all too well how First Contact would spiral out of control.

Breezy pulled the trigger on Buster, but not out of malice or hate. She was manipulated into killing him. She was sincere, conscientious, dedicated, devoted, passionate, and patriotic. And all of that was used against her. All of those attributes were weaponized for a cause she didn't even understand. Hell, her unwavering commitment made her an easy mark for Johnson. He used her as he would a car or a knife. She was disposable. It hurts to admit this to herself, but it's true. She wasn't a fool. She wasn't dumb. She was naive. She trusted in the wrong cause. She allowed herself to be used.

Breezy knows what would happen. Nations haggle for influence and power all the time. Countries have gone to war for far less than what's on offer with First Contact. Breezy can see how their rancor would be amplified in the presence of an intelligent species with the ability to leap between stars. Gaining access to even a fraction of that scientific understanding would allow them to dominate other nations. When it comes to politics, the end justifies the means—war would be the logical outcome. And it would be waged by people just like her. They'd be brave and loyal, diligent and committed to their tribe. And just like her, they'd think nothing of pulling the trigger on someone like Buster.

Grock is conspicuously silent. Breezy goes on to say to Olivia, "War would be inevitable. If not with these guys, then with each other. If Grock

375

turned up at the UN, it would be like lighting a match and tossing it in gasoline."

"But why?" Olivia asks.

Breezy says, "Any time there's something to gain, there's something to lose. And no one wants to be a loser."

Grock says, "And yet, if everyone wins, there's nothing to lose."

"But we'll never believe that, huh?" Breezy says. "We're too afraid of losing. We've convinced ourselves we're playing a zero-sum game—only it's a lie. It doesn't exist."

Grock says. "The problem is, lies are the default on your world."

"He's right," Breezy says. "Lies are a tool. They're a lever. They allow people to move others with a minimum of effort. Politically, that makes them more valuable than the truth."

Olivia asks. "Why would anyone lie about First Contact?"

"Why wouldn't they?" Breezy asks. "We lie for a reason. We lie to manipulate others into doing things for us. We lie to gain an advantage we shouldn't have. Once someone falls for a lie, the next one comes all the more easily.

"Look at us! Lies have become so common, we can't agree on anything. Hell, a pandemic ripped around the world and an entire political class talked people *out* of vaccines. That's like telling a drowning man he doesn't need a lifejacket. We humans are stubborn. We will get what we want regardless of whoever stands in our way. And if we can't, we'll lie and cheat and bitch and moan and steal until we do. Lies come easy. They're cheap."

"And they cost lives," Grock says.

"So lies would lead to war?" Olivia asks.

Breezy says, "Lies *are* weapons of war. They're bullets fired without the need for gunpowder."

"So what do we do? What's the answer?" Olivia asks.

"Break the cycle," Grock says. "Open their eyes. Expose *The Spectacle* for what it is—an illusion of importance, a mirage, a fake."

"It's an illusion of our own making," Breezy says.

"A house of cards," Olivia says.

"Yes." Grock gets to his feet. "This has been a good discussion, but you're tired. Please, rest. I'll wake you when we arrive."

"Thank you," Olivia says.

Grock bows slightly and walks away. The two women watch as he walks on nothing but darkness. Stars drift by beneath his feet. The closer he gets to the distant, fiery ring surrounding them, the more his body seems to blend with the flames. There comes a point where he disappears into the light.

"Where do you think they're taking us? To their homeworld?"

"I don't think so," Breezy says. "Grock said he wants to show us something that's ours."

"What does that mean?" Olivia asks. "How can anything beyond Earth be ours?"

Breezy shrugs. She lies back on the soft, lumpy, invisible surface. Out on the edge of her vision, the fiery ring blazes around them. Above her, the stars are magnificent. They're beautiful. She lies there wondering which ones contain life.

Her eyelids grow heavy. Breezy wants to stay awake, but she can't.

ΛLIΞNS

"We're here," a gentle voice says, touching lightly at Breezy's shoulder.

She rolls over, struggling to open her eyes as she mumbles, "I had the weirdest dream."

"Really?" a kind voice asks.

Breezy looks up. She blinks, seeing Grock down on his haunches, crouching beside her. Behind him, the ring of fire glows softly.

He asks, "What did you—"

"Not a dream," she says, pushing herself back a little and sitting up. Olivia's beside her. She nudges her awake.

"Hey," Olivia says, rubbing her eyes.

"I thought you would like to see the approach," Grock says.

"Approach?" Breezy asks, confused. But it's not just his words that confuse her. There's something different about her body. She's not in pain. There are no aches. She reaches up, touching at her ear. The cut is

379

gone. There's no swelling. Her teeth no longer hurt. Damn, these guys could put dentists and doctors out of work.

Grock points above and behind the two women, wanting them to turn and look. Olivia and Breezy exchange a knowing glance. Their worldview is about to change in a way they cannot fathom—and that's *after* being snatched by extraterrestrials and soaring through the depths of outer space.

They turn slowly.

Breezy says, "Oh—My."

Followed by, "God," from Olivia.

"It's beautiful, isn't it?" Grock says, smiling. The women are in shock at the sight before them. It's nothing they haven't seen before, but the scale is mind-boggling. Ammonia clouds glisten tens of thousands of miles away, swirling within the jet stream on Saturn. Intricate patterns form like ribbons blowing in a breeze. Golden clouds entwine themselves with streams of white. They curl around the gas giant, forming distinct bands that stretch around the planet. Sunlight catches different colored clouds at various altitudes. They stir together, mixing in with each other, moving like foam. Shadows are cast by some of the cloud banks, providing a sense of height. Cyclones break through the cloud tops in one region. Eddies twist and turn, dragging behind the storm.

The sheer size of the planet is overwhelming. It stretches back into the darkness. Lightning ripples through the night side, lighting up the clouds.

"The rings!" Olivia says, looking up.

Breezy struggles to pull her eyes away from the planet. Far from being a screenshot on the internet, Saturn is alive with motion. It's subtle, and Breezy has no doubt the winds in the atmosphere are raging at hundreds of miles an hour, but to her, the gas giant behaves like cream swirling in coffee. There's a beauty to the way the gases interact. They move like fluids in a drink, teasing each other as they rise and fall.

Olivia taps Breezy's arm, pointing up.

Breezy knows what the rings of Saturn look like. She's seen a bazillion photos online and yet nothing prepares her for what she sees stretching out above her. The rings are magnificent! They feel as though they're so close she could reach out and touch them. Sunlight catches the frozen fragments, causing them to glisten like diamonds. They're immense. The alien spacecraft seems tiny by comparison. The rings stretch out in a vast curve curling around the planet, soaring out into space. They're regal in appearance, being refined and surprisingly flat.

To her surprise, there are rings within the rings, forming bands. It's the density. In some places, there are gaps. Close to Saturn, the rings are translucent, being almost ghostly in appearance. Then there's a series of thick golden bands. In between, hundreds of thousands of massive icebergs curl in orbit around the gas giant. To Breezy's surprise, some rings are visibly thicker than others, casting shadows. It's as though Saturn has its own celestial barcode.

The rings are in motion. The inner rings move faster than the outer ones. At first, Breezy wasn't sure if it was just her eyes playing tricks on her, but they're swirling around the planet in their own orbits rather than moving as one.

"Moons," Olivia says, pointing.

"Oh, as if this wasn't enough," Breezy chuckles, feeling a sense of childlike delight at the splendor of the gas giant.

One of the moons looks like Saturn itself, minus the rings. It's cloudy, being surrounded by a thick, golden haze. Some moons are rocky, while others are bluish and white, which is a surprising combination.

Grock sits crosslegged behind the women as they kneel in what seems to be outer space, but it can't be. They couldn't survive in a vacuum. The planet and its rings tilt. It takes Breezy a second to realize Saturn hasn't moved—it's their orientation that's changed. The glowing ring of the spacecraft accelerates, taking them out from beneath the icy rings.

"Okay," Breezy says. "I'm convinced."

"Oh," Grock says. "This is not what we wanted you to see."

"It's not?" Olivia asks.

"What awaits is something far more grand, something far more rare and precious." He points at an icy moon rapidly growing in size before them.

Craters pockmark the white billiard ball floating in front of them in the darkness of space, but the impacts have peppered just one region in what to Breezy looks like the northeast. Deep green lines run through ice-like veins to the south. They curl around the moon. There are canyons and crevasses, but they bunch up along the edge of what appears to be plates of glacial ice.

As their craft descends, the surface of the tiny world reminds her of an ice skating rink. Lines crisscross the surface, but they largely follow the same direction in each area. At one point, they'll be transverse, running across in front of her, then they'll abruptly change direction by thirty degrees, forty-five degrees, ninety degrees. The result is a patchwork quilt of streaked ice.

The alien spacecraft races across the surface at an altitude of a few hundred miles. Mountains and ridges pass beneath them. Often, they're bunched up like the edge of a sheet thrown lazily over a bed.

The craft descends, lowering itself within a broad crevasse curling around the glistening moon. On either side of them, walls of ice tower over the spacecraft. They descend deeper into the valley, winding their way through the fractured ice.

"There," Grock says. "We are just in time."

"In time for what?" Olivia asks as the craft descends toward a plateau about halfway down the side of the valley. Fine snow is kicked up as the ship settles, forming a brief whiteout. It disperses, settling back to the surface.

"This fissure extends another fifteen miles beneath the ice," he says, pointing at the deep crack running along the valley floor.

The glowing ring around them softens and fades from sight now that the craft is resting on the surface of the ice moon. A small cigar-shaped craft departs the mothership, becoming visible as it rises above them. It's dark, almost black in color. It shoots along the canyon like a missile, disappearing from sight.

"We'll take samples to show you," Grock says. He points along the glacial canyon, saying, "Any moment now."

The women peer down the valley. Although they're suspended a few feet above the ice, they can feel the surface tremble through the invisible hull of the spacecraft. Ahead, boulders the size of buildings crumble from the walls, falling into the valley. Their motion is slow. They crumple, breaking apart as they slide into the chasm, leaving fractured blue/white cliffs behind.

With Saturn at their backs and the sun glistening off the ice, the dark of space is disturbing to behold. The sky should be blue. The pitch-black rising over them feels ominous. Tremors continue to shake the craft. Out on the horizon, a curtain rises. Breezy's not sure what she's looking at. Everything unfolds in utter silence—the falling ice, the streams of white rising high into the darkness, the boulders crashing into the chasm. All she can hear is her heart thumping inside her chest.

"See?" Grock says, smiling.

A curtain is raised, lifting from the ice toward the sky. It's semi-transparent. Streaks line the curves racing into the darkness. Ice crystals spray out into space. As the broad stream rises, it thins, dispersing high overhead.

"What is that?" she asks.

"A geyser," Grock says. "The moon flexes, the pressure builds, the ice fractures and the sea bursts forth from beneath."

"There's water down there?" Olivia asks. "Beneath the ice?"

"More water than in Lake Baikal, the largest freshwater lake on Earth. There's almost as much as is found in the Caspian Sea."

"You brought us here to show us water on another world?" Breezy asks.

"Not just water," Grock says as the thin black shuttle returns to the invisible mothership. The craft glides above them. The slick skin is so close Breezy could reach out and touch it. A panel slides open. Grock reaches and pulls out a hollow box. Twelve chrome struts form a cube enclosing a shard of blue ice almost a foot in length. It's suspended within the cube without any visible means of support.

"Look," he says, holding the cube before the women as the craft retreats.

Although the fractured ice is solid, it's largely transparent. The center hasn't frozen. Water sloshes around within it. No, wait. Breezy looks closer. Tiny worm-like creatures wriggle within the fluid.

"Life!" Olivia says, barely able to speak.

"You are not alone," Grock says. "Not even in your own system."

"And this is what you showed Buster?" Breezy asks.

"We wanted him to see. We wanted him to understand. Life does not end at the edge of your atmosphere."

"How is this possible?" Olivia asks.

"Your system has been stable for over four billion of your years. It is plenty of time for life to arise."

"So out there?" Breezy asks, gesturing to the dark void of space overhead.

"There is life," Grock says. "Not everywhere. Not around every star. But given time, given a stable environment, life will arise. It is as natural as any planet."

The glowing ring appears again as the spacecraft lifts off the surface of the icy moon. The vast crevasse falls away. Fresh cracks mark the ice. The geyser continues to erupt, sending ice crystals racing hundreds of miles into the sky. Over the course of a few minutes, the spacecraft flips over and flies away. As they can barely feel the motion, it seems as though it's the tiny moon that's moving, swinging around and above them. Saturn itself, along with its stunning rings, seems to invert and recede from them.

"We have a long flight back to Earth," Grock says. "You should rest."

HOME

Olivia has a thumping headache. She's dehydrated. She reaches up, pressing her palm hard against her temple, trying to cancel out the pain. She rolls her hand around, soothing the storm raging within her head.

Cars drive past, but they're barely a monotonous drone whizzing by on some distant freeway. She sits up. Her clothes are damp from the dew forming on the grass. Her eyes struggle to focus in the darkness. Lights blur before her. She squints. A boat pushes on against the current. Its navigation lights blink, sending reflections racing across the Potomac.

"What the hell?" she mutters, feeling unsteady as she gets to her feet. The silhouette of the trees looming over her darkens the sky. Around her, the wreckage of the circus lies scattered throughout the forest. A string of dead lightbulbs hangs from a branch. A sign lies crooked against a bush. Carefully calligraphed words read: *The Greatest Show on Earth*. A popcorn stand has flipped over.

The glass in a ticket booth has been smashed. The flimsy structure has collapsed on two sides. In the moonlight, the joyful red and white strips look pale and grey. A tree branch has punctured one of the panels like a sword thrust into its side.

"Was any of that real?" she mumbles, followed by, "I gotta stop doing drugs."

Olivia steps through the undergrowth on the edge of the forest. Rugged boot prints mark where police officers in tactical gear must have trod through the grass, exposing the mud beneath. She stops and leans down, picking up a rainbow-colored clown wig for no other reason than to touch something.

Olivia tosses the wig to one side and stares down at her feet. She's got a dirty sock on one foot while her other foot is bare, reminding her of her time in the high-altitude desert plateaus of central Asia.

There's talking nearby.

Someone's whispering.

Soft voices drift on the wind.

"Breezy? Is that you?"

They fall quiet.

Olivia whispers, "Breezy, I really need to know that's you and not god-knows-what-else."

There's no answer.

Olivia pushes off a tree, staggering toward the collapsed big top. Ropes and wires stretch across the ground. Steel pegs have been wrenched from the earth, dragging clods of grass and soil with them. The frame of the rollercoaster lies crumpled in the distance. The various flimsy buildings and tents within the sideshow alley have been flattened.

"Where are you?" she asks the darkness.

Olivia is unsure about what lies hidden around her in the night. A cool wind curls through the trees. Scraps of paper lift off the ground, tumbling across the grass.

Over by the grandstand, an abandoned police car lies on its roof. Claws have scratched the paint on one of the doors. The trunk is open. Its contents have fallen in a heap on the ground.

There's more talking. It's hurried. Olivia can make out the direction but not the words. She walks forward.

Hundreds of broken mirrors lie scattered on the nearby grass. The dark glass reflects the stars back at her. As she's barefoot, Olivia steps away from the shattered fragments. She walks on the fallen canvas. Bleachers and poles have scattered beneath the tent, making it impossible to walk in a straight line. Out across the open field beyond the circus, she sees a car parked on the road. A set of emergency lights sit idle on its roof. From the front seat, there's a slight glow. Someone's looking at a smartphone. *Fuck.* It's got to be a cop keeping watch over the ruins of the circus.

"Breezy. I need you."

"Olivia?" a familiar voice replies from out of the darkness.

"Where are you."

"I—I'm over here."

In the dead of night, that's no help. Olivia turns, not seeing her friend.

"By the cages."

She doubles back toward the forest. The ruined remains of several animal cages have been strung out in a row toward a thicket on the edge of the woods. Most of them have been crushed. Their steel bars have skewed sideways. The cage doors have swung open.

"Hang on," Olivia says. She finds Breezy half-buried by the fallen canvas next to an overturned cage. How did she end up here? When the aliens dropped them in the desert, they were within a few feet of each other. Why is it different this time?

"Are you okay?" Olivia asks, offering her a hand.

Breezy accepts, getting to her feet with a bit of help. "Yeah. I'm good."

"Is something wrong?" Olivia asks, feeling Breezy's on edge.

"No. Nothing."

"Did you hear someone else moving around?"

"No."

"I heard whispering," Olivia says softly. "I think there's someone else hiding in here."

"There's no one," Breezy replies, but she's too confident. How could she know for sure? Olivia's convinced she heard voices. Breezy seems to read her mind. She says, "It's just us."

As if to contradict her, a spotlight ripples across the fallen tent and a male voice bellows, "Who's there?"

Olivia jumps in fright. She preferred the soft whispers. She and Breezy crouch beside the wheel of a cage lying on its side. The spotlight catches grease dripping from a broken axle.

"This is a crime scene. You shouldn't be here!"

"Who's that?" Breezy asks, confused.

"It's a cop," she whispers. "This way."

Olivia leads Breezy sideways, slightly below the brow of the hill, staying low among the debris, keeping to the edge of the fallen tent.

"If I catch you kids, you're in so much trouble," the officer bellows, but he's looking in the wrong place. He's walked toward the forest. As useful as his flashlight is, it's also a tell. It not only allows them to see where he is but in which direction he's facing. The two women stay low, working their way toward the far fence line. Olivia grabs the chainlink fence with both hands. She looks up at the barbed wire, preparing herself for the agony of going over the top.

"No," Breezy says, pointing toward the road. "There's a gap in the fence. Up there. By the stables."

The cop circles around. He stays wide of the fallen big top, calling out, "I know you're here. You'd better run back to Mommy, 'cause if I catch you...."

Breezy pulls on the wire, holding the gap in the fence open for Olivia. She scoots through and then reaches back, holding the fence up as Breezy crawls through on her hands and knees. A flicker of light brushes across them and passes on, rippling over the trees. Fractions of a second later, it swings back, illuminating them. Breezy grabs Olivia's hand and dashes into the bushes on the vacant lot next to the fairgrounds, rustling leaves and breaking twigs.

"Yeah, you'd better run," the cop yells, jogging up to the fence. He's overweight and out of shape. He stops beside the gap in the fence and shines the light back and forth, scanning for them. The two women hide behind a couple of trees not more than twenty feet away. After he's satisfied they're gone, the officer marches back through the long grass toward his car. His radio squawks with traffic, but he doesn't report anything about what he must assume was a couple of teens out trophy hunting.

Breezy and Olivia make their way to the road. As the cop car is sitting in the gravel parking lot in front of the circus, facing the river, they can see him silhouetted back in the warmth of his front seat.

"Quick," Breezy says, but Olivia's struggling on the rough ground. Broken twigs dig into the soft soles of her feet, making it painful to rush. Breezy's already on the other side of the road, taking shelter behind a brick wall. Olivia dances over the sharp gravel on the edge of the concrete. Ouch! She doesn't even bother looking to see which way the cop is looking now. She doesn't care. This is worse than being caught. She might as well be walking on LEGOs scattered on the carpet.

Breezy beckons for her to hurry, waving her arms in the shadows. Olivia hobbles over the road and joins her.

"I hope you've got a plan," Olivia says. "I can't go on like this much longer."

Breezy looks her in the eyes. "We've got to warn the Vice President. He knows there's a coup in motion, but he doesn't know where it's coming from so he can't stop it."

"And how are *we* going to do that?"

"I'm still figuring that bit out," Breezy says, creeping down an alley running parallel with the road leading to the fairgrounds. To one side, there are the rear entrances to garages and stores. On the other side, there are ramshackle homes. Solid steel doors along with bars on the windows give a clear indication of the crime rates in the area. A rickety wooden fence runs along the far side of the alley. Houses sit in darkness. Their occupants are asleep. A narrow side alley leads the two women back to the main road. The cop car is out of sight, being just over the brow of the hill.

"Do you like motorcycles?" Breezy asks, pointing further down the road.

"You're going to steal some wheels from the White Lords? Are you insane?"

"It'll be dawn before they notice," Breezy says, walking down the street and keeping to the shadows. As the sky to the east is already starting to lighten, that's little comfort to Olivia.

The gang's sleazy bar is several hundred yards away. A neon light flashes out the front, but there's no movement within. If anyone's awake, they haven't turned on any lights. The gang must own the buildings on either side as the windows are open. Curtains blow in the breeze. It seems the one thing they're not afraid of is being robbed. A row of motorcycles has been lined up in front of the bar. Several of them have scratched chrome mufflers and dented fuel tanks.

Olivia whispers, "Why do I get the feeling you really hate these guys?"

Breezy grins. She crouches, moving between bikes, feeling around beneath the speedometers on the handlebars.

Olivia should be quiet, but she can't help herself.

"What are you doing?"

"Shush."

A shadow moves within the bar. Someone's walking around in there. The two women duck down between the bikes. They're illuminated by a streetlight, so they're hardly out of sight.

Breezy continues fiddling with something beneath the center console of each bike. She's feeling for something specific. Olivia trails along a few bikes behind her, keeping her back to the street, watching the vast folding glass windows within the bar. They're shut, but they provide a clear view both ways. She catches sight of someone jogging up a set of internal stairs.

Above them, the sky fades from pitch black to dark blue. Clouds up high in the stratosphere light up with shades of pink and red. Hints of yellow catch the leading edge of the thin clouds. In any other context, it would be an absolutely beautiful dawn. For Olivia, it's terrifying. She's waiting for someone to yell at them, catching them in the act of stealing from a bunch of jacked-up white supremacists.

Breezy pauses. She holds still between two bikes, looking across the street away from the bar. Her lips move but there's no sound. It's as though she's talking to someone but no one's there.

"What is it?" Olivia asks, crouching and looking in the same direction. "What can you see?"

Olivia doesn't see anything beyond shuttered windows, steel roller doors and graffiti. She's more worried about someone spotting them from the darkened bar behind the two of them. Olivia's anxious to get moving.

"Come on," Olivia whispers, feeling exposed. She reaches out, touching Breezy's shoulder. Breezy turns and looks at her as though she's seen a ghost.

"Are you all right?" Olivia asks. "Is everything okay?"

"Fine," Breezy says, creeping around to face the next motorcycle. A one-word answer is not convincing.

"Got it," Breezy finally says, crouching beside the second-to-last motorbike. She's turning something with both hands. It's the locking ring surrounding the ignition cylinder. She pulls the cylinder out. Wires hang from the device. Several support prongs protrude from beneath it.

"I hope you know what you're doing."

"Almost there."

A dog barks from out the back of the bar. At first, it's sporadic, but the dog grows more agitated. Someone yells, "Shut up!" But that only infuriates the dog. It barks, becoming more aggravated. The dog tugs at its chain. Steel links rattle as it tries to get to a fence in the alley beside the bar. The dog must be able to smell them.

Someone throws something out a window at the back of the second floor. It hits the dog, and the poor creature yelps and sulks away.

Breezy digs around inside the console, using the prongs on the cylinder to jimmy the lock. She grimaces, twisting hard. There's a click.

"Got you!"

She fiddles with the cylinder and twists a few wires together before draping it over the side of the gas tank. Lights glow softly on the console of the motorcycle.

"Come on," Breezy says, gesturing for Olivia to join her.

Quietly, Breezy flicks the kickstand and walks the bike out onto the road. She straddles the seat, using her feet to flick the gear lever and ensure the bike is in neutral. Olivia climbs on the back of the seat. Breezy pushes the motorbike along with both legs. At this point on the hill, the slope is gentle. They roll away in near silence. As the road gets steeper, they go faster. Once they're roughly fifty yards away, Breezy slips the bike into second gear and pops the clutch. The bike lurches. The engine starts.

"Nice," Olivia says with her arms around her waist. "Where to?"

Breezy leans into a corner, riding toward the freeway onramp. She calls out, "Neither of us can go home. We'll head to Susan's hospital apartment. She'll have spare clothes and a shower."

"A shower?" Olivia says. "Oh, hell yeah."

Olivia holds on tight as Breezy accelerates. Olivia's out of ideas. For now, racing along on the back of a bike with the wind catching her hair is as good as anything. The hum of the engine gives her time to think. Right now, any plan that involves a hot shower and a change of clothes gets her vote. As for stopping a coup or dealing with aliens, Olivia's happy to leave that to Breezy. She's just along for the ride—literally.

The sky is a stunning shade of purple and pink by the time they turn into an alley beside the VA hospital on the outskirts of DC. A light blue glow reaches along the horizon to the east. Breezy parks the bike out of sight from the road, bringing it around behind a dumpster.

"This way," she says as they hop off. Breezy jogs across the parking lot separating the hospital from an apartment complex. Olivia tries to keep up, but her feet hurt.

The reception area is brightly lit. There's a security guard at the desk.

"Breezy?" he asks, getting to his feet as she walks in.

Olivia's waiting for Breezy to take him down and club him with his own baton, but she says, "Hey, George. Is Susan here?"

"Ah, yeah," he says, glancing down at a printout. "She's in 4C. Are you okay? Is everything all right?"

Olivia interrupts, feeling she might have a slight advantage being unknown but still obviously with Breezy. "We were mugged," she says, holding her hands out and gesturing at her filthy, torn clothes and lack of shoes.

"Do you need me to call the cops?" the guard asks.

Breezy turns to Olivia with raised eyebrows as if to say, *What the hell? Shut up!*

"The cops?" Olivia says with exaggerated emphasis. "Oh, we've just come from the precinct. Those pricks wouldn't even give us a lift home. Can you believe that? Two gals out on the town for a good time. Get jumped by a mugger. And all they care about is filling out their goddamn paperwork."

The guard walks over to the elevator, hailing it for them. He waves his security card over a sensor, saying, "They're useless, huh?"

"You got that," Olivia says, smiling at him and making eye contact.

"Well, you two take care," the guard says. Breezy hits the button for the fourth floor.

"Will do. Thanks, George," Breezy says, looking relieved.

The elevator doors close. The two women sigh. For Olivia, there's a sublime, serene beauty about being in a small steel box, riding between floors. After traveling for millions of miles in an open spacecraft, the sense of claustrophobia is welcome—it's the bright lights shining overhead, the glow of the buttons, the mirrors on the walls, the polished handrails, the maintenance hatch in the ceiling. They're familiar. She looks awful. Olivia ruffles her hair, fussing with it in the mirror but to no avail.

"This way," Breezy says as the doors open. She leads her down the corridor and knocks on a nearby door briskly. There's no answer. Breezy knocks again.

"Hang on. Hang on," a woman's voice says from the other side.

The door opens a fraction, being secured by a chain. A pair of eyes peer out from the darkness within. The chain rattles as the lock is released.

"Breeze? Oh, my god, Breezy. What happened to you?"

"Hi," Olivia says, leaning around Breezy and waving. "You must be Susan."

"What is going on?" Susan asks, opening the door and turning on a light.

A teenage girl is sleeping on the couch within the tiny apartment. She sits up, rubbing her eyes. "Mom?"

"Alice," Breezy says, rushing over and hugging her. Susan joins them, but she seems alarmed by Breezy's dirty, torn, bloody clothing. She fusses with her shirt.

"I'm Olivia, by the way."

No one responds. They're too busy hugging each other. Okay. Whatever. Olivia closes the door.

"Do you mind if I?" Olivia asks, pointing at the fridge in the kitchenette. The three of them are too busy sobbing and mumbling through their tears.

"You were right," Breezy says, looking deep into Susan's eyes and holding her with trembling hands. "You were right and I was wrong."

"OJ," Olivia says, looking inside the fridge. She picks up the container. There's not much left. "If you don't mind, I'm just going to chug this."

No one responds so she knocks it back. Not-so-freshly-squeezed orange juice that's actually made from reconstituted frozen pulp has never tasted so goddamn good. Olivia puts the empty plastic bottle on the bench and closes the fridge.

"May I?" she asks to no reply, pointing at the fruit bowl. The other three are too busy pushing their foreheads together. Tears run down their cheeks. Breezy says the word *stupid* far too often for Olivia's liking, but she's referring to herself. Olivia's never been one for making up after a breakup. She rolls on. That's more her style, but she can see the emotion shared by Breezy, Susan and Alice. It's real. Their anguish is visceral.

Olivia peels a banana. It's a little overripe, but it tastes a helluva lot better than goat's cheese in salty flatbread. She sits at a small round table and kicks her feet up on one of the other chairs.

"What's going on?" Susan finally asks, sitting back on the couch next to Breezy and Alice. "Are you guys in some kind of trouble?"

Breezy replies, "Ah, Olivia is a witness."

"A witness?" Olivia says. That is *not* the way she sees herself, but okay. She waits to see where Breezy is going with this.

"There's been a breach in the security profile around the—"

Olivia interrupts. "Have you seen *Star Wars*?"

"What are you doing?" Breezy asks, narrowing her eyebrows as she glares at Olivia.

Olivia doesn't care. She points at Susan, saying, "Do you want the long-winded version or the summary?"

Susan shrugs.

Alice says, "*Star Wars*?"

"Yeah. Number two. Or is it number five? I get confused. The one with the big walking dog machine things in the snow."

"*The Empire Strikes Back*?" Susan says with a worried look on her face.

"That's it," Olivia says. "We've been there. To Hoth. The ice moon."

"What is she talking about?" Susan asks, shaking her head in disbelief and turning to Breezy.

"You know about the clowns, right?" Olivia asks.

Susan and Alice nod.

"They're aliens," Breezy says.

"They're what?"

"It's true," Olivia says.

Alice lowers her head, looking at Olivia with a befuddled expression on her face. "The clowns are aliens, and they took you to a fictional planet that doesn't exist?"

"Oh, it's real," Olivia says. "It's a moon in orbit around Saturn. I saw the rings and everything for myself!"

"Enceladus?" Susan asks, wanting clarification.

"That's it," Olivia says, snapping her fingers and pointing at her. "I knew it was something like Hoth or Enchilada or something crazy like that." She laughs at herself.

Susan looks at Breezy, who's conspicuously silent. "Have you taken any drugs I should know about?"

Olivia says, "It's no wonder Buster couldn't get anyone to believe him."

"I know it sounds crazy," Breezy says. "Look. I have proof."

"You do?" Olivia says. She's more surprised than either Susan or Alice, who seem utterly confused.

"Look at the leg of my jeans," Breezy says, shifting forward on the couch and positioning her knee well out in front of her. "Look at the dried blood. Look at the way the denim has torn. You've got an entry point and an exit wound, but...."

"But no wound," Susan says, leaning forward and touching the frayed material.

"You're an ER doctor," Breezy says. "You tell me what you're looking at."

"Ah," Susan says, twisting her head slightly as she runs her fingers over the denim. "I mean, it's consistent with a handgun entry/exit, but you'd have no knee. A 9mm round would have punched through the cartilage and bone like a box of tissues. From the angle, it would have severed the posterior tibial artery or at least crushed it."

"And it did," Breezy says. "And it hurt like *fuck!*"

"The bleeding would have been profuse. If—If you presented with that in Emergency, you'd lose your lower leg! The damage would just be too great."

"I know," Breezy says.

"But?"

"Aliens," Olivia says, raising her eyebrows.

"Aliens isn't a rational explanation," Susan says. "You might as well say, magic!"

"Uh, oh," Alice says, interrupting. "That thing Clarke said. Remember?"

"Clarke?" Breezy asks, unsure who her daughter is referring to.

"Arthur C. Clarke," Susan says. "Ah, he said, any sufficiently advanced alien technology would seem like magic to us. Kinda like showing a caveman an iPhone."

Breezy laughs. "Have you been geeking out with my daughter again?"

"I might have been," Susan says with a smile.

"So they're real?" Alice asks with unbridled enthusiasm. "You've seen them?"

"Oh, we've seen *something*," Olivia says, but she's not quite as enthusiastic. "And these aren't your anal-probe aliens of conspiracy lore. They're real."

"*Olivia!*" Breezy says with a stern look on her face.

"What?" Olivia replies, holding her hands out in her defense. "You think she hasn't heard of—"

"Don't," Breezy says, cutting her off and pointing a stern finger at her.

Susan says, "Can we get back to the aliens? Who are they? Are they going to land and make contact?"

"They already have," Breezy says. "One of their shuttlecraft crashed in the mountains north of Afghanistan."

Olivia clarifies. "It was one of the 'Stans but not Afghanistan."

Susan shakes her head. It's a point that doesn't seem important to her.

"That's where they met Buster," Olivia says.

"And?" Susan asks.

"It's complicated," Breezy says.

"They're worried about going public," Olivia says. "Based on what they've seen on social media, they think we'll tear ourselves apart."

"Huh," Susan says. "Well, they're not wrong on that count. The President has stood down the military, but Congress has branded the Clowns as a terrorist organization. And the people have reacted. There are protests in most major cities."

Breezy buries her head in her hands, rocking forward and leaning on her knees as she says, "We've got to figure this thing out. I don't understand what Johnson is doing or why."

"Easy," Susan says, rubbing her back. "It's okay. You're here now. You're safe. Deep breaths."

"Um," Olivia says. "You wouldn't happen to have a change of clothes, would you?"

"Oh, sure," Susan replies, getting to her feet. "Of course. Alice, can you run Olivia a shower? I'll get her some clothing."

Alice leads Olivia to a bathroom next to the tiny bedroom. Both are just off the kitchenette. Several cardboard boxes have been stacked in the bedroom. Susan rummages through them.

As Olivia squeezes past into the bathroom, Alice says, "You smell like a zoo."

Olivia sticks her head back out of the doorway and addresses Breezy. "I really like this kid!"

"Not a kid," Alice says, walking away and leaving her to start the shower.

Once the water is up to temperature, Olivia dumps her clothing in the corner of the bathroom and steps into the shower. Hot water streams over her body, soothing her aching muscles. She faces the jets, allowing them to massage her cheeks and forehead. Steam fogs the glass. She rubs shampoo through her hair and scrubs her body with soap before rinsing her hair and rubbing in some conditioner. There's a knock at the door. At first, Olivia assumes it's a hurry-up signal from Breezy, but the door cracks open and some folded clothing is placed on the floor along with a towel.

"Thanks."

Olivia could stand there forever beneath the shower. It's with reluctance that she turns off the water. Susan's given her some fresh underwear, jeans and a plain pink t-shirt but no bra. That's no surprise as sizing is individual, but it means Olivia's got to put her smelly, sweat-ridden bra back on. She gives it a few squirts of perfume, spraying the sweet smell of jasmine on the cotton. For now, that'll have to do.

Once she's dressed, she opens the door to see Breezy standing there with a towel and fresh clothing, ready for her turn.

"It's good," Olivia says. "Real good. So so good."

Breezy chuckles. "Oh, I can't wait."

Susan hands Olivia a mug. "Coffee?"

"Oh, yes. Yes!"

"What was it like?" Alice asks, sitting at the table with Olivia and Susan.

"Better than any movie," Olivia replies. She turns to Susan. "Did Breezy tell you about our time in the *Stan*?"

"She said something about an anti-aircraft gun on the back of a flatbed truck."

"Oh, she wanted to fire that thing so badly."

"I bet. But she didn't, right?"

"No," Olivia says, laughing. "Ah, we met Buster's twin brother, Chester. He's a legend. He smuggles refugees to Europe. Mostly women and children on the run. He told us about them."

"Them?" Susan asks, wanting clarification.

"The aliens. I think they wanted us to hear about the clowns from him."

"And them?" Alice asks. She's got her elbows on the table and her chin resting against her hands. "What do they look like?"

"We never saw them," Olivia says. "They were worried it would freak us out. Like being abducted by aliens and whisked away past the moon toward deep space wouldn't freak us out! We spoke to someone that looks like Buster. I guess it was a robot or something."

"And they took you to Saturn?" Susan asks.

"Yes. The rings are—well, they're huge! As big as you might think they are, they're bigger. And they're thin. And they're in motion. Everything's moving. I mean, it's like the pictures you see from NASA and yet it's not. It's—it's real."

404

"And they took you to Enceladus?"

"They said it was ours," Olivia says. "I think they meant: it's life in our solar system, so it's part of our home. Funny, I'd only ever thought of Earth as home, but I guess it's the whole thing."

"So there's life on Enceladus?" Susan asks.

"Beneath the ice," Olivia says. She holds up her thumb and forefinger to show the size. "Worm things."

"Worms?" Alice says, screwing up her nose at the idea.

"Life is a big deal," Susan says. "Any kind of life beyond Earth rewrites the science textbooks."

"I guess," Alice says. "But worms?"

"Worms," Olivia says, shrugging.

Susan says, "As simple as it seems, that would set the scientific community alight."

Breezy comes out of the bathroom, rubbing her hair dry with a towel.

"That was quick," Alice says.

"I think that's the quickest shower you've ever had," Susan says.

"Too much to do," Breezy replies.

"Coffee?" Susan asks.

"I'd love one," Breezy says, sitting at the table.

"So, what's the plan?" Olivia asks.

"The plan is simple: warn the Vice President that Director Johnson is the one behind the coup."

"Okay. How?"

"An old friend of mine, Agent John Alexander, can get us inside," she says, followed by, "Susan, can I use your phone?"

"Sure," Susan says, unlocking it and handing it to her.

"But," Olivia says, sensing there's something still bugging Breezy.

"But there's a problem," Breezy says, tapping on the smartphone and looking up a phone number.

Olivia knows. "Too many unanswered questions."

"Yep."

"I don't understand," Susan says.

Olivia says, "We know what he's doing. We don't know why."

"Exactly," Breezy says. "What does Director Johnson get from all this? What does he gain?"

Olivia says, "When Buster and I were with the VP, he thought Senator Langford was behind all this."

"Did he say why?" Breezy asks.

"No," Olivia replies. "Just that he was being a pest."

"Why does Johnson want Langford to be the next President?" Susan asks. "What does the director get out of that?"

"I don't know," Breezy says.

"And why complicate all this?" Olivia asks. "Why frame the Clowns?"

Breezy sips her coffee slowly.

Susan says, "That's a good point. They could frame anyone, right? I mean, why leave a trail? A lone wolf makes more sense than an organization. All they need to do is snuff out their Lee Harvey Oswald and the trail goes cold. A fake trail is dangerous. It could lead back to them. Isn't a dead-end a better option?"

Breezy stares blindly into the kitchenette, not making eye contact with anyone. She finishes her coffee, saying, "He knows something we don't."

"What do you mean?"

"Johnson's been playing cat and mouse with the Clowns for years—across multiple administrations. Suddenly, all that changes. Suddenly, he starts poking and prodding them. Why?"

Olivia says, "And don't forget—they struck back. They destroyed that building downtown."

The doubt in Susan's voice is apparent, but she seems compelled to ask, "Is he trying to start a war?"

Breezy nods, saying, "Maybe that's it. Langford's a war hawk. Johnson needs a President that's prepared to go into battle."

"Are you serious?" Olivia says, not liking what she's hearing.

"It's the reason for all the churn. It's the only thing that makes any sense. Johnson wants to go public. For that, he needs public outrage. And when he does go public, he needs someone that won't shrink from a fight."

"That's insane," Olivia says. "He can't for a moment think he'll win. These guys can fly between stars! Hell, it took us less than a day to get to Saturn. What's that for one of our rockets. Weeks? Months?"

"Years," Susan says.

"We're not going to win a war against them," Olivia says. "Sure, we've got nukes. But what have they got? They could have planet killers."

"It makes no sense," Susan says.

"Unless," Breezy says.

"Unless what?"

"Unless something's changed. Unless he's figured out some way to tip the balance in his favor."

"You think he wants to catch them?" Susan asks, raising her eyebrows in surprise.

"I think he's tempted to try."

Olivia says, "*Fuck!*"

THE WEST WING

Olivia's lived in D.C. for almost a decade. She knows what it's like when the place gets locked down with security for a head of state visit or when protest marches hit town. After all that's gone on over the past few days, including two jets colliding and crashing near the White House, she's expecting empty roads. The streets are crowded. People are walking on the edge of the road because the sidewalks are packed.

"What's going on?"

Susan keeps her eyes on the road. "You guys are what's going on. It's the clowns. They're shutting everything down. It's like this in capital cities all around the world."

"But it's over," Olivia says. "Buster's dead. There are no more clowns."

"Apparently, they disagree," Susan replies. "Buster may have died. The revolution lives on."

"And the police aren't trying to break them up?" Olivia asks.

"It's hard for police to form a line against other police officers," Susan says. "No one knew just how deep the clowns had penetrated society. Theirs has been a quiet revolution."

Olivia watches as a skinhead with tattoos wrapping around his neck helps an elderly black lady across the street. She's frail with a stooped back, carrying a sign that reads, "*If not now, when?*"

"I don't get it. How is this possible?" Olivia asks, leaning forward from the back seat and pulling against her seatbelt as she points at the two of them.

"We rally around things we share," Susan says. "In the past, that's been skin color or gender, country or culture. I think the clowns got through to us. What we really share is life. That's all that defines the tribe. Nothing more. Nothing less."

Ahead, the crowd swells, covering the street, but the protest is orderly. There's no chanting or yelling. There are very few placards. People are marching to be seen, not to cause a stir. The sheer number of people on the streets speaks loudly enough. A band is playing from a balcony. The lead singer is a woman in her early twenties. She's wearing hippie clothes and belting out John Lennon's classic, *Give Peace a Chance*. The song is easily fifty years old. Peace has long been out of reach, but the desire is still there. The crowd marching past sings along with the chorus.

"We're not going to make it to Lafayette Park," Susan says, turning onto a side street. "You're going to have to walk from here."

"Are you okay?" Olivia asks Breezy, tapping on her shoulder from the back of the car. Breezy's sitting in the front passenger's seat. She's quiet, which is out of character for her.

"Yeah, fine. Just nerves, I guess."

Before Olivia can respond, Susan says, "You be careful. Okay?"

"Will do."

Olivia wants to ask Breezy about her nerves but the moment is gone. In the time Olivia's known her, Breezy has been anything but nervous. She rescued her from the hospital and took on a stupid number of cops at the circus. She faced down armed bandits in the desert with ice in her veins. She was ready to slit the throat of the guard in the *Kindzhak* jail. When a drunk pissed against the tire of one of the trucks, Olivia was sure Breezy was going to plunge her glass shiv into the guy's neck. This is the woman that wanted to shoot an anti-aircraft cannon at anyone that followed them. Why is she anxious?

Susan brings the car to a stop by the curb and puts the gear shifter in park. She pops her seatbelt and leans over, kissing Breezy on the cheek. "Come back to me, okay?"

"And me," Alice says from the backseat beside Olivia. "I want you back too."

"And me?" Olivia jokes.

"You come back too," Susan says, squeezing Olivia's knee.

Olivia and Breezy get out of the vehicle. Susan waves as she drives off. Olivia waves back. Breezy just stands there, looking into the distance. She's staring away from the White House, peering down the street in the wrong direction, looking at the crowd walking toward them. She's focused, but on what? Her lips move. She's mumbling.

"Is everything okay?" Olivia asks.

Breezy snaps. "Everything's fine!"

After all they've been through, it's disconcerting to see Breezy cracking under pressure. The strain is starting to show.

"Is something wrong?" Olivia asks.

"No. Nothing," Breezy says, being unusually adamant.

411

"And you're sure you're up for this?"

"Yes," Breezy says, snapping herself out of whatever anxiety has been bouncing around inside her head. "It would be nice if we had some backup, you know?"

"Hey, I don't want to go in there either," Olivia says. "I'm quite happy to talk to the Vice President over the phone. We can still do that."

"No, no," Breezy says, turning and walking toward Lafayette Square. The White House is visible beyond the lush oak trees in the park. She says, "As it is, it will be difficult to convince him we're sane. We stand a chance if we're face to face. Over the phone, he'll just hang up on a couple of wackos."

As they walk on, they pass uniformed police officers on the various street corners. They're more interested in keeping people moving and turning vehicles around than deterring the protests. They joke with people in the crowd. Once the two women are in the park, they're forced onto the grass to make any headway.

"And John's going to get us in there?" Olivia asks, pointing at the White House as they cross Pennsylvania Ave. "Without ID?"

"He'll work some magic," Breezy says.

"But he thinks I'm a terrorist, right?"

"He saw me shoot Buster," Breezy says. "He thinks I'm one of the good guys. If I say you're a deep-cover operative, he'll buy it."

"I hope you're right."

The protesters in front of the White House are carrying placards.

No More Lies

No More Excuses

412

No More Delays

In any other context, the confusion of different banners for multiple, different causes wouldn't make any sense. Seen together, they would dilute each other, but the underlying principle behind all of these causes is the same: the need for change.

Moms Demand Action

Bring Down the Cis-tem

Keep your religious hands off my body

Gun Sense is Common Sense

Quit Clowning Around with Our Climate Future

The Time for Change was Yesterday

The two women push their way through the crowd and past the circular drive leading to the White House front entrance. On reaching the Marine post on the side road separating the West Wing from the Executive Office building, Olivia says, "This is good. There's so much chaos out here, the Secret Service will be distracted. They're going to be looking for anything and everything other than someone knocking on the door."

Agent John Alexander stands back from the Marine post on the side street. The soldiers' eyes might be facing outward at the crowd, but his are directed at his phone. Breezy uses Susan's phone to send him a message.

Look up!

No sooner has she hit send than he looks up and peers around for a few seconds before recognizing her. He talks to one of the Marines and waves them over. There's some discussion about identification and procedure, but he convinces the Marines to let them approach the guardhouse, probably because Breezy is a Secret Service agent.

"De la Cruz," he says, greeting her warmly and wrapping his arms around her. "What the hell happened to you?"

"It's been a long week," she replies as he steps back. "We're gonna need to debrief over beers."

"Hah, I hear you on that one," he gestures to the crowd. "Can you believe this crap? These assholes are everywhere. They won't go away. They're making our lives hell. Johnson is running double shifts to ensure everything is secure."

"And the Vice President?" Breezy asks.

"He's in his office. Come on. Even without ID, I need you to sign in. You know the drill. Fingerprints and facial scans."

The two women go through the security screening process. The Marines keep a close eye on them. They walk through a metal detector.

"And this is her?" Agent Alexander asks. "She's the one that led Buster into the trap?"

"Yep," Olivia and Breezy both say in unison, which isn't overly convincing, but Agent Alexander doesn't care.

They walk down the long driveway with the agent, making their way toward the side entrance on the West Wing. Olivia was here just a few days ago in the Jaguar convertible. As complex as things were back then, they were simple by comparison. As she gets closer, she notices the concrete where Buster fell. It's been bleached. The bushes have been pruned. Fresh mulch has been laid in the garden bed. The paint on the wall appears glossy and pristine. If there's one thing humans are good at, it's covering shit up and pretending nothing bad ever happened.

Her heart aches at the sight of a few dark red spots that have been missed on the rim of the concrete surrounding the garden bed. To anyone else, they could be bits of dirt, but they've landed in thin streaks and been overlooked by the cleaners.

Agent Alexander leads them past the Marine on duty by the entrance. Once inside, he walks them around an empty desk and opens the door to the Vice President's office. Where's the secretary? For that matter, where's the internal security checkpoint? Olivia's about to say something, but Breezy's already stepping inside the office. The agent shuts the door behind them.

The first time Olivia walked into the Vice President's office, she was in awe of the occasion. She felt overwhelmed. Buster was relaxed. She was as nervous as hell. She focused more on the man than the furniture and decor. This time, she's circumspect. Something feels wrong, but she's not sure what. She scans the room, unsure what she's looking for but feeling there's something out of place.

The office is considerably larger than her living room. To one side, there are three tall, floor-to-ceiling windows with white lace curtains diffusing the sunlight. Portraits of John Adams and Thomas Jefferson hang in the gaps between the windows. Each painting has been framed with ornate, polished oak, which has been meticulously gilded with threads of gold. Two couches face each other in the middle of the room, but it seems neither has ever been used. The seats are taut. The cushions are plush and plump. There's a drinks cabinet on the far wall with an all too familiar bottle of Scotch sitting on a silver tray. Two flags flank the antique wooden desk at the far end of the room. They've been mounted on brass stands with polished wooden poles.

The Vice President is seated at his desk, but his plush, high-back leather office chair has been swung around away from them. He's leaning forward, hunching over a laptop on the counter behind his desk. Perhaps

Olivia's reading too much into it, but she's surprised he didn't turn to face them. He had to have heard them enter.

"Mr. Vice President," Breezy says.

The chair swivels.

"Ah, Breezy. Olivia," he says warmly, giving them his full attention. The Vice President clutches his hands on the desk, which seems forced to Olivia. He's the one in a position of power, not them, and yet he gives them his sole focus. He doesn't look relaxed. Nervous is the wrong term. Concerned? What is he worried about? Then it hits her.

Olivia blurts out. "It's a trap!"

"What do you mean?" the Vice President says, looking befuddled, but the expression on his face isn't convincing. He's putting on a show.

Olivia looks around the office. "We've got to get out of here. Now!"

"What's wrong?" Breezy asks, looking confused.

"He knows my name," she says, pointing at the Vice President, who keeps his fingers clenched in front of him, looking earnest and sincere. For Olivia, nothing feels right. Agent Alexander was relaxed when he should have been on edge given all the commotion beyond the gates. He didn't even ask them why they wanted to speak to the Vice President. There was no internal security. The secretary was missing. Isn't the White House supposed to be on high alert?

"Buster," Olivia says. "He only ever called me Lisa in front of him. It was a fake name to get us through security." She addresses the Vice President. "How do you know my name?"

"I read it somewhere."

"He's lying."

"Why would he lie?" Breezy asks. She looks confused.

"I'm telling you, this has all been too easy. They're setting us up."

"Who's setting us up?" Breezy asks.

The Vice President reaches below his desk and pulls out a phone. A call is in progress. Calmly, he places it face-up on the polished wooden surface.

"I think this is as far as we're going to get," he says, addressing someone on the active call. "You might as well come in."

The hairs on Olivia's arms rise in alarm.

There are two doors leading into the office. Both of them are behind her, being separated by an ornate fireplace.

"What's going on?" Breezy asks as several Secret Service agents walk in. They take up positions around the room, effectively surrounding the two women.

"We're fucked, aren't we?" Olivia says, turning and looking at the muscle-bound agents in their suits. "Totally fucked."

Within seconds, there are six agents evenly spaced around the windows. They remain back against the walls, leaving the couches between them, but Olivia has no doubt they could vault those in a heartbeat if needed.

"You disappoint me, Breezy," a deep voice says from the far doorway.

"Who is this asshole?" Olivia asks.

"Director Johnson," Breezy replies, facing him with clenched fists held by her side.

"Wait," Olivia says, pointing at the director and then at the Vice President. "I don't get it. Wasn't he trying to roll him?"

"Oh, she gets it," the director says as Breezy hangs her head.

"What is going on?" Olivia asks. Neither the director nor the Vice President answers.

"They played us to get to them," Breezy says.

"So the affair? The deep fake?"

"It was for an audience from another planet," the director replies, addressing Olivia. "Honestly, I thought we'd blown it at the mall. I thought we'd overplayed our hand. There were too many agents there from too many agencies. I worried we were going to scare them off."

"It was always too easy," Olivia says as the realization dawns. "You let me go."

Director Johnson nods. "We baited them to intervene. We needed you to lead us to them."

"But me?" Breezy asks. "How did I get dragged into all this?"

"That was a stroke of luck," the director says, walking up to her. "Or was it? After they lost FBI Agent Zambarrow, the Clowns were always going to recruit someone else. It makes sense that they'd switch agencies and try to go deeper. I suspect they saw what you did to save that security guard. I think Buster went to the precinct knowing you were inside, knowing I'd take you along to the interrogation. He certainly wasn't surprised you were there. He looked right at you. It was as though he could see through that one-way mirror. Perhaps he could."

Breezy steps back slowly as he speaks, wanting to keep her distance.

"You're tracking them," she says. "That's why you needed us. You needed someone that could draw in their spacecraft."

"What are you talking about?" Olivia asks.

The Vice President says, "Chess, my dear."

"They were becoming more aloof," the director says. "We needed something that made them nervous. We needed to bring them in close."

"I don't understand," Olivia says.

Breezy says, "You're probing, testing their responses." The director nods as she continues. "It's like a game of chess. You've been moving pieces around the board, setting up for one final move."

The director asks her, "How do you catch the invisible man? How do you even know he's there? We needed to gather data. We needed to know when they were present so we could calibrate our systems. We had to be sure they would show up."

"Why?" Olivia asks. "What's your next move?"

"Checkmate," the Vice President says, leaning back on his desk. He's far too relaxed.

"But you can't see them," Olivia says. "You said it yourself. Their ships are invisible."

"They were," the Vice President says.

"They're good," the director says. "The problem is, they're too good."

"Problem?" Breezy asks, confused.

"They're so good, their shields stop everything." He smiles. He's arrogant. Olivia's seen plenty of men like this over the years. He's been blinded by his own ego. The director goes on to say, "Every second, roughly two hundred randomly scattered particles soar through your body. They're the result of high-altitude collisions with cosmic rays. They're always present except—"

"Except when *they're* overhead," Breezy says, realizing the implications.

"And just like that. We can see them." The director waves his hand in the air, gesturing at the roof. "But we needed to eliminate any false positives and understand false negatives. We needed some test flights. We needed to know it would work. And that's where you came in."

Breezy says, "You're trying to catch them? That's what all this is about?"

"That's crazy," Olivia says. "They'll wipe you out."

"Will they?" the director asks. "Or will they back off, realizing they're far more exposed than they thought? There's one of them. That's all. Just one ship and a bunch of lifeboats. This is our home turf. We hold the advantage. They're isolated. They might have their technology, but we have numeric superiority."

"My god. What have you done?" Olivia asks the Vice President, turning to him with a look of horror on her face.

He's not worried. He says, "We've upgraded our missile defense systems. We're ready for anything they throw at us."

"You're going to start a war," Olivia says.

"The war's been raging for over a decade," the director replies. "They've been infiltrating our society, molding our culture, spreading their lies about *The Spectacle*. Don't you see? They're termites destroying the house from within. And they're winning. We have to hit back. They have no right to interfere with our lives!"

"But you have that right, huh?" Olivia says. "You don't mind *fucking* with people's lives. You killed my sister, you asshole!"

She slaps him across the face. His head rocks sideways. Several agents step forward, prepared to restrain her, but he holds out his hand, signaling for them to wait. Red welts form on his cheek.

"There are casualties in any war," he says.

"You bastard," Olivia replies. The veins on her neck strain as she grinds her teeth and clenches her fists. If she could, she'd throttle him. As it is, the agents make it clear they won't tolerate anything else. One of them slips his hand inside his jacket pocket, ready to draw a gun.

"No, it's okay," the director says.

"You're insane," Breezy says. "They are *thousands* of years more advanced than us!"

Director Johnson counters with, "And yet the Taliban hit one of their shuttles with Soviet-era artillery."

The look of shock on Breezy's face says more than words ever could.

"Buster didn't tell you that, did he?" the director asks. "The Taliban were shelling rebels in the Afghan province of Kunduz and they clipped one of them by accident. We tracked the damaged craft across the border with a drone. Don't you see? They're not invincible. Oh, they'd like you to think they are, but they're not."

Breezy is exasperated. Her voice breaks as she speaks. "They'll wipe us out."

"Will they?" the director asks, walking around her. "They didn't retaliate against the Taliban. Don't you get it? They're alone. And as any military analyst will tell you, that makes them vulnerable. Why do you think they hide from us? They know their weaknesses. And the biggest is they're a helluva long way from home. There's no chance for resupply. One hit on that mothership and it's over. They're not going to risk open warfare with us."

"But why would you do this?" Olivia asks, shaking her head in disbelief.

"Because we're not dumb," the director replies. "We're not inferior to them. We're intelligent. We're their equal. We *will* have that technology. We'll take it from them if we have to!"

"Don't do this," Breezy says, pointing toward the Executive Office building visible out the window. "There are no winners in war. Only losers. Think of everyone you lost in that base across the road."

"Hah," the director says, smiling. "Did you really think I would show you a top-secret command center and then stand by and wait for them to strike? That base was empty within ten minutes of you leaving for the hospital."

"You have no idea what's happening here," the Vice President says, joining the director. "We've been two steps ahead of them at every juncture."

The director signals with his head, nodding toward the door. The agents herd the women into the corridor as he says, "And now we're going to bring one of them down. Let's see how they feel when they start losing lifeboats."

"And us?" Olivia asks as their hands are zip-tied behind their backs.

"You're the bait!"

With that, black hoods are slipped over their heads.

BAIT

"Where are you taking us?" Olivia yells as she's marched outside. Being unable to see, everything becomes a trip hazard. Her shoes scuff the sill in the doorway. The drop to the concrete pad outside takes her by surprise. Her feet barely touch the ground as she steps onto the driveway. She moves her legs, but the agents on either side of her are carrying most of her weight.

A car door is opened—no, it's something bigger than a car. The door sounds heavy. Solid. Hinges move. Steel parts clip into place. Without any sense of sight and being in a state of utter panic, Olivia's hearing is heightened. Birds chirp in the trees. Cars drive past easily a block away. None of this helps.

Olivia's expecting to be shoved sideways into the back of a car. She bends her neck, lowering her head, not wanting to hit the edge of the door as she's pushed into the backseat. What she isn't ready for is being bundled longways into the back of what feels like a van. The agents holding her arms grab her legs, and she topples forward, unable to catch herself. Her lower lip hits the back tray of the vehicle as she's shoved inside. Blood oozes out within the black hood over her head.

Olivia is shoved sideways. She crumples against the hard, unforgiving sheet metal. Breezy is pushed in behind her. Doors are slammed. More doors are opened. The order seems wrong. Doors are slammed yet again. The sounds reverberating around her seem amplified, which is terrifying.

"I need to pee," she whispers. "I knew I should have gone before we left."

"Shush," Breezy whispers in reply. "I need to listen."

The engine is running. It's deep and throaty. The parking brake is released. The vehicle rocks slightly. The shifter is put into drive and the vehicle pulls away, but it's slow, crawling forward at no more than five mph.

"Where are you taking us?" Olivia calls out. No one replies.

Breezy whispers. "South 150 meters... Turning East."

She must be mentally mapping their journey. Hearing her mark waypoints is reassuring. It's a way of wrestling back control. It's an illusion of control, but Olivia quickly pushes that realization from her mind. At the moment, she'll cling to any comfort she can.

The vehicle accelerates, joining traffic. Within a hundred yards, it turns again.

"South," Breezy whispers.

"I wanna speak to my lawyer," Olivia calls out. "I've got rights."

"They're not going to talk to you," Breezy says, but she's no longer whispering. Instead, she speaks in a clear voice. "We're in a black Chevy Suburban SUV with four agents wearing body armor. The two in the backseat are carrying MP5s while the two in the front have standard-issue Glocks."

"Where are they taking us?" Olivia asks.

"Andrews Air Force Base," Breezy says.

"How do you know that?"

"I don't. It's a guess," Breezy replies. "But that soft squelch just then was the guy on the right turning around on the leather seat to make sure our hoods were still secure. And that tells me I'm right."

Her words are followed by a slight rocking from the backseat. It's subtle, but it's in response to Breezy's comment.

"Now the other guy is quietly remonstrating him for information leakage. Relax guys. You've got one of your own back here. I know all the processes and procedures you use."

There's no reply. The vehicle turns again. Breezy says, "East."

Olivia wriggles. She's struggling with the sense of claustrophobia that comes from having a dark hood drawn around her neck. As the vehicle turns, the weight of her head pulling on the thick material is enough to draw the cord a little tighter. It's all she can do not to spiral into a panic attack. Breezy, by comparison, is calm. It seems her nerves are gone. Olivia doesn't understand her. Stand on a street corner and she's nervous and distracted. Get kidnapped and she's got ice in her veins again.

"They're by-passing Fort McNair and Joint Base Anacostia-Bolling. We just turned onto the parkway. We're going southeast."

Breezy's talking loud enough to be heard by the agents. They don't respond. Olivia's not sure about her strategy. Perhaps she's trying to unsettle them, but she could be wrong. With a dark hood over her head, it's difficult to tell anything at all other than that they're driving along a road.

"How do you know?" Olivia asks in a whisper. "How can you be so sure?"

"Trust me."

"I trust you," Olivia says. "Now, how are we going to escape?"

"I don't know that we are," Breezy replies.

"That's not what I wanted to hear."

"Just... trust me."

It's another twenty minutes before the SUV pulls up at what Olivia guesses is a security gate. There's considerable discussion with the guard on duty. The driver gets out, leaving the vehicle running. Olivia can feel Breezy working with her zip-ties, trying to get her hands free. She rocks back and forth. Olivia's curious. She rolls slightly, feeling for Breezy behind her. Breezy's got hold of a metal cargo hook on the floor of the vehicle. She's working her zip-tie against it like a saw.

"Shhh."

After a few minutes, the vehicle continues on within the military base. The front window is down. The a/c is still running. Cool air spills out of vents in the roof, but the heat and humidity of the day overwhelm her. Sweat breaks out on Olivia's forehead, soaking the lining within the black hood.

The SUV is following another car. From the way the engine of the other vehicle roars, it's heavy. It must be a military humvee.

Their SUV turns in a wide half-circle, swinging around and coming to a halt facing in the direction it came. Wherever they're going, they've arrived—that much is clear as all the agents get out. Seconds later, the back of the SUV is thrown open and the women are dragged out.

Olivia's curious as to how Breezy is going to play this. If she starts kicking and wriggling as she's hauled over the tailgate, Olivia will do likewise, following her lead. As it is, Breezy doesn't offer any resistance.

The two women are marched across a broad, open concrete slab. There's nothing for Olivia to trip on. The echo suggests they're in a hangar.

"What's so important about you two?" the director asks as their hoods are removed. Immediately, Breezy looks around. Olivia's more interested in the director. He's perspiring. Sweat soaks through his white shirt. His suit jacket looks hot and heavy.

Breezy's thinking about their options. Olivia tries to buy her some time and space by wrestling to get away from the agents holding her back. They tighten their grips on her upper arms. She was never going to break free, but it wasn't about escaping; it was about ensuring Breezy went unnoticed for a moment. After all they've been through, Olivia's confident Breezy will think of a way to escape.

"Why do they care so much about you?" the director asks again, taking hold of Olivia's jaw and turning her head to one side. "What's so special about you that they stay so close?"

Neither woman responds.

The hangar is empty. It's big enough to hold several jets side by side. Out on the edge of the shadows cast by the roof, there's a military-grade trailer painted with army camouflage. It's covered in netting, with bits of fake foliage sticking out of the weave. It strikes Olivia as dumb at an airport with vast concrete runways separated by grassy fields that reach up no more than a foot in height. The trailer looks stupidly fake, like a square box of trees dumped on the edge of the hangar. If this were a video game, she'd complain about the lack of realism.

Several soldiers and aircrew engineers open side panels on the trailer. One of them starts a diesel generator while the others work at various controls. Steel legs take the weight off the wheels, keeping the trailer level. A small set of stairs allows the soldiers to work at a rugged console on the side. A radar dish is raised and pointed back toward Washington.

The vast air force base is idle. There are no planes on the tarmac. Olivia hears one of the support crew saying, "Flight operations are suspended. We've got a six-hour window."

"They're out there, you know," the director says as they walk over to the trailer. He raises his hand toward the clear blue sky. "When Buster went to the White House, they sat up at a hundred thousand feet. But you... For you, they're circling between a thousand and ten thousand feet. Why? Why are they so damn interested in you?"

"Fuck off," Olivia says as they come to a halt roughly fifteen feet from the trailer.

The director laughs, turning his attention to Breezy. "What about you? What do you have to say for yourself?"

"I'm not afraid of you."

"Oh, you should be."

The director towers over her. Breezy refuses to take a backward step.

"Have you ever heard of a Glaswegian kiss?" she asks. Before he can reply, Breezy springs forward, jumping off her feet and slamming the brow of her forehead into his face. She takes the agents holding her by surprise and manages to connect with the bridge of his nose, cracking the fragile bone. Blood explodes across his cheeks.

"You—*fucking*—bitch!" he yells, grabbing his nose and staggering backward. Blood streaks down his face and onto his tie, turning his white shirt bright red. Several agents rush to his aid. An agent behind Breezy smacks her on the side of her head with an extendable baton. Blood runs down her neck. She staggers to one side, looking back at him with eyes that could kill.

"You're next, Anders," she mutters.

Director Johnson is enraged. He grabs a Glock from one of the agents and marches over to Breezy with the gun held out in front of him, threatening to kill her. He pulls back on the slide, loading a round into the chamber. His finger is on the trigger. He aims at the center of her chest.

"Do it," she yells, pulling against the agents holding her back, refusing to shrink from him. "Go on! Kill an unarmed woman in front of your agents. Kill a prisoner in front of the military. Show them all what a fucking *coward* you are!"

The director pistol-whips Breezy. He uses a back-fist strike, raking both his clenched fist and the gun across her face. Her head rocks under the force of the blow. Blood flies from her lips, but still she's defiant.

"I bet that felt good," she says with blood staining her teeth. "Do you like hitting women? Does it make you feel good? Because I think you're piss-ant weak. You're a loser."

Incensed by her, the director raises the gun, shifting his aim to the middle of her forehead at a distance of no more than a foot.

"What are you waiting for?" Breezy yells, trying to wrestle herself away from the agents struggling to hold her back. "Show them! Show them who you really are! Do it! Do it now!"

Director Johnson bares his teeth. The veins in his neck go taut. With a clenched jaw, he takes aim. His fingers tighten around the grip of the pistol. Rage consumes his eyes.

Breezy marches forward toward him, dragging the agents along with her. With her arms pinned behind her back, she pushes her forehead against the barrel of the Glock. Tears stream down her face, lining her cheeks with streaks. Her lips tremble. Although she sounds defiant, there's a quiver in her voice. Regardless, she continues to goad him.

"What are you afraid of? Just squeeze the trigger. You know you want to. It's not so damn easy when there's a life at the other end of the barrel, is it? It's not as easy as shooting targets at the range, huh?"

Director Johnson screws the barrel of the gun sideways, working it hard against the skin on her forehead. The two of them lean into each other, pressing against the gun held between them.

"Breezy, please," Olivia says, pleading for her to back down. Olivia turns to the agent beside her, saying, "Do something. Don't let this happen."

The director growls, "You think you're so smart—"

"And you're an asshole," Breezy yells at him, looking past the barrel at his bloody face. "You're pathetic!"

"Sir," one of the agents says, coming up beside him and gently putting his hand over the Glock. He gets him to lower the gun. "Please, sir. This is not right."

The director's arm falls loosely to his side. The gun remains in his clenched fist. The agents beside Breezy drag her back, holding her next to Olivia.

"You," the director says, turning as he walks away. He points the gun back at her, adding, "I *will* kill you."

Breezy spits blood on the concrete. "Not if I kill you first."

"Jesus," Olivia says under her breath. "What the hell are you doing?"

"Trying to stop a war," Breezy replies. Her body goes limp. She hangs her head. Her legs buckle beneath her as the agents hold her aloft. She stutters. "I—I need time. I need more time."

The emotional toll on her is obvious. Her arms are shaking. The agents seem to pity her, allowing her to crumple to her knees on the concrete. They each keep a hand on her shoulder, preventing her from rising, but they needn't. She looks spent. Breezy stares down at the concrete. Her shoulders are stooped. All the fire is gone. She's mumbling, but she's not making sense.

"I can't do this alone... I need help."

Olivia's confused. Who's Breezy speaking to? Her? It sounds as though she's talking to someone else, but that's not possible. If she's trying to rattle the agents behind her, wanting to unsettle them and appeal to their conscience, it's not working. They're stone-faced.

"We've got a bogey on approach," an Air Force officer says, looking at what appears to be a radar image on the control panel.

"Don't do this," Olivia yells, trying to give Breezy the time she needs for whatever crazy plan she's concocting. "Captain *whoever* and Lieutenant ^. You don't have to do this."

"Shut up," the director says, wiping the blood from his face with the back of his hand. Thick, coagulated blood clings to his nose, dripping over the corner of his lips. One of the ground crew brings over a damp rag. The director wipes his face, smearing but not clearing the blood from his chin.

"Think for yourselves," Olivia says. "You don't have to obey an unlawful order."

Olivia has no idea what Breezy's doing on her knees. If she didn't know better, she'd think she was praying. All Olivia knows is Breezy needs more time. Perhaps she's working with her plastic zip-tie. Maybe she's on the verge of breaking it and just needs a few more seconds to bust free. Olivia's got to run interference for her.

"You're making a mistake," she calls out, addressing the ground crew working with the guidance system controls. "You do not want to start an interstellar war!"

"That's enough!" the director says, looking at her with anger in his eyes.

"What you're doing is wrong. You can't fire on them."

"I said, shut—the—*fuck*—up!"

"Or what?" Olivia asks, echoing Breezy's logic at him. "Are you going to threaten to shoot me as well? I'm unarmed. I'm in cuffs. How brave of you."

"Are the missiles online?" the director asks, ignoring her.

The senior officer says, "Ah, we're running hot, but this is just a demonstration, right? I was told this was a dress rehearsal of the system."

The officer looks worried. Seeing the confrontation between Breezy and the director has left him rattled. He was seconds away from witnessing a murder. He's nervous. He looks around for support from the others. This is not what he signed up for.

One of the radar operators says, "The bogey is passing over the southern end of the airfield, crossing the main runway at an altitude of 1500 meters. The heading is 10 degrees northeast at a rate of 90 knots. They'll cross the second runway in about 30 seconds."

The agents holding Olivia look out across the runway, staring up into the clear blue sky. Like all of them, they're curious, but there's nothing there.

"This is a proof of concept," the senior officer says. "We've got two hundred sensors out there calibrated to detect them, but we're not going to shoot them down, right?"

"You will give the order, or you will be relieved of your command," the director says.

"I'm not sure you have the—"

The director pushes past the officer and steps up beside the console operator, saying, "Fire!"

The operator looks briefly at his commanding officer. He's got his hand on a circular switch. A key protrudes from a glowing green plastic ring the size of a quarter. His fingers grip the tab surrounding the key. The director reaches out and grabs his hand, twisting it sideways and turning the key. The color of the ring changes from green to red, arming the system. Before the operator can react, the director slams his hand down on the launch button on the command console.

"Noooooo!" Olivia yells.

From the far end of the base, several hundred yards away, a missile launches into the air. Its sleek body is barely distinguishable from its fiery exhaust and the billowing trail of pungent, white smoke curling behind it. Far from being refined or something like the launch of a space rocket, the missile is crude. The only consideration is speed. It rips into the air, leaving a cloud of fumes in its wake. Olivia trembles. The glowing rocket engine rises high into the sky, twisting slightly as it locks onto its target. Its white nose cone appears as thin and as sharp as a needle.

Breezy is still on her knees. She's not even watching. Her lips are moving.

The missile strikes something in midair. An explosion breaks in the clear blue sky. A deafening boom thunders over the airbase. Bits of burning metal rain down on the roof of the hangar. Out of nowhere, an alien spacecraft appears. It's an elongated cylinder reminiscent of a cigar. They've hit one of the shuttles.

The craft is streamlined, but it's traveling sideways. The black skin of the shuttle is punctuated with silver disks, making its rotation apparent. Rather than falling from the sky, it seems to roll toward the ground, slowly losing altitude.

The soldiers, aircrew, officers and Secret Service agents walk forward in astonishment, watching as the craft rolls past, slowly descending to the tarmac. As the craft is over a hundred yards long and coming down sideways, it easily spans both runways.

The missile struck almost dead center. The gaping hole rotates with the craft. Metal glows, burning white-hot in the brilliance of the noonday summer sun.

"Sweet Jesus," one of the agents says. He's got Breezy by the collar, marching her forward alongside Olivia. For her part, Breezy's looking at the fall of her feet, not the spacecraft. She's still mumbling.

The doomed craft twists in the air. It crashes further down the runway. Explosions rise from within. Flames leap into the sky as another deafening boom washes over them.

Breezy looks up. She shakes her head as though waking from a dream. "You did it. You actually *fucking* did it. You goddamn fool!"

"Hah," the director says, turning to her and gloating. "Now, *this* is First Contact!"

There's confusion on the base. Fire crews rush to put out the flames burning within the crumpled remains of the alien spacecraft, but it's much larger than any fighter craft, and it's lying sideways, straddling both tarmacs, scorching the grass in between. Emergency response vehicles rush past with sirens blazing and lights flashing. Within seconds, thick white foam blankets the far end of the burning craft. Steam rises into the air.

The director addresses the aircrew standing on the raised platform in front of the trailer. "Stay alert. There are other bogeys out there. We need to increase the scan range. McClusky, I want confirmation that Aegis, Patriot and THAAD are ready to respond to any targeting we provide them. Bring the *whole* goddamn network online. Now!"

He turns to his agents, waving with the Glock in his hand. "And bring the two of them. I want them to see this."

The director strides forward, cutting across the grass and onto one of the taxiways as he makes his way toward the fallen alien spacecraft. Sections of the craft collapse, breaking apart under the intense heat raging within the fuselage. More firefighters arrive and begin hosing down the flames.

Olivia and Breezy follow along behind the director. To their surprise, the agents let them go. They walk along behind them, but they're no longer holding them, and their pace is slowing. They fall behind, coming to a halt on the side of the runway, allowing the two women to walk on over the grass. It seems their conscience has finally got the better of them.

The director doesn't notice. He's too focused on the burning wreckage.

Olivia could run away at this point. No one is forcing her to go with the director. She should sprint over behind the edge of the hangar. But where would she go from there? She's in the middle of a military base with her hands pinned behind her back. Breezy's not going anywhere other than forward. Olivia decides to stay by Breezy's side, saying, "We're fucked. We are so *fucking* fucked."

"Are we?" Breezy asks, smiling as she looks sideways at her. "Or is he?"

"What do you mean?"

"Look at this," the director yells, raising his arms as he turns to face them, rejoicing at his prize. "We've done it! We've done the impossible! We've brought down an alien spacecraft!"

"Have you?" Breezy asks, stepping up onto the concrete taxiway about thirty feet behind him. "Take a closer look."

"What?" he says, unsure of himself.

The director walks across the field toward a smoldering line of blackened grass burning beneath the crumpled remains of the alien vessel. The hull near the nose cone collapses, falling apart, revealing a hollow interior. The skin of the spacecraft appears to dissolve as flames lap at the strange metal, leaving the large, thin rings of the supporting superstructure behind. They rise like the ribcage of a skeleton, but these, too, collapse moments later, disappearing in the flames engulfing the ground.

Fire suppression foam blankets the middle of the vessel, but this section also collapses onto the grass. There's little to nothing left of the spacecraft beyond a burning husk.

"What's happening?" he asks, turning toward Breezy as she steps down into the grass behind him. Olivia stays close by her side.

"The aliens asked me to give you a message," Breezy says. "They said to tell you, مات. Although they say most Iranians put the emphasis on the leading s—as in sss-shah mat!"

"What?" he asks, confused. The gun hangs from his right hand, almost falling from his fingers into the grass. Smoke drifts around his legs.

"Checkmate!"

The director walks over to a curved section of the hull, watching as it burns up, disappearing into pungent black smoke. "I don't understand."

"It's fake," she says. "It's a decoy."

The director yells at her, "Breezy! What have you done?"

She ignores him, asking, "Have you seen enough, Mr. President?"

Olivia's eyes go wide. "*Who* are you talking to?"

From the far end of the tarmac, a series of black SUVs rush along with their red and blue lights flashing. Olivia counts six vehicles in the motorcade, entering from the south side of the runway, turning toward them easily a quarter of a mile away. The director sees them.

"You bitch," he says, raising his gun and pointing it at Breezy.

"It's over," Breezy says. She flexes her arms and shoulders, breaking the zip-tie around her wrists and freeing her hands. "You lost. You know it. They know it. The President knows it. You've failed. You're going down."

"If I'm going to hell," the director says, "you're coming with me!"

"No!" Olivia shouts.

Gunfire erupts at the airbase. The first bullet strikes Breezy in the center of her chest. She reels to one side, staggering backward. Blood oozes from between her fingers as she grabs at her shirt. Her feet shuffle through the grass. She struggles to keep her balance.

The director continues firing as he advances on her, walking through the grass between the runways. In his rage, several shots miss. Chips of concrete are dug out of the taxiway as bullets ricochet across the tarmac.

Breezy turns side on to the director, doubling over as she struggles to stay on her feet. The director shoots her in the shoulder. Blood sprays out behind her. Two more bullets punch through her clothing. The shots are deafening, breaking like thunder in the clear blue sky.

Breezy's back arches with another impact. She stumbles onto the taxiway, finding firmer ground on the concrete. Thick, red blood drips onto the tarmac. Her hair flies around with each thundering impact. Four, five, six shots hit her. Each one causes her to shudder and grimace, but somehow she remains on her feet. She locks her knees together, refusing to fall to the concrete. Breezy's on the verge of keeling over. She leans forward, rocking slightly. Blood and saliva drip from her lips, staining the concrete.

The director closes on her. She sways, unable to straighten but refusing to fall to the tarmac.

Olivia runs. With her arms still strapped behind her back, she charges at the director. He's so obsessed with Breezy that he doesn't see her until the last moment. She collides with him from the side. The crown of her head catches the underside of his jaw, sending his head rocking back. Blood flies from between his teeth.

Olivia falls into a drainage ditch. The director staggers to one side, stunned. He almost drops his gun. Hatred swells within his eyes. She's given him another target. Olivia grimaces, waiting for the inevitable.

Grass sways around her. To her surprise, the Glock slips from the director's hand—only it doesn't fall. It rises above his outstretched fingers. He watches in awe as the pistol grip slides away from his open palm.

"What is going on?"

Olivia knows.

The grass around her loses its natural curl, rising straight up in the air. The director's shoes lift off the dirt.

"What? Wait," he yells.

Breezy is already twenty feet up. Drops of blood float beside her. She's doubled over in pain but still appears conscious.

A dark shadow blots out the sun. A deep hum fills the air. The mile-wide alien mothership hovers several hundred feet above the tarmac. It bristles with spikes.

This is the first time Olivia's seen the craft in the daylight. Whereas the alien shuttles are smooth, the mothership is a chaotic mess of equipment packed together. Nothing is streamlined or aerodynamic. There are domes and antennae, concave dishes and racks that look like they hold missiles. Dozens of turrets rotate. Cannons point at various potential threats around the airbase. Like a porcupine flexing its quills, the starship screams, *Don't fuck with me!*

As Olivia's in a drainage ditch, the pull on her isn't enough to draw her off the ground. She peers across the taxiway. Stones and bits of gravel hover a few feet up, but the beam is focused on Breezy and the director. In the distance, the black SUVs have surrounded the camouflaged trailer. Roughly a dozen soldiers and aircrew lie flat on the ground as the agents from the SUVs point their guns at them. No one is dumb enough to fire on the mothership.

The firefighters further down the runway stand there in awe of the alien spacecraft looming overhead. Breezy and the director disappear into an open hatch. And in a heartbeat, the spacecraft disappears. Olivia squints, reacting to the sudden rush of sunlight around her. The clear blue sky stretches out overhead once again. White, fluffy clouds drift on the horizon. Several Secret Service agents come running over to her, but no one has a gun drawn. They're coming to help.

Tiny bits of rock and concrete fall back to the tarmac along with drops of blood. The Glock clatters on the taxiway.

Olivia sinks back into the ditch. Long grass curls around her. The sun warms her face. It's over. They're gone. It's not just that the craft has turned invisible. This time, it feels different. Regardless of what happens to Breezy and the director, this is the end. Olivia knows. The aliens aren't going to play any more stupid games. They've been pushed too far. Humanity fucked around and found out. Chester was right. The US didn't fare any better than chimpanzees hurling feces at explorers in the jungle.

"We've blown it," she mutters to herself, remembering something her Polish grandmother used to say, "*Nie mój cyrk, nie moje małpy.*" She shakes her head, mumbling, "Not my circus, not my monkeys."

She knows that's what Grock will be thinking. He did his best to coax humanity into building a real civilization. He didn't have to help Buster. Just like Chester didn't have to help those women escape. The difference is that those women appreciate all Chester is doing for them.

Olivia hangs her head. Secret Service agents gather around her, standing on the edge of the ditch.

"Hey," one of them says, reaching out and offering to help her up, but her arms are still pinned behind her back. He's confused, not realizing why she doesn't take his hand. He drops down beside her in the ditch.

"It's okay," he says, seeing how her arms are bound. He cuts her loose and helps her stand. "Everything's going to be okay."

"No," she replies, rubbing her wrists and shaking her head. "No, it won't."

Tears roll down her cheeks. She's not talking about herself. She feels the loss of First Contact. Olivia understands the conclusion Grock and his people will reach. Humans are self-absorbed. They're trapped in

The Spectacle. It's all about humanity. Only it isn't. These aliens don't need petty attitudes and vicious attacks. There's a whole galaxy out there waiting for them. There are hundreds of billions of stars just beyond the stunning blue skies of Earth. They have other worlds to explore. Olivia's heart sinks. Once again, humanity is on its own.

The End

EPILOGUE

"Oh, you have no idea how good this tastes," Olivia says, sitting in a booth within a colorful Georgetown restaurant overlooking the Potomac. It's been twenty-four hours since the events at Andrews Air Force Base.

"Is everything okay?" a handsome middle-aged man in a striking grey suit asks. He's trim and athletic with a smile that could melt ice.

"Perfect. Thanks, Joe."

He walks off.

Under her breath, Breezy says, "That's *Joe the Dildo?*"

"Joe the who?" Alice says, leaning forward and glaring at her mother.

"Hush," Breezy says. "You didn't hear anything."

Susan laughs.

"Yes. That's Joe," Olivia says, picking up another slice of pizza. "Isn't this place great? And the food! Oh, My God. This cheese is from

443

Switzerland. The pepperoni is from Italy. The olive oil is from Greece. The rosemary is from Cyprus. While the flour that makes this dough is from the wheat fields of Ukraine. It's perfect!"

"It's so much better than goat's curd in a wrap," Breezy says, agreeing with her.

"So what happened?" Susan asks. "Can you tell us? Or is it classified?"

"Come on, Mom," Alice says. "Tell us."

"Okay, okay," Breezy says, gesturing for them to be a little quieter and not attract any more attention within the busy restaurant.

She sips at her Coke before saying, "On our way back from Saturn, I couldn't sleep. Olivia was snoring, but not me. I lay there looking at the stars. I was too damn nervous. I'd killed Buster. I'd ruined everything. I knew how easily I'd been used and I worried about what would happen once we got back here. How many more people would Director Johnson manipulate to get his way?"

"And?" Susan asks.

"Grock came over. We sat there talking for hours. He said they couldn't intervene directly. It was too risky. If anything was to happen, it had to be us that took action. Humanity had to fight for humanity. Change has to come from within. At that point, I was feeling pretty damn helpless. I knew Johnson had something planned. I was sure we were walking into a trap back here."

"And?" Alice asks, sipping a chocolate milkshake.

"And I'm starving," Breezy says, wanting a little patience from her daughter as she bites into a slice of hot pizza. She talks with her mouth full, covering her lips with one hand. "I told Grock I feared for our lives. I said I didn't think we could do this alone.

444

"The aliens knew Johnson was planning something, but they didn't know what. They doubted any human technology would work against them. I told them it was a risk neither side could take.

"At that point, I wasn't sure what part the Vice President played, but I knew the President was clean. He'd had no involvement throughout any of this. And he was the target. He was the one they were trying to bounce. I pointed that out to Grock, telling him the US President was going to be replaced. Logically, that made the President the only one we could trust in all this. We needed him on our side."

"So?" Susan asks.

"So we decided to take him for a ride," Breezy says with a grin.

"A ride? You took the President of the United States of America for a ride in an alien spaceship?"

Breezy laughs. "Yep. There he is, getting ready for bed in the White House—the most secure building on the planet—and I'm outside knocking on the French doors. He pulled back the curtains and saw me standing there. He knew me from my time on the outer perimeter detail. I pointed at the clear night sky behind me, saying, *Sir, would you like to see the Space Station?* He's such a geek. He downplays it with the media as they mock him about it, but he loves anything to do with space. He was excited. He opened the door and walked out to the balustrades running around the balcony, asking, *Where is it?* I pointed at a bright star and he said, *Oh, yeah. I can see it.*"

"You lied to him?" Susan asks.

"I didn't say *who's* space station we were looking at!" Breezy replies, laughing. "We were over near the broad, winding staircase leading down to the South Lawn. I gave him a pair of binoculars as a distraction. He was so intent on seeing the space station, I don't think he felt his feet lift off the marble floor. By the time he realized what was happening, we were drifting over the gravel driveway behind the White House. He looked at me with raised eyebrows and I said, *It's okay, sir. I do this all the time.*"

Alice laughs.

Susan asks, "What did he say to that?"

Breezy says, "He panicked. I think he was expecting to fall. There he is, looking down at the grass as we're drawn inside an invisible alien shuttlecraft."

"And then what happened?" Alice asks.

"Well, Grock wanted to take him out past the Moon to give him a really good look at the planet. We got him into a Low Earth Orbit and that was enough. He was convinced. I think he was struggling not to vomit. I don't think he does well with heights. He really, really wanted to get back down on the ground.

"I explained what was happening. The three of us agreed it wasn't enough to nab Director Johnson. We needed to know how deep this ran and who was cooperating with him within the government, within the Secret Service, and within the military."

"And then at the airbase?" Olivia asks. "When you were mumbling?"

"Once we knew what they were doing, we needed a decoy."

"That's why you needed more time."

"Yes," Breezy says. "The aliens were building a dummy shuttle in the sky above us as that whole shit show was going down in the hangar."

"That's why you were down on your knees."

"Yep. There was too much going on. I couldn't talk to you and the aliens and the President all at once. I was down on the concrete, mumbling, and they were picking me up through a hidden communicator. Buster used something similar back at the police precinct. He pretended to use an electronic earpiece, but it was a bluff. He was using alien technology—and that stuff picks up everything. You can hear the heartbeat of a mouse from a mile away!"

"You were talking to them? So they were listening to us the whole time?" Olivia asks. "The President and the aliens? While we were in the Vice President's office? While we were in the back of the SUV?"

Breezy says, "They were tracking us from above. They were telling *me* where we were going!"

"Oh, now I get it," Olivia says, pointing at her. "That's how you knew which roads we were on."

"Yes. But they couldn't see us within the airbase. Once we were inside the hangar, things got dicey."

"They couldn't see you," Olivia says. "So when Director Johnson held his gun on you, you weren't talking to him. You were talking to them when you said, *What are you waiting for? Show them who you really are!*"

"Yep," Breezy says, chuckling. "You've got to remember—they could only see body heat through the hangar roof. I had to describe everything. So when I'm yelling at him about murdering an unarmed woman, I'm trying to tell them this shit is going south fast. And there they were blabbering in my ear. Both of them were telling me they needed more time. The President was rushing there from the White House, while the aliens were constructing a dummy target in the sky. And me? I've got a gun to my forehead. Dear god, it was frustrating."

"Why didn't you tell me you could talk to them?" Olivia asks.

"I needed to fool Director Johnson," Breezy replies. "I needed him to think we were helpless. It was the only way to expose the whole operation. I needed you to be convincing. Besides, as it was, you almost blew it."

"Me?" Olivia asks, surprised by that point.

"Back at the circus?"

"How?"

"We were hovering over the circus, and you were starting to wake. Grock didn't want to blow the plan, so he set the two of us down. The implant they'd given me hadn't taken. I had an alien working on it while you started wandering through the trees, calling out my name."

"You were whispering to each other," Olivia says, laughing. "I *knew* something was going on."

"Yes. One of the aliens was under there with me. He was lying on his side beneath the canvas, fiddling with the bug behind my ear. I think you stood on him."

"No way!"

"And then you attracted that cop. So there I am, trying to lead you out of the fairgrounds without getting caught, hoping the cop doesn't stumble on the alien technician hidden under the canvas."

"Haha. That is so funny," Olivia says. She waves a finger at Breezy. "But I knew. I knew you wouldn't be so nervous. And you kept getting distracted. Like that time when you froze between the motorcycles."

"It was too damn sensitive," Breezy says. "I was still getting used to how it worked. Someone started talking a block away and suddenly I'm listening to them complaining about running out of fresh coffee beans. So I'm madly trying to get Grock to dial back the sensitivity."

"What could you hear?" Susan asks.

"On the base? The President, Grock, and just about everyone at Andrews."

"But you were shot, right?" Alice asks, screwing up her face at the thought of losing her Mom.

"Several times," Breezy says. "Thankfully, they're pretty good at patching up human biology. I guess they've had plenty of time to study us."

"And Johnson?" Olivia asks. "They took him up there as well."

"Oh, they wanted to flush him out into space," she says. "But I convinced them to turn him over to us to stand trial."

"So what now?" Susan asks. "What happens next?"

"Well, the President wants to dismiss the whole thing at the airbase as a—"

"A weather balloon, right?" Alice says dryly, looking at her mother with disdain.

"Something like that."

"They can't just cover it up," Olivia says. "Too many people saw that thing."

"But what did they see?" Breezy asks. "They saw a blimp crash. It was hollow. Empty. It burned to a crisp. That's the one thing everyone agrees on. Oh, there will be conspiracy theories, but there are *always* conspiracy theories, right? Who cares?"

"And the clowns?" Susan asks. "The aliens?"

"Let's just say, the President is no longer bound by *The Spectacle*. I think you're going to see change—a lot of change! It's going to raise eyebrows. It will get some resistance along the way, but change has always been inevitable. It's the pace of change that's been the problem. Now's our chance to turn on the heat."

"And us?" Susan asks. "What's next for us?"

"I was thinking we should take a vacation. All four of us."

"Sounds great," Alice says, getting excited.

"Where?" Susan asks.

"I know this little village near a quiet lake."

"Oh, no," Olivia says.

"It's up high in the desert. And at night, the stars shine like diamonds."

"No, no, no."

"And there's this amazing traveling circus!"

"Nope," Olivia says, shaking her head, but she can't suppress the smile lighting up her face.

Susan says. "I don't have a passport."

Breezy grins. "When you're flying with these guys, you don't need one."

AFTERWORD

Thank you for supporting independent science fiction.

If you've enjoyed this novel, I hope you'll leave a review and tell a friend. If you liked the creepy cover, go back and look at the eyes. *Oh, the eyes!*

Clowns offers one possible explanation for the Great Silence. Perhaps the reason we haven't made contact with an extraterrestrial intelligence is no one wants to talk to us. As a species, we're capable of speech, but it's not necessarily intelligent. More often than not, it centers around our own self-interest and desires. We cannot speak as one. Like howler monkeys screeching in the trees, all we offer is a cacophony of noise about this form of politics or that, this religion or that, this celebrity or that. Oh, there might be one or two people ET could talk to down here, but they would be drowned out by everyone else clamoring to be heard.

As with all of my novels, I try to ground the story in actual science and plausible, real-world details. Here are some of the concepts woven into this story.

ET & Philosophy

This novel was born out of the question: *What would an intelligent extraterrestrial species make of our intelligence?*

Rather than adopting a black and white stance, I wanted to explore our complex and often contradictory existence as a species. Most of us go through life with barely any thought about the drivers behind society, but what would aliens make of our various human cultures?

Modern political life is highly polarized. Terms like capitalism, socialism and communism are largely meaningless in the 21st Century as they're used either as insults or ideals devoid of any real substance. They've become abstracts. They're oversimplified and poorly understood. Visit China and it seems communism is misunderstood by communists themselves. Walk down a busy street in Shanghai and you'll see five-story high digital ads for Omega Watches, Giorgio Armani and Hugo Boss.

Complex subjects are difficult to grasp, so we tend to reduce them to simple axioms. Capitalism is liberating. Communism is oppressive. Socialism is the conveyer belt between the two. The truth is more nuanced. The free market is not as free as most people think.

Modern capitalism would be unrecognizable to the 18th Century economist Adam Smith. As an example, he could not have conceived of a single company like Facebook being worth hundreds of billions of dollars and amassing billions of devotees around the world. Its active user base is twice the size of the population of China! It's a single company with more power and influence than any empire the world has ever known. And it's amoral, existing only for the sake of generating money. And it's unregulated. As such, it has a history of being exploited. It's been used to propagate lies about vaccines, influence elections and even facilitate genocide. And all for a lousy buck. But capitalism is good. Capitalism cannot be questioned. No interference is allowed or we stray into the evils of communism—apparently.

Adam Smith is best known as the author of *An Inquiry into the Nature and Causes of the Wealth of Nations*, which is credited as the foundation of modern capitalism. Few people realize he published *two* critical works on life in the Industrial Age, not one. He's largely forgotten as the author of *The Theory of Moral Sentiments*.

Despite what you're told in the news and by political pundits, Adam Smith never intended capitalism to be devoid of morals.

"...To admire, and almost to worship, the rich and the powerful, and to despise... [the] poor... [is] the great and most universal cause of the corruption of our moral sentiments." Does that sound like an endorsement of billionaires to you? Two hundred years later and the poor are still despised. We blame them for their lack of standing in society. If only they worked harder. In truth, they're the hardest workers of all.

As for celebrity worship, he said, *"To superficial minds, the vices of the great seem at all times agreeable."* Being famous, it seems, has always been a license to sin. To paraphrase Adam Smith, money is no substitute for morals.

Far from being a rugged libertarian individualist, Adam Smith was a socialist. He said, *"The most sacred laws of justice are the laws which guard the life and person of our neighbor,"* not ourselves!

Somewhat prophetically, he also said, *"The great source of both the misery and disorders of human life, seems to arise from over-rating the difference between one permanent situation and another."* Could it be that socialism is misunderstood? Could it be that capitalism is overrated? Could these misplaced attitudes be a *"great source of... misery"* in our world?

What would an extraterrestrial intelligence capable of looking objectively at our economic systems think about modern capitalism? I think they'd see through the facade.

We need to dispel the myths surrounding capitalism. It is not a system of market forces achieving a natural, healthy balance for society. Not even Adam Smith thought that was true. This position might not be obvious, it might be contentious, but it's a position that would be immediately recognized by an objective observer looking at us from without. An extraterrestrial intelligence would deconstruct the convenient web of lies that supports capitalism. They'd see through the flaws in unbridled greed just as surely as Adam Smith himself once did.

So how would aliens view our world? I think they'd largely echo the words of our own oft-ignored philosophers.

In his book *How We Became Human and Why We Need to Change*, Australian philosopher Tim Dean deconstructs the outrage machine that is social media and talks about how the attributes that brought us to this point in time are insufficient to carry us forward. We've reached an impasse in our development as a species. We can't rely on our instincts anymore. We need to embrace reason. We need to embrace change if we want to move forward. If we keep doing what we've always done, we'll get the same results, which have been catastrophic for the natural world.

The 19th Century German philosopher Friedrich Nietzsche said, *"We belong to a period of which culture is in danger of being destroyed by the appliances of culture."* In other words, he saw culture being replaced by things. Sound familiar? Today, we call this consumerism. Every ad you've ever seen for any product, be it Coca-Cola, a new 4x4 truck, or a candy bar, has sold you on a feeling. It's sold you on emotions—on a lifestyle of happiness and joy. It's sold you an illusion.

In 1967, Guy Debord published his theory of *The Spectacle,* which has been discussed at length in this novel. In summary, we're like crows going after shiny objects. We become mesmerized by them, attributing our happiness to them. We inflate their sense of worth beyond what's reasonable. We crave the latest and greatest. And these things take on a life of their own. The companies that promote them achieve an almost god-like status in society. Companies like Apple, Instagram, Google, Tesla, and SpaceX, etc. can seemingly do no wrong. Even when corporate shenanigans are exposed, companies like Amazon, Meta, and Exxon still ride high on the stock market. Nietzsche was right. Appliances have replaced culture.

We're living in *The Spectacle*. Our minds are mesmerized by *The Dazzle* of the lights on this ethereal Broadway.

Whether we're flicking through Facebook, watching celebrities at the Oscars, or grabbing a burger from a fast-food outlet, we're divorced from reality. Want a cup of coffee? It's instant. Only it isn't. Someone grew the beans. Someone else harvested and dried them. Someone roasted them. Someone else ground them and packaged them and shipped them halfway around the world. Someone else stacked them on the shelves of your supermarket. As wonderful and convenient as capitalism is, it's an illusion. The all-important profit margin means companies pay the least amount possible for products and services, often exploiting people along the way, and then charge as much as they can to squeeze every cent from the dollar.

Over the past two hundred years, capitalism has brought about tremendous social and political change. There's no doubt it has improved our quality of life. Unbridled capitalism, though, has unleashed more damage than all our wars combined.

As an example, the fossil fuel industry has known about climate change for over forty years. And what has it done with that knowledge? It's lied. It's cheated. It's misled the public. It's bribed governments to get its way. It's manipulated the market. It's focused on short-term monetary gains at the expense of irreparable long-term ecological damage. It has waged a war of denial against science and society. The sad irony is that no one is exempt from the ravages of climate change. Not you or me or even the families of those that have plundered the land.

Far from being an abstract ideological battle, unbridled capitalism has real consequences. We're losing species at a scary rate. We're living through a mass extinction event, but it's not being caused by an asteroid or volcanic activity—it's being caused by us burying our heads in the sand. We're so caught up in *The Spectacle,* we can't see what's happening around us. We're losing species at a rate faster than any period of time since a lump of rock ten kilometers in diameter struck the Chicxulub peninsula in Mexico and all but wiped out the dinosaurs! And yet we're still steeped in denial. And for what? All for a lousy buck. Unbridled capitalism is the most destructive force in the last 65 million years!

Ursula K. Le Guin said it best. *"We live in capitalism. Its power seems inescapable. But then, so did the divine right of kings. Any human power can be resisted and changed by human beings."*

We can no longer allow greed to dictate its terms to us. We can no longer tolerate selfishness as an excuse for raping the natural world. Step outside *The Spectacle* and you'll see the most important aspects of life are devoid of monetary value. Hoarding wealth is a losing strategy. If we are to thrive as a species, we have to start thinking about how we structure the post-capitalist world.

Voltaire said, *"Every man is a creature of the age in which he lives. Few are able to raise themselves above the ideas of their time."* Are we any different? Can we be different? It all comes down to our willingness to embrace reason-based change. It's not that the protests of the youth of today are iconoclastic, simply wanting to overthrow the old order for the sake of it. The future is theirs. They understand the damage that's been done to the world they're inheriting. For us older folk, it's cowardice to ignore the impact of unbridled capitalism. Reason demands change.

In my admittedly naive view, capitalism needs consequences to be brought to heel. As long as it's more profitable to lie, steal, cheat and pollute, companies will. Modern capitalism lacks the morals espoused by its founder, Adam Smith.

I know this will raise the heckles of those that despise government intrusion, but the market will *not* regulate itself. It can't. Imagine a game of football without a referee—that's the free market! Left to themselves, companies will continue to lie and cheat and cut corners in order to beat each other and make a buck.

Governments have their own unique problems, like corruption and bureaucratic incompetence, but they are "*of the people, by the people, for the people.*" Their role is to represent *us* and *our* best interests—not those of corporations. When it comes to capitalism, governments should provide the bit and bridle in the horse's mouth to stop it from charging off the path and into the nearest pasture.

Subjects like politics, economics, and climate change are polarizing. We, humans, are tribal. We love to take sides in an argument, but the side we take is largely based on emotion, not logic. People decide they're for something, be that the free market or socialism, but we fail to see we need *both* sides to work together to solve the problems we face.

The free market should not be free to harm the public.

So what would an extraterrestrial intelligence make of our intelligence? They'd be saddened by how we've deluded ourselves, surrounding ourselves with *The Spectacle*. Our love for shiny things at the expense of all else would put us on par with crows!

Earth

Grock was right. We've given our planet the wrong name. Not only is Earth a water world, with over 70% of the surface covered in water rather than land, our bodies share similar proportions. Our muscle tissue is comprised of 60% water, while the heart and brains reach 73% and the lungs top out at 83%. Even unlikely contenders like bones come in at 31% water, although it sounds low in comparison, a third of your bone mass is nothing but liquid!

Deep Fakes & Electronic Fingerprints

In this story, Buster exposes Olivia's video as a deep fake by saying it failed to match the electronic fingerprint of the power grid. This is a legitimate way of disproving deep fakes.

Deep fake videos are set to become an enormous problem over the next decade. They're videos that are deliberately misleading. They're produced with such fidelity that it's impossible to tell they're not real. Take, for example, the video of Tom Cruise on TikTok. It's convincing. It looks real, but it's the result of artificial intelligence using footage from various Tom Cruise movies to change the face of an impersonator. At the moment, it's silly, harmless fun, but what happens when there's a deep fake of a US President wanting to start a nuclear war?

The ability of bad-faith actors to fake videos and mislead people is only going to increase. The arm wrestle between the political left and right often comes down to swing voters, being reasonable people that can be swayed one way or the other. Even if a deep fake is called out as a lie, it'll still introduce doubt and uncertainty in that central group. Out on the fringes, no questions will be asked either way.

How can we avoid being hoodwinked by deep fakes? By looking for factors beyond the video contents that confirm or refute its authenticity. Electrical Network Frequency (ENF) is the only means of verifying a video. It identifies the time and location where a video or audio recording was recorded. It's the only effective way of countering deep fakes.

ENF analysis matches the faint background hum of electrical equipment against power company logs with the timestamp of a particular audio/video clip. It's not perfect and sometimes relies on harmonics, but it can be startlingly accurate as demonstrated by Tom Scott in this video.

What exactly is ENF? In essence, the alternating current found in our homes isn't exactly 60 Hertz. It wavers, hovering around that value, but it isn't perfect. It varies slightly according to supply and demand. Over the period of a minute, it traces a wiggly line that is as unique as a fingerprint. Although it's invisible to us, forensic investigators can compare the logs of various power companies with the background hum in a video to determine when a recording was made. It's possible to isolate both audio and video to within a second using this technique.

Faking an ENF fingerprint is extraordinarily complex, so ENF is our best defense against deep fake videos. In the Tom Cruise video, as an example, it would be possible to figure out exactly when and where the video was recorded and then match that with Tom's actual location at that time. The challenge is that this takes time, and social media is anything but patient.

Drowning in the Desert

In this story, Breezy and Olivia almost drown in a bone-dry desert in central Asia. As strange as it seems, according to the United States Geological Survey, more people die in the desert from drowning than dehydration! It sounds crazy, but it's true. Flash flooding can arrive from miles away, submerging dry riverbeds in minutes.

Eighty-One Deaths

459

While talking with Susan, Breezy spoke about eighty-one people being brutally executed in Saudi Arabia, with a number of them being killed for *"disrupting the social fabric and national cohesion,"* as well as *"participating in and inciting sit-ins and protests."* In other words, free speech. Some were ostensibly executed for crimes of terrorism and murder, but their confessions were obtained under torture, as evident by their lack of teeth!

How do we stop this? How do we change this barbaric behavior?

Like many conservatives, Breezy advocates for a shepherd to protect the sheep. That's her solution to stopping it from happening *here*—wherever *here* may be.

Susan adopts the liberal position that such change can only come about as people change their values.

Who's right?

I'd like to think that change is possible, but we tend to be willfully blind to our own shortcomings. There's no indication that Saudi Arabia, Iran, or any other repressive country will change any time soon, so perhaps I'm naive. Regardless, any intelligent extraterrestrial species examining the various societies of *Homo sapiens* (the supposed wisest of the hominids) would be appalled and disgusted by this abuse of power. Their conclusion would be that selfishness and greed are of greater value to us than intelligence and honesty.

Acid Attacks

In this novel, Chester smuggles refugees out of oppressive countries, leading them to Europe.

Regardless of whether it's the United Kingdom, the United States or Australia, there's a considerable backlash against refugees in the current political climate. People react as though they're cheats, as though they're stealing jobs, or they don't belong here. Here as in where? Earth?

Refugees are the most vulnerable people on the planet—and none more so than women subject to acid attacks. Each year, more than a thousand women are disfigured by acid being thrown at them out of spite, with the most common reasons being: suspicion of cheating in a marriage, denying a marriage proposal, and fathers attacking their daughters for *"looking at boys."* What's worse, *"90% of the reported cases are not settled because of the perpetrators' wealth. Rich individuals are more easily able to evade the legal system."*

Our claim to be an intelligent species is laughable. Putting people on the Moon and inventing smartphones is a decent start, but our shortfallings are far more revealing than our achievements. In the words of futurist Jacque Fresco, *"The question is not whether there is intelligent life out there. The question is whether there is intelligent life down here. As long as you have war, police, prisons and crime, you are in the early stages of civilization."*

Our Senses

While on their way to Saturn, Grock describes how difficult it is for him to appreciate human senses like taste. He uses bananas and oranges as an example. To us, they're entirely different fruits. They look different, smell different and taste entirely different, but at a molecular level, they're surprisingly similar.

$CH_3CO_2CH_2(CH_2)_3CH_3$ is the flavor of a banana.

$CH_3CO_2CH_2(CH_2)_6CH_3$ is the flavor of an orange.

If/when we do make First Contact with an extraterrestrial intelligence, there's no doubt they'll be fascinated by our senses. They'll marvel that we see such a marked difference in what are very similar molecules. They'll also be fascinated by our insistence on colors being real when color simply doesn't exist outside of our heads. If you want to learn more about this concept, it's discussed in my novels *Cold Eyes* and *But the Stars*.

Saturn & Enceladus

For the most part, every photo you've ever seen of various celestial objects has been enhanced in some way. The point is not to mislead anyone but to compensate for the limitations of our eyes. Humans have wonderful eyes for life on Earth. Our eyes are adapted for bright sunlight and dim evenings, but they're not that great for the subtleties of astronomy.

The sunlight that falls on Saturn is roughly 1/5th of what we experience here on Earth. Were you to journey there and see the gas giant up close with your own eyes it would appear quite dim, a lot dimmer than any photo you've seen. The same's true of Mars, Jupiter, Neptune and Uranus, etc, with the amount of sunlight reaching Pluto being around 0.1% of what we experience during the day. High noon on Pluto equates to roughly 90 minutes after sunset on Earth. To compensate for this, the images we see from NASA are enhanced and brightened.

In some cases, like the tiger stripes on Enceladus, some features are accentuated by NASA to make them clearer. They're there, but they're not obvious to our eyes, so we process the images to make them more apparent. In this novel, I've taken the same liberty with what Breezy and Olivia saw while in orbit around Saturn.

If you've enjoyed this afterword and would like to learn more, be sure to read the blog entry on thinkingscifi called After the Afterword where I go into a bit more detail behind some of these concepts.

Thank You

Thank you for taking a chance on *Clowns*.

I'd like to thank my wife for her support along with a bunch of enthusiastic beta-readers that helped refine this story: Terry Grindstaff, Ian Forsdike, Chris Fox, John Larisch, Petr Melechin, and Didi Kanjahn. In addition to this, John Stephens and David Jaffe went back through the novel a second time to pick up on loose ends.

Independent publishing is tough. You won't find *Clowns* in your local bookstore or see it being nominated for any awards. You will find a bunch of one-star reviews on Amazon, though, as I'm always annoying someone along the way.

When it comes to *The Spectacle* and the drudgery of our daily lives, paying bills and doing human stuff, remember the advice of Oscar Wilde: *We're all in the gutter, but some of us are looking at the stars!*

If you've enjoyed this story, jump on GoodReads or Amazon and leave a review. Be sure to tell a friend it's worth reading.

Peter Cawdron

Brisbane, Australia

Printed in Great Britain
by Amazon

81304647R00271